THE RELUCTANT AGENT

MICHAEL TEFFT

In loving memory of my mother, Myrtle Tefft

CHAPTER 1

"Bloody Hell," muttered Captain Malcolm Robertson of His Majesty's Airship *Daedalus*.

Sand, sand, and more sand, as far as the eye can see, he thought, as he scanned the horizon with his binoculars. When Italy bombarded the port of Tripoli in October of 1911, the British Government was keen to prevent the Ottoman Empire from sending troops through its Egyptian protectorate. To show their sincerity, they dispatched the flagship of the Air Service to enforce their will.

That had been nearly four months ago. When the *Daedalus* first arrived in Egypt, seeing the Great Pyramids and the Sphinx every morning, as they lifted off to begin their patrol, filled Malcolm with awe. The sun and warmth was a welcome change from the cold, wet, grey weather of England. But four monotonous months of flying over the Egyptian desert had changed Malcolm's view of Egypt.

The warmth, that at first had been welcome, quickly became oppressive. The bright sun, a welcome sight after a long English autumn, became blinding after weeks; so much so that Malcolm had bought several sheets of coloured glass to put inside the windows of the bridge to cut the glare. It wasn't strictly regulation, but it helped. And the sand! Malcolm only left the ship when they ended their week of patrol and resupply. But those trips resulted in sand ending up in places he never thought sand could find.

"Commander Saxon, anything to report?" Malcolm asked absently.

"Nothing but sand," drolled Commander Saxon, Malcolm's second-in-command. "I thought I saw a camel, but it was just a sand dune. Whom did you anger to get this plum assignment?"

"I have no idea," said Malcolm. He sighed, looking at the seemingly endless expanse of desert. "You have the bridge; I'm going to my office. I can't believe I'm saying this, but even paperwork is preferable to this."

"Are you sure you don't need any assistance? Surely there's something I need to do, or something you can lose, and I can redo?"

"No, the problem is you're too efficient. You have all your work done on time, and it's always impeccably neat. Think of this as your reward for a job well done," Malcolm joked.

"Thank you, Captain, you are too kind," Saxon said, his voice dripping with sarcasm. With any other officer, Malcolm might chide him for his sarcasm, but Charles Saxon was more than his second-in-command; he was Malcolm's friend. Both were thrust into command two years ago, when a saboteur's bomb destroyed the bridge of the *Daedalus*, killing the command crew. The subsequent mission to retrieve a Martian spaceship from the Russian steppe built a strong bond between the two men.

Malcolm and Charles were as different as could be. Malcolm came from a working class Scottish family, while Charles was related to the Royal Family, albeit distantly. Malcolm was bold, decisive, and boisterous; Charles was calculating, and charming. Malcolm sometimes wondered how they worked so well together, and was often at a loss to understand.

Malcolm took one last scan with his binoculars, from east to west, when he stopped. To the west, it looked like the sand was moving. He fiddled with his binoculars, struggling to focus. Suddenly, a wall of sand leapt into focus.

Malcolm returned to the ship's wheel. The *Daedalus'* first captain insisted on using a naval ship's wheel, and Malcolm, although he refused to admit it, liked it as well. He spun the wheel quickly, turning the *Daedalus* away from the storm.

"What is it, sir?" Saxon asked, once again all business.

"Sandstorm, coming in from the west. We need to get as much distance between us and it as possible."

Saxon looked through his binoculars. "It's a large one. Do you think we'll be able to outrun it?"

"No, but I am hoping that we can get above it," Malcolm said. He grabbed the handset and called the Engine Room. "Mr. Jennings, give us as much speed as you can, and release the emergency ballast."

"Begging your pardon, sir, but is that a wise idea? The engines don't like all the sand that gets in them, and we might burn them out," Chief Engineer Jennings offered.

"Understood, Mr. Jennings, but if we don't put some distance between us and an incoming wall of sand, it's a moot point," Malcolm said calmly. "Full speed, Mr. Jennings, if you please."

"Fine," Jennings said. "I still think this is a bad idea."

"Noted," said Malcolm, a little testily. "Give us full speed, and release the ballast."

"Yes, sir," Jennings said.

"Mr. Jennings, please see me in my office tonight when you finish your shift."

"Aye, sir," Jennings said.

Malcolm hung up the handset and concentrated on the task at hand; getting as much distance and elevation from the sandstorm as possible.

Malcolm heard the thrum of the engines, and felt the ship pick up speed. He watched with growing impatience as the speedometer slowly crept up past their typical cruising speed of 30 miles per hour. After the initial boost in altitude from the release of the emergency ballast, Malcolm watched the altimeter slow its upward travel. The added push from the engines provided more lift from the rear flaps, but Malcolm felt like the tortoise racing the hare. But this time, it was unlikely that the hare would stop to take a nap.

"Rear Observation, what's the situation?" Malcolm said into his handset.

"Not good, sir," the airman said. "The storm is gaining on us. I think we may have a few minutes until it reaches us."

"Acknowledged," Malcolm said. "What about altitude? Have we climbed over the top of it?"

"Not yet, sir," the airman replied. "It's going to be pretty close."

"Understood. Give me a report every minute, and let me know when we are about a minute away from impact."

"Aye, aye sir," said the airman.

"If anyone has any ideas on how we can escape a sandstorm, please don't feel shy about sharing them," Malcolm announced to the bridge crew. Malcolm wished he had the engine from the Martian spaceship he recovered two years ago – a short burst of that engine would put some distance between them and the storm.

That thought gave Malcolm an idea, although there wasn't much time to implement it. He grabbed the headset and called the Engine Room. "Mr. Jennings, how are our fractional distillers running?"

"Fine," Jennings said cautiously. "Why?"

"Do you think you can vent helium through the back of the ship?" Malcolm asked.

"Yes, sir, the port exhaust is… what do you have in mind, sir?" asked Jennings, a nervous tone creeping into his voice.

"I want to concentrate the helium through the port exhaust to give us extra thrust. Rather like letting go of a child's balloon. On my mark, prepare to vent the helium from the forward balloons with as much pressure as you can. You have about," Malcolm said, checking his granda's watch, "about three minutes to make it so."

"Aye, sir, I'm sending the crew out now," said Jennings.

"What do you have in mind?" Saxon asked, joining Malcolm at the wheel.

"I think we might be a wee bit too close to the top of that sandstorm, and I want the best possible chance to clear that storm. The sand might very well cut the balloon to shreds if we're not careful. I hope that if we can vent enough pressured gas at the right time, we might get a bit of a push to clear the sandstorm."

"Isn't a bit risky venting helium, since we're counting on that to take us over the top?" Saxon asked.

"Aye, but first we'll gain momentum from the vented gas. I'm hoping that buys us a few more seconds to clear the top. By the time our nose begins to dip, the aft side should be clear of the storm."

"If you say so," said Saxon. "I think it's going to be a bumpy ride."

"That," Malcolm said in a serious tone, "is exactly what it will be."

CHAPTER 2

Malcolm locked the wheel into position, and pulled his slide rule from its holster on his belt. He was the only captain in the Air Service to wear a slide rule, but old habits die hard. Particularly when it came in useful at moments like now. Malcolm used the time of the two reports from Rear Observation, and estimated the distance to get a rough idea of the speed of the storm. Malcolm guessed that the storm was driving towards them at somewhere around 50 miles per hour, give or take 10 miles per hour. The *Daedalus* was currently pushing its engines at 45 miles per hour. At its current rate of ascent, Malcolm thought that they might just clear the top of the sandstorm, but it was only a guess at this point.

Malcolm's handset rang. "We have about one minute, sir," said the airman manning the Rear Observation bubble.

"Understood. Get yourself out of there, and hunker down somewhere," Malcolm said. He would have to ask Saxon who had been assigned to Rear Observation duty, as the airman had certainly earned his pay today.

"You don't have to tell me twice," said the airman. He then remembered who he was addressing, and quickly added a hasty "sir".

Malcolm flipped the controls for the handset for a ship-wide broadcast. "This is the Captain. All hands, grab on to something, and hunker down. We're about to attempt to fly over the top of a sandstorm, and it might get rough. As they used to say aboard ship, batten down the hatches!"

The bridge crew secured themselves with belts that had long ago been added to chairs on the bridge. Malcolm grabbed the two leather thongs that had been attached to the wheel, and lashed one hand to the wheel.

Then Malcolm heard it; a low rumble. The rumble increased, until it sounded like the roar of waterfall, and showed no sign of decreasing in volume. Malcolm grabbed the headset and yelled, "Mr. Jennings, vent now! I repeat, vent now!"

Malcolm dropped the handset, and wrapped his hand in the other leather thong. Malcolm felt a small push of acceleration as the ship moved up. The roar increased to the point that Malcolm could hear nothing else.

And then, Malcolm was thrown off his feet, and he banged into the wheel. Malcolm caught a quick glimpse of the sand from the window before he was knocked off his feet, and it seemed that the ship had cleared the wall of sand. It was all Malcolm could do to hold the wheel, as the storm's wind tossed the airship around with ease. The bridge crew remained in their seats, but maps and papers flew around the bridge, making it difficult to see. After several seconds, the airship settled down.

Malcolm pulled himself up using the wheel and checked the situation. They seemed to have forward momentum, but the engines had stopped. They had plenty of altitude, but the nose was drooping and they seemed to be slowly descending, no doubt due to the vented helium.

Malcolm picked up the headset and flipped the controls to shipwide communication. "We seem to be over the worst. All sections, report current situation."

One by one, each section reported. All in all, it seemed there were minor injuries and minor damage, as anything that wasn't bolted down had flown around the wind-tossed ship. When all the sections reported, except Engineering, Malcolm called the Engine Room. "Engine Room, please report." Silence. "Engine Room, report. That's an order!"

"Aye sir, it's Airman Mackenzie, sir."

"Where's Mr. Jennings?" Malcolm asked, with a note of annoyance in his voice.

"I don't know, sir. The engines are down, plugged with sand, I think, Mr. Jennings went to the vent control below us, and we haven't heard anything from him. I sent Eddie, I mean Airman Hall, down to see what happened."

"Very good, I'm on my way now with a corpsman. Make sure the fractional distillers are online and working at maximum, and see what you can do about getting those engines cleaned up, Airman Mackenzie."

"Aye, sir."

Malcolm rang Sick Bay, and arranged for a corpsman team to meet him in the vent control. Malcolm hung up the handset, and untied his hand from the wheel. "Mr. Saxon, you have the bridge. I'm going to Engineering to see what happened to our Chief Engineer."

"And lend a hand, if necessary?" Saxon said, arching one eyebrow.

"If necessary. I haven't been to the Engine Room since..."

"Since last month when you manufactured an excuse to assist on the teardown of the main engine," Saxon pointed out.

"Fine, you made your point. But if Mr. Jennings is hurt, they'll..."

"Yes, need your expertise," said Saxon. "Once an engineer, always an engineer."

"Very funny," said Malcolm. "You have the bridge," Malcolm said, as he walked to the bulkhead. He turned and saw the disarray of papers and maps. "Such as it is."

Malcolm worked his way through the main hall of the *Daedalus*. It seemed to have survived the sandstorm with minimal damage. Malcolm thought that their descent was slowing, and the nose of the airship was beginning to level out. As Malcolm descended the stairs at the aft of the ship, he caught up with the corpsmen as they attempted to bring a stretcher down through the twisty circular stairs that led to the Engine Room.

As he slowly descended the stairs behind the corpsmen, Malcolm thought back to his conversation with Jennings. He suddenly remembered an eerily similar conversation he'd had with Commander Arthur Bromley nearly four years ago. Commander Bromley ordered Malcolm to run the engines at full. Malcolm protested very strongly, nearly to the point of insubordination, against running them at full. And in that case, he'd been correct; after several hours, the engines did in fact seize up. *It was different*, Malcolm thought, *we didn't need to run at full; it was Bromley's pride.* In the Engine Room, he had no way of knowing why he was ordered to run the engine at full. He chuckled to himself; no wonder Bromley hated him so much. He had a very different reaction being on the other side of the conversation.

They reached the Engine Room, and Malcolm was relieved to see that Mr. Jennings was back, and directing the men to tear down the engines. He had an oily rag wrapped around his forehead, covering a bruise that had split open, although it was hard to tell blood from oil on the dirty rag.

"Mr. Jennings, I'm glad to see you up. I was a little worried when you didn't report," Malcolm said.

"Sorry, sir," replied Jennings. "To build up the pressure you wanted, I gradually released the helium from the forward balloons, but kept the port exhaust vent closed. The pressure made it a bastard to get open, pardon my language, sir."

"Nothing I haven't said myself on many occasions," chuckled Malcolm. Here Jennings was banged up, and probably saved the ship, and he was worried about offending the captain. *He'd have to work hard to offend me with his language*, thought Malcolm. He had said that, and much worse. When he was Chief Engineer, the enlisted men remarked that they had never met an officer who could out-curse them until they had met Malcolm.

"Thank you, sir," Jennings continued. "Once I received your signal, I released the valve and when the ship jumped, I was thrown back against the wall. That's when I must have gotten this," he said, pointing to his forehead. "I didn't know what happened next until Airman Clarke roused me. I'd just arrived in the Engine Room, and was assessing the mess when you arrived."

"Very good, Mr. Jennings," Malcolm said. He wanted to take off his uniform jacket, roll up his sleeves, and dive in to help. But he realised in that moment that he had done that too frequently. Jennings had just done something potentially dangerous, rather than letting any of the other men do it. He deserved the respect he enjoyed from his men, and Malcolm knew that playing engineer would undermine Jennings.

"When you have everything settled here, report to Sick Bay and get that bump looked at. I'd daresay that you're not doing it any favours covering it with that dirty rag. I'd find something else to cover it with before you see Dr. Jenkins, or the headache you'll get might not be from the bump on the head. And, Mr. Jennings, stop by my office after you see Dr. Jenkins."

"Aye, sir," Jennings said, a touch of resignation in his voice.

"Corpsmen, you can return to Sick Bay. Let Dr. Jenkins know to expect Mr. Jennings in a while. Mr. Jennings, I'll leave you to it. Let me know when the engines are working."

"Aye, sir," Jennings said. Malcolm returned to the bridge, and was not surprised to see that Commander Saxon already had it in order. Saxon was meticulous, and Malcolm relied on him to keep things ship-shape. If left to his own devices, Malcolm's office looked like controlled chaos. Saxon often reminded him when the piles of paper in his office seemed to take on a life of their own.

When he opened the door to his office, he wished that he had asked for Commander Saxon's organisational skills. Papers were strewn across the room, lending the impression that a blizzard of paper had occurred in the room. Malcolm sighed, and began the task of gathering the papers and other items strewn all over the room.

Since becoming Captain nearly a year and half ago, the Captain's Office now contained much more of the character of its current occupant than its former, the late Captain Archibald Collins. All of Collins' effects were sent to his family long ago, except for the globe that now lay on its side on the floor. The globe had red x's marking all the places that Captain Collins had visited in his illustrious career. Malcolm had marked the globe with blue x's to indicate the places he had visited in his own career.

Malcolm carefully replaced the books on his bookshelf. The books, titles such as Newton's *Principia Mathematica*; *Radioactivity* and *Radioactive Transformations* signed by their author, Ernest Rutherford; *A Text Book of Electrical Engineering* by Adolf Thomälen; *Origin of Species* by Charles Darwin, and a dog-eared copy of *The Mechanical Engineers Pocket-Book* by William Kent, were stacked next to his copies of naval regulations, ceremonies, and military law. Next to these were stacked nearly twenty different technical journals covering disciplines such as material science, thermodynamics, and modern physics. Behind these, Malcolm hid a copy of *The Scented Garden* translated by Sir Richard Francis Burton, a gift from his lover Joan.

Malcolm looked down and picked up the framed photograph of Joan de St. Leger, whom he met when he was just an acting Captain. She was a smart, strong woman who might intimidate many men. Malcolm found her captivating, if not sometimes frustrating. Not long after they met, Malcolm deduced that she was a spy for the British Secret Service. She might have killed him for discovering her secret, were it not for Malcolm's quick thinking, and a bed pan. The two came to an uneasy truce, before realising that each had feelings for the other. At the end of the mission, Matthew Frye, a German spy who had been one of Malcolm's closest friends, shot her in the abdomen before escaping. She faked her death, and let Malcolm believe that she was dead for over three months, before she revealed that she had assumed a new identity as Madame Charlotte De Marnier, a wealthy widow. Malcolm and Joan saw each other when they could. Malcolm stopped to recall the last time they had seen each other, and realised that it had been over a year.

And it would likely be many more months, Malcolm thought. He gently placed the frame on his desk with a sigh. Malcolm looked at the picture for a second longer, and continued with the task of restoring some semblance of order to his office.

Malcolm sat down at his desk and reached for the first report when there was a knock at the door. "Come in," Malcolm said, his hand going to the revolver he kept strapped to the bottom of his desk. After the incident with Frye, Malcolm was very cautious of being alone with anyone.

"Lieutenant Commander Jennings, reporting as ordered, sir," Jennings said, standing smartly and saluting.

Malcolm returned the salute. "At ease, Mr. Jennings. Please have a seat," Malcolm said, pointing to chair in front of desk.

"If it's all the same to you, sir, I'd rather stand," Jennings replied, still holding himself at attention.

"Well, for God's sake, you don't have to stand at attention. I don't know what you're expecting, but it's not a dressing down. I just want to talk."

"You're not reprimanding me?" Jennings asked tentatively.

"Good Lord, no. I just want to talk; clear the air; make sure we're both working together."

"Oh," said Jennings. He lost some of his rigid stance as he considered what he should do.

"Please, sit, Mr. Jennings. You're making me nervous."

"Yes, sir," Jennings said and quickly sat in the seat, hands resting on his knees.

"Let me reassure you that this is not a dressing down," Malcolm began. "Well, maybe I might have thought that when I was on the bridge. But on my way to Engineering, I recalled a certain Chief Engineer, who was nearly charged with insubordination for questioning the order of his commander. That Chief Engineer was me. At the time, I was right that the Commander's order was a stupid order, and was going to ruin the engines. But now that I'm the one on the bridge, I see why Commander Bromley wanted to charge me with insubordination. Lucky for me, I was right that Bromley was trying to show off."

"You absolutely did the right thing in telling me that the engines weren't in shape for a prolonged run at full power. However, I could see that sandstorm coming and knew if we didn't get some height, the engines might be the least of our worries. Based on the information I had, I knew that I was choosing the lesser of two evils."

"Permission to speak freely, sir?" Jennings said tentatively.

"Absolutely. That's the point of this meeting," Malcolm said, smiling.

"I don't quite know how to put this without offending you, but I felt that you were interfering with the Engine Room, because..." he trailed off.

Malcolm waited a beat and continued, "because I wanted to be back in Engineering?"

"Yes, sir," Jennings said, looking relieved that Malcolm hadn't made him say it.

"It's true, I miss being an engineer; I miss working on the engines, and doing things with my hands. And I've probably not been an easy Captain to please, because I know as much about the ship as you do. But please know, Mr. Jennings, although I like to get my hands dirty once in a while, I have no intention of taking your job away from you. And I will do my best to give you leave to run the Engine Room as you see fit."

Jennings exhaled, and visibly relaxed. "Thank you, sir. I was worried you might get mad."

"No," Malcolm laughed. "Commander Saxon reminded me exactly how often I like to meddle in Engineering before I left the bridge. It was, in fact, the reason I left you to get the Engine Room settled."

"Thank you, sir," said Jennings.

"I think you're a top-notch engineer, Mr. Jennings, and a credit to this ship. I absolutely insist that you tell me when one of my ideas is totally daft, and will put the ship in danger. But also know, sometimes I only have a choice between something daft that might kill us, or something that will definitely kill us."

"Yes, sir," said Jennings.

"How's your head?" Malcolm asked, pointing to the bandage.

"I imagine I'll have a quite a bruise tomorrow; and you were right, Dr. Jenkins gave me a tongue lashing for stopping the blood with a greasy rag. He made a big deal about having to clean the wound, but I think I'll be right as rain in a few days."

"I'm glad to hear it. I don't want my Chief Engineer laid up," Malcolm said, smiling. "One last thing I wanted to say. Thank you for personally seeing to the venting of the helium. It made a difference, and while not many others know that, I know it. And it will most definitely be noted in my log." Malcolm rose and offered his hand. "Thank you, Mr. Jennings," he said as he shook the engineer's hand.

"Thank you, sir," Jennings said, suddenly embarrassed by the attention.

"Once you have everything set in the Engine Room, take the rest of the night off. You've earned it."

"Thank you again, sir," Jennings said as he left the office.

Malcolm returned his attention to the pile of reports, and picked up the top report. *No rest for the wicked,* he thought.

CHAPTER 3

The *Daedalus* slowly made its way back to the British Army base at Tel El Kebir, just outside of Cairo. Ordinarily, the *Daedalus* would resupply at the Royal Naval base in Malta. But to keep up the patrols over Egypt, the *Daedalus* was ordered to use the Army base as its base of operations. Malcolm always dreaded their arrival at the base. It meant that he had to trudge across the camp and report to the base commander, and then trudge back to the *Daedalus* to radio his reports to the Royal Naval base at Malta.

The walk through the base was always troublesome. There was no love lost between the Army and the Royal Navy. And since Malcolm was a "fly-boy" as they called him, he received even less respect than his naval counterparts. And the mismatch in ranks between the services compounded it even further. While Malcolm's Royal Navy rank of Captain outranked Lt. Colonel Beauchamp, the commander of the Tel El Kebir base, he pretended that Malcolm's rank of Captain was the same as an Army captain. That meant he treated Malcolm with the same disdain he showed his junior staff.

Once the *Daedalus* was moored, Malcolm disembarked and began the long trudge through the camp, while the late day Egyptian sun beat down on him. By the time he reached the Lt. Colonel's office, his shirt was drenched and he wanted a large glass of anything wet. Malcolm saluted the guards outside the building and made his way inside. It was only slightly cooler in the building, as the ceiling fans circulated the hot air. But even that breeze was a relief from the burning sun. Malcolm announced himself to the Lt. Colonel's aide and waited. And as was his wont, Beauchamp made Malcolm wait for ten minutes before he opened his door. "Ah, Captain Robertson, back so soon?"

Malcolm gave a perfunctory salute, out of habit more than respect. "Yes, Lt. Colonel. I've come to give my report."

"Well, let's hear it," Beauchamp said dismissively. "I have an Army base to run, but I wouldn't expect you to understand," he said.

"No, sir, I don't suppose I understand the complexity of running a base that always stays in one place," Malcolm said.

"Are you being smart with me, Robertson?" Beauchamp sputtered.

"No sir," Malcolm said. *It would be decidedly ungentlemanly to engage him in a battle of wits, Malcolm thought. Especially since he's so woefully unarmed.*

"See that you aren't," Beauchamp warned. "Spit it out, I don't have all day."

Malcolm recounted the day's events, ending with the encounter with the sand storm, and loping back to the base.

"Any damage to your giant gas bag?" Beauchamp asked.

"The only giant gas bag around here is you," Malcolm muttered under his breath.

"What was that? Speak up, man, and stop your muttering!"

"Only minimal damage. The outer surface was scuffed up quite a bit, and we're overhauling the engines now to get the sand out of them."

"Good," said Beauchamp. "That means you'll be ready to leave in the morning."

"Leave?" asked Malcolm.

"Yes. Leave. I have orders for you to report to the Royal Naval Base in Malta immediately." Beauchamp handed Malcolm the orders.

Beauchamp was correct; the *Daedalus* was to report to Malta, and from there, they would receive their orders.

"Well, sir, it's been a pleasure," Malcolm lied, as he extended his hand to Beauchamp, who just stared at him. "A pleasure to see the backside of this flea-infested base," he said as he pulled back his offered hand.

"What did you say about my base? I'll have you up for insubordination, Robertson!" Beauchamp huffed.

"Technically, you can't do that. As you seem to have conveniently forgotten, a Royal Navy Captain outranks a Lieutenant Colonel," Malcolm said, pointedly emphasising the word *lieutenant*. "Since you have treated me with nothing less than utter contempt, perhaps I should bring *you* up on insubordination charges. I imagine that I could easily entice your aide into testifying, seeing how you treat him."

"You wouldn't dare," sneered Beauchamp.

"I would dare, but it would mean I'd have to either stick around this Godforsaken flea trap or, worse yet, come back. You're not worth the aggravation. Good evening, Lt. Colonel, and good bye," Malcolm said. This time Malcolm stood there without offering a salute to make his point.

Beauchamp sneered at Malcolm. "If you think, I'm going to salute you, you've got another think coming."

"I'll be sure to tell the supply officers in Malta about the level of respect you showed the Air Service here. It would be most unfortunate if there were some supply problems, and you couldn't get your ale. That would indeed be most unfortunate."

"Are you threatening me?" sneered Beauchamp, his face turning beet red.

"Not at all," Malcolm said. "I'm just remarking how unfortunate it would be if paperwork were misplaced and supplies, like ale, for instance, were sent somewhere else. It is the military; mistakes happen all of the time."

Beauchamp glared at Malcolm for another five seconds, and then finally snapped a very quick salute. Malcolm graciously returned the salute and left the office.

Malcolm returned to the blazing heat of the outside, and trudged back to the radio shed, and relayed his report to Malta. They confirmed the orders he received from Beauchamp, and acknowledged that the *Daedalus* would depart for Malta in the morning.

Malcolm returned to his ship and asked Commander Saxon to meet him in his office. Malcolm also sent a midshipman for a large pitcher of water, which Malcolm almost singlehandedly finished before Saxon arrived. When Saxon settled into his customary chair, Malcolm handed the orders to Saxon. "What do you think?" asked Malcolm.

Saxon furrowed his brow as he read the orders. He looked up and handed them back to Malcolm. "Curious. I thought we were supposed to be here another two months."

"As did I," said Malcolm. "Not that I'm sad to be leaving the desert, but I can't for the life of me understand why we're leaving."

"Maybe because our patrols were so effective in scaring away the Turks, that the Admiralty thinks they don't need us here anymore."

"Possibly, but I bet that it's something else. In the meantime, we need to get ship-shape. We've got just under two days to pass muster when we land in Malta. I, for one, don't want the Air Services' flagship looking anything else but top notch."

Malcolm and Saxon spent the next hour listing duties and inspections that would need to be completed, to get everything in place for their arrival in Malta. After mess that evening, Malcolm assembled the senior officers, and handed them specific duties for each section to ready the ship for its landing.

The airship was like a beehive that had been whacked by a stick. Crews were dispatched in the night, to fix and repaint the balloon and gondola, where it had been buffed by the sandstorm. Early that morning, as the paint was still drying, the *Daedalus* took off, and headed across the Mediterranean to the island of Malta.

As the *Daedalus* floated over the Mediterranean on its way to Malta, the crew was busy cleaning, polishing, and doing everything necessary to make the *Daedalus* look its best. Malcolm and Saxon never had a moment's peace from receiving status updates, requesting status updates, and staging inspections. The frenetic pace continued until the final approach to Malta. Once the island came into sight, Malcolm gave the order for the crew to put on their full-dress uniforms, and prepare for landing.

As the *Daedalus* approached the city of Valletta, Malcolm again marvelled at the beauty of the baroque city, whose fortress walls loomed over the Mediterranean. Malcolm could easily spot the basilica of the Carmelite Church that dominated the city's skyline; Fort St. Elmo, guarding the approach into the Grand Harbour; and numerous churches, hotels, and buildings that seemingly crammed into every nook and cranny of the peninsula. Malcolm took the wheel, and slowly guided the airship to the east side of the city, and quickly found the airship field just away from the harbour where the ships of the Mediterranean Fleet were anchored. Malcolm quickly spotted the *HMS Inflexible* and the *HMS Invincible*. They were a new class of ship called a battlecruiser; heavily armed like a battleship, but fast like an armoured cruiser. Nestled between the two battlecruisers was the flagship of the Mediterranean Fleet, the battleship *HMS Exmouth*.

Malcolm could see throngs of people coming out of buildings, and pointing to the sky to watch the arrival of an airship. The arrival of an airship in a small city like Valletta was still an exciting event. Malcolm guided the *Daedalus* to the airship field, and brought the ship to a gentle stop. Within seconds, the ground crews attached the lines to several winches that pulled the *Daedalus* to the ground.

Once the ship was secured, Malcolm and Saxon left the bridge and joined their escort in the cargo bay. He nodded, and the crew opened the doors and lowered the gangplank. Malcolm gave the order and the honour guard marched out of the *Daedalus*. He looked down the gangplank to the receiving party, and saw Admiral Edmund Pöe, Commander In Chief of the Mediterranean Fleet. Malcolm coughed to get Saxon's attention. He nodded toward the receiving party, and saw Saxon raise an eyebrow when he saw the admiral. Malcolm gave an almost imperceptible shrug as they continued to the end of the gangplank.

Bloody hell, thought Malcolm. *It's never a good thing when the Commander In Chief of the fleet is here to greet your arrival.* He took a deep breath, something that Joan had once told him would help calm his nerves. It wasn't working. Malcolm steeled himself and threw his smartest salute. "Permission to land," he said, holding the salute.

"Permission granted," said Admiral Pöe. The admiral looked every bit the part of a high-ranking British naval officer – white hair with a full beard and mustache. He had a bit of a squint, like he had spent many years on the deck of a ship staring into the sun. Malcolm somehow doubted that he had seen the deck of a ship in a very long time. "Captain Robertson, your men are to secure the *Daedalus* and await further orders. You and Lt. Commander Saxon are to follow me to headquarters. Get your men in order and return to my car immediately."

"Yes, sir," Malcolm said, and turned with Saxon back to his ship.

"What was that about? Have you done something that you haven't told me about, Malcolm?" Saxon asked.

"I honestly have no idea," Malcolm said.

CHAPTER 4

Malcolm turned back to the ship and found Lt. Commander Jennings. "Lt. Commander Jennings, You're in charge now. The crew is to secure the *Daedalus* and wait for further orders. Commander Saxon and I must report to the Admiral's office."

Jennings, thinking Malcolm was kidding with him, smiled. But as Malcolm continued to look at Jennings, the smile slowly faded from Jennings face, and was replaced with a look of sheer terror. "Me, sir? In charge? I don't know the first thing about running a whole airship."

"I'll wager that you won't have to for very long. I'm sure that we'll be back shortly. You can handle this, Mr. Jennings. Your orders are to secure the *Daedalus* and wait for us to return."

"Yes, sir," said Jennings. "Do you have any idea when you may return?"

"I have no idea," said Malcolm. "Until then, follow orders and keep your head down."

"Aye, sir," said Jennings. "I'll keep the *Daedalus* ship-shape until your return."

"Thank you, Lt. Commander Jennings," Malcolm said. "I know I can count on you."

Malcolm turned to Saxon, "Are you ready to face the firing squad?"

"Really, Malcolm, you must get a better handle on military law. They can only execute us for treason," Saxon said. After a beat, he added, "You haven't committed treason lately, have you, Malcolm?"

"Damned if I know," Malcolm said. Malcolm and Saxon strode to the Admiral's car and awaited further orders. They were shown into the back of a Crossley Model 15 with two burly Royal Marines. Malcolm noted that they hadn't been shackled, which was a hopeful sign. When Admiral Poë returned to his car, the procession left the airfield and headed to the Admiralty House on South Street. It was only a few blocks from the airfield, and all Malcolm could see was a blur of white stone buildings, and glimpses of the blue sky and ocean. He turned, looked at one of the marines, and nodded. The marine was as stony-faced as if Malcolm had not been there at all.

This is shaping up to be one bad day, Malcolm thought. Having to report to an admiral's office was rarely a good sign. Malcolm tried to recall if he had done something wrong. Their mission was routine patrol, and as nearly as Malcolm could recollect, the mission ran by the book.

The cars pulled up in front of the ornate entry to the Admiralty House. The baroque portico loomed over the entryway, held aloft by two ornate columns. The white-washed plaster looked sand-colored in the afternoon sun. Two marines stood guard in front of the large oak door. As the cars came to a stop, soldiers rushed to open the Admiral's door and escort him into the headquarters. Malcolm and Saxon, on the other hand, were alternatively pushed and pulled out of the car, and pushed forward into the headquarters.

Malcolm tried very hard not to drop his jaw as they entered the Admiralty House. Malcolm had heard that it had once been a palace, but was not prepared for the spectacle. The whole room glowed as the sunlight hit the white marble. Ornate corbels shouldered a balcony that ran along three of the walls. Two stairways arced gracefully to the top of the balcony, rimmed by balustrades. The party climbed the left stairway and continued down a long hallway. A third of the way down the hall, Malcolm caught sight of two Marines standing attention by a doorway, and assumed that that must be the Admiral's office.

Malcolm's assumption proved correct, and the party entered the doorway. The room was a large office with several ornate desks stationed around the room with a single door against the left-hand wall. This could only be the Admiral's office. At the desk nearest the door to the Admiral's office, Malcolm saw a Captain who somehow looked familiar to Malcolm, but he was sure he had never met him. He must be the Admiral's aide.

"Captain Bromley, please join us," the Admiral said as strode into his office, never stopping to acknowledge anyone in the room.

Bromley, thought Malcolm. Before becoming Captain of the *Daedalus*, Malcolm had had more run-ins with Commander Arthur Bromley than he could ever count. Commander Bromley perished when the bridge of the *Daedalus* was destroyed by a saboteur's bomb. And the captain before him could only be Bromley's brother, Charles. *This day just keeps getting better*, Malcolm thought ruefully.

Bromley glared at Malcolm as the party passed his desk. He rose, followed them in, and when the guard left, he closed the doors, and took his place beside the admiral.

Malcolm and Saxon remained at attention. The Admiral was intently reading something on his desk, apparently forgetting Malcolm and Saxon. After a very long minute, he looked up and said, "Sit."

Malcolm and Saxon quickly settled into the chairs before the Admiral's large ornate desk.

"Well, what do you have to say for yourselves?" Admiral asked.

"I'm afraid I don't understand, sir," said Malcolm.

"Do you have any idea why the Admiralty would order you to return to Kingsnorth, and abandon the patrol of Egypt?"

"I honestly have no idea, sir. I was hoping that you were going to tell us."

"I think he's lying, sir," said Captain Bromley. "I think Captain Robertson thinks his current duty is beneath him, and asked Admiral

Beatty to get them out of their current assignment." Malcolm had to give Bromley credit; he had never met someone who made the word *captain* drip which such contempt.

"Captain Bromley, how could I contact the Admiralty back home with any radio I have access to while I've been here?" Malcolm asked with all the courtesy he could muster. He had to tread very lightly here, which was not his strong suit.

"Sir," Malcolm said, addressing the Admiral. "All I can say is that I've executed my duties to the best of my abilities. My log speaks for itself, and I know of no reason why we would be ordered to return."

Admiral Poë considered Malcolm for a few seconds. "I agree, Captain Robertson. I supposed that this isn't your fault, probably just a manoeuvre by one of the other Admirals to weaken my position. Blasted Fleet politics!"

"Perhaps that was their mission all along, sir," suggested Bromley. Malcolm was beginning to quickly dislike Bromley more than his brother, who was a bully.

The admiral sighed, "Bromley, that's enough. I know that you blame Captain Robertson for the death of your brother, but the inquiry completely cleared him of any wrongdoing."

"As you say, sir," said Bromley. But his eyes showed the anger that he directed at Malcolm; he knew in an instant that nothing he did or said would placate Bromley.

"You do," said the Admiral, "have new orders." Captain Bromley politely handed Commander Saxon a thick envelope, and shoved Malcolm's envelope into his hands, as if Bromley feared contamination from Malcolm's touch. Malcolm gave Bromley a smile and said, "Thank you, Captain."

"You are to transport a Mrs. Charlotte De Marnier, a Professor Nigel Sinclair, and a shipment of religious artifacts from Rome to London. I don't know who these people are, but the Air Service is not a civilian air service!"

"I suggest that the two of you get your ship ready to depart for Rome in the morning," indicating Malcolm and Saxon. "The rest of the details are there in your orders. You are dismissed," the Admiral said, already starting to read a report.

"Yes, sir," Malcolm and Saxon said in near unison. Both gave a sharp salute and left the Admiral's office.

25

CHAPTER 5

The car was waiting to take them back to the *Daedalus*. Once in the car, Malcolm read his orders, and confirmed what the Admiral had said. The *Daedalus* was to escort Mrs. Charlotte De Marnier, Doctor Nigel Sinclair, and a shipment of religious artifacts from Rome to their home base in Kingsnorth, where they would receive additional orders.

Malcolm was now worried. If he was transporting Joan, in her identity as Charlotte De Marnier, that could only mean the Secret Service was involved. Although Malcolm would be glad to see Joan, things were complicated when they had to work together. Malcolm was concerned because he had never heard of Dr. Nigel Sinclair, and had no idea why Joan would be working with him, when she usually preferred to work alone.

"What's wrong?" Saxon asked. "Are you concerned about our orders? It seems straightforward. Do you know either of our passengers?"

"Yes, you could say I do," said Malcolm. "I met Madame De Marnier when I visited Joan's grave before taking command of the *Daedalus.*"

"Interesting," said Saxon. "Do you think that's why we were picked?"

"That, and other reasons that will eventually make themselves apparent." Malcolm longed to tell Saxon the truth about the mysterious woman, but this was not the time nor place. And, it wasn't Malcolm's decision to make. Joan had made it clear that he was not to tell anyone she was still alive, and that included Saxon.

The car arrived at the landing field, and the two men returned to the ship to prepare to leave the next morning. Again, the ship was a beehive of activity, as supplies and fuel were loaded for the long trip to England. Malcolm and Saxon calmly dealt with all the emergencies. By late that evening, the ship was ready to depart for Rome, and subsequently return to England.

The morning's weather was picture perfect, and it appeared that they would have a smooth, uneventful trip to Rome. Malcolm was fully prepared for some unanticipated disaster, or a sudden storm to blow up, and throw them way off course. But the *Daedalus* flew smoothly over the Mediterranean, and landed in Rome late that night. Even the field was adequately lit, so that bringing the *Daedalus* in for a landing was easy as well.

Upon arriving, a messenger appeared with a letter for Malcolm. He recognised the handwriting on the letter at once; it was a letter from Joan:

"Dear Captain Robertson,

Bonjour! I hope this letter finds you well.

I will arrive tomorrow morning with the cargo that must be transported to England. Dr. Sinclair will not be joining us tomorrow. I will explain that and more when we meet on the morrow.

Until then,

Madame Charlotte De Marnier"

Malcolm could smell her perfume on the letter. The letter troubled Malcolm; more for what was left unsaid than its actual contents. Malcolm recognised Joan's very careful wording, done so that if other people read the letter, it would seem innocuous. *I knew today was too good to be true*, Malcolm thought.

After Malcolm ensured that the ship was secure, and ready to receive its cargo and passengers, he asked Saxon to come to his office for a nightcap. Some time ago, Malcolm recognised that his friend did not share his own appreciation for whisky. Malcolm bought several bottles of excellent gin, and had worked with Chef and his quartermaster to secure a supply of limes. When Saxon arrived, he went straight to the bar and fixed himself a gimlet, his drink of choice. Malcolm, as always, poured himself a measure of *Auchentoshan*, his favourite whisky.

As they savoured their drinks, Malcolm showed the letter to Saxon. Saxon read it and furrowed his brow. "I'm not sure what to make of it. Our orders explicitly tell us to return to London with Dr. Sinclair and yet, it appears that we are to leave Rome without him."

"Aye, that's what I thought," said Malcolm.

"What do you know of either of them? Madame De Marnier, or Dr. Sinclair?"

"As I said, I've met Madame De Marnier. We talked for a bit, but I didn't learn much about her. Other than that her husband had been an airship captain, and he had died rather recently." Malcolm hated repeating this lie to his best friend, but he was more afraid of Joan's wrath. *Besides, soon the cat would be out of the bag,*" Malcolm thought.

"Somehow that name Nigel Sinclair seems familiar to me," said Saxon. He sat staring at his drink when he jumped up. "Now I know where I heard that name. I believe he's a Reader at Oxford. Yes, now I remember. His interest is in anthropology, particularly in the area of folklore and myth. From what I understand, he's an accomplished linguist and archaeologist as well. There was a fascinating piece on his work at Calleva Atrebatum." Malcolm looked blankly at Saxon. "You know, the ruins of the Roman town discovered near Silchester?"

"Never heard of it," said Malcolm. "Seems very dry reading."

Saxon laughed. "This coming from a man whose idea of a good time is to read technical journals?"

Malcolm laughed. He raised his glass to his friend and said, "to each his own."

"I'll drink to that," said Saxon. After a moment, he stopped with a thoughtful look on his face. "What does a Reader in Anthropology, a widowed owner of an airship company, and a cargo of religious artifacts have to do with us?"

Malcolm took a long sip of his whisky. "I don't know, but I bet that it means trouble."

CHAPTER 6

$\mathcal{M}$alcolm woke at dawn, anxious both to see Joan, and understand this mission. It was a grey morning, and it seemed as if the sun never rose. Before long, it began to rain. Malcolm thought it odd, because the weather reports he received the evening before did not indicate any storms in the area.

Malcolm ordered the crew to prepare two cabins for their guests, and assigned Joan the cabin nearest to his. Ever since his first mission as captain, there was always a need for cabin space for some guest or another. Sick of having to displace his officers, Malcolm refitted a few store rooms and offices on the main deck, so that at least four cabins were free at any time.

At nearly 0900 hours, a black car, and a transport truck, drove up to the *Daedalus*. The black car, with a long sleek front hood, had its roof pulled up to protect its occupants from the ongoing rain. Malcolm put on his waterproof and led a detachment of his men down the gangplank of the *Daedalus*. He directed his men to assist with unloading the truck, while he made his way to the car. He watched as the chauffeur hurried, and opened the back door. He was happy to drink in the sight of Joan as she emerged out of the car, and immediately raised her parasol. She wore a navy-blue jacket over her empire dress. Her now raven hair fell in ringlets from under a small fedora. He couldn't help but smile when he saw her. She caught his eye and flashed a momentary smile, but quickly turned her attention back to the chauffeur, and concluded her business.

Malcolm used all his self-control to walk, and not run, to Joan. When he got to her, he reached for her hand and gave it a gentlemanly kiss. "Madame De Marnier, it is my pleasure to welcome you aboard the *Daedalus*."

Joan whispered in her low husky voice, "I was hoping it would be my pleasure." She winked and said, "Thank you, Captain. Perhaps we can dispense with the formalities, and get inside out of this beastly rain."

Malcolm gave her his arm and, to his surprise, was pulled as Joan started running towards the *Daedalus*. Malcolm soon caught up with her, and they dashed inside. "If you give me a moment, Madame, I will oversee the transport of the cargo, and then it will be my pleasure to escort you to your cabin."

"That is most kind of you, Captain… Robertson, isn't it?" she said. "Do make sure that your men are careful with my steamer trunk."

"I'll see to it personally, Madame."

Malcolm dashed out into the rain and supervised, as his men unloaded half a dozen large crates, and Joan's steamer trunk. When the cargo was safely inside the *Daedalus*, the truck and car departed. The cargo and Joan's trunk were weighed before the cargo was stored. A crewman brought Joan's trunk to her, and Malcolm ordered the crewman to take it to Joan's cabin. The crew in the cargo bay relayed the weights of the new cargo to Chief Engineer Jennings, who would adjust the ballast, based on the added weights to the ship.

Malcolm offered her his arm, and they started out of the cargo room to Joan's cabin. In a low voice, Malcolm asked, "Where is our other passenger? Are we really to leave without him?"

"Yes. He was to meet me in Rome several days ago on a train from Romania. The train arrived with no Nigel, but a note that said if he did not arrive by the time of the trip, to come and get him at Tismana in Romania."

"Romania?" Malcolm said, a little more loudly than he intended. He continued in a whisper, "You do know that Romanian sovereignty is a sore issue with the Austro-Hungarian Empire with whom our government has, what could best be described, as a fragile relationship?"

"Of course, I do, you ninny," she said.

"So how are we to get to Tismana?" Malcolm asked.

"It's been worked out. I have updated orders that you may verify at your leisure."

At this point, they reached Joan's cabin. Joan looked down the hallway, and noted with delight that Malcolm's cabin was only two doors down. Malcolm opened the door for her and she swept into her cabin. As she entered, she grabbed Malcolm firmly by the wrist, pulled the surprised captain into her room, and closed the door behind them.

Immediately, she wrapped her arms around him and kissed him passionately. After momentarily being taken aback, Malcolm responded in kind. Joan broke the kiss and sighed, "It's been way too long since I've been able to do that."

"I agree. Although you know, we could just get married, and then we'd be able to..." The words were out of Malcolm's mouth before he could stop them.

"To what? Steal moments when you are at Kingsnorth? Me sit around while you're off having some sort of adventure? We've been through this a hundred times, Malcolm!" She paused, and softened her voice. "Can't we just enjoy our time together when we get it?" asked pleadingly. "I've only just arrived and I don't want to start a row."

"Very well," sighed Malcolm. "I'll let the subject drop. For now," he said, as he reached to kiss her again.

Joan put her finger to his lips. "You have a job to do, Captain. I believe we are to take off shortly? For now, set a heading due east, and send for me when we are safely away."

"I thought I was the Captain here," Malcolm said.

"You are – I'm just the woman who is helping you do the right thing."

"So, that's what it is?" he said. He stole a quick kiss, and then adjusted his uniform, so that he was the model of an Air Service Captain. He opened her cabin door and said loudly, "Anything else I can get you, Madame?"

"No, I believe I am fine. You have been most generous with your time," she said, while pantomiming wiping her mouth. Malcolm took out his handkerchief and wiped off Joan's lipstick. He looked quickly at the wall mirror, and tried to wipe the rest away before leaving.

"God, that woman is so infuriating," Malcolm fumed as he slipped into his own cabin to wash the lipstick off his face. "She won't hear of marriage, but then bosses me around like a wife." Malcolm left his cabin and returned to the bridge. He was not surprised to see that Commander Saxon had everything ready for lift off, and the crew was waiting for the word from the captain.

Malcolm heard a loud boom and realised that it was thunder. "When did this storm blow up?" asked Malcolm.

"Literally, just as you walked onto the bridge," Saxon said. "It had been raining, but there was no thunder until you walked in. Should we wait to see if the storm will blow over?"

"I'd rather not wait. Let's see if we can get above it before it has time to build." Malcolm reached for the handset, and flicked the switch to address the whole ship. "Attention crew, prepare for lift off. All crew to lift off stations."

Malcolm flipped the switch to call the Engine Room. "Mr. Jennings, are we ready for lift off?"

"Aye, aye sir," said Mr. Jennings. "The engines are ready when you give the word."

"Thank you, Mr. Jennings," said Malcolm. He switched back to the crew, "Initiate lift off."

Crewmen signaled to the ground crew to untie the lines. When the ground crew finished, they signaled the *Daedalus* that it was untethered. Malcolm increased speed, and pointed the *Daedalus* skyward. As the *Daedalus* lifted to the sky, Malcolm jumped when a bolt of lightning flashed near by the *Daedalus*. Although a lightning strike would not ignite the inert helium gas they used for their airship, it would wreak havoc with the *Daedalus'* electrical systems.

The rain streaked over the main window of the bridge, making it difficult to see out of the window. Malcolm, at this point, trusted his compass and altimeter to guide him. He set a course of due east, and increased engine speed sooner than he might in normal circumstances.

It was bumpy as the *Daedalus* rose above the turbulent storm clouds, but soon settled once it broke the top of clouds. As Malcolm looked out the main window, he was surprised to see that the storm had been localised around Rome, and very soon, they had escaped its grasp.

"Mr. Saxon, please join me in my office. Mr. Barrows, please escort Madame De Marnier to my office, and see if Chef can muster up some tea and biscuits. Mr. Hensley, you have the bridge."

Malcolm and Saxon left the bridge, and went to Malcolm's office. They settled in at the round table. Early in his tenure as captain, Malcolm replaced the long table that Captain Collins had favoured. Malcolm wanted all the officers to feel that they were on equal footing; no one more important than any other. In more fanciful moments, he thought of it as his Round Table, like King Arthur. Shortly, a midshipman arrived with a tray of tea and biscuits. Malcolm was thankful to note that they were honest-to-goodness biscuits, and not ship biscuits.

Malcolm poured tea for Saxon and himself, but caught himself before he poured tea for Joan. He knew how Joan took her tea, but he was not supposed to know how Madame De Marnier took her tea. Malcolm drank his black tea, and was pleasantly surprised to find it was not thick enough to tar the skin of the airship.

There was a knock on the door. Mr. Barrows opened the door and Joan swept into the room. Even though he had seen her minutes ago, the sight of her still made his heart jump. Malcolm and Saxon rose, and before Malcolm could move, Saxon had already pulled out a chair for her.

"Madame De Marnier, may I present Commander Charles Saxon."

"Madame de Marnier, it is a pleasure to meet you," Saxon said. He took her hand and gently kissed it. When he looked at her, he paused for a moment. "Have we met before?" asked. "I have the distinct feeling that I have met you before, but I can't for the life of me remember where."

"That is funny," she said, with a slight French accent. "I feel like I have met you before as well." Malcolm was amazed that she could keep a straight face. Malcolm realised that Joan would make a game of this; to see how long it would take before Saxon would recognise her. "Please, sit down. It is not often I am in the presence of two such handsome men."

"Madame, may I offer you some tea and biscuits? I'm afraid the fare on our airship may not be up to your standards."

"Oh, I'm sure it will be fine. Cream and two lumps of sugar would be fine," Joan said.

Malcolm looked at the sugar bowl, and guessed how many spoonfuls made up a cube. "Here you are, Madame."

"Merci," she said, as she took the cup from Malcolm. He thought he caught a glimpse of a wink.

The three sat in silence as they sipped their tea. Saxon broke the silence first. "Am I correct in understanding that you own an airship company?"

"*Oui*," she said. "It was my husband's company. He died piloting one of his experimental designs. I took over and have run it ever since."

"I'm sorry for your loss," said Saxon. Malcolm had to look at his tea to stop from laughing. "Malcolm tells me he met you in a cemetery, of all places."

"*Oui*. I was visiting my husband's grave, when I saw a handsome man weeping at a grave. I was so touched; I had to offer my condolences. That is how we met."

"Handsome man? You are talking about this man, Malcolm Robertson?" asked Saxon with a smile. Saxon looked at her. First, the smile faded from his face, and then his brows furrowed. After a few moments, his face was transformed into a look of shock. "Joan?" he whispered.

"*Oui*," she said, smiling.

Saxon turned on Malcolm. "You knew she was alive all this time? And you didn't say a word to me?"

Before Malcolm could speak, Joan interjected, "Yes, I told him in no uncertain terms that he should not tell anyone that I was alive. And you know how persuasive I can be."

"But how? We saw you die!" Saxon sputtered.

"You saw Frye shoot me. After surgery, I convinced the doctor and Mycroft to tell everyone I was dead. My identity as a spy had become public knowledge, and I was worried that someone would come after Malcolm. I intended to continue to play dead for a long time, but I found I missed Malcolm too much. I arranged for him to meet me at the cemetery that contains my grave. He saw through my disguise immediately."

"Yes, about that," said Malcolm. "How did you know I would come, based on Mycroft's rather cryptic visit?"

"Really, Malcolm. I knew that you would think his visit strange, and that there would be some ulterior motive to him telling you where I was buried. It really was rather obvious."

"You think you have me wrapped around your finger?" Malcolm asked.

"Absolutely, my darling," she said, putting her gloved hand over his for the briefest of moments.

"I take it that this visit, and our orders, are not just an excuse to rendezvous with Malcolm?" asked Saxon.

"No. It was happenstance that the *Daedalus* was on patrol here when I started this mission. I have been working on an extended loan of religious artifacts from the Vatican, and the Orthodox Church. My partner," Malcolm tried not to bristle at the word, "Dr. Nigel Sinclair was to lead the negotiations with the Vatican, but was unexpectedly called away before we even started. He left for Bucharest, and said that he would return by train a week ago. The train arrived, and Nigel was not on board, and but he sent a letter asking us to pick him up at

Tismana in Romania. I have spent the last week diverting the *Daedalus* and arranging for us to travel to Romania. And here we are," she said, as she pulled a large, sealed envelope from her purse. She handed it to Malcolm.

He examined the envelope, which bore the seal of the British Embassy in Rome. He broke the seal, opened the envelope, and began to read. His brow furrowed as he read. The orders took the *Daedalus* to Constantinople, where they would pick up more religious artifacts. From there, they would head north to Romania, rendezvous with Dr. Sinclair, and return to London. Malcolm frowned, and handed the orders to Saxon.

"Why are we collecting so many religious artifacts? Has Mycroft suddenly found religion?" Mycroft Holmes, Head of the British Secret Service, was a notorious religious skeptic.

"Hardly," said Joan. "But, I'm sure it will be made clear... eventually." She said the last word with a tone of bitterness in her voice.

"So you don't know what's going on either?" Malcolm asked. *That is not a good omen,* Malcolm thought.

"I've been told very little, other than we need to collect these artifacts and return them to Britain. I've been told that all will be made clear once we are there."

"Does your partner, Dr. Sinclair, know why we're chasing all over Europe for religious artifacts?" Malcolm asked.

"I don't believe so, although he left when we arrived in Rome. A telegraph was waiting for him when we arrived, and he immediately left for Romania."

"What can you tell me about your... partner, Dr. Sinclair?" Malcolm asked. He hadn't meant to pause, but he couldn't help it.

Joan picked up on his hesitation and smiled. "Nigel," she said, emphasising the familiar use of his first name, "is absolutely brilliant. He holds doctorates in Anthropology, Theology, and Classics. The man speaks more languages than I do. His area of expertise is in folklore and mythology. He has been called in from time to time for consulting work with the Secret Service. I've had the pleasure of working with him on multiple occasions. He's very dashing and very handsome," Joan said, looking directly at Malcolm. "I'm surprised that you have not heard of him," she continued. "He was featured in most of the newspapers, and magazines, for his work in the excavation of the Roman town at Calleva Atrebatum."

"Yes, I read all about his work. Fascinating," said Saxon. "I was telling Malcolm about it last night, in fact."

"Malcolm, what am I going to do with you? Do you read anything but your technical journals?" she asked playfully.

"Reading technical journals has held me in good stead," Malcolm replied grumpily.

"There are more things in heaven and earth, Malcolm, than are dreamt of in your science," Joan said teasingly.

Malcolm sighed. *This is going to be a long trip,* he thought to himself. "Is there anything else we should know?" he asked.

"Not that I've been told. All requests for the religious artifacts, save for the one for the Vatican, had already been arranged before I was involved in the mission. I don't know what diverted Nigel from this mission, so I'm not sure what we'll find when we get there."

Malcolm frowned. "What's wrong?" Joan asked. "The mission seems very straightforward and, dare I say it, routine?"

"Aye," said Malcolm. "That's what has me worried."

CHAPTER 7

$\mathcal{M}$alcolm, Saxon, and Joan broke up their meeting, with Malcolm and Saxon returning to the bridge, and Joan returning to her cabin. On the way to the bridge, Malcolm stopped Saxon in the hall. "Charles, what do you think of the mission?"

"It seems straightforward enough," Saxon said. "But this is the Secret Service, so it can't be that straightforward. Do you think Joan… Madame De Marnier," he said, quickly correcting himself, "is telling us all she knows?"

"Damned if I know." Malcolm said. "I think so. I trust Madame De Marnier, but I don't trust her boss."

"I see your point," Saxon said.

"Let's be prepared for anything," Malcolm said.

"Agreed. Fortune favours the prepared," Saxon said.

"Or the foolish," Malcolm added.

Saxon laughed. "That too." The two men continued to the bridge. Malcolm gave the navigators the new destinations, and put them to work on plotting the new courses. He informed the officers that there would be a formal dinner in the Officer's Mess tonight. Many of them groaned, but knew it was to honour their guest, Madame De Marnier. Malcolm had done away with the formal Officer's Dinner that

Captain Collins insisted on when starting a new mission. Malcolm, instead, favoured working dinners where they could discuss the mission, and eat in a more relaxed environment. But with a guest, it was to be a formal dinner with dress uniforms.

Malcolm made arrangements for the evening's dinner with Chef. To his amazement, Chef had done some trading when they resupplied in Malta, and had acquired a large quantity of fresh seafood, and fresh vegetables. Malcolm decided he would not enquire as to how Chef obtained this, because he suspected that it wasn't strictly regulation.

With dinner arranged with his staff, Malcolm stopped by Joan's cabin. He knocked, and patiently waited for her to answer the door. "Madame De Marnier, I hope you will do me and my officers the honour of joining us, for a formal dinner in the Officer's Mess at 7:00 this evening."

"Why, thank you, Captain," Joan said coyly. "Perhaps, you can help me? I'm having difficulties opening the closet."

"Let me see what I can do," Malcolm said. Before he had taken three steps into the room, Joan had the door shut, locked, and for the second time today, he found himself being kissed. Again, he melted into her kiss for several long moments, before breaking off. "You know, we're not going to be able to keep doing this," he said, holding her in his arms.

"I know, but I thought I'd take advantage of the few moments that I can. Do you think I'll be able to see you tonight? I get so lonely in this big room," she pouted.

"You are a temptress, woman," Malcolm laughed. "I think something can be arranged. And now, if you can keep your hands to yourself for a few minutes, I have work to do before dinner tonight."

"You think you're so irresistible that I can't keep my hands off you?" Joan asked, with a hint of laughter in her voice.

"You are the one who has grabbed me twice," he offered.

"Touché," she laughed. "I will try to be the model of decorum."

"Starting tomorrow, I hope," Malcolm said with a leer.

"We'll see," she smiled.

Malcolm gave her one last kiss, reluctantly pulled himself away, and returned to his office. He carefully reviewed the orders, and found himself puzzled. The mission appeared straightforward enough; pick up cargo from two major capitals, and return to London. But the question that stuck in Malcolm's mind was *Why? Why divert the flagship of the Air Service on a cargo run?* he thought. *And why was Joan involved?* Her involvement in this meant the involvement of the Secret Service, and that was something that didn't bode well.

Malcolm continued to ponder these questions for another hour, before reaching the conclusion that he wouldn't know the answers to the questions until he got to London. And despite the relative ease of this mission, Malcolm could not shake a certain sense of uneasiness about it.

He turned back to the pile of reports that had gathered on his desk. As he made his way through the pile, he found a copy of Gentleman's Quarterly, with an extensive article on Dr. Nigel Sinclair, undoubtedly placed there by his second-in-command. He decided he ought to learn more about Joan's partner, and read the article.

It confirmed much of what everyone had already said; Dr. Nigel Sinclair was a Reader at Oxford with Doctorates in Anthropology, Theology, and Classics; he specialised in mythology, folklore, and lost cultures; he spoke almost every major language on the European Continent, and could read almost as many ancient tongues. The article mentioned in passing that Dr. Sinclair had been involved in the excavation at Calleva Atrebatum because of his expertise in lost cultures. The Roman town was abandoned sometime in the fourth to sixth century. Unlike other former Roman towns, no mediaeval town sprung up in its place. The whole area had been abandoned.

The drawings in the magazine depicted a man of approximately Malcolm's age, with dark hair, and a distinctive handlebar mustache. The drawing showed him outfitted in a bowler hat, a suit with a smart waistcoat, and a very sturdy walking stick. Malcolm grudgingly conceded Joan's point, that he was a handsome man. While Malcolm could see him as an academic, he found it hard to believe that the man also did extensive work in the field, and had travelled deep into the jungles of Africa, Asia, and South America looking for various lost or legendary tribes or cities.

Malcolm set the article aside for the moment. Why would such an eminent archaeologist gather up religious artifacts? And partnered with a Secret Service agent? The more he thought about this mission, the less sense it made. And Malcolm liked things to make logical sense. The sense of unease that he felt earlier became dread now.

Malcolm tried to clear his head and look at the other reports. He managed to distract himself from the sense of dread he now felt, with the myriad issues he faced in running the airship. He forced himself to read through his officers' reports, wrote several new orders for the next day, and approved the shift rotation for the trip to Constantinople.

The ship's clock rang two bells, startling Malcolm from his paperwork. He left his office and returned to his cabin to begin his ablutions for the formal dinner. Malcolm's cabin was much larger and better appointed than his cabin when he was Chief Engineer. A large, canopied four-poster bed took up almost one wall. A couple of burgundy-upholstered chairs huddled around a small table, stacked with books and magazines. On the wall opposite the bed was a proper closet, and next to that, the door to his private bath. Malcolm cared very little for the accouterments of being captain, save this. He relished having his own private bath, even if it was small.

Malcolm showered, shaved, and put on his full-dress uniform. He retrieved a small lock box from his trunk, opened it, and put on his decorations. The first was for conspicuous gallantry for engineering the *Daedalus'* escape from a German zeppelin, with no bridge, and no engines. The second was the decoration of which he was the proudest; the Victoria Cross, the highest decoration in the British military. He received that for rescuing his men from a German encampment, and singlehandedly defeating four German zeppelins, to return a Martian spaceship to Britain. He retrieved his uniform sword. He drew the blade from its scabbard and looked at it, thinking back to his duel with the traitor Matthew Frye, and the moment when Frye shot Joan. Not wanting to relive that memory any more, he slid the blade back into the scabbard, and looked in the mirror.

Malcolm looked at the reflection in the mirror wistfully. His hair was beginning to grey at his temples, and the crow's feet were more pronounced, but he still had the rugged handsomeness that attracted Joan. But Malcolm couldn't help but see the day when there would be less time ahead of him than behind him. He wanted to spend those days with Joan. Every attempt to broach the subject of marriage with her ended in a huge row. Malcolm learned as a young man to be frugal, so he managed to save a great deal of his salary. But it had surprised him when he found it so easy to spend a great deal of that money on a ring for Joan; a ring he still hadn't given her because he couldn't bear the rejection. It was one thing to talk in abstract terms about marriage and fight about that; it was another to propose, and be refused. Malcolm looked at the ring box sitting in his lock box. For just a moment, he took it out of the lock box and opened it, so he could look at the ring. He looked for a few seconds, sighed, and placed the box back inside his lock box.

Malcolm checked his granda's pocket watch, and saw that he was right on time to pick up Joan. He left his room and took the short walk down the hall. He knocked, announced himself, and waited for Joan to appear. When she opened the door, Malcolm felt his breath catch. Joan looked gorgeous in a perfectly tailored black jacket, frilled collared blouse, and a long straight skirt that did much to emphasise her impressive curves.

Malcolm took her gloved hand and kissed it. "Madame De Marnier, you look positively beautiful tonight. You will definitely make quite an impression on my crew."

"Oh, Captain Robertson," she said, with her hint of a French accent, "I am sure you say that to all of your female passengers."

"I do, actually," he said, as he offered her his arm to escort her to the Officer's Mess. As she looped her arm through his, she gave Malcolm a quick dig in the rib cage for his cheek.

Arm in arm, they walked to the Officer's Mess. When they arrived at the door, the midshipman opened the door, and announced the

Captain and Madame De Marnier. The officers stood in unison, as Malcolm escorted Joan to the seat reserved for the guest of honour, and held the chair for her as she sat. Malcolm saw the looks on his officers' faces. If it were any other woman other than Joan, he would have to do his best to defend the woman's honour. In this case, he felt sorry for his men.

Malcolm sat down, and his men followed suit. Soon, midshipmen arrived with wine, as Malcolm introduced the officers to Madame De Marnier. Some had been onboard when Joan had last been onboard, but many were new, and had not met her before. Only one, Dr. Jenkins, the Ship's Surgeon, knew that Madame De Marnier was, in fact, Joan. When Malcolm introduced Dr. Jenkins, he remarked, "You may not remember me, Madame, but I believe that we have met before, and I'm most relieved to see you are in excellent health."

"Oh, but how can I forget such a distinguished man, such as yourself?" she replied. "I am in fine health, thanks to your most able assistance." Turning to the other officers; "Some time ago, I was out with my husband and I was overcome by the heat of London. Fortunately for me, Dr. Jenkins happened to be at the restaurant, and he attended to me. You have a fine physician on your ship; you should consider yourselves very fortunate." Joan told the story with such a convincing demeanour that *he* almost believed it, and he knew better. She smiled at Jenkins, and he smiled back, his eyes twinkling.

With the pleasantries out of the way, the midshipmen brought in the meal. Dinner started with *aljotta*, a Maltese seafood soup with fish, tomato, lemon, and mint. To Malcolm's surprise, it was very delicious. *I might have to give Chef a promotion*, he thought to himself. The main course was a pasta dish called *seafood fra Diablo* which was as spicy as it sounded. Most of Malcolm's crew, himself included, were not used to the art of eating pasta, and struggled to keep the linguine on their forks. Only Joan and Saxon successfully ate the pasta by using both fork and spoon. The crew watched in amazement as they wound the pasta around their forks with ease, using the spoon to hold it on the fork. Malcolm and his crew imitated them, with degrees of success varying from limited to none. Malcolm considered the whole endeavour rather much like putting an octopus in a mesh bag. He looked down, and knew that he would need to have his dress uniform laundered. As he looked around the room, most of his officers seemed to be in the same predicament.

The midshipmen cleared the pasta away, and dessert appeared in its place. It was a fresh berry cobbler; a simple dessert, but the kind that Malcolm preferred. Port arrived for the officers, and whisky for Malcolm. Malcolm hated port and since he was Captain, he didn't have to drink it anymore. But as a good Captain, he wouldn't take it away from those who enjoyed it.

As his officers sipped their port, Malcolm outlined their new mission; the stops in Constantinople, Romania, and finally back to their base. His men asked the same question repeatedly: why was the *Daedalus* taken from a vital, if not boring, duty for a glorified cargo run? Malcolm had the self-same question and deferred to Joan, who in her practiced manner said a great deal to allay suspicions, and not say anything at all.

At length, the men left the Officer's Mess. While Malcolm was giving final orders to Lieutenant Hensley, he glanced up to see several his men bidding good night to Joan. He stopped mid-sentence in his orders, feeling a wave of anger and jealousy wash over him. He quickly caught himself, and continued discussing how long it would take to complete each leg of the journey. Mr. Hensley guessed that they should be in Constantinople in two days, another day to Tismana, and another three days until they returned to base in Kingsnorth, not allowing for any other stops along the way.

One by one, the officers took their leave, and soon the only people left were Malcolm, Saxon, and Joan. "I see that it's just the three of us," Saxon said. "Which means it is my cue to bid you a good evening." He kissed Joan's hand and left the Officer's Mess.

"Well, Captain, you seem to have me all to yourself," she said in a husky voice that suggested seduction.

"That I do," Malcolm replied. "May I escort you to my quarters where we can continue this discussion in earnest?" Malcolm offered her his arm, and she slipped her arm through quickly.

They strolled at a leisurely pace to Malcolm's quarters, and waited until the hallway was clear before they entered his cabin. He was taking a big chance bringing her to his cabin, but their previous embraces had left him wanting more.

Malcolm barely closed the door when Joan grabbed him, and kissed him with urgency. Malcolm returned the kiss with equal ardour, and soon hands were running over each other's bodies, looking for buttons and zips.

Malcolm broke the clinch. "Hold that thought. I should hang up my dress uniform before it gets wrinkled. It would be out of character, and we don't want to arouse any suspicion. You get into something more comfortable, and wait for me on the bed. I'll be but a moment." Malcolm went to his water closet, and closed the door behind him.

Joan took the opportunity to remove her jacket, get out of her dress, and loosen her corset. She draped her jacket and dress over Malcolm's chair, and moved to the bed. As she did, she noticed Malcolm's trunk was open, and that he had left his lockbox open. In it, she saw a ring box from a top-notch London jeweller. She opened it and gasped; it was an engagement ring. Once the shock wore off, her anger began to rise. Clenching her fists, she sputtered as she marched over to the door to his private bath, and began banging on it.

"What's the matter?" Malcolm said, flinging the door open. "Is something the matter?"

"What is this?" she asked, thrusting the ring box in his face.

"What? How did you find that?" he asked, flustered.

"Your lockbox was open where anyone could see it. I recognised the jeweller's name. Now, answer my question; what is this?" The volume of her voice was beginning to increase.

"It's… it's… it's an engagement ring," he muttered.

"I can see that. To whom do you wish to propose? Is there someone else?"

"Of course not, you silly woman!" Malcolm retorted.

"You don't think you're giving it to me, do you?" she said. "We've had this discussion. We're not getting married."

"*You've* had this discussion, you mean," Malcolm replied, anger rising in his voice. "Every time we have this 'discussion', as you put it, you yell at me and stomp off, before you even hear what I have to say!"

"That's exactly what I intend to do this time," she said. She began to get dressed, but since she had loosened her corset, the dress was even tighter fitting than usual. She let out an exasperated breath, as she tried to dress and leave the cabin.

"Why are you so afraid to even discuss it?" he said.

"Because I don't want to be trapped."

"Am I really that awful to be around? That you feel trapped?"

"No, that's not it. It's… I watched my grandmother and mother become dependent on their lovers, and it cost them so much. I vowed I would never depend on a man… for anything."

"See, that's the problem. You see it as chains that bind you, and keep you down. I see it as spending our lives together, hand in hand."

"Suddenly you're a poet, and not an engineer?"

"What the hell is that supposed to mean?" he asked.

"Now that you have this engagement ring, you talk about love and connection. I thought you were a man."

"What the bloody hell do you mean by that?" Malcolm snapped.

"You think a pretty bauble and some silky words would make me weak in the knees, and I'd say yes?"

"When did I become the villain here?" Malcolm asked in disbelief. "You're the one that went through my lockbox."

"For your information, the box was already open and just sitting there. I happened to notice it." Joan had her dress on, and was beginning to pull on her jacket.

"Be that as it may, you shouldn't have been looking though my belongings."

"I'll bet you left it out because you wanted me to see it!" she yelled.

"No, I left it out, you daft cow, because I needed to put these," holding up his military decorations, "back in the box when the evening was done." He angrily tossed his medals into the lock box, grabbed the ring box from Joan, and made to put it in the lock box.

"Don't put it away on my account. You know I can open that," she sneered.

"It keeps the honest folks out," he said. He shut the lock box, but left the ring box in his hand.

"You think I'm dishonest?" she yelled.

"You are a spy. Honesty is something that doesn't come easily to you."

"Oh, so I'm dishonest? Anything else you want to get off your chest? If I'm such a horrible person, why don't you find someone else to receive that ring?" Joan hollered.

"Maybe I will!" Malcolm yelled back.

"Fine, you do that," she said. She stomped to the door and flung it wide open.

"Fine. Wait a minute, let me at least escort you to your room," he said.

"I can find my own way!" she said as she stomped down the hallway.

Malcolm followed her to the door, and looked down the hall after Joan. As soon as Malcolm's head popped past the doorway, nearly a dozen doors all along the corridor shut. Malcolm watched as Joan opened her door and slammed it; the sound reverberating down the hall.

He slowly shut the door. He locked both the lock box and the trunk before slumping on to his bed. *That's not the way I saw the evening ending*, he thought, as his heart felt like a lead weight in his chest.

CHAPTER 8

Malcolm tossed and turned all night; his mind replaying the fight with Joan. This was a bad fight, even by their standards. He said things that he had not meant. Joan was skilled at irritating him into saying something mean, and suddenly, he became the villain. He knew he had to apologise because he needed to work with her for the duration of the mission.

But Joan had hurt him last night. He had done nothing but treat her with love, and received nothing but scorn in return. He had been foolish to leave the engagement ring out where she could see it, but he hadn't thought she would fly off the handle.

Still groggy from a night of bad sleep, Malcolm washed, dressed, and went down the hall to Joan's cabin. He knocked three times on the door, but received no answer. As he was turning to leave, one of the crewman asked, "Are you looking for Madame De Marnier? She's in the mess, having breakfast with Commander Saxon."

"Very good. Thank you," Malcolm said. The crewman saluted. Malcolm returned the salute, and headed to the mess hall. When he arrived, he did, in fact, see Joan having an animated conversation with Saxon. Both looked in his direction when he entered, and returned to their conversation. Malcolm got a very large mug of strong tea, and patiently waited in line for breakfast. Today, it was beans on toast.

"May I join you?" Malcolm asked, as he approached the table.

"Yes, for a moment. I was just leaving. I must get to the bridge. The Captain is a slave driver." Saxon said, trying to elicit a smile from either of them. He was afraid that the frostiness of the two stares might freeze his tea, and left the room quickly.

"I was just about to return to my cabin," Joan said, as she started to rise.

"Please, Madame," Malcolm said, touching her arm. "Please stay for a moment. I wish to apologise for," he hesitated, realising that there were many eyes on them, "… for getting off on the wrong foot last night. Many things were said and I, for my part, would like to apologise."

"Apology accepted, Captain," she said through tight lips as she sat down. Malcolm waited for a second, and sat down across from her.

He waited, expecting to hear an apology in return. He waited several more seconds and sighed, as he started to eat his breakfast.

"If you are sulking and expecting an apology from me, you will not have it," she said.

"Figures," Malcolm muttered, as he shovelled a forkful of beans into his mouth.

"What was that?" she asked.

"Nothing, I was just enjoying my breakfast," Malcolm replied. He wasn't enjoying it at all. The beans, although decent by usual standards, were sitting like lead weights in his stomach. He felt his blood begin to boil, as he realised that Joan had no intention of apologising.

"What are your plans today, Madame?" he asked, with all the politeness and sincerity he could muster.

"I thought I would stay in my cabin today. I have a great deal of correspondence that I must send."

"I was hoping we would have the honour of your company on the bridge."

"I'm afraid I have to decline," she said.

"More's the pity. Would you care to dine with me tonight in the Officer's Mess?"

"I think that might not be wise, Captain. I think neither of us want a repeat of last night."

"No, that would be unwise," Malcolm said. He rose and picked up the tray containing his half-eaten breakfast. "I do not wish to impose upon you any longer. I'll send one of my men to notify you when we reach Constantinople."

"That would be most kind," she said. The words were civil, as was the tone, but each word had a frostiness that seemed to cool the room several degrees.

Malcolm gave a nod of his head, and left Joan at her table. He returned his tray, refilled his tea, and left for the bridge. Although Malcolm hoped otherwise, he knew that the crew heard their argument, and knew that she had flown from his quarters in a rage. And while it was the largest ship in the Air Service, when it came to gossip like this, it was very small. As he reached the bulkhead for the bridge, he stopped and took a deep breath before entering. Joan had told him that deep breathing was good for centring oneself. It wasn't working this morning. He pushed open the bulkhead door, and strode in with a sense of confidence that he didn't have. He noticed a couple of the junior navigators looking up at him and whispering, so he walked over to the two of them who immediately turned their attention to their maps.

"Anything you wish to share, Mr. Blackburn? Mr. Croft?" he asked.

"No sir," the young lieutenants replied in near unison.

"Very good. Let's keep it that way." Malcolm rested a hand on each of the young officers' shoulders. "You're both doing such a fine job on the bridge, it would be a shame if you were reassigned to oversee and clean the wastewater treatment plant."

"Yes, sir," they replied.

"Glad we understand each other, gentlemen." He looked up and saw Commander Saxon at his station. "Commander Saxon, what is our status?"

"We are currently over Albania. We should reach Constantinople by tomorrow morning."

"Excellent," Malcolm said. He sat in his chair and read the morning status reports. When he finished, he turned to Saxon and said, "Commander Saxon, could you join me in my office?"

"Yes, sir," Saxon replied. The two officers left the bridge and went to Malcolm's office just down the hall.

They took their customary positions in Malcolm's office, Malcolm behind the desk, and Saxon in the chair opposite.

"What were you and Madame De Marnier talking about this morning when I saw you in the mess?"

Saxon sighed. "What do you think we were talking about? The weather? Of course we were talking about your fight last night."

"You heard that?" Malcolm asked sheepishly.

"I'd be surprised if they hadn't heard it in Constantinople." Saxon said. "Everybody on this hall certainly heard it. By now everyone else on the ship knows that Madame De Marnier left the captain's cabin after a loud argument. Mercifully, it seems the crew is ignorant of the cause of the argument."

"But you know?" Malcolm asked.

"Yes, Jo… Madame De Marnier told me. Malcolm, you have to be careful."

"Me? Did she tell you I started the fight?"

"No, she said that she started it when you tried to propose to her."

"Ah, well, that's not exactly the way it happened. I left my lock box open that had the ring I intend to give her when we can have a reasoned discussion about it. She found it and started in on me."

"Ah, that's a very different picture than what I got from her. She said you were pressuring her to accept your proposal, and when she wouldn't say yes, you started harassing her." Saxon paused. "Of the two, your account seems far more likely." He paused again, choosing his words carefully. "The two of you are going to have to work together, at least for the time being. Can you do that?"

"I can. I, for my part, have already apologised. I'm still waiting for her to apologise to me."

"You may have to wait quite a while," Saxon offered with a careful tone. "She feels like you're pressuring her into doing something she doesn't want to do."

"I had no plans to even discuss it last night. She found it because she was snooping, like she always does. Then she started at me like a rabid terrier."

"You can't be mad at her for snooping, can you? You know what she does for a living."

Malcolm sighed, and buried his face in his hands. "What do I do, Charles?"

"Lord knows, I'm no expert on women, but it seems like your best option is to keep your distance, and let her simmer down. This ship is a small place. She'll calm down... eventually. And when she does, just say it was your fault."

"But I didn't start it!" Malcolm objected.

"That may be true," Saxon replied, "but it's been my experience that the man is always wrong, especially when he isn't." Malcolm managed a weak laugh. "For what it's worth, I think she does care about you. I think that's why she's so mad."

"That's oddly comforting... I think," Malcolm said. "Thank you, Charles. Now that we've solved my personal problems, let's prepare for tomorrow's landing in Constantinople."

The two made plans for their arrival in Constantinople. Malcolm tasked Saxon with talking to Joan, to understand the arrangements that had been made to pick up the religious artifacts. Saxon returned some time later. The relics were stored at the Cathedral of St. George, the seat of the senior patriarchate of the Greek Orthodox Church. Across the street from the Cathedral was a large park where the *Daedalus* would land, and receive the artifacts. It seemed that the Ottoman Empire was happy to get the infidel artifacts out of its capital, and the Greek Orthodox Church was likewise happy to relocate the artifacts somewhere else.

When everything was in order, Saxon returned to the bridge, and Malcolm issued orders for the crew to prepare for the landing. All crew were required to be in full dress when they arrived, as it seemed that Patriarch Joachim III himself wished to bless the crew, and ship, before its departure. The bridge officers groaned, as they all knew that they had to find a way to clean the pasta sauce from their uniforms. Malcolm sighed. He was out of his league with these diplomatic missions, and needed Joan's expertise. At the very least, he was going to need her to translate. But that might be difficult, since she wouldn't speak to him.

Malcolm spent the rest of the day and most of the evening in his office, even having a midshipman bring his meal to his office. Malcolm buried himself in his work, and was startled in the evening when there was a knock on his door. "Come in," he said, not looking up from his work. Joan entered and closed the door behind her without saying a word.

After a few seconds of silence, Malcolm looked up from his work. "Yes?" he said, before realising it was Joan. "Oh, it's you. What can I do for you, Madame De Marnier?" Malcolm didn't rise as he would customarily do when a lady entered the room.

"We land tomorrow in Constantinople, and I wondered if you needed any assistance in the preparations," she said. She sat down at the chair in front of his desk.

"I believe we are set for the preparations. I will need your assistance tomorrow when we greet the Patriarch. In addition to knowing not a single word of Greek, I am a bit lost as to the correct protocol."

"I will assist to the best of my ability," she said flatly. She could see that Malcolm was still hurt, and she did her best to keep her voice emotionless. "If you're not too busy, we could go over the protocol now," she offered.

"If you want," Malcolm said. He put his pen down, and sat back in his chair regarding her.

Joan started to explain the proper protocol for greeting the religious leader. Malcolm listened attentively, as if he was listening to a university lecture. When she finished her dissertation on the protocol of greeting the Patriarch, Joan took a deep breath. "Captain Robertson, there is one more thing."

"Yes?" he asked, looking up from the notes that he had written, after it became obvious that the greeting protocol was rather involved. Her lesson also included a quick overview of the Greek Orthodox Church, and its difference from the Anglican Church.

"It has been brought to my attention," she said, and then stopped as if unsure how to continue. Malcolm was puzzled. The word 'unsure' was never used to describe anything that Joan did. "I might have slightly overreacted last night, and I apologise for any hurt I may have caused."

Slightly overreacted? Malcolm thought to himself. *How about completely overreacted?* He closed his eyes, took a deep breath, then opened his eyes and said, "I accept your apology."

Joan seemed visibly relieved, and some of her confidence seemed to return.

"However," he continued, and her posture immediately snapped to ramrod straight, fire beginning to flash in her eyes. "After the mission, we will discuss the matter in more detail. For now, we both have jobs to do, and we can't afford the distraction."

"I agree," she said. "Thank you, Captain." His expression softened slightly. She stood to leave and this time, Malcolm rose as well. "I should return to my cabin, so that I'm rested and prepared for the morning."

Malcolm walked around the desk and offered her his elbow. She linked her arm in it, and they walked to the door, then he took her hand and gave it a gentlemanly kiss. "Thank you, Madame. I look forward to working closely with you again," placing an ever so slight emphasis on the word 'closely'.

"As do I," she said, as a smile flickered across her face. Malcolm watched as she glided down the hall to her cabin. *That's not the way I saw the evening ending,* he thought, as his heart felt a little less heavy.

CHAPTER 9

The next morning, the *Daedalus* began its descent, and approach, to the city of Constantinople. Flying over the Mediterranean, the *Daedalus* approached by the Bosphorus strait, and made the graceful turn around the Golden Horn near the Maiden's Tower. From the bridge, the view of Constantinople showed the unique blend of architecture that made up the city; the ancient walls built by the Western and Eastern Roman Empires, the mosques and minarets of the conquering Ottomans, and the Byzantine churches and palaces, culminating in the great Hagia Sofia. Once a great basilica and now a mosque, it dominated the skyline of Constantinople. The waterways buzzed with ships; large oceangoing vessels travelling into or out of the Bosphorus, smaller ships and tugs hauling cargo around the city, and even a few sailboats.

Since becoming captain, Malcolm never tired of watching the approach to a city. In his years in the Engine Room, he rarely saw the destination until after they landed. Malcolm delighted in watching the city appear from afar, and grow, until he could make out the individual details of its buildings.

Malcolm remembered his last visit to Constantinople. The

Daedalus had been in a race with the Germans, to supply the Ottoman Empire with military advisors, as the empire sought to modernise its forces. The overeager second-in-command, Commander Bromley, ordered Malcolm to run the overworked engines at full speed all night. Malcolm protested, nearly going so far as to disobey a direct order. In the end, he did as he was ordered and shortly afterwards, the engines overheated and seized up. Malcolm went to extraordinary lengths to get them repaired. The *Daedalus* limped into Constantinople ahead of the Germans, allowing the British to cultivate a valuable ally, and secure contracts for naval and air ships. Malcolm received a commendation for his efforts, and Bromley received a rebuke from the captain.

How much has changed since my last visit? Malcolm thought. As he looked away from the view, he noticed that Joan had entered the bridge unobserved. She was dressed in a shapeless black dress, that hid her curves, and wore a matching hat with a lace veil over her face.

"Madame De Marnier, I was just going to send for you. We are just approaching the landing site." He looked at her quizzically, indicating her dress with a nod of his head.

"Both the Ottomans and the Patriarch believe that women should remain modest, and keep their faces covered. While it is a backward notion, I follow it so as not to offend our hosts."

"Very good. As you can see," he said, indicating the main window, "we are making our final descent. Excuse me as I concentrate on our approach and landing."

"Yes. Don't mind me," she said, as she found an inconspicuous place to wait.

Malcolm guided the ship over the waterway, and to the park, with an ease learned over the last two years. As the airship neared the park, he saw the landing crew ready to receive the *Daedalus*. He ordered the crew to drop the mooring lines, and for Engineering to cut the power. The *Daedalus* slowly floated down to the ground, and Malcolm timed his approach so that the landing crews could grab the mooring lines, and quickly attach them to the weighted winches. The *Daedalus* was now in the hands of the landing crew. Malcolm's only job at this point was to make sure that the rudder remained steady in case of wind.

Malcolm was relieved that he had completed a textbook landing. When the ship was secured, he offered his arm and escorted Joan to the gangway in the cargo hold, where they would meet the Patriarch and other dignitaries. When they arrived at the cargo hold, Joan removed her arm from Malcolm's saying, "They would consider it unseemly for you to touch a woman who is not your spouse," she said.

"Huh, that's interesting," Malcolm said. He immediately regretted the words as they came out of his mouth. Joan shot him a venomous look before regaining her composure. She took a step away, to leave an even larger distance between Malcolm and her.

Malcolm looked down the gangway and saw the Patriarch Joachim III ready to greet them. The Patriarch looked the part of a holy man; bedecked in black robes, with a black kalimavkion and a black veil covering the back of his head. Coupled with his long, white beard, his overall look was severe, but Malcolm could see compassion in the Patriarch's eyes.

Malcolm took a deep breath and prepared to greet the Patriarch, as Joan had instructed him last night. When he arrived before the Patriarch, he bowed, reached down with his right hand, and touched the ground. He placed his right hand over his left with his palms facing up and said, "Bless, All Holiness" in Greek.

The Patriarch answered in Greek, "May the Lord bless you and your crew." He made the Sign of the Cross, placed his right hand on Malcolm's, and Malcolm kissed the holy man's hand. Joan repeated the ritual. When she was finished, she took her place beside Malcolm, and acted as interpreter as Malcolm began.

"Your All Holiness, in the name of King George V, by the Grace of God, of the United Kingdom of Great Britain and Ireland, and of the British Dominions beyond the Seas, King, Emperor of India, I thank you for your blessing, and your generous loan of the artifacts of your great church." Malcolm purposely left out the King's title of "Defender of the Faith", as Joan indicated that it might offend the Patriarch. Joan effortlessly translated Malcolm's words into Greek, and the Patriarch's response into English.

"He says that he is glad to be of service, and glad that His Majesty will look after the artifacts of his church. But he asks one thing in return."

"What is that?" Malcolm asked. He was worried that he would have to renegotiate the terms on the loan of the artifacts, and had no idea of the protocol involved.

"He would like to have a ride in the *Daedalus*."

"Please tell His Holiness that it would be my most distinct pleasure to fulfill his wish."

When Joan relayed this to the Patriarch, he smiled. *He looks less the solemn priest, and more like Father Christmas*, Malcolm thought. Malcolm led the way as the Patriarch slowly made his way up the gangplank. When reaching the cargo bay, Malcolm ordered one of his crew to contact the ground crew, and let them know that the *Daedalus* would be lifting off momentarily, and ordered another crewman to inform the bridge as well.

He returned to Joan and the Patriarch. He gave the Patriarch a tour of the *Daedalus*, ending at the bridge. He led the Patriarch to the main windows at the front of the bridge, so he could see everything. Within a few minutes of reaching the bridge, the arrangements for the flight were complete, and Malcolm slowly angled the *Daedalus* back into the sky.

Malcolm focused on piloting the *Daedalus* over and around Constantinople, traveling up the Bospherus, over the Golden Horn, over the Mediterranean, before returning to the park, where Malcolm made another nearly perfect landing. During the whole trip, the Patriarch stared in wide-eyed amazement. When they landed, the Patriarch started talking very quickly and excitedly in Greek. When he finished, Joan turned and said, "He wishes to tell you that he never thought in his life, he would be able to see his city as God sees it. He thinks that you must be a holy man as well, as you spend so much time in the sky with God. He obviously doesn't know you," she said in a much lower voice, that only Malcolm heard.

Malcolm ignored Joan's barb, and replied, "I don't know about that, Your All Holiness, but it does give one a different perspective." Joan again translated; Malcolm hoped that she was using his words, and not her own.

Malcolm escorted the Patriarch back through the ship. The Patriarch signalled his staff, and they brought forth numerous crates. A priest handed the Patriarch a bundle. The Patriarch blessed it, and handed it to Malcolm. Joan translated, "Please take this icon of St. Nicholas, who is master of Air and Tempest. May he bless your ship and its crew, as you take our most holy relics for safekeeping."

"I am most honoured, Your All Holiness. I will keep this on the bridge so that through St. Nicholas, God may watch over us." As Joan translated, she gave a brief nod of approval.

The Patriarch raised his arms and began to recite in Greek. Malcolm looked at Joan, who indicated that they should kneel. They knelt as the Patriarch continued his recitation in Greek, and approached the *Daedalus*. Malcolm started to move, but Joan put a hand on his arm to indicate that he should let matters be. The Patriarch continued toward the *Daedalus*, and produced an aspergillum that he used to splash the *Daedalus* with holy water. When the Patriarch finished, he returned to Malcolm and Joan, who were still kneeling. He made the sign of the Cross over both, and offered his hand first to Malcolm. Malcolm kissed the Patriarch's ring and again offered, "Bless, All Holiness" in the Greek that Joan had taught him. The Patriarch indicated that they should rise. He made a final benediction, and then turned and left. "Bless you Captain, and may the angels of God himself watch over you as fly." Joan translated.

When the Patriarch left, the real work began, as the crates were loaded onto the *Daedalus*. Malcolm decided that given the significance of these artifacts to the Church, that he would oversee the loading. Malcolm could not shake a sense of foreboding since the start of this mission, and even the blessings of the Patriarch of the Eastern Orthodox Church did little to diminish that feeling.

When the crew had secured the cargo to Malcolm's satisfaction, he and Joan returned to the bridge. Once there, he ordered a midshipman to find the ship's carpenter to hang the icon of St. Nicholas. Joan looked at him quizzically. Malcolm replied, "I'm not a heathen. And besides, given the number of things that could go wrong, I'd rather err on the side of having the support of the Master of Air and Tempest."

Malcolm began the pre-flight checks, and soon the bridge and ship were a whirl of activity. Malcolm radioed the Engine Room, and addressed the ship to be ready for liftoff. Joan watched in fascination as Malcolm coordinated the myriad of activities, like a maestro conducting a symphony. He cued every crewman, and each performed his duty with well-practiced precision.

Soon, the *Daedalus* rose over Constantinople and headed north to Romania. Again, the feeling of dread filled Malcolm. Although it had become an independent country, Romania was sandwiched between the Austro-Hungarian and Ottoman Empires; two empires often working at countermeasures to Great Britain. The Balkans were a political powder keg ready to explode, as the collection of small Balkan states all clamoured for independence from the Ottoman Empire. Malcolm tried to console himself with the thought that the mission had gone well so far, his fight with Joan notwithstanding.

Once the *Daedalus* was well on its way, Malcolm asked for Saxon and Joan to join him in his office. Malcolm brought another seat to the front of his desk. He settled behind his desk, and waited for first Saxon, and then Joan, to enter. Joan had changed from the shapeless black dress to a much more form fitting forest green dress with a jacket. It made it very difficult for him to both concentrate, and hold onto his anger about their fight.

"What do we know about our visit to Romania?" Malcolm asked.

"Very little." Saxon replied.

"Tismana is a fortified monastery built on Starmina Mountain," Joan said. "It is part of the Romanian Orthodox Church. It has impressive fortress walls that encircle the church at the centre. I have been there only once, but I believe that the *Daedalus* must land outside the walls, as I don't believe it will fit inside." Again, Malcolm was amazed at the places that Joan had been in her life.

"Why would Dr. Sinclair go there, and not rendezvous with us in Bucharest?" Malcolm asked.

"I don't know. Perhaps he needed to retrieve additional religious artifacts. That seems to be the purpose of this trip."

Malcolm could tell that Joan had suspicions about why they were going to Tismana, and she wasn't telling him. "You don't sound convinced that that's the reason he's there," Malcolm prodded. "What exactly does Dr. Sinclair do for the Secret Service? His credentials don't seem to be very useful in the spy business."

"True," Joan said, hesitating. "What I'm about to say must not leave this room, and I ask you, especially you, Malcolm, to keep an open mind."

"What's that supposed to mean?" Malcolm asked, as his temper started to flare.

"It means that you are a man of science and rational thought. Dr. Sinclair deals with things that defy science and rational thought."

"I don't follow," said Malcolm.

"Dr. Nigel Sinclair works for a top-secret branch of the Secret Service, tasked with investigating supernatural threats to the Empire and, if necessary, eliminating them."

Malcolm could not help but laugh. "Supernatural threats? You mean he chases the bogey man?"

"No," Joan said, with a hint of irritation in her voice. "This is exactly why I was hesitant to tell you. The things that Nigel faces are some of the most dangerous and deadly foes in all of creation. I know little about the work that he does, but what little I do know makes me glad that it is not my job."

Malcolm started to make another joke, but saw the serious look on Joan's face and decided he better not. Joan continued, "It's possible that he has had to deal with some sort of supernatural agent, and the sacred ground of the monastery gives him some measure of protection. It's my understanding that most supernatural entities cannot step on hallowed ground, like that of a church, or in this case, a monastery."

"If he is hiding from some supernatural agent, as you put it, and we have to land outside of the monastery walls…"

"The *Daedalus* has no protection from whatever chased Nigel inside the monastery," Joan said.

CHAPTER 10

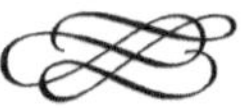

*M*alcolm laughed. "You don't seriously believe that, do you?"

Joan hesitated. "Like you, I found it difficult to believe. I have seen glimpses of the enemies that Nigel fights, and I believe it's a real threat." Joan was deadly serious.

Malcolm knew better than to contradict her. "Do you have any suggestions?"

"Land and leave as soon as possible. And do it in the daylight."

"Charles, you've been silent. What do you think?"

"I'm inclined to agree with Madame De Marnier," he said reluctantly. "We don't know the real reason Dr. Sinclair came to Tismana. I suggest we remain on alert, and as Madame De Marnier suggested, we spend as little time on the ground as possible."

Malcolm sighed. He couldn't believe that he was having this discussion with two rational people. "Very well," he said, after a notable pause. "If there's nothing else, we should prepare for our landing tomorrow."

Joan and Saxon took that as their cue that the meeting was over, and left Malcolm's office. *Could they be correct? Could there be supernat-*

ural forces at work in the world? he thought. Malcolm found it difficult to believe, but then again, two years ago, he never thought that Martians existed.

Malcolm finished his work in his office and returned to the bridge. The weather ahead of them looked dismal. Low, grey storm clouds hung low to the ground. Malcolm ordered the crew to fly up above the clouds. The navigators were going to have to earn their money today, Malcolm thought. Navigation by instrument was possible, but it was much more difficult and required exact information on heading and speed. Malcolm returned to his office to tackle the never-ending pile of paperwork that screamed for his attention. Sometime later, Saxon joined Malcolm in his office.

"Do you believe that we could be dealing with supernatural forces?"

"Probably not," Saxon hesitated. "But in my travels, I've lived in many old homes. Once, while my family was staying at Windsor Castle, I saw this translucent figure pass right through a closed door. I followed it, and there was no one in the room. The temperature of the room was a good ten degrees colder than the hall. I later identified the face as King George III from a portrait." He paused before continuing, his face taking on a very serious demeanour. "I'm inclined to believe that there is more than can be described by science."

Malcolm had no idea how to respond to this. Here was his friend, a man whose judgement he trusted as much as his own, telling him he believed in ghosts and the supernatural. Maybe Charles was correct; maybe there was more in the universe than could be described by science. Or rather, the science had not caught up to be able to explain the phenomena. *After all, who would think that in the last thirty years, airships such as the Daedalus would ply the air, or steam-powered vehicles would replace the horse and carriage?* Malcolm thought. The study of radiation was a whole new science. Could there be the creation of a whole new science needed to explain the so-called supernatural?

Malcolm left the bridge to Saxon, returning to his office where he reviewed reports and arrangements for their landing in Tismana.

Malcolm again sought out Joan for dinner, but his knocks on her door were left unanswered. *Damn that woman and her pride*, Malcolm thought, before he gave up and had his meal brought to his office where he ate alone.

Malcolm woke from a fitful sleep full of dreams of arguments with Joan, while being chased by transparent entities that travelled through doors. *No more ghost stories for me*, Malcolm thought, as he trudged to the mess for a mug of very strong tea. When he returned to the bridge, Sub-Lieutenant Blackburn informed him that they would arrive at Tismana within the next hour. Moments later, Saxon joined him on the bridge, and Malcolm sent a crewman to fetch Joan. Then he ordered the crew to begin the descent.

Sometime later, Joan joined them on the bridge, but Malcolm scarcely noticed her. To get below the cloud cover, the *Daedalus* was barely skimming the treetops of the forests that went as far as the eye could see. Malcolm had briefly spotted the monastery during a break in the clouds. It was nestled on the side of a valley. It was going to be a narrow fit for the *Daedalus*. Malcolm reduced the speed to almost nothing, and tried to manoeuvre the great airship with all the precision he could muster. A few times, Malcolm heard the tops of the trees scraping the gondola.

After a long, gruelling, nerve-wracking descent, Malcolm manoeuvred the *Daedalus* to a clearing just outside of the main gate of the monastery. The crew quickly tied down the great airship, and Malcolm, Saxon, and Joan headed toward the main gangplank in the main cargo bay.

As they descended the gangplank, a tall, impeccably-dressed man hurried from the gate of the monastery, and approached the party. "Ah, Madame De Marnier, you received my cable! I was worried that I would be stuck here for some time." The man came to Joan, and kissed her on the cheek.

"Of course, Dr. Sinclair," Joan said. "I sent a cable when we left Malta letting you know to expect us today."

"I did not receive it," the man muttered. "Communications don't always reach this monastery."

Malcolm cleared his throat, and Joan said, "Dr. Nigel Sinclair, may I introduce Captain Malcolm Robertson, and Commander Charles Saxon, of His Majesty's Airship *Daedalus*?"

Malcolm offered his hand, "A pleasure to meet you, sir," he said. "I've heard so much about you." He looked at Joan, who shot him a withering look.

"Pleasure to meet you, Captain. But at the risk of sounding rude, would it be possible to suspend the pleasantries so that we may leave immediately?"

"Well, yes, that's fine," Malcolm said, caught off guard by the abruptness of the request. "How much time do you need to be ready to leave?"

"I believe that we will be ready to leave within the hour," he said.

"We?" Joan asked.

"Yes, my assistant Miss Deirdre Hastings-Elliott is here as well. It is a long story, and one best told when we have distance between us and this location. Excuse me, and I will get everything ready for our departure." And with that, Dr. Sinclair hurried back to the monastery, leaving a very confused trio.

"Is he always so… abrupt?" Saxon asked.

"No," Joan observed. "He's usually very polite and circumspect. It concerns me that he wishes to leave here so abruptly."

"Me, too," added Malcolm. "But the sooner we leave here, the happier I'll be." There was a chill in the foggy air that disquieted Malcolm. The fog seemed to weigh down on him in a way different than the familiar fog of London.

The three waited for twenty minutes before a young, attractive, blonde woman approached them. She wore a blue Empire dress with a fur cape draped across her shoulders. Her bright blonde hair fell in ringlets from beneath a wide brimmed hat. "Good day. I am Deirdre Hastings-Elliott, the Doctor's assistant." She offered her gloved hand which Malcolm took and kissed.

"I am Captain Malcolm Robertson of His Majesty's Airship *Daedalus*. This is Commander Charles Saxon, and Madame Charlotte

De Marnier," indicating the two. He was sure that he saw a glint of anger in Joan's eyes.

"Delighted to make your acquaintances," she said. Malcolm had to admit; she was far more charming than her boss. "In addition to my trunk, I have acquired several new dresses from my travels that I would like to bring aboard, if that would not be too much trouble?"

"No, no trouble at all. I'll have my men assist you," Malcolm replied. He signalled for two crew members to join him.

"That is most kind. I'd appreciate it if you wouldn't mention this to Dr. Sinclair. He constantly berates me for my shopping."

"Of course, Miss Hastings-Elliott. I will be the soul of discretion," Malcolm said, smiling. Again, out of the corner of his eyes, he saw the nasty glance that Joan gave him.

"Please, I insist that you call me Deirdre. I hate such formality between friends. And I think we should be very good friends," she said as she smiled. The warmth of her smile took Malcolm off guard.

"Very well, Deirdre. Then you must call me Malcolm." Again, Joan's eyes looked like they might set fire to him.

The two crewmen arrived. "Please assist Miss Hastings-Elliott. She has some cargo she needs brought aboard."

"Thank you, Malcolm. You are most kind. I'd like it brought to my cabin, if that's not too much of an inconvenience."

"No inconvenience at all."

Deirdre turned and escorted the two crew men off to an area to collect her trunk. Malcolm felt a sharp pain in his side, and turned to realise that Joan had poked him very hard in the ribs. "What?" asked.

"She certainly has you eating out of her hand," she snapped.

"What's that supposed to mean?" .

"… 'I think we should be very good friends'," Joan mimicked. "All she had to do was bat her eyes at you, and you were putty."

"I beg your pardon, Madame De Marnier," Malcolm said pointedly. "I do believe that you made it very clear that there are no ties between us."

Joan started to retort when Saxon stepped between them, and said,

"Do I have to separate you two children, or can you both behave like adults?"

Joan took a breath and straightened herself. "I'm certainly capable of behaving with the proper decorum, if the Captain can think with his brain as opposed to other parts of his anatomy…"

Malcolm started to retort, but saw the serious look on Saxon's face. He was right; this was not the time or place to get into this discussion again. "I am more than capable of making rational decisions."

"That remains to be seen," Joan muttered under her breath.

"Madame De Marnier, must I have you restricted to your quarters?" Saxon asked.

"No, Commander," she said sullenly. "Perhaps I'll see if Nigel needs any assistance," she said, as she stomped toward the monastery gates.

When she left, Malcolm said, "Thank you, Charles. I don't know what got into her."

"Malcolm, she was right. You all but swooned over the young lady."

"I did not," Malcolm retorted. After a beat, he said "Alright, maybe a little."

"And you made Joan very jealous," added Saxon.

"Good, she deserves it," Malcolm pouted.

"Be that as it may, I don't want to play diplomat between the two of you for the rest of our flight. I joined the military, not the diplomatic corps."

"You're right," Malcolm said. "I will try not to provoke her. I can't say she will do the same."

"That's half the battle," Saxon said. "Try not to act like a besotted school boy when Miss Hastings-Elliott is around."

"Yes, Charles," Malcolm said.

Six crewmen arrived, carrying the large crate followed by Deirdre. "Captain, I believe it's customary for me to ask for permission to come aboard? May I have permission to come aboard?" she asked coyly.

"Of course, Deirdre. Permission granted," Malcolm said, trying to sound like a mature, capable captain.

"Thank you, Malcolm," Deirdre said, as she slipped her arm through his. "Perhaps you will escort me to my quarters?" she asked.

Malcolm looked into her large blue eyes. He swallowed and gently untangled himself from her grasp. "It would be my pleasure, Deirdre, but I think that Commander Saxon should escort you to your quarters. I need to oversee the preparations for lift off. Duty calls," he said playfully.

Deirdre looked Malcolm in the eyes and said, "What a shame, but I understand. Perhaps, later, you can give me a private tour of your airship. I think I would like that very much," she said.

"If my duties permit," Malcolm blurted. "I leave you in the capable hands of Commander Saxon," Malcolm said. He decided that this was the moment to personally supervise the placement of the cargo.

A few minutes later, Dr. Sinclair and Joan returned with several suitcases. Malcolm ordered his men to take the cases from them. When the duo approached Malcolm, Dr. Sinclair immediately asked "Is my assistant aboard? I looked for her in the monastery, and did not find her there."

"Yes, she and her cargo are aboard," Malcolm said.

"I must apologise for my rudeness, but we need to leave as soon as possible," Dr. Sinclair cautioned.

"I believe all is in order now that you have arrived. Madame De Marnier, perhaps you will escort the doctor to his cabin, while I make the final preparations for lift off."

"As you say, Captain," Joan said. "Come Nigel, let us leave the Captain to his work." She linked her arm around Sinclair's, and directed him out of the cargo bay. Malcolm tried not to let it bother him, but snapped at the first crewman who asked him a question, then he stalked off to the bridge.

Everything was ready for lift off when Malcolm arrived. Within minutes, the *Daedalus* started its long trip back to its base at Kingsnorth. Once the crew settled the course, Malcolm had crewmen gather Madame De Marnier, Dr. Sinclair, and Miss Hastings-Elliott for a conference in the Officer's Mess. He also sent a midshipman to round up a light lunch of sandwiches and tea.

Malcolm and Saxon adjourned to the Officer's Mess, and waited for their guests.

Soon, the trio arrived and everyone was silent as the midshipman served the group. Malcolm, sensing there would be no discussion until the midshipman left the room, dismissed the midshipman, telling him that he could clean up when the meeting was over. As the door closed, Malcolm waited for Dr. Sinclair to start the conversation. After several long seconds, Malcolm finally let out an exasperated sigh, and said, "Dr. Sinclair, I believe you were going to explain our abrupt departure."

Dr. Sinclair, deep in thought, realised that Malcolm had addressed him. "I'm sorry, what did you say, Captain?"

"I said," Malcolm repeated, a hint of irritation in his voice, "you were going to explain our abrupt departure?"

"Yes, yes," he said, somewhat flustered. He started hesitantly. "How much do you know of my work?"

"I know that you have Doctorates in Anthropology, Theology, and Classics; you specialise in mythology, folklore, and lost cultures; you speak and read more languages than I have fingers and toes; and I've been told that you investigate things that go bump in the night," Malcolm said. Joan shot him a withering stare, but Malcolm didn't care.

"Things that go bump in the night?" Sinclair laughed. "An apt, if not colourful, description for what I do."

"Why did we have to leave so abruptly? Why did you have to depart Rome in the first place?"

Sinclair looked at Joan for an indication of whether he should proceed. Malcolm saw her give him an almost imperceptible nod. Sinclair took a deep breath and began.

"Everything you have said is true. Although I am primarily a Reader at Oxford, I do work in a very secret capacity for the Secret Service. I investigate, and sometimes deal with, those things that defy logical, scientific description. By that I mean, the science that we currently have at our disposal."

"I'm sorry, I'm not following. What is it you investigate?"

Sinclair spoke slowly as if explaining to a child. "I study the supernatural and paranormal sciences."

"The para-what?" asked Malcolm.

"Paranormal," Sinclair said. Malcolm thought his tone rather reminded him of one of the Readers he had had in university. "Paranormal; things outside the scope of our current scientific understanding. Things like clairvoyance, telepathy, telekinesis... and even those things considered supernatural."

Malcolm drew in a breath to speak, and Sinclair cut him off. "Yes, I know, you want to understand why I'm here, and we had to leave so suddenly."

"You can tell, us, Nigel," Joan said soothingly. "We will not judge you. Will we, Captain?" Her look told Malcolm that she would not stand for any disagreement.

"No, we won't judge you," Malcolm said defensively.

"Very well. As you know, my expertise is in so called 'lost civilisations'. To that end, my research has led me to books that not only describe long lost places, but also contain dark, forbidden knowledge." He paused, choosing his words carefully as he continued.

"I received a telegram from my assistant, Miss Hastings-Elliott, that a fragment of one such book was going to be auctioned in Bucharest. She was already in Bucharest when I received the telegraph. By the time I arrived, Miss Hastings-Elliott had secured the fragment. This fragment had some bearing on our mission."

Malcolm glanced over at Deirdre and caught her eye. She smiled at Malcolm who immediately return his attention to Dr. Sinclair.

"A book of forbidden knowledge has bearing on our mission? How?" Malcolm asked.

"I'm afraid I am not allowed to explain any farther," Nigel said.

"Of course," Malcolm snorted. "How, then, did you arrive in Tismana?" Malcolm asked.

"Although the fragment was not of great assistance, it did suggest that that something useful for our mission might be found in Sarmizegetusa Regia. This was the capital of the Dacian Empire. At the site are ruins of their temples, and a structure very like Stonehenge."

"And how does this relate to our mission?" Malcolm interrupted.

Nigel let out an exasperated sigh, but took a breath before continuing. "Again, I can't tell you in detail. But we were there looking for something useful at the temple ruins when we had... an encounter with the local people."

Malcolm waited before prompting, "What kind of an encounter?"

"When we arrived at the nearby village, we told the locals that we would be scouting for an archaeological excavation to occur later. The villagers regarded us warmly, as many locals seek work as diggers or labourers. Over the next few days as we explored the ruined temples. I had the distinct feeling we were being watched, and Miss Hastings-Elliott, whose instincts about such things are more acute than mine, agreed. We weren't in any real danger until we stayed out after dark." Again, Malcolm looked at Deirdre when Sinclair mentioned her part in the story. This time, Malcolm was sure that she had winked at him. He looked away and caught Joan's glance, which was murderous if nothing else.

Malcolm felt warm, and suddenly felt as if his collar were choking him. "Why would you look for anything in the dark? Wouldn't it have made sense to wait until the morning?" Malcolm asked.

"In this case, we needed the alignment of the moon and certain stars," Nigel said in clipped tones. "And, as misfortune would have it, it was a full moon."

"Wouldn't that allow you to see more clearly?" Malcolm asked.

Nigel paused, as if considering his words carefully. "Do you know what the word Dacian means?"

"Someone from Dacia?" Malcolm quipped.

Nigel sighed. "Yes, of course it means that. But the word means 'wolf people'. They believed that they could be possessed by the spirit of the wolf, and had a ritual to transform themselves into wolves. They were successful. Residents of that area who are descended from the Dacians can become afflicted with lycanthropy."

"What is that?" Malcolm asked.

"In medical terms, lycanthropy means the delusion that one is a wolf. In this case, it means that they were able to transform themselves into actual wolves."

"Surely, you don't expect me to believe that people can turn into wolves," Malcolm scoffed.

"I don't care what you believe," Nigel said. His eyes flashed in anger. "You asked why we were here. Do you want me to continue?"

"I'm sorry," Malcolm said. "Please, continue."

"Miss Hastings-Elliott and I were able to find a hidden, subterranean chamber through information from the book fragment. After careful searching, we found the object of our search. As we climbed out of the chamber, a pack of wolves with glowing, red eyes circled the exit. We had the forethought to bring our guns, and we chased the pack away. We then returned to the village and arranged to leave immediately. It was difficult to find someone willing to leave during the full moon, but we offered one of the young men in the village enough money that he was willing to take us."

"I'm sorry, I'm having problems following," Malcolm asked. "What does the full moon have to do with this?"

"The actual transformation from man to wolf only occurs during the time that the moon is full. That is why the locals refuse to leave the safety of their homes during the full moon."

"Were you pursued?" Malcolm asked.

"Yes, for a time," Nigel said. "This time, we were prepared, and we were able to keep our pursuers at bay."

"How?" Malcolm asked.

"Silver has a particularly nasty effect on lycanthropes, and in fact, supernatural entities as a whole. As the pack neared our wagon, we fired a shotgun loaded with silver shot. Several rounds from the gun finally persuaded them to break off pursuit."

"Why come to Tismana?" Joan asked.

"Holy places tend to offer some level of protection from the supernatural. I had been to Tismana before, and believed that the monks would take us in. The fortified nature of the monastery was also a consideration. And as it turns out, I was able to negotiate the loan of some of the monastery's artifacts."

"Why were you in such a hurry to leave?" Malcolm asked.

"I wanted to leave well before nightfall, and another full moon."

"So we are not at risk from being pursued by something more sinister?" Joan asked.

"Not at this time," Nigel said.

"That, at least, is comforting," Malcolm said. "Do you know why we have a cargo hold full of religious artifacts from both the Roman Catholic and Greek Orthodox churches?"

"I do," Nigel said. "But I have express orders from Mycroft not to divulge the reason until we return to London. And quite frankly, if I did tell you, I daresay that you would not believe me."

Malcolm sighed. "Very well. Is there anything that you can tell us?"

"Nothing, save that it is important we reach London as soon as possible."

Malcolm waited for more information, and after several seconds of silence, he said. "Well, it appears that we have covered all that we are allowed to know." Joan shot him another angered look which he ignored. "Dr. Sinclair and Miss Hastings-Elliott, it would be my distinct pleasure if you would join me in a formal dinner with my officers in the Officer's Mess this evening."

"I don't think that..." began Sinclair, before his assistant interrupted him.

"It would be our pleasure," Deirdre said. "I think it would help us all to get to know each other." She turned her luminous blue eyes to Malcolm. "I, for one, would like to know more about our dashing captain."

His mind was overwhelmed by those beautiful blue eyes; he was lost for words when a loud cough from Joan brought his thoughts back to the here and now. Malcolm cleared his own throat and stood. "Very good," he said. "If we are done, I have to inform the crew, and make arrangements for dinner. Commander Saxon and Madame De Marnier, perhaps you will escort our guests to their cabins."

"Captain, I'd like to have a word with you. Perhaps Commander Saxon can escort our guests?" Joan said in a cheery voice.

Saxon looked between Malcolm and Joan, trying to determine if he should stay behind to referee. Malcolm saw Saxon's indecision and said, "Anything to accommodate our guests, Madame. Commander, I hope that you don't mind escorting our guests?" He gave Saxon the tiniest of nods to indicate that he would do his part to remain calm. Saxon put on a charming smile and offered his elbow to Deirdre. "Of course, sir." He led the two out of the office and room, already chatting amiably about the ship as the trio walked down the hall.

Joan stalked to the door and shut it hard. "What the hell are you playing at, Malcolm?"

Malcolm sighed. "I'm not playing at anything," he said in a tone of utter resignation. Whatever was bothering Joan was obviously his fault, and he needed to placate her if he were to have a moment's peace.

"You insulted Nigel with your disbelief, and you were all but drooling at that blonde tart!" she said.

Malcolm felt his anger rise, but he forced himself to keep it in check. "I found much of what Dr. Sinclair said to be quite outlandish, but I take him at his word. But to do my duty as captain, I need information and there has been deucedly little available to date. If I pushed too hard in trying to find out why we were in Romania, I will apologise to him at dinner. And as for the 'tart' as you put it, yes, she does distract me. I'm unaccustomed to having beautiful women focus that much attention on me."

Malcolm saw Joan take a deep breath, and he suspected that she was about to launch into another tirade, but he put his hand up to forestall her and continued. "There is only one woman whose attention I want to have, and to whom I would give everything, and that's you," he offered softly and gently.

Joan fumed and sputtered like a boiling tea kettle before saying, "Malcolm, how can I be mad at you when you say something like that?"

Malcolm walked over to her, and gently put his hands on her arms.

"That was rather the point. I don't want to fight with you. We spend so little time together that I don't want to spend it at each other's throats. Especially," he said as he brought a hand to gently caress her cheek, "when there are much more interesting ways to spend our time."

The tension and anger in Joan's body seemed to release with his touch. She lowered her face, ashamed that she had been mad at a man who could be so tender. "Neither do I," she said in a low voice.

Malcolm gently raised her chin until she looked at him and met his gaze. She could see the love in those blue-grey eyes, and the colour rose in her cheeks at the realisation that he did only have eyes for her. "I'm sorry for being so jealous. I should have known better."

Malcolm smiled. "Well, you do have green eyes," he said.

Joan drew herself up, ready for a fight. "What's that supposed to mean?"

Before she could say another word, Malcolm stopped her lips with a kiss. For a moment she resisted, and then melted into the kiss, allowing Malcolm to hold her in his arms.

"It was, my dearest, a very sad attempt at humour. Jealousy is often referred to as the green-eyed monster." She took a breath; ready to say something, and he put a finger to her lips. "It was a feeble attempt at humour, and I apologise."

Joan looked up at him and smiled. "Actually, that was quite apt. Not bad for an engineer," she said with a playful grin.

"Thank you," he said. They stood there for a moment holding each other and saying nothing. "Are we alright now?"

Joan said, "Yes."

Malcolm smiled. "Good, Charles will be relieved that he won't have to play referee between the two of us for the rest of the trip to London."

She laughed. "With our tempers and prides, I wouldn't wish that fate on anyone." She reached up and pulled Malcolm into a kiss. It was soft and tender. Before it could become passionate, she pulled away and took a step back from Malcolm. "Malcolm, please don't think I'm being jealous; perhaps I am. But hear me out. Something about Miss

Hastings-Elliott rings false." Malcolm started to say something, but this time she put her hand up. "I know, I may not be objective about her, but you know that I can read people. And there is something there that I can't quite figure out. Malcolm, please be careful around her."

Malcolm could sense that there was real concern in Joan's voice, and that she wasn't just being jealous. "Very well, I will keep on my guard."

"Thank you, Malcolm," Joan said. "That woman strikes me as a real man eater."

CHAPTER 11

*A*fter Joan left, Malcolm made preparations for the dinner with their new guests. Another groan arose from the officers on the bridge when Malcolm informed them of the formal dinner that evening. It was unprecedented; two formal dinners in such a short time span. When Malcolm told Chef, he grumbled, "This is an airship, not some bloody restaurant."

Malcolm smiled, "Chef, I don't think we'll ever have to worry about confusing the *Daedalus* with a restaurant. I'm sure that you will be able to come up with something; you usually do."

Malcolm returned to his office, and asked a midshipman to bring Commander Saxon to his office. Saxon entered and settled into his customary chair. Before Malcolm could say a word, Saxon asked, "What did Madame De Marnier want? You seem to be none the worse for wear."

"Oh, she was ready to rip me limb from limb, but I reassured her, and I think everything is settled between us." After a beat, he added, "Mostly."

Saxon arched an eyebrow quizzically. "And you managed to do this without, say, a blow to the head?"

Malcolm laughed, "Why does everyone think I can't be diplomatic?"

"Because your usual approach is to taunt and goad people into anger," Saxon said.

"Touché," Malcolm replied. He paused for a bit before asking, "What's your impression of our guests?"

Saxon stopped to consider his response for a moment. "Dr. Sinclair is not what I expected. I assumed that he would be much more pleasant and forthcoming with information."

Malcolm hesitated for a moment and asked, "And his assistant?"

Saxon shifted uncomfortably in his chair. "She is a most beautiful and charming young lady. And she only seems to have eyes for you, Malcolm. When I escorted her to her cabin, she was polite, but I could tell she was merely tolerating my presence."

"Madame De Marnier told me to keep a close eye on her, and that she feels something is not quite right."

"Is she jealous of the attention Miss Hastings-Elliott is giving you?" Saxon asked.

"Most definitely. She all but admitted that. But she doesn't think that's all that it is. She's an excellent judge of people, and I think she was being objective; well, as objective as she can be. Can you keep an eye on her for me? You seem to be immune to her charms."

"That's because they are not levelled at me," Saxon replied quickly. "I will do my best to keep an eye on her. You give me all of the difficult assignments," he said with a smile. The smile slowly faded. "I do think Madame De Marnier is correct; I think it would be best to keep the two of you separated as much as possible."

"In more ways than one," Malcolm said. The two friends laughed, and turned to the details of their trip. The *Daedalus'* return to London found them retracing their path back to Rome, travelling north through Italy to France, and on to London. It was the long way, but the direct route involved seeking approval from either the Austro-Hungarian Empire or the German Empire. Given Malcolm's drubbing of several of Germany's zeppelins, he doubted very much that he would receive such approval.

Mr. Hensley's initial estimate of three days to return to London was nearly perfect; the *Daedalus* was, indeed, scheduled to arrive in London in three days. Malcolm was hoping that he would find answers waiting for them when they arrived. But since the Secret Service was involved, he had his doubts.

"I can't, for the life of me, figure out what we're doing," Malcolm said, exasperated.

"I trust you're talking about this mission, and not some deeper meaning," Saxon joked.

"Yes. I was hoping that Dr. Sinclair would provide some information on what we're really doing."

"Yes, I noticed that he wasn't forthcoming with information. Do you think there is more to this than simply transporting religious artifacts? I'm sure much of this cargo is priceless, and it makes sense that such important cargo be treated as such."

"I would tend to agree, although this is a Secret Service initiative. Mycroft wants those artifacts for a reason, but my head hurts when I try to unravel his puzzles. I'm sure his plans have plans." Malcolm sighed, "I guess we'll just have to wait until we arrive in London, and hope that Mycroft deigns to enlighten us." Malcolm picked up one of the many reports on his desk. Malcolm and Saxon spent the rest of the afternoon reviewing duty rosters and reports. Saxon excused himself to prepare for the dinner, and Malcolm returned to his quarters not long after him.

As Malcolm prepared for the dinner, this time he ensured that his lock box containing the ring was closed, locked, and hidden, within his closed and locked trunk. Joan would not be able to accuse him of leaving it out on purpose if she were to come back to his cabin. He took one last look at himself in the mirror, and was satisfied that all was in order. He left his cabin, walked the short distance to Joan's quarters, and knocked on her door. A few seconds later, Joan came to the door, and was startled to see Malcolm. "Oh, I thought you would be escorting Dr. Sinclair and Miss Hastings-Elliott."

"No, I ordered Commander Saxon to escort them to dinner. I

reserved the right to escort the most beautiful woman on the ship to dinner."

"Are you talking about me?" she purred. She wore a form fitting emerald gown that matched her eyes. Her raven hair was pulled up, with two ringlets hanging down to perfectly frame her face.

"Most definitely. May I have the honour of escorting you to dinner, Madame De Marnier?" he said, offering his arm.

"I would like that very much," she said, looping her arm in his. Together, they strolled down the hall, making their way to the Officer's Mess. As they approached, they met Commander Saxon, escorting Dr. Sinclair and Miss Hastings-Elliott. The young woman's eyes momentarily flashed as she saw Malcolm and Joan. Joan gave Malcolm's arm a light squeeze to indicate that she had noticed the look, and Malcolm patted her arm to let her know that he had seen it as well.

As his officers arrived, they seem to make a bee-line for Miss Hastings-Elliott, and keep her surrounded. She politely chatted with all of them, but Malcolm could see that she was trying to get away, and make her way over to him. For his part, Malcolm kept close to Joan.

Soon a midshipman announced that dinner was ready. Before Miss Hastings-Elliott could react, Malcolm took Joan by the arm and escorted her to a seat to the right of where Malcolm would sit. He looked at Saxon, who nodded and retrieved Dr. Sinclair and Miss Hastings-Elliott. Before anyone could say anything, Malcolm indicated the chair to his left. "Please, Dr. Sinclair, have a seat here. I would love to hear more about your exploits." Saxon pulled out the chair next to Dr. Sinclair, and held it for a clearly disappointed Miss Hastings-Elliott. Saxon moved to a place next to Joan, his usual spot taken by Dr. Sinclair. Malcolm caught Joan's eyes, and saw a glimmer of approval.

After the midshipmen brought bowls of French onion soup, Malcolm decided to start the conversation. "Dr. Sinclair, I understand you are an expert in lost civilisations?"

"Yes," said Sinclair, barely looking up from his soup bowl.

A few seconds of silence passed. Malcolm tried again. "I understand that you've been all over the world looking for various lost tribes or lost cities."

"Yes," replied Sinclair, again barely acknowledging Malcolm.

Silence lingered for a few seconds. Malcolm found his patience with this man nearing its end. He took a deep breath and tried again. He guessed that, like himself, if Sinclair started talking about his subject, he would talk more freely. Malcolm knew that he would have to engage the professorial side of Sinclair.

"After all that travel, it must have been refreshing to find a 'lost' tribe so close to home in Silchester."

"Yes, it was," Sinclair replied.

"I read the article about your work there. It was fascinating. Although I don't happen to recall if you ever mentioned a theory to explain what happened."

"I did not," Sinclair said in a flat voice. He was now looking at Malcolm.

"Do you have a theory about what happened at Calleva Atrebatum?" Malcolm probed.

"Yes, I do," Sinclair said.

A few beats of silence. "Would you care to share that with us?"

"No, I would not," said Sinclair. Silence fell over the table. Joan and Saxon looked over at Malcolm; both afraid he'd lose his temper, and make this situation worse. Sinclair broke the silence first. "Look, Captain Robertson, I realise that you're trying to be polite, but we have nothing in common. I know that you don't believe in the work I do, so let's drop the pretences. The sooner we stop talking, the sooner dinner will be over, and we can get away from one another."

"Oh, Nigel," said Deirdre. "Stop being so beastly to the captain. He's trying to get to know you better. It wouldn't hurt to answer some of his questions."

"And you need to stop making doe eyes at the Captain like a besotted schoolgirl, and keep focused on our mission."

Malcolm stood, "Alright, that is quite enough. If you want to be beastly to me that's fine, but do not take it out on Miss Hastings-Elliott. I meant this dinner as a courtesy to you, and a chance to get to know one another in a congenial manner. If you don't want this to continue, I'll have this, and every meal, brought to your cabin, so you don't have to face any of us again. The choice is yours, Dr. Sinclair – do we continue dinner as civilised adults, or do I send you to your cabin with your dinner like a misbehaving schoolboy?"

Joan and Saxon could tell that Malcolm was angry, but had a firm command on his emotions. Joan looked at Nigel who suddenly turned red, although Joan was unsure if it was embarrassment or anger, or both.

Silence lingered for a few seconds before Nigel said "I'm sorry, Captain. I have behaved abominably, and if I have not caused too much offence, I would like to stay and enjoy the dinner that you have arranged for us."

Malcolm sat down. "Thank you, Dr. Sinclair. Apology accepted. Perhaps you should suggest the topic of conversation, Dr. Sinclair."

"Very well," Nigel said, taken off guard. "How long have you commanded the *Daedalus?*"

"A little more than two years," Malcolm said.

Nigel stared at him. "You don't seem like the typical captain of an airship." Some barely-contained snorts from some of the officers could be heard down the table, before Nigel quickly added, "I meant no offence."

Malcolm laughed, "None taken. You're quite correct; I am definitely not a typical captain." Malcolm explained how he became Captain when a bomb destroyed the bridge of the Daedalus, and most of its command crew. He told Sinclair about their trip to Russia, how the ship was taken over by German spies, how they eventually escaped, and returned to Britain. During the tale, Malcolm was relieved to see that Sinclair had a real interest.

"What an extraordinary story, Captain. Thank you for sharing. I'm afraid that I have misjudged you. You have talents, and know how to do things other than just give orders."

"Thank you, Dr. Sinclair. Although if you talk to my crew, I think they'd say all I know how to do is give orders." A polite laugh came from Malcolm's officers at the table.

"You were asking about my work at Calleva Atrebatum? You wanted to know if I had a theory for why the city essentially disappeared?"

"Yes," Malcolm replied.

"After much excavation and study of the remains, I believe the city was quarantined by all of the other nearby settlements, and it eventually died a slow death."

"Oh, Nigel, must you talk about such gloomy topics?" Deirdre interrupted. "Tell the Captain the story of your expedition looking for the Temple of the Midnight Sun."

"The one where I was nearly killed by natives, spent the rest of the expedition laying in a tent, fighting dengue fever, and wishing someone would put me out of my misery? I'm sure that would be excellent dinner conversation," Sinclair said. Malcolm laughed, and he could see that Sinclair had, in fact, relaxed and was much more open and outgoing. "How about my time with the Dörpfeld expedition excavating the ruins of Ancient Troy, the city made famous by Homer?"

The evening flew by as Sinclair told stories of his travels to various archaeological sites throughout the world. As the tales went on, Malcolm, who fancied himself a world traveller, seemed much more poorly travelled than the professor. By the time the after-dinner drinks were served, the coldness and silence from the start of the dinner was a distant memory.

As Dr. Sinclair and Deirdre left, Sinclair stopped to shake Malcolm's hand. "Thank you, Captain. This was, in the end, a most enjoyable evening. I apologise for my behaviour earlier. If possible, I'd like to speak with you privately, after I escort Miss Hastings-Elliott to her cabin."

"Very well, I must escort Madame De Marnier to her room. Perhaps you can join me in my office."

"Thank you, Captain," Sinclair said. He offered his arm to Deirdre, who again looked disappointed that Malcolm would not escort her to her room.

Joan came up next to him, and whispered into his ear. "You're staring."

Malcolm jumped with surprise; he hadn't heard her move up next to him. "I was not staring."

Joan said, "I believe the phrase is 'pull the other one, it has bells on it'?"

Malcolm decided the best response was to change the subject. Offering her his arm, "May I escort you to your cabin?"

"I'd rather you escort me to yours," she whispered.

"I would too, but Dr. Sinclair wants to talk. No rest for the wicked."

"Funny, that's what I intended," she whispered in his ear.

"This is one of those times where I hate being captain," he whispered back. He took her arm and they walked together back to her cabin. At the door, he chastely kissed her hand. "Good night, Madame." He lowered his voice and whispered, "If my visit with Dr. Sinclair doesn't take too long, perhaps we can compare notes."

"Is that what we're calling it now?" she she said, her eyes twinkling with mischief. "I would like that very much," she said. "Until later?"

"Until later." He released her hand, and watched as she let herself into her cabin.

Malcolm sighed wistfully, and returned to his office. While he waited for Nigel, he busied himself reading through reports. He barely looked up from his reports when he heard a knock on his door. "Come in," he said as he finished reading the report.

He was surprised to find Deirdre standing in the doorway. He rose immediately and said, "Deirdre, I'm surprised to see you. Didn't Professor Sinclair escort you back to your room? I'm to meet him momentarily."

"Yes, I know," she said, her voice husky. She slinked over to stand next to him. "That's why I'm here. He wanted to me to show you something," she said, as she unbuttoned the top buttons of her dress.

"Deirdre, I think you have the wrong idea about me," Malcolm said as he took a step back.

"Nonsense, Malcolm. I want to show you what we found at the

temple. I think it will be of great interest to you," she said, as she continued to unbutton her dress and step towards him.

"I don't feel this is appropriate, Deirdre," Malcolm said, as he backed away.

"Nonsense," she said, as she pulled open her dress to reveal an amulet. The amulet was black as obsidian, but had a metallic glint. The face of the amulet was an octopus, with mechanical tentacles splayed out as if it were a hideous compass rose. The ends of the tentacles weren't visible, as they stopped at her chest. She pulled the amulet over her head and when she did, the tentacles pulled themselves out of her chest, blood seeping from the holes. She stepped forward to put the amulet over Malcolm's head, and as she did, the metallic tentacles flailed towards Malcolm, attempting to grab him.

Malcolm immediately stepped back and said, "What is that thing?"

"This is the answer to all of your questions," she said as she stepped forward. There was no trace of her sparkling blue eyes, as the irises of her eyes were completely black.

The door to his office flung open, and Nigel raced in, shouting, "Stay away from her!"

CHAPTER 12

"This isn't what it seems," Malcolm began.

"I know," Nigel shouted. "Deirdre, drop the amulet immediately!"

"No!" came a voice from Deirdre's lips that was not her own. It was deep and metallic. "I must bond with the captain!"

"Deirdre, put it down! I beg of you! Break its hold on you! Remember your training!" Nigel pleaded.

"I can't! It's too strong," she said, her normal voice returning. It was soft and barely audible.

Nigel produced a silver amulet inscribed with a line with five branches. "In the name of the Elder Ones, I rebuke you! You have no power over this woman!" As he spoke, a bright light flared from the amulet, momentarily blinding Malcolm.

Deirdre, dazed by the light, dropped the black amulet. As soon as it left her hand, she crumpled to the floor. The amulet clanked on the floor when it fell. Malcolm watched in amazement as the mechanical tentacles pushed themselves outside the amulet, and began moving toward him, looking like a mechanical crab.

"Stay back!" Nigel shouted. "Don't let it touch you!"

"I don't intend to." Malcolm said. He continued to back away as the amulet awkwardly advanced on its metal tentacles. Much to his dismay, it seemed to be closing the distance.

A shot rang out, deafening Malcolm. The amulet was flung in the air, and when it landed, the metallic tentacles fell off as the shot had torn the amulet asunder. The amulet was a twisted piece of metal that started to smoulder, and dissolve into an acrid puff of smoke.

Nigel rushed to Deirdre and started to examine her. She had eight wounds where the amulet had buried itself into her chest. None of the wounds seemed life threatening. "Deirdre, are you all right? It's over. It's been destroyed!"

Deirdre's eyes fluttered open. "Nigel! I'm so sorry! It was too strong! I knew it was wrong to take it from the monastery, but I couldn't help myself. It kept calling to me."

Nigel tried to quiet her. "Deirdre, you're alright. It's been destroyed. Just rest." Looking up at Malcolm, "I assume you have a surgeon on board? We need to clean these wounds immediately."

"Of course," Malcolm said, barely hearing anything over the ringing in his ears. Before Malcolm could call for assistance, several crewmen burst in with weapons drawn. "All clear. There is no danger now. Please escort Professor Sinclair and Miss Hastings-Elliott to Sick Bay. Professor, once you have Miss Hastings-Elliott settled, perhaps you can enlighten me on what just happened."

"Yes, of course," Nigel said as he helped Deirdre to her feet. She seemed weak, but able to move of her own volition. "Can you wait a moment while I retrieve a few items from my cabin?" he said to the crewmen. They nodded and Nigel ran from the room. In a few moments, he returned with a valise. He put Deirdre's arm around his shoulder, and they left Malcolm's office.

Shortly after they left, Saxon and Joan burst into his office. "Everything is fine now. Let me pour us all drinks, and I'll explain what happened," Malcolm said as he went to the bar. He made a gimlet for Saxon. He looked, and was happy to discover that he still had some vodka left from a bottle confiscated from the German spy Frye. He poured a generous helping for Joan. After pouring a generous helping of whisky, Malcolm sat at this desk and relayed the events of the last few minutes.

"What you say is impossible," Saxon said. "Amulets don't come to life on their own."

Malcolm got up and moved to the spot where the amulet had dissolved. There was a dark oily stain on the floor. As Malcolm showed them the spot, he noticed a shiny object embedded in the floor. Taking the letter opener from his desk, he pried the object loose, and picked it up to examine it more closely. To his amazement, it was a silver bullet.

"I'm not making this up," he said as he showed the bullet to Saxon and Joan.

"I'm sorry I doubted you, Malcolm," Saxon said. "What was that thing that Miss Hastings-Elliott tried to put around your neck?"

"I don't know. A mechanical octopus is the best way to describe it," Malcolm said. "It definitely exerted some form of mental control over her. I have no idea what it wanted with me," he said.

"As the Captain of an Airship, you would be able to take it anywhere in the world," Joan said. "Now tell me again. How did she display the amulet? You say she unbuttoned her dress? She just came in and unbuttoned her dress?" Joan stared at Malcolm, using her eyes to burn him.

"Joan, it happened exactly as I said. I barely glanced up from my paperwork when I realised she was in the room. I didn't lay a finger on her, I swear!"

"Did you enjoy the show?" Joan accused.

"Joan! No! I was confused, and then that thing came for me. I backed away as fast as I could. If it hadn't been for Nigel, I might have succumbed to that thing."

"Interesting choice of words," Joan said. "Succumbed." Her voice accused Malcolm of all manner of things.

"Joan, that's enough," Saxon ordered. Malcolm and Joan both jumped at the sudden authority. "Malcolm did nothing wrong, and for you to accuse him of anything else is unfair, unkind, and untrue. He mopes around like a puppy dog when he's around you. He has no interest in Miss Hastings-Elliott, or any woman other than you."

Joan had started to respond, but the words never left her mouth. She sat for several moments in silence, before looking down and whispering, "I'm sorry, Malcolm. I was wrong."

Malcolm had a sharp retort on his lips, but as he looked at Joan, he saw a vulnerability. It might have been a trick of the light, but he thought he saw her eyes glistening with tears. Malcolm left his chair and kneeled next to Joan. "Thank you, Joan. I swear that I feel no more for Miss Hastings-Elliott than I do for any of my crew." Malcolm put his hand over hers.

"Well, I, for one, am insulted," Saxon said with a smile. "I thought we were friends."

Joan and Malcolm laughed and the tension broke. They sipped their drinks and talked of other things until Nigel returned.

"Can I get you anything to drink, Dr. Sinclair?" Malcolm asked.

"Do you have brandy?" asked. "I could do with a very large brandy."

Malcolm filled the brandy snifter and gave it to Nigel, who immediately took a large drink.

"How is Miss Hastings-Eliott? Is she alright?" Malcolm asked.

"Yes, she is resting. She will be fine in time," Nigel said. He took another drink before asking, "Captain, what happened prior to my arrival?"

Malcom relayed the events one more time. Nigel listened intently, nodding at times with the story.

Nigel took another drink before beginning. "I escorted Deirdre back to her cabin. As she opened her cabin door, she grabbed my arm, pulled me into the room, and hit me on the back of the head. I went down. When I came to, I hurried back to your office, because I thought there had been something odd about her behaviour during our earlier meeting, and dinner." Malcolm looked at Joan, who looked away immediately.

"It wasn't until I arrived at your office, and saw Deirdre with the amulet, that everything fell into place," Nigel said.

"I don't follow," Malcolm said.

"Let me start again. This afternoon, I told you that we discovered an object related to our mission. That thing was the amulet. When we found it, I should have left it there. Deirdre discovered the amulet, and pulled it from its hiding place. Her hands were gloved, so I didn't think it would be able to influence her. But on the way to Tismana, she wouldn't let it out of her sight. At that point, I knew the amulet had some sort of influence over her."

"When we arrived in Tismana, I realised how dangerous this amulet would be if I brought it back to London. With the assistance of the abbot of the monastery, we performed a ritual to seal it in a container, and prevent its evil influence from affecting anyone."

Nigel took another drink and continued. "The reason that I was short with you when you arrived, was because I wanted to get Deirdre away from that amulet. When we first arrived at Tismana, she was very anxious and didn't want to be far from it. After I sealed it away, the anxiety disappeared, and I attributed it to the ritual. We now know that she stole the amulet and, by putting it on, fell to the dark power within."

"What was that… thing?" Malcolm asked.

"It's called the Amulet of R'lyeh. It was constructed of a metal not found on this earth, and carved in the likeness of an ancient entity of evil. I'm afraid I can't tell you any more than that, other than that a tiny portion of that entity's essence was imbued within the amulet."

"Did that thing actually have its claws in Miss Hastings-Eliott?" Malcolm asked.

"Yes." Nigel said. "It is how it gains power. Once worn, the tentacles of the amulet embed themselves in the wearer, drawing sustenance, and wielding its control over its host." Nigel stopped to take another sip of brandy.

Nigel continued, "I realised that Deirdre had the amulet, and was likely attempting to put you under its power. Fortunately for me, I had my own amulet that acts as a ward against the entity depicted on the amulet. Using my amulet, I disrupted its control, so that Deirdre dropped the amulet. When it came after you, I used my revolver and shot it."

"With this?" Malcolm asked, as he held out the silver bullet.

"Yes. It turns out that silver is very useful against… things that go bump in the night, as you said."

"It was a bloody excellent shot," Malcolm said.

"Thank you," Nigel said.

"Will Miss Hastings-Elliott recover?" Joan asked.

"I believe so," Nigel said. "She is resting now. It took a great deal of effort, but I convinced your surgeon to allow me to administer a special salve for the wounds. It contains silver, holy water, and several other herbs. It's very potent against wounds of a supernatural nature. Now that the amulet is no more, it shouldn't bother her any more once we heal the wounds."

Malcolm looked at this pocket watch, and it was nearly midnight. "It's rather late. I suggest we all return to our cabins and try to get some sleep."

They departed Malcolm's office, while Malcolm escorted Joan to her room for the second time that night.

"If you don't mind, I think I should return to my room. I don't know if I can take much more excitement tonight." Malcolm said when they reached the door to Joan's cabin.

"Who said you were invited?" Joan said.

"Madame, we have been through this. I have no designs on Miss Hastings-Elliott. I only have eyes for you."

"So you say," Joan said pointedly.

"Very well, I will not overstay my welcome. *Bonne nuit*, Madame," Malcolm said as he turned and strode to his own cabin.

CHAPTER 13

Malcolm tossed and turned all night. Visions of the mechanical monstrosity scuttled after him, often succeeding in burying its mechanical tentacles in him. Malcolm rose, and once dressed, stumbled to the Mess for breakfast and the strongest cup of tea he could find.

He returned to his office, and ordered a crewman to have Commander Saxon report to his office at his earliest convenience. Saxon arrived a few minutes later.

"Do you think that the amulet has something to do with the reason we're carrying all of these religious artifacts?" Saxon asked.

"I have no idea. He said that the amulet might be useful for our mission. I can't possibly see what good that thing could do!"

"Neither do I. What do we do now?" Saxon asked.

"We fly like the wind to get these artifacts to London as soon as possible."

The two settled down to the business of running the ship. They reviewed the crew assignments, and called in Lieutenant Hensley to see if there was any way to cut time from their journey home. After a great deal of consulting and debate, the trio decided that while it might take longer, the safest route was the route they were taking, and they couldn't cut significant time from their journey.

Malcolm sent for Chief Engineer Jennings to discuss options for increasing speed. The two engineers were soon engrossed in discussions of engine optimisations, and tune ups. Commander Saxon stopped listening after a while, and let the two men discuss. After a somewhat heated debate, Malcolm and Jennings came to an agreement on things they could do to drive a little more efficiency out of the engines, and speed their journey. However, the best combination of navigation and speed would only cut a few hours from their journey, but Malcolm was glad for that.

As night fell, the *Daedalus* encountered a large storm. The large cumulonimbus clouds towered ahead like forbidding guardians barring their way. The *Daedalus* kept its distance, but thunderclaps could still be heard throughout the ship, and it was a very bumpy night.

With morning light, it was clear that any advantage they received from adjusting engine performance would be nullified by flying around the storm. The day turned out to be a rather easy day of flying. Malcolm did not see Joan during the day, or at any meal. Before turning in, he knocked on her door.

"Who is it?" he heard her ask from behind the closed door.

"Captain Robertson. I have not seen you all day, and wished to find out if you are well."

"I am fine. I have been occupied with correspondence today," she said.

"Would you mind if I came in? It's deucedly difficult to conduct a conversation through a closed door," Malcolm said.

"Who said I wanted to converse?" asked Joan.

"Please, Madame De Marnier. I want to work out the issue between us."

"There's no issue, Captain."

Bloody hell, Malcolm thought. He rummaged through his key ring, and found the key to the lock on the door. He unlocked the door and the next thing he knew, he felt a sharp blow to his head, and he was lying on the floor. He rubbed his head, "What the bloody hell did you do that for?"

"You came uninvited into my cabin. A woman has a right to defend herself."

"I let myself in because this could be our last night together for some time, and I was hoping to spend it together." He pulled himself up to stand in front of her. "But, I see that you are not interested, and far be it from me to force my intentions on someone who doesn't want them." He turned to leave when he felt the touch of her hand on his shoulder.

"No. Don't go," she whispered.

"Are you going to hit me again, or throw me to the ground?" Malcolm asked grumpily.

"No... not unless you want me to," Joan said, in her very husky voice.

"I'd prefer it if you didn't," Malcolm said. He turned around and faced her. Her eyes and nose were red, as if she had been crying. He thought about asking her the cause of her tears, but quickly dismissed it. "Are you alright? I let myself in only to make sure you were fine."

"Yes... no... I don't know. Malcolm, I may have been a bit hasty in accusing you of taking advantage of Miss Hasting-Eliott's advances."

A bit? thought Malcolm, who wisely bit his tongue before his thoughts could betray him.

"I want so much to be with you, but I keep pushing you away, and I don't know why," she said.

"You're not pushing me away now," he said gently. Her other hand went to his shoulder. She was now an arm's length away.

"I know."

"Let's just enjoy each other's company tonight, and not think about this too much," he said as he took a step towards her, and put his hands on her waist.

"That sounds... nice," she said, taking a step towards him. Her hands moved from his shoulders to just behind his neck.

"I think we could both use some nice," he said as stepped towards her, and pulled her into a kiss.

CHAPTER 14

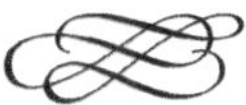

Malcolm slipped out from Joan's embrace sometime in the wee hours of the morning. He dressed and, before he left, gently kissed her forehead without stirring her. He cautiously opened the door and was relieved to see that no one was in the main hall. He slipped out of the cabin and returned to his own room. While he had faith that his men would not report his fraternisation with Joan, he did know that they liked to talk, and talk like that had a way of drifting up the ranks. Malcolm's rise to Captain had rankled many of the traditionalists in the Air Service. He wasn't a gentleman of note, as were many airship captains. He was a Scot, and he was an engineer. Much of the command scoffed at how someone like Malcolm could possibly be a Captain. Rumours of him fraternising with guests on the airship would most certainly be used against him, to bust him back down to the Engine Room where they thought he belonged.

Making his way back to his quarters unseen, he let out a sigh of relief and prepared for the day ahead. He showered, shaved, and prepared his dress uniform. The *Daedalus* would reach Kingsnorth in the late afternoon. Tradition dictated that the crew wear their dress uniforms, and Malcolm found it a comforting tradition. And, he chuckled to himself, it didn't hurt the crew's chances with the ladies if they were given liberty.

Once dressed, he made his way to the mess. To Malcolm's surprise, Chef had prepared a full English breakfast for the crew and passengers; fried eggs, bacon, bangers, grilled tomatoes, and baked beans. It was probably just as well, Malcolm thought. The crew would be much busier as they approached Kingsnorth later in the morning, and there would be no time for lunch. Malcolm washed down the veritable feast with strong tea, and when he was done, refilled his mug, and went to the bridge.

Malcolm loved this time of the morning; the last few minutes before dawn. In the east, Malcolm could already see the sky brightening. The light, at first orange, quickly shifted to red, and to Malcolm's surprise, intensified to blood red. Soon, the sun was visible; a blood red disc, bleeding its light onto the clouds below the *Daedalus*. All Malcolm could think of was the sailor rhyme: "Red sky in the morning; sailors take warning", and he frowned.

Malcolm sent crewmen to the radio room to get the current weather reports for France and England. He worked with the navigators to determine their exact location. When the crewman returned with the weather reports, Malcolm's frown was joined by furrowed eyebrows. A large storm was sitting over much of France and England. The reports indicated strong winds, thunder, lightning, and driving rain. The *Daedalus* could fly above the storm, but they were going to have to descend through the storm if they intended on landing today. Malcolm sighed, knowing he had little choice but to bring the *Daedalus* down through the tempest.

As Malcolm saw it, he had two choices: begin a gradual descent that would bring them into the storm for a longer time, but give them a controlled descent; or continue to fly above the clouds, and try to descend nearly vertically. Malcolm didn't like either option, as the former left the *Daedalus* exposed to the danger of winds and lightning for a longer time, and the latter left them with little control as they descended through the clouds. Descending in an airship was always a tricky matter; most of the descent was accomplished by letting out the helium. Some aerodynamic tricks that Malcolm had picked up from Professor Nikolay Zhukovsky on his mission to Russia were of some use, but the trick was the delicate balance between adjusting the airship's lift, and the force of gravity.

Malcolm gathered the senior officers for a final meeting before landing. The first part of the meeting was spent hammering out the preparations and inspections for landing; the rest of the meeting was spent analysing the weather, and determining the best approach for landing. The officers were evenly divided over a longer, slower descent, or a short, nearly vertical descent. Malcolm frowned; he had hoped that his officers would see something he hadn't.

"Excuse me," said the Gunnery Officer, Lieutenant Brown. "I know I'm not a navigator, but would it be possible to find a middle ground? What if you spiral past the storm, and come down from the north?" He indicated the path on the map with his finger. "It seems to me that the amount of time spent in the storm would be much more manageable."

Malcolm looked at the map, cursing himself for not thinking of it himself. To the north of Kingsnorth, the storm weakened; coming from the north only meant twenty or thirty miles of inclement weather. "That, Mr. Brown, is an excellent suggestion. What do you think?" he asked his officers. After some discussion, the group agreed that Brown's plan was the best option. It would add extra hours to their trip, but everyone thought the delay would be well worth the safety it might afford.

After the staff meeting broke, the *Daedalus* was abuzz with activity. Crews polished every surface; equipment was arranged in an orderly, but accessible fashion. As a precaution, Malcolm dispatched a few crewmen to lash down the religious artifacts in case the storm shook the ship. Malcolm did not want to be responsible for breaking a priceless relic.

As the *Daedalus* approached northern France, the storm was easily visible. The storm seemed to engulf Normandy, the Channel, and the whole southern coast of England. Malcolm had only a vague idea where to find London or Kingsnorth; the coast was covered in dark, evil looking clouds. Even from this distance, Malcolm could see lightning in the clouds below. Mr. Brown's suggestion had been a wise course; ahead of them was a wall of cumulonimbus clouds. The *Daedalus* would travel to Land's End on the Cornish coast, northwest towards Leicester, start a circle through Cambridge, Colchester, and Chelmsford, and then south to Kingsnorth. *Certainly going around Robin Hood's barn*, Malcolm thought.

The initial approach was easy. Malcolm steered the *Daedalus* to the west, past the edge of the storm. As he approached Land's End, he began a very slow and steady descent on route to Leicester. By the time the *Daedalus* reached Colchester, they had descended below the clouds, and had entered the storm. As Malcolm saw the approaching wall of rain, he looked to the icon of St. Nicholas that he'd had the crew install on the bridge. *Saint Nicholas, we most certainly could use your favour now*, Malcolm thought. He opened a channel to the whole ship, "All hands, secure yourselves. Things are about to get a wee bit bumpy."

The moment the ship entered the tempest, Malcolm found it was all he could do to hold the great wheel steady. According to his navigators, the *Daedalus* was still nearly fifty miles from Kingsnorth, but the *Daedalus* could have been in Timbuktu for all Malcolm knew. It felt like the *Daedalus* was flying underwater as it pushed through the wall of rain. The black clouds above them hid the late day sun, and it looked more like night than late afternoon. Malcolm continued the slow descent, and tried to use the coast line to keep his bearings.

The winds buffeted the *Daedalus*, particularly as they crossed the meeting point of the Thames and the Atlantic Ocean. The winds that usually came from the ocean seemed to be pushing the *Daedalus* out to sea, as if the storm itself did not want the *Daedalus* to land. As the *Daedalus* crossed the Thames, the storm intensified in strength. Malcolm fought to hold the course towards Kingsnorth.

Lightning flashed all around the *Daedalus*; each flash appearing nearer and nearer to the *Daedalus*. Suddenly, a loud boom deafened the crew, and the view in front of the bridge was filled with blinding light. When Malcolm's vision and hearing returned, he attempted to call the Engine Room on the radio. It was dead. Malcolm guessed that the bolt had hit the *Daedalus'* main antenna. As Malcolm surveyed the bridge, he realised that electricity throughout the bridge was out. He was officially flying blind, with no radio guidance.

Malcolm looked up at St. Nicholas. "We could really use your help about now," he muttered. "If you're not too busy, perhaps you can do something about this storm?" A loud clap of thunder was Malcolm's response. Malcolm sent a crewman to the Engine Room, to have Chief Engineer Jennings begin a damage control assessment of the ship. From the map, and the bearings that he did have, he figured they were now less than twenty miles away. Malcolm continued to wrestle the ship through the storm, but it was like walking through a vat of oatmeal. The ship's response was sluggish, and the winds kept pushing the ship towards the sea.

Suddenly, a flash illuminated the bridge, and another boom rocked the whole ship. Malcolm looked at the flight controls and realised, to his dismay, that the main engine was no longer working. It had probably been hit by the lightning and was wrecked. Malcolm ordered any able crewman on the bridge to the Engine Room, to assist with whatever was needed. Without the main engine, Malcolm had little hope of getting the *Daedalus* anywhere. They would be blown out to sea where Malcolm could only imagine the storm would be worse.

Malcolm silently prayed to himself; *God, spare my men and this ship from your wrath. If you want me, take me, but save my men. Amen.* As soon as he finished, he felt the pull against the wheel from the wind lighten ever so slightly. Malcolm blinked. The wall of rain had lessened to a drizzle, and the clouds suddenly seemed to brighten. Malcolm could now see the air base in the distance, with its landing beacons and searchlight pointing the way home. Malcolm stopped for a moment, and looked again at the icon of St. Nicholas. "Thank you," he said. Malcolm returned his attention to the task at hand, of landing the *Daedalus.* Even without the main engine, the landing was easy now that the raging tempest was reduced to a drizzle.

As Malcolm brought the *Daedalus* to its landing platform, and the ground crew tied the landing cables to winches on the ground below,

Malcolm gathered the senior crew for a quick briefing on the status of the *Daedalus*. As Malcolm had expected, the first lightning strike burned out the radio and electrical system; the second wrecked the main engine, and started a small fire that Chief Engineer Jennings and his crew had swiftly extinguished.

Malcolm waited for the crew to assemble in the main cargo room. When they were ready, the crew lowered the gangplank, and Malcolm went out to meet Wing Commander Woodcock, the base commander. He saluted his commanding officer who was standing under an umbrella held by a very wet and miserable looking lieutenant. "Permission to land," Malcolm said.

"Permission granted," said Woodcock, returning the salute. "What in the devil are you doing, Malcolm?" he asked. "We ordered you to abort your landing some time ago."

"It must have been after we lost the radio from a lightning strike," Malcolm said. "We lost the main engine from another. We're rather fortunate to have made it here, I think."

"Yes, you are," Woodcock said.

"What are our orders, sir?" Malcolm asked.

"Your crew has been granted one-week liberty, after which, they will work on getting the *Daedalus* airworthy. However, you and Commander Saxon are expected at the Admiralty in the morning," he said, handing over two sets of sealed orders. "The two of you will be escorting your guests and cargo to London."

"No rest for the wicked," Malcolm said.

"Apparently," Woodcock agreed. "Cars are waiting to carry you and Saxon, along with your guests, to London. Accommodations have been made for all of you. Apparently, someone is very eager to see you."

"That's a first; someone in the Admiralty eager to see me," Malcolm laughed.

"Yes, I did find it rather odd," Woodcock said. "You'd best get moving."

"Aye, sir," Malcolm said. He saluted his commander and returned to the *Daedalus*. Malcolm was happy to give the men liberty; they had been in Egypt for several months, and he knew they looked forward to being home. Malcolm dismissed his crew and asked Saxon to join him. Together, they read their orders. They were ordered to escort their guests to the Admiralty, and would be stationed there until further notice.

"Apparently, we have no time to waste," Saxon said. "What have you done this time, Malcolm?"

"Damned if I know. Let's get our guests and head out."

Malcolm had crewmen gather his trunk; Malcolm was always prepared when he returned to base. In his youth, he would be ready to leave as soon as the word was given. Saxon returned to his cabin to pack; he was very meticulous, so Malcolm knew it was best to leave him to it. He walked back to Dr. Sinclair's cabin and knocked on the door. A weak voice called out, "Come in." Malcolm entered and found Dr. Sinclair white as a ghost, with a cloth over his forehead. "Are you alright, Dr. Sinclair? Shall I fetch the surgeon?"

"No, no, I'm fine. Just a bout of air sickness. The rough descent triggered it. Give me a moment, and I should be fine."

"I'm glad to hear it, because we have orders to depart immediately for London. Cars are waiting to escort us and our cargo to the Admiralty."

"Very good," Sinclair said, who already had some colour returning to his face. "I will tell Deirdre, and get her ready for the trip."

"Thank you," Malcolm said, relieved that he could avoid Deirdre and another fight with Joan.

"I am on my way to fetch Madame De Marnier. When we are all assembled, we will leave. While I believe that the Admiralty would rather have us in London immediately, I see no reason to leave before you are ready."

"Thank you; that is most kind."

"I'll leave a crewman at your disposal," Malcolm said as he left. Malcolm grabbed one of the crewman who had yet to leave, and ordered him to take care of Dr. Sinclair and Miss Hastings-Elliott. Hearing her name made the crewman brighten.

Malcolm continued down the hall and stopped at Joan's cabin. He knocked on the door. "Who is it?" he heard from the other side.

"Madame, it's Captain Robertson. We have landed, and we have orders to leave for London."

Joan opened the door, and Malcolm couldn't help but take in a quick breath. Joan's porcelain skin was a sharp contrast with her bright red lips, and the long black dress she wore under a black coat. Malcolm wasn't sure if he had ever seen her look more beautiful. She looked up and saw he was staring. "What?" she asked.

"I don't think I've ever seen you look more lovely," Malcolm said.

"Oh?" she asked, raising one eyebrow provocatively. "And what do you intend to do about that?" she enquired, as she sauntered over to him.

"This," Malcolm said, and swept her into his embrace and kissed her for a very long time. When they parted, Joan looked and laughed. "Oh dear, I do believe you are wearing more of my lipstick than I am."

Malcolm took his handkerchief and rubbed his mouth; the cloth coming away with streaks of red. He went to the mirror over the chest of drawers, and rubbed until he had removed all of the colour. Joan laughed as he struggled to remove the lipstick. When he was finished, she picked up a wash cloth, opened a jar of beauty cream, dabbed some on her face, and effortlessly removed hers. She carefully wiped off the cream, and effortlessly reapplied her lipstick. "Now, if you can control yourself, we can go now."

"No promises," he said. He sighed, saddened at the thought that they would not spend any time together while he was at the Admiralty. He held out his arm and escorted Joan out of her room. On their way, Malcolm sent a crewman to fetch Joan's trunk. As they left the *Daedalus*, Malcolm was relieved to see that the sun had started to break through the clouds. He loved the smell of the air after a thunderstorm. The world smelled clean, fresh, and earthy. Malcolm wrinkled his nose as he stepped out of the ship. The smell that reached his nose was fetid, spoiled, and mouldy.

Joan noticed his reaction. "What's wrong?" she asked.

"Do you smell that? It doesn't smell like the air after a thunderstorm. It smells of decay."

"What are you talking about, Captain? It smells..." Joan stopped mid-sentence. "Yes, there is something off about it. What do you think it is?"

"I don't know," Malcolm said. "But I'm sure it isn't good."

CHAPTER 15

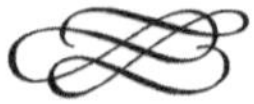

By the time Saxon, Dr. Sinclair, and Miss Hastings-Elliott, joined Malcolm, the ground crew had loaded the *Daedalus'* cargo onto waiting lorries. The great steam-powered machines looked like steel boxes, with small half circles of wheels visible just under the bottom edge of each lorry's body. Everything was the colour of gun metal. A large exhaust cylinder poked out of the top, and two large exhaust pipes arced down from behind the lorry's cabin, and ran along the bottom of the lorry for some distance; the exhaust at the top vented the smoke from the coal that fuelled it, while the side exhausts were used to vent steam.

While the design of the lorries was functional, the design of the automobiles that awaited the group was slightly more luxurious. The automobiles truly resembled motorised carriages. A short hood flowed down from the cabin, while the back stuck out only slightly from the cabin. The inside was upholstered in red velvet, and heavy curtains hung over the rear side windows. Dr. Sinclair, Miss Hastings-Elliott, and Saxon took one car, while Malcolm and Joan took the other. When all were settled, the caravan started its procession to London.

Since Malcolm had to feign a disinterest in Joan, he took out a technical journal from his satchel, and started to read in the fading daylight. Joan, who at first watched the Kentish countryside fly past them, saw that Malcolm was engrossed in his technical journals, and pulled her sketchbook from her purse. Not long after they had first met, she spent part of an afternoon watching the new captain work, and had sketched him at his desk. There was an innocence and sense of trepidation to that sketch. Now, the sketch of Malcolm came easy, and it had a sense of intimacy. She used the dramatic lighting caused by the late day sun, which cast deep shadows, to add a touch of drama to the sketch.

Their activities were interrupted just over an hour later, as the caravan slowed to enter the heart of London. Dusk was beginning to fall and the gaslights of London twinkled on one by one. As they drew closer to the Admiralty, Malcolm could make out the landmarks of London bathed in gaslight; the rotunda of St. Paul's Cathedral, Monument, and the spires of nearly a dozen churches. Malcolm caught his first glimpse of Admiralty Arch, now finished, and full of Naval offices. When the car came to a stop in front of the Admiralty building, Malcolm got out and crossed behind the car to open the door for Joan. She looked at him in surprise, and said, "I'm sorry, didn't you know? Nigel and I are going somewhere else."

"Oh," said Malcolm. "So, this is goodbye?"

"For now," Joan said. "I have a feeling we will see each other again very soon."

Malcolm started to ask, but thought better of it. He reached over and kissed her hand in a very gentlemanly fashion. "Madame De Marnier, it's been a pleasure as always. I wish you safe travels."

"Likewise, *mon capitaine*," she said as she closed the door. Malcolm watched as the automobile pulled away, wondering what she had meant by "see each other again very soon." Malcolm shook his head as he realised one of the marines was directing him to follow him. He realised that in the short time he had spoken to Joan, the marines had unloaded his trunk and were carrying it down the street.

Saxon soon fell into step with Malcolm, as they followed the squad to the flats they would use for the night. Saxon leaned close to

Malcolm and whispered, "Something doesn't seem right about this, don't you think?"

Malcolm had been so focused on Joan's last words that he hadn't given the current situation much thought. "How so?" he whispered.

"I can't put my finger on it exactly, but something seems amiss about this," Saxon said.

"I, for one, am looking forward to a meal not cooked by Chef, and a good bed," said Malcolm.

"Yes, that will be a welcome change," Saxon said. He still thought there was something odd about their reception, but he tried to put it out of his mind.

Soon, Malcolm and Saxon were settled in their respective flats, each finding orders to report the Admiralty at 0900. At first, Malcolm thought nothing of it, but then considered Saxon's concern. Malcolm, too, began to suspect that something was amiss, but like his friend, he couldn't put his finger on it either. Over dinner and a few drinks at a nearby pub, they found that each was to report to a different office in the Admiralty. This generated further concern, but neither of them could think of what was happening. They both decided to get an early night, to be prepared for whatever might come their way.

The next morning, Malcolm showered, shaved, and dressed in his duty uniform. He met Saxon in the building's lobby, and together they went to the Admiralty. They made their way through the building. When Saxon reached his destination, he nodded to Malcolm, and entered. Malcolm continued down the hall a little farther until he found his destination. He looked at the name plate on the door, and swallowed hard. Commodore Godfrey Paine. Malcolm swallowed again. Commodore Paine oversaw all the airships in the Royal Naval Air Service. *Bloody hell, this can't be good*, Malcolm thought. He also knew that Commodore Paine did not think much of Malcolm, and had tried to transfer Malcolm away from the *Daedalus* on more than one occasion.

Malcolm took a deep breath, and knocked on the door. "Enter," the voice said in a perfunctory manner. He opened the office door and found a young ensign at the desk. "Captain Malcolm Robertson, to see Commodore Paine."

"Go in, the Commodore is expecting you," the young ensign said. He didn't look up from his typing, and refused to even make eye contact with Malcolm. Malcolm's stomach began to churn; this most assuredly was not a good sign. Nevertheless, he pulled himself erect, and entered the office with a feigned confidence. Once inside, he threw his smartest salute, "Captain Malcolm Robertson, reporting as ordered, sir."

The Commodore looked up and smiled. He half-heartedly returned the salute and said simply, "Sit." Malcolm almost bristled at being treated like a dog, but reminded himself that this was his superior officer, and no good would come from losing his temper. Malcolm sat, again holding himself rigidly, setting his cap neatly on his lap.

"Read this," Paine said, as he thrust a piece of paper at Malcolm, "and sign it." He indicated a pen that sat on the desk in front of him. Confused, Malcolm took the paper and dutifully read. It was a letter, dated today, that simply read:

"*I, Captain Malcolm Francis Robertson, do hereby resign my commission in the Royal Naval Air Service, effective immediately.*"

Malcolm felt like he had been hit by a physical blow. "I'm sorry, sir. I don't understand."

"Then let me spell it out for you," Paine said maliciously. "I have received reports of you... fraternising with guests on your ship. First, Miss Joan de St. Leger, and most recently, Madame Charlotte de Marnier, who you picked up on your return to Britain."

"Commodore, there must be some mistake," Malcolm began.

"Do you wish to add lying to a superior officer to your charges as well?" Paine said. "There are those within the Admiralty that sing your praises. I am not one of them. However, since these people wield significant power, I'm giving you the option of resigning quietly, and sparing both yourself, and the Air Service, the disgrace of dragging you through a court martial."

"Sir, I've done my best to-" Malcolm began.

"What? Disgrace the Air Service? As if you weren't enough of a disgrace to the Air Service to begin with, you sully it with cheap affairs with obviously brazen women aboard a Naval Airship."

Malcolm's temper rose. He maintained his composure by gripping his cap until his knuckles were white. He cleared his throat and said, "Sir, I'd thank you not to refer to these women as brazen. Also, I hardly think I am the first captain of a ship to 'fraternise', as you say. Or would you prefer that I buggered one of my crew in the naval tradition?"

Paine's face darkened more, and Malcolm knew at once he had made a mistake. "It certainly wouldn't surprise me. You are Scottish, are you not? I'd be surprised if you hadn't had relations with a sheep!"

Malcolm felt the urge to rise, but swallowed his anger, and sat impassively. Paine continued. "What Admiral Beatty ever saw in you is beyond me. You were satisfactory as an engineer, I suppose. But you most definitely should never have been made Captain of the Royal Naval Air Service's flagship!"

"And why is that, sir?" Malcolm hissed through clenched teeth.

"Do I have to spell it out for you?" Paine said. He snorted. "I suppose I must. First, you are Scottish. If that alone is not enough of a disqualifying reason, the fact that you are the son of a shipyard worker should suffice."

"So, you are saying there is no place in the Royal Navy for a self-made man?" Malcolm said, straining not to yell, or even strike the man in front of him.

"Not if it's you," Paine said with contempt. "And now your conduct has demonstrated just how unsuitable you are. Now, sign that paper, or I will order a guard to arrest you, and you will be held in the brig until a court martial can be arranged. And that may take some time," he said, with a certain gladness in his voice.

Malcolm swallowed. He was caught, there was no way out of the situation. If he resigned his commission, there might still be a way to return some day, especially if Paine was no longer part of the Air Service. But if he were dishonourably discharged, there would never be a way back. He looked up with a glare, reached for the pen, signed his name, and flung the paper at the commodore. "Satisfied?" Malcolm asked.

"Very much so," replied Paine. "Now, if you would be as kind as to leave, I have work to do," he said, emphasising 'work'. "Oh, and by the way, you'll find your trunk has been brought back from the flat. It will be waiting for you on the street. If you continue to stay on Admiralty property, you will be considered a trespasser. Good day."

Malcolm rose, considered several choice responses, each containing several curses, but thought better of it. With the little bit of dignity he had left, he put on his cap, and left the office. Once in the hallway, two marines escorted him directly out of the building where he found his trunk. He looked to his right and recognised Saxon's trunk. Within a few seconds, Saxon arrived, also escorted by two Marines. Saxon looked as pale as a ghost. He looked down at his trunk and looked up. "Malcolm, you too?"

Malcolm nodded. "It was either resign or sit through a court martial for fraternising with guests. But you, what possible charge could they have to make you resign?"

Saxon looked up, the colour draining further from his face. "I... I'd rather not say here. Suffice it to say, I was offered the same option."

Malcolm sat on his trunk, and Saxon followed suit. Saxon said, "I don't know how this day could possibly get any worse."

The two men started as a car honked its klaxon. They looked up and saw a large black steam-powered car with an elegant long hood, and large closed cabin in the back with black windows. The back window rolled down, and Mycroft Holmes stuck his head out of the window. "I understand you gentlemen may need new jobs, and a place to stay. Would you care to join me?"

Malcolm looked at Saxon. "You spoke too soon."

CHAPTER 16

With a heavy sigh, Malcolm stood up and went to pick up his trunk when, to his surprise, the driver had already got out of the car, pulled the trunk out of his hands, and deposited it in the back of the car. He likewise took Saxon's trunk and when he loaded that, held open the back door of the vehicle. There were two upholstered benches in black velvet. Sitting on the back bench was Mycroft Holmes. He was a large man, both tall and portly. He was balding, and the hair that circled his head was mostly grey. He had a look of permanent disapproval on his face. Both Malcolm and Saxon had spent a very eventful trip to Russia and back with the enigmatic gentleman.

Malcolm and Saxon took the opposite bench, and soon the car pulled into the London traffic. The silence wore on for several seconds before Malcolm broke the silence. "I suppose that you are responsible for our sudden 'career changes'?"

"I am sure I don't know to what you are referring," Holmes drawled. "I had heard that charges might be filed against the two of you, and I simply wanted to secure your services before someone else snatched you up."

"Secure our services?" Malcolm said incredulously. "I was

drummed out for 'fraternising' with Joan, and Madame De Marnier. Since we had only just landed, and came straight to London, I can only assume that that accusation came straight from you."

"Touché," said Mycroft. "You are correct. I engineered the charges, because I need the two of you for a delicate mission."

"So that's why you dragged Madame De Marnier into this? So you could ensnare me? Did you order her to make love to me?" Malcolm demanded angrily. The thought that Joan might be complicit in his departure from the Air Service angered him.

"No, Madame De Marnier was an unknowing player in this little game. Do not be angry at her, Malcolm. This was solely my doing," Mycroft said, somewhat sympathetically.

Malcolm stewed in silence for several seconds. "What's so bloody important that you couldn't just have us transferred, instead of destroying our careers?"

"The mission within which I intend to use the two of you is one of the highest secrecy and, dare I say, delicacy. There can be no link between you, and the Royal Navy. Hence, the charade of having the two of you resign under a cloud of scandal."

"What, pray tell, is this mission?" Malcolm said cheerlessly.

"Ah, we have reached our destination," Mycroft said, as the car slowed. The car arrived in front of the Charing Cross Rail Station. The driver opened the door and Mycroft was up and out of the car.

"Are we going on a trip?" Malcolm called after him.

Mycroft stopped, realising that Malcolm was still in the car. "Yes, come along, we have a train to catch. My driver will ensure that your luggage follows. Come, time waits for no man," he said as he turned and strode towards the station.

Malcolm turned to Saxon. "What do you think?"

"Well, since we don't seem to have any better offers at the present, we should see what he has to say."

"Aye, I suppose," Malcolm said begrudgingly.

"Malcolm, I know you are angry. As am I. But we'll never find out what was so bloody important if we sulk like children."

"I suppose you're right. Let's follow him before we lose him,"

Malcolm said. The two men left the car and ran to catch up with Mycroft, whose long strides had nearly brought him inside.

"Excellent. Stay close to me, it's rather confusing here if you don't know your way around."

Malcolm felt confident that he could find his way around the station, as he had been there on several occasions. However, his confidence began to erode after they left the main lobby with its newsagents and sandwich stands, went up and down several stairs, and through several hallways, until they came to a gate that Malcolm was sure he had never seen. A disinterested ticket agent sat in his kiosk, and looked up when he saw the trio approach. Mycroft approached the kiosk, and slid three tickets to the agent, as he said "I understand the peonies are in bloom in Hyde Park."

"I hear that the chrysanthemums in Regents Park are not to be missed," the ticket agent said, as he opened the gate. The two men nodded to one another, and the agent opened the gate to allow the trio to enter, shutting it abruptly as soon as they were past. They continued down another hall that twisted and turned, ascended and descended, until Malcolm, who usually had a strong sense of direction, could not tell where they were. The trio arrived at a platform where a train with a single car waited. The car was obviously not used in the regular Underground service. The interior beamed with polished mahogany, with richly upholstered burgundy coloured seats. A pot of tea, a plate of biscuits, three cups and saucers, a creamer, and sugar pot rested on a small table.

"This certainly isn't the Metropolitan Line," quipped Saxon, as the trio entered the carriage. Within moments, Malcolm heard the hiss of pneumatic doors, and the train was in motion. Mycroft poured tea for the two men. Neither was surprised that the tea was at the perfect temperature for drinking. In the time it took to finish the tea, and eat a couple of biscuits, the train arrived at its destination; a nondescript platform that could be any platform in the London Underground, except for its small size. The platform covered the length of their car, no more. The pneumatic doors hissed open, and the trio disembarked. Mycroft strode to a door directly in front of them, and when he opened it, Malcolm was not surprised to see a brass gilt lift waiting for them. They entered the lift, Mycroft closing first the door and then the gate. They slowly ascended for several seconds until the lift came to gentle halt. Mycroft opened the gate and a solid oak door. The door opened into a long hallway panelled with oak. A dark green carpet ran the length of the hall, which ended at two large double doors. On either side of the hall were several doors with plates on each, designating a number.

"Gentlemen, welcome to the home of the Secret Service," Mycroft added. "Please follow me, and I will answer all of your questions about the mission." Mycroft swept out of the lift, and continued to the double doors at the end of the hallway. He opened the double doors and led them into a large library. Two floors of cast iron stairways, balconies, and book shelves formed the walls of the room. Two figures sat at a large round table in the center of the room. Malcolm quickly recognised the two figures as Nigel Sinclair and Joan.

Mycroft sat in a large upholstered high back chair that could only be his. To Malcolm, it looked as if he was sitting on a throne. Malcolm took a seat next to Joan, while Saxon sat on the other side next to Dr. Sinclair. Joan was happy to see Malcolm, but she was perplexed when her smile was met with a scowl. Malcolm sat back in his chair, arms crossed. Joan put her hand on his arm, and leaned over and whispered, "Is something the matter?"

Malcolm recoiled and said, "No. I don't want to talk about it."

Joan removed her hand and stared at Malcolm. She could not, for the life of her, understand why he would be mad at her.

Mycroft cleared his throat. "Before we begin, we have one important matter to resolve. This meeting must strictly involve Secret Service personnel only. While Dr. Sinclair and Madame De Marnier are members of the Secret Service, Messrs. Robertson and Saxon are not. To that end, please review and sign these before we begin." Mycroft handed letters to Malcolm and Saxon. Malcolm pulled his from the envelope, and began to skim through it.

His brow furrowed. "This is an employment contract?" Malcolm asked.

"Yes," Mycroft said. "You will find that your salary more than matches your previous pay grade in the Air Service, and includes a very handsome expense account. It basically makes you a member of the Secret Service for the duration of this mission, with an option for either side to renew the contract at the end of the mission."

"But," Malcolm interrupted, "we can't learn the nature of the mission until we sign?"

"Yes," Mycroft said. "That is rather the way it works."

Malcolm threw the contract down. "Please explain to me why I would want to be a part of this? First, you connive for me to lose my commission. Then you expect me to be grateful, and willingly sign on to a mission that could very well be a suicide mission?"

"Yes, I do." said Mycroft matter-of-factly. "First, you are currently unemployed, and not likely to receive as generous an offer as this. Second, while I would not like to do it, it would be nothing for me to have the investigation of the explosion on the *Daedalus* reopened, and for incriminating evidence to be uncovered that would convince anyone that you were a member of the plot."

"Why do you want me so badly that you're willing to ruin my life to coerce my cooperation?" Malcolm retorted.

"Because, quite simply, I need your talents," Mycroft said. "While we have many talented engineers that design remarkable equipment for us, we have very few people who are able to think on their feet and improvise solutions. And you have intangible qualities that lend themselves to this particular mission."

"And as for Mr. Saxon," said Mycroft, "his familial connections might be useful in this mission. And I do believe that, should he wish it, he has the talent to make an excellent agent."

"And I wouldn't?" Malcolm retorted.

"While I believe you possess skills that would be a great aid to you as an agent, you lack the moral flexibility necessary to be a great agent."

"Moral flexibility?" Malcolm.

"Yes. Agents have to sometimes make decisions that are, shall we say, morally ambiguous." Mycroft saw the look of confusion on

Malcolm's face and continued. "Imagine if you will, you have information that a person is planning a crime that will injure hundreds of people. But at this current point in time, he has not done a single illegal thing. What would you do?"

"I'd keep him under surveillance, and arrest him before he executed his crime."

"So, you wouldn't consider killing that person, knowing that the one death could prevent hundreds or thousands?"

"No, you can't go around killing people based on the fact that they *may* commit a crime. Bloody hell, if everyone were treated that way, everyone would be dead."

"That's what I'm talking about, Malcolm. If I had strong evidence that someone would commit a crime that could kill hundreds of people, I would use every method at my disposal to make sure that it doesn't happen. That is why you would make a poor agent; you believe in justice, honour, and truth, and that they should mean something in the world. While I commend you for that, I am not so blessed. And I would truly hate myself if I was responsible for making you betray those beliefs."

"Then why are you coercing me into becoming an agent?" said Malcolm.

"Because for this mission, we need those ideals. And I'm afraid we're fresh out of them in the Secret Service."

Malcolm thought it over. While part of him bristled at complying with Mycroft's demand out of sheer spite, he didn't have a better offer.

"Assuming I accept," Malcolm said, "I have a condition of my own."

"Which is?" Mycroft asked.

"If I complete this mission, you will use the same skills that forced my resignation from the Air Service, to reinstate me as Captain of the *Daedalus*."

"While I don't have absolute control over the Admiralty, and cannot guarantee my success, I will do everything in my power to make that happen."

"So, I'm to trust the word of someone who is 'morally ambiguous'?"

"Yes," Mycroft said.

Malcolm sighed. "I'm sure I'll live to regret it, but I'll hold you to your word." He picked up the contract, finished his review, and signed the document. As he handed it Mycroft, he said, "Why do I feel like I just made a deal with the devil? Should I have signed it in blood?"

"Stop being so melodramatic, Malcolm," Mycroft sighed. "And you, Charles?"

Saxon handed the contract to Mycroft. "I agree with Mr. Holmes, Malcolm. I signed mine immediately."

Mycroft nodded. "Thank you. Now that that particular bit of drama has played out, we can begin. To begin, however, we need to take a trip to the past."

"Is H.G. Wells joining us?" Malcolm muttered.

"No, Malcolm. Now if you would stop pouting and listen," Mycroft continued, "it will become crystal clear as to why we took such pains to secure your services."

"Hmmph," Malcolm snorted and simply glared at Mycroft.

"To bring Nigel up to date, we start three years ago, when a large explosion occurred over the Siberian tundra. The following summer, an expedition led by myself, Malcolm, and Charles, investigated the crash site, and found what the Secret Service had conjectured as the cause of the explosion: a spaceship from Mars."

Mycroft looked at Sinclair, "This shouldn't come as a surprise, as I believe that you have reviewed the files on the incident at Horsell Common."

"Yes, I have," Sinclair said. "I still don't understand why this involves me. Aliens are out of my area of expertise."

"Yes, I am coming to that," Mycroft said. "On that mission, we recovered an intact Martian spacecraft and four aliens, one who did not survive the crash. The other three were sealed in tubes that kept them in some sort of deep sleep; a hibernation, if you will."

"After we brought the spacecraft back to Britain, we immediately started to analyse its technology. One year ago, we accidentally reactivated what we called the hibernation tubes, and the three Martians were brought back to consciousness."

Malcolm started at this news. He had been disinterested in Mycroft's recitation, but real live Martians? Walking on this Earth? His disinterest melted, and he listened keenly.

"We spent the next six months learning to communicate with the creatures. For that, Madame De Marnier's linguistics skills have been a blessing. Apparently, Martians use some sort of telepathic means to communicate with one another, but this telepathic communication does not appear to work on humans. With Madame De Marnier's patience and assistance, and Martian technology, we've been able to bridge the gap, and have been able to communicate with the Martians."

"It appears that our visitors," Mycroft continued, "are a diplomatic entourage sent here to enlist the aid of the Earth's governments, in a mission that will save two worlds. I think that you should hear these words directly. If you will all follow me," Mycroft said, as he rose from his chair and strode to one of the bookshelves on the wall. He pulled a book from the shelf, and a door opened in front of him. *Of course there's a secret door here*, Malcolm thought to himself.

The group followed Mycroft down a narrow hall that ended in another lift. This one was less ornate than the one Malcolm had taken to the headquarters; it looked like the kind of lift used to move goods throughout the complex. Once everyone had squeezed into the lift, Mycroft pushed an unmarked button and the elevator descended. Some thirty seconds later, the lift stopped. Mycroft led them to another room with two guards standing at attention. He nodded, and the guards opened the heavy steel door, then they entered a small room with a similar door on the other side, with a red light glowing over the doorway. When everyone was in, the guard shut the door.

"In case you're wondering, we are waiting for this room to bathe us with filtered air, to minimise any bacteria or microbes we might bring from the surface. In addition, our guests are also similarly bathed to minimise any naturally occurring bacteria or microbes.

After the disaster at Horsell Common, where the Martian died after being exposed to earthly microbes, we learned our lesson."

Suddenly, there was a whoosh of air in the chamber, and Malcolm felt air blowing all over him. When the burst of air quieted, the light above the door changed from red to green, and Malcolm heard a click ahead of them. Mycroft quickly opened the door before adding, "Watch your step. We needed to change the gravity in this area to accommodate the lesser gravity to which the Martians are accustomed."

"Change the gravity?" Malcolm sputtered. "That's impossible! You can't change the laws of physics!"

"Apparently, Malcolm," replied Mycroft, "the Martians can, because we were able to use an apparatus from their ship to provide a localised adjustment to the gravitational field. Or so my engineers tell me."

As they stepped into the room, Malcolm did feel the change in gravity. As he stepped, he felt as if he almost floated. The large room was panelled with mahogany, and would be appropriate for any gentleman's society or club in London, save for the fact that a large glass wall bisected the room. Two long tables had been placed on either side of the glass to give the illusion that it was one large table. The illumination in the room was very dim, and Malcolm could barely make out a figure sitting in a large upholstered chair in one corner. The figure was covered in a robe, a hood hiding its wearer's face. The figure looked up, rose, and made its way to the table.

"Ladies and Gentlemen, may I introduce to you C'thwan T'plua, Crown Prince of the Martian Empire?" Mycroft and Joan bowed, and the others followed suit, not sure of the protocol for introductions to an extraterrestrial monarch. "How did I do this time, Your Majesty?"

"Much better," said C'thwan in an impeccable British accent. "But you missed the swallowed sound between the C and thwan."

"Your Majesty, may I introduce your visitors. Of course, you know Madame De Marnier," he said, indicating Joan. The Martian inclined his head as Mycroft continued. "This," Mycroft said, as he indicated Malcolm and Saxon," is Malcolm Robertson, former Captain of the airship that retrieved you and your crew, and his former second in command, Charles Saxon." The two men bowed again as the prince again nodded.

"And finally, this is Nigel Sinclair, an expert in the folklore and mythologies of our world." Nigel likewise bowed, and received a nod from the figure.

"Captain," said the Prince. "You have my thanks for rescuing me and my crew. You have done the Martian Empire a great service."

"I am happy that I could be of service," Malcolm replied.

"Yet, I sense you are perplexed. What is troubling you?" said the Prince.

"It's just, you've only been speaking English for the last six months, yet you speak it like a native speaker." Malcolm said.

"Ah, easily explained, Captain. On Mars, we use telepathy to communicate, but our powers don't seem to work on humans. Using some of the technology from our ship, we have constructed these portable translation units that allow us to communicate our thoughts in the language that you most understand. To you, our speech sounds like impeccable English, while to Madame De Marnier, I imagine that we speak in a mixture of languages, is that correct?"

"*Oui*," Joan said.

"The hard part for us was to comprehend your speech. Since you do not have a telepathic means to express your thoughts, we have had to devise a mechanism to distill your words into thoughts that we can understand. It has taken a great deal of time, and dare I say, a great deal of embarrassment."

"Perhaps I may impose upon Your Majesty to relay to my compatriots what led you to come to Earth?" asked Mycroft.

"Of course, Mycroft. Please sit and I will tell my tale." The Martian sat in a chair on his side of the table and once he was seated, the others followed. "As Mycroft has said, I am the Crown Prince of the Martian Empire. My father, the Emperor, asked that I personally lead a delegation to request the aid of the Earth in a matter of mutual importance to both our worlds."

The Martian continued. "After the failure of our first attempt at contact, many of our people disagreed with my father's decision to send another envoy. So much, in fact, that we were pursued by a rival House. There was a battle near your moon in which we prevailed, but our ship was badly damaged. To allow as many of the crew to live as possible, my pilot, and cousin, C'thwan N'pagu, set us in our hibernation tubes, I believe you call them, and attempted to land."

"From what we've been told, it appears that one of the engines exploded not long after entering your atmosphere, and we lost much of our ability to control the landing. My cousin crashed the ship in a deserted corner of your world, until we were discovered and released from our hibernation. He did not survive the impact."

"As for my mission, its origins begin in the ancient past of Mars," the Martian continued. "Millions of years ago, our world was not the vast red desert that it is now. Our world had water and an atmosphere not unlike that of Earth. At this time, a great god came to our planet, and created the first Martians in his own image."

With this, the Crown Prince pulled back the hood, and Malcolm once again looked upon the face of a Martian. Now, unobscured by the tube or damaged in a crash, Malcolm saw how a Martian truly appeared. It had a large bulbous head resembling an octopus. Two large luminous black eyes seemed to dominate the face. It had a beak where its nose and mouth should be. Below the mouth were nearly a dozen tentacles of different sizes. Several of the larger tentacles disappeared beneath the robe, while other smaller tentacles undulated around its mouth. Its skin was grey and wet looking.

"Your Majesty, does your God have a name?" Nigel asked.

"Yes, we call him 'Cthulhu', although we do not use the name openly. Use of His name gives him more energy, and shortens the time of his slumber."

Nigel looked shocked. He whispered "*Ph'nglui mglw'nafh Cthulhu R'lyeh wgah'nagl fhtagn.*"

The Crown Prince's tentacles flapped excitedly. "How do you know that? Those are the words to the Invocation, and are forbidden."

"Yes, they are forbidden words," said Nigel. "I read those words in a book called the *Necronomicon*. It was written by a mad man that talks of Cthulhu." After a pause, he added. "And others."

The Crown Prince nodded. "Yes, there are Others to whom He is simply a priest. But on our world, He was a god. But our God was a mad one. He created our race, but treated us like his playthings. He helped us discover technology, but otherwise kept us as slaves. He would experiment on us, mutate us, force us to fight for his amusement. Finally, it became too much for many of our people. That was the start of the Great Schism. Many in our world thought that our God could be destroyed with the very technology he had given us; others clung to the old ways."

"The resulting war was devastating. We unleashed weapons of such great destruction that we did, in fact, wound our God enough that he left Mars. However, this act destroyed our atmosphere, and caused the surface water of Mars to evaporate into space. Our race was almost decimated. We retreated to underground caverns, where we were able to reproduce our atmosphere and access water."

"You wonder how this involves Earth? When our God left Mars, he travelled to the only similar world he could find: Earth. His arrival caused a great shift in your climate, that may have been responsible for the extinction of the creatures you call dinosaurs. The gravity of Earth was stronger than Mars, so He retreated to the ocean, where the buoyance of the water reduces the effects of gravity. He has rested there for millions of years, rebuilding His strength. However, we have reason to believe that He is about to rise again, enslave Earth, and use its inhabitants to destroy Mars."

The Crown Prince continued, "We have felt His pull, even on Mars. My people came here in 1894 with the intent of peaceful contact so that together, we may prevent the destruction of both worlds. Our first contact was disastrous, as I believe you know, although I do believe your Mr. Wells greatly exaggerated our 'invasion'. After that, there was little appetite among my people to deal with the barbarous Earthlings, and many of my race started to prepare for the inevitable battle. However, my father felt that one last try was necessary."

"Pardon me, Your Majesty, but if your people only wounded him with your advanced weaponry, how are us 'barbarous Earthlings' supposed to assist you?" Malcolm asked. Mycroft shot Malcolm a withering look, but Malcolm didn't care. He did not want to be here, and something in this story didn't add up to him.

"An excellent question. While it is true that our weaponry is far more advanced than that of Earth, you humans have a power all of your own, that you do not even realise."

"I beg your pardon?" Malcolm asked, before hastily adding, "Your Majesty."

"It appears that you humans seem to have an ability to imbue items with psychic energy. You don't even know that you do it, but nevertheless, it is there. Our God does not exist completely in this plane of existence. But He does feel psychic energy keenly. He fed on the energy of my people; we were unsure of how human psychic energy would affect Him until recently."

The Martian produced a small statue, and placed it on the table. It was made of blackest obsidian, and seemed to almost drain the light in the room. Its form was a hideous being seated on a throne. Its head was that of a giant octopus; the body was roughly humanoid with two legs and two arms, each ending in webbed appendages with huge claws. Two bat-like wings shrouded the back of the creature, and a long tail coiled at its feet. Malcolm found something fundamentally disturbing about the creature, but familiar. Then he realised that this creature was the creature depicted in the Amulet of R'lyeh.

"This," the Crown Prince said, "is an idol said to be touched by the God himself."

"Nigel, this is why you are here. Please display the relic that I instructed you to bring," Mycroft said.

Nigel reached down and produced a cloth parcel. He laid it gingerly on the table and carefully unwrapped the parcel. When he was done, a small sliver of wood lay on the table. "This is a piece of the True Cross, given to us by the Vatican, and brought here by the *Daedalus* and her crew."

The Crown Prince slid the statue right up against the glass. "Now, slide that towards the statue." Nigel nodded and slid the sliver towards the glass. As he did, it seemed to glow with a bluish light, and as it got closer to the glass, Malcolm watched in disbelief as the Martian artifact slid back from the glass. It was like he was watching two magnets with the same poles facing each other, pushing each other away.

"Yes," the Crown Prince said. Malcolm found the Martian's voice disconcerting as it produced little sense of emotion. It was almost a mechanical voice, as if it was being spoken by a machine. Malcolm realised that that was in fact the case. The Martian's machine that changed Martian thoughts to human thoughts and words likely stripped out any emotion from the words.

The Crown Prince continued. "It was as we thought; the psychic energy invested in your relic is in direct opposition to His. A very powerful source of that energy could be used to wound him, and drive him back to His slumber. Though it has been millions of years, all Martians feel the pull of our God even now. On this planet, I feel it much more strongly. He is waking and when he does, our two planets will be consumed by His fury."

"Do you have any idea when He might awaken?" Nigel asked.

"Nothing definitive. However, in our ancient texts, it appears that His power ebbs and flows with the alignment of the stars and planets."

"As a result, I have resources scouring the world for news of a planetary alignment," Mycroft said. "While I am certain we will find the when and where, what I am most concerned about is finding a weapon we can use to defeat this entity. This is where you come in Malcolm, and Nigel."

"Me?" asked a confused Malcolm. "I don't know anything about psychic energy. I'm an engineer, not a medium."

"Precisely. Nigel believes that psychic energy can be measured; that it is simply a form of energy that we haven't identified. While I have excellent engineers at my disposal, I do not want them learning any more about this than is humanly possible. You, Malcolm, have been brought here because of both your engineering expertise, and your knowledge of the Martians. You and Nigel will find a way to measure the strength of the relics that we have found, and we will attempt to ascertain if any can be used as a weapon."

Malcolm crossed his arms. "Why don't you get Excalibur or the Holy Grail or something?"

Mycroft let out an exasperated sigh. "Do you honestly think we haven't thought of that? The present owner of Excalibur will not give it back, no matter how we ask her, and the Grail cannot leave its home, or it will be lost for all time. The relics you have brought back are our best hope."

"There is one other," Nigel said.

Mycroft raised his hand to cut him off. "No, we will pursue that lead only when all other avenues have been exhausted." Nigel made to speak when Mycroft again interrupted. "There will be no more discussion on the matter. Do I make myself clear?" Nigel nodded and sagged in his chair.

"I believe we have trespassed on the patience of the Crown Prince long enough. Your Majesty, thank you for your assistance." Mycroft stood and bowed; the Martian tipped his head almost imperceptibly.

"If you will all follow me, we will continue our briefing upstairs." Mycroft strode out of the room. Malcolm rose and bowed toward the Crown Prince. For a moment, he felt like the Martian was eyeing him as prey, and a shiver ran down his spine. Malcolm stopped and looked at the Martian, and the Martian returned his gaze and cocked its head, as if inviting a question. Instead, Malcolm nodded and turned, leaving the room.

Joan ran up to catch Malcolm. "What was that about?" she whispered.

"I'm not sure," Malcolm said. "But I had the distinct feeling that he was the person looking at a fish in a fishbowl, and I was the fish."

CHAPTER 17

The rest of the briefing was mundane after the interview with the Crown Prince of Mars. Mycroft assigned Malcolm to work with Nigel, to create a device to measure psychic energy, and use it to measure the relative energy of the relics that the Secret Service had assembled. It appeared that the Secret Service had gone to the four corners of the world, seeking artifacts and relics from nearly every religion on earth. The list included artifacts from every religion imaginable; from Christianity, Islam, Judaism, and Hinduism, to the varied religions of the aboriginal people of North and South America, Africa, Asia, and Australia. It appeared that no stone had been left unturned in the search.

Mycroft assigned Saxon to a different mission with Joan; something that seemed to involve some diplomatic manoeuvring. Malcolm hadn't listened; he kept going over the encounter with the Martian Crown Prince. Something about it felt off; he just could not put his finger on it. Perhaps it was just the oddness of being in the presence of a being from another world. Gone were the subtle nuances of body language, and tone that could communicate as much or more than the words. And he still couldn't shake the feeling of being eyed as prey.

After several more hours of discussion, to which Malcolm half-listened, Mycroft dismissed the meeting, and staff of the Secret Service arrived to lead Malcolm and Saxon to their new quarters. As it turned out, Malcolm and Saxon were not allowed to leave the Secret Service Building, because they would not be able to find their way back. Malcolm's quarters were rather well appointed, reminding him of his cabin on the *Daedalus*. He sighed; he hadn't been gone one day yet, and he already missed the ship. He missed the routine, the smells of the engines; he found he was even missing Chef's food, if that were possible. The longing gave way to anger, as he realised just how little effort it took for Mycroft to take it away from him.

Why was he here? There were plenty of engineers in the world who could build this contraption; why him? Mycroft's motives were always riddles, wrapped in mysteries, inside enigmas. Mycroft had an endgame for blackmailing Malcolm into joining this endeavour; what it was, was anyone's guess. Malcolm felt like a beginning chess player paired against a grandmaster; he could only see the present, and a few moves ahead. Mycroft saw not only that, but had likely played out every variation of this game. Malcolm sighed; he would just have to go along to see how this would play out. But, he thought, he didn't have to like it.

After a few minutes, another Secret Service employee, who announced himself as Geoffrey Pembroke, came to escort him to his work area. Malcolm reluctantly followed. Geoffrey led him through the corridors, and noted their path for Malcolm to find his way back to his quarters. After several turns, and a descent down several flights of stairs, they came to a set of double doors made of heavy steel. In fact, it looked disconcertingly like doors to a great safe; either keeping something valuable or dangerous on the inside. Geoffrey presented Malcolm with a large, elaborate key, and showed him how to unlock the door. The key itself seemed to work in all three dimensions; there were a series of knobby projections and holes, as well as the typically notched surface of a typical key. The key itself was several inches long, and nearly three inches wide. Malcolm slid the key into the lock, and felt a satisfying click when it was in place. He turned the lock and the heavy doors seemed to release a seal, as Malcolm felt a breeze wash over him that smelled of ozone and diesel.

Malcolm's jaw dropped; he literally couldn't speak. The doors revealed a huge room arrayed with workbenches, and scientific equipment of every type imaginable. In the back of the room were two gigantic generators powering the lights over each of the workbenches. The left wall was lined with shelves running the whole length of the room. On one set of shelves were dozens of scientific instruments, Malcolm recognised signal generators, volt meters, and oscillographs, as well as many unknown instruments. Another section of the wall contained shelves of bottles and jars; likely chemicals, Malcolm imagined. The right wall contained a series of specialised work areas; one looked much like a blacksmith's forge. Malcolm easily recognised the anvil, crucible, and the forge, bringing back memories of his granda's shop. Next to that was a glass blower's shop. As Malcolm looked along the wall, he saw there were areas for metal working, wood working, leather and fabric working, and any other craft he could imagine. Mixed in this jumble were at least three shining computators, their brass gears shining in the light. In front of Malcolm were three men in white lab coats standing attentively.

"Mr. Robertson," Geoffrey said, "this is your lab, and may I introduce your lab assistants? This is Albert Bennet; accomplished blacksmith, metal worker, and glass blower." Geoffrey indicated a middle-aged man, who nodded at Malcolm with calm neutrality. Stepping to the next man. "This is Percy Griffiths, our resident chemistry expert". Griffiths was tall and slender, with a mop of yellow hair on top of a long face that reminded Malcolm of a basset hound. "And finally," Geoffrey continued, "this is Quentin Boothroyd. He is our newest member, but has a talent for making almost anything." Quentin was young; he looked like he was barely out of school, let alone university. He had dark wavy hair, and bright, perceptive eyes.

"And with that, I'll leave you to get acquainted. I'll be back to escort you to dinner." Geoffrey turned and left the room.

Malcolm didn't quite know what to do. "I'm Malcolm. I'm at a bit of a loss here to know what to do. Why don't you show me the laboratory?"

Quentin quickly piped up, "It would be our pleasure, wouldn't it?" Quentin was obviously excited, Albert looked disdainful, and Percy looked bored. Quentin excitedly showed Malcolm all the instruments at their disposal. When they reached the chemical shelves, Percy listed off their inventory in a monotone; Malcolm had a hard time not letting his attention wander.

Albert started to explain the workings of the blacksmith's forge; his voice dripping with disdain, until Malcolm jumped in and explained the purpose of each piece of equipment. Albert's manner changed when Malcolm told him about being raised in his granda's tinker shop, which had been the village smithy. To Quentin's dismay, Albert and Malcolm were soon swapping stories of forge work. Quentin finally interrupted them, so he could show him the rest of the fabrication areas. Malcolm took great interest in them as well, and by the end of the little tour, felt at ease with both Albert and Quentin. Percy, with his perpetual hang-dog expression, was difficult to read. Malcolm couldn't tell if the man was bored out of his mind, or if his dog had just been shot in front of him.

Malcolm took the opportunity to tell the men about his background; working in his granda's shop, going to University, leaving to join the Royal Navy to complete his studies, and his assignment on various ships and airships. Malcolm decided not to tell them about his assignment as captain, as he didn't want them to think he felt superior in anyway. Because he didn't. He felt like he was way out of his league. Experimental engineering was not his forte; he'd always had an acute grasp of practical engineering. He had no idea whatsoever as to how they would measure stored psychic energy.

As he finished his biography, Nigel entered the room, pushing a sample cart in front of him. Whatever was on the cart was covered in a sheet, but Malcolm could already tell what was on it; it was that malignant statue that the Martian Crown Prince had shown them. He didn't need any apparatus to feel the psychic energy emanating from that monstrosity. The room seemed to get darker, the shadows more foreboding. The hair on the back of Malcolm's neck felt like it was standing on end.

"While science is not my area of expertise, I do know enough to know that to measure anything, you need a reference against which to measure," Nigel said, indicating the covered statue.

"Bloody hell," Malcolm sputtered. "Does it have to be that abomination?"

Nigel considered the point for a moment. "I think it does. Anything that we would want to use as a weapon would need to be much stronger than that. I fear almost all of the relics we've collected will not be up to the task."

Malcolm gathered the men around the cart. "Alright, gentlemen. Can you feel the energy coming from that… thing? We need to be able to measure and quantify it. Nigel," he said, realising he hadn't introduced him to the lab, "believes it might be some sort of electromagnetic energy, or perhaps radiation, that we have yet to detect. If anyone has any ideas on how to begin, please feel free to share them."

The men stood in silence for several moments, and soon each was proposing one or more experiments that might be able to quantify this strange energy. The three men ran off in different directions, each looking for the equipment for their experiments. As the day wore on, they tried several experiments, each no more successful than the next.

Before Malcolm knew it, it was quitting time and he wished the trio a good night as they left to return to their lives. Malcolm envied them; the life he had known, such as it was, had been taken away from him. *Is this all I have to look forward to for the rest of my life?* he thought. *Stuck in a dungeon of the Secret Service building gadgets?* He could feel his anger at Mycroft boiling up inside him. *What gives that sanctimonious bastard the right to ruin my life?* he fumed.

"Are you ready for dinner?" a female voice said from the door. Malcolm turned and saw Joan. She looked radiant; Malcolm was uncertain if she was wearing a new outfit, or the one from that morning. At first, he was happy to see her, but as he remembered why he was here in the first place, he quickly frowned.

"What's wrong?" Joan asked gently. She could see from the look on his face that a storm was brewing, and she didn't particularly want to be here when it let loose.

"This!" Malcolm thundered, indicating the room around him. "What am I doing here? I should be onboard the *Daedalus*, not cooped up in a dungeon!"

"I don't understand," she said.

"Your boss blackmailed me into resigning my commission, or face a court martial for fraternising with you. Didn't he tell you that?"

"No," Joan said darkly. "I had no idea."

"Now I'm stuck in this bloody dungeon with no bloody idea what I'm doing! And I can't even leave because I can't find my way back, and I have nowhere to go!"

Joan nodded as Malcolm continued to rant.

"And who does he think he is that he can treat all of us like his own bloody marionettes? Who is he to play with people's lives? Doesn't he have anything better to do than play God?"

Malcolm sputtered on for two more minutes before his vitriol for Mycroft and the situation were spent. She walked to him and grasped both of his hands.

"Malcolm," she said softly, "Mycroft has his reasons. Yes, they may be selfish and uncaring, but he is always looking at the bigger picture. I know it seems like he has done you a great wrong." Malcolm started to interrupt when Joan put a finger softly against his lips. "And he has. It was wrong to coerce you into joining the Secret Service. But look at the bright side."

"Bright side? What bright side?! I'm stuck in this bloody dungeon."

Joan put her finger again to his lips. "And is that really so bad? You've been wanting to be an engineer for a while now; here's your chance. And, I think you'll find there are certain… fringe benefits to staying here." She took his hands and placed them on her waist, and pressed herself against him. She looked him in the eyes, "There are no rules about fraternisation in the Secret Service," she said, her voice sounding like honey and whisky. She pulled him close and kissed him.

Maybe this place isn't so bad after all, Malcolm thought as he returned the kiss.

CHAPTER 18

$\mathcal{M}$alcolm was forced to admit that Joan was right to a certain degree; it wasn't so bad working for the Secret Service. His days were spent trying to figure out a means to measure the psychic energy of the idol. Evenings he dined with Joan and Charles; often they would be joined by Nigel and Geoffrey Pembroke. It seemed that Geoffrey and Charles had struck up a very quick friendship, and spent a great deal of time in each other's company. The one rule the group held was that no one would talk about their work, for the very practical reason that each of them might be working on something above someone else's security level. Instead, they talked about books, music, art, and even science. The group often adjourned to a parlour room where they played cards, chess, or mah-jongg. Later, Malcolm and Joan would spend the night wrapped in each other's arms.

Malcolm struggled every day to think of new ways to detect psychic energy. Every day, he wracked his brain and tried every idea he could conceive; new approaches, a previous approach with a subtle change, a previous approach in the hope that it would work this time. He was still no further ahead than he was on day one.

By the end of the first week, Mycroft had taken to visiting the laboratory, looking for progress. As the second week progressed, Mycroft appeared more frequently. If Malcolm was in the middle of another experiment, Mycroft started looking over Malcolm's shoulder. After the third day in a row of this, Malcolm turned around, handing a screwdriver to Mycroft and asked, "Do you want to do this?" He politely declined, and found a reason to return to his office. As Mycroft exited, Malcolm cursed under his breath.

When they were alone later that night, Malcolm relayed the events to Joan, who was mortified. "Malcolm, you didn't really do that, did you?"

"I most certainly did. I don't know how he bloody well thought standing over my shoulder would make me miraculously figure out the solution!"

"He obviously wants this figured out as soon as possible. He's a very busy man, and the fact that he's stopping in every day to check on the progress means it is very important that this is solved quickly."

"What the bloody hell do you think I'm doing? I want out of this bloody situation so I can get back to the *Daedalus*. His standing over me like a disapproving parent is not going to make anything happen faster!"

Three days later, Malcolm sat in his laboratory looking at the idol for what seemed like the thousandth time, trying to come up with some idea, when the double doors to the laboratory opened. "I rather thought that's what you engineers did; sitting around and waiting for us great scientists to tell you what to do!" a familiar voice said with a hint of humour.

Malcolm turned, and was astonished to find his friend, the physicist, Ernest Rutherford standing at the door, smiling. He still looked every bit the proper English gentleman; hair and mustache precisely trimmed, a perfectly tailored grey suit, and a starched high collar shirt showing an exquisite blue silk tie. Malcolm rose and walked to the door to greet his friend. They shook hands and hugged.

"What in the world are you doing here, Ernest?" Malcolm asked.

"I could ask the same of you," Ernest said.

"I was... let's just say I was between a rock and a hard place, and I took the lesser of two evils," Malcolm said.

Looking around, Ernest said, "If this was the lesser of the two evils, I hate to see what the other choice was." He smiled and Malcolm knew he was just ribbing him. Malcolm and Ernest had got off to a very bad start when they met on Malcolm's mission to Russia; in fact, the physicist had taken a swing at Malcolm. But the two realised that they had come from very similar backgrounds, and shared a great love of science. They continued to correspond after the mission, and Ernest sent him signed copies of his works on radioactivity. Malcolm considered them among his prized possessions.

Malcolm introduced his assistants to Ernest, and even Percy seemed mildly excited by the chance to meet Ernest Rutherford. "You still haven't answered my question; what are you doing here?" Malcolm asked.

"I've been doing some consulting for Mycroft, and he asked if I would look at your problem and offer some guidance. Now, exactly what is it you're trying to do?"

"Please don't laugh, but I've been asked to come up with a means to measure..." He paused, and took a deep breath before saying, "psychic energy."

Ernest started to laugh, but saw the discomfort on Malcolm's face, and tried to change the laugh into a cough. "Surely, you're not serious?"

"I wish I wasn't, but yes, Mycroft has me in this dungeon trying to concoct a machine to measure psychic energy." Malcolm went on to explain Nigel's theory that psychic energy was some sort of electromagnetic energy, and that it could be stored in items. Malcolm brought him to the workbench and uncovered the idol.

Ernest immediately recoiled. "What, pray tell, is that monstrosity?"

"This," Malcolm said grimly, "is my reference standard. It gives off negative energy. I intend to use that as a base line for my measurements... if I can ever think of a way to measure it."

"What have you tried?" Ernest asked, and Malcolm listed the litany of approaches he and his assistants had tried in the last two weeks.

"I'm sorry, can you cover that thing? For some reason, it discomforts me and I can't think."

"My pleasure," said Malcolm as he put the cover over the idol.

Ernest stood in thought for a long time, and Malcolm was loathe to bother him; especially if he had an idea.

"I wonder," Ernest said, "have you thought to approach it from a radioactive model? Not so much as a continuous source of energy, but something that is decaying? It might be emitting some sort of energetic particle of some kind."

"I tried using x-ray and photographic plates," Malcolm said.

Ernest thought more. "I wonder," he said. "Do you have paper and a pen?"

"Yes, here," Malcolm said, leading Ernest to his desk.

Ernest sat down and immediately began sketching a device. "When I was at Victoria University in Manchester, I had an assistant, Hans Geiger, who designed an experiment to capture the scattering of alpha particles. He used a glass tube filled with an inert gas, say neon. The walls of the tube were treated to become a conductor, turning it into a cathode; a wire is run through it, acting as an anode. In our experiment, we used a fluorescent screen to track the particles' path. I daresay you are only interested in detecting particles so it might be easier."

Malcolm watched in amazement, as Rutherford continued to sketch and describe the experiment. At first, Ernest's explanations were over Malcolm's head, but he began to slowly get the general gist of the explanation. The radiation would interact with the gas in the tube, and it would eventually create an electrical current. And that could be measured.

Malcolm brought Albert over to the design that Ernest had sketched out. "Do you think you can make this?"

"Aye, I've had a fair bit of luck making cathode ray tubes; not so very different."

Now that Malcolm had a general idea of how to begin, he leapt into action. Ernest and Malcolm worked with Albert to create the glass tube according to Rutherford's specifications. Malcolm decided that silver should be used as the conductor inside the tube, as it was an excellent conductor of electricity, and he knew that it had some reaction with the supernatural. When the tube was finished, Malcolm attached it first to a power source to charge the tube, and then connected the anode to an oscillograph. Malcolm placed the idol on the cart, and wheeled it nearly ten feet away from the contraption on the workbench. Ernest and Malcolm's lab assistants donned goggles and stepped back, well away from the workbench.

Malcolm donned his own goggles, and tentatively applied the power from the power source. Immediately, signals jumped to life on the oscillograph. Although very faint, there seemed to be a detectable signal on the paper. Malcolm slowly pushed the cart towards the workbench. For the first five feet, the activity on the oscillograph was nearly unchanged. As the cart came within five feet of the bench, the oscillograph began to become more animated. Each step forward caused the oscillograph pen to move more wildly, and a high-pitched hum could be heard. Each step caused the hum to increase in pitch and volume. When Malcolm succeeded in moving the idol so that it was all but touching the tube, the hum reached an earsplitting level. Suddenly, there was a burst of light and an explosion of glass, as the tube could no longer bear the intensity. Malcolm ducked behind the cart which shielded him from the shards of glass.

"I think that you might be on to something," Ernest said wryly. "I think my work here is done."

"Ernest, I can't tell you how grateful I am for your assistance. I would never have come up with anything like this."

"It actually seems to be an interesting area of investigation. I'd encourage you to write a paper on your results, but I honestly don't know where it could possibly be published. Good luck, Malcolm," he said, shaking his hand. "Next time you're near Cambridge, please look me up."

"I might very well take you up on that," Malcolm said.

"Is that a promise or a threat?" Ernest said with a smile.

"Both."

Ernest left Malcolm to the work of refining his design. Over the next few days, Malcolm engaged all his assistants. Albert spent most of his time creating a large supply of what they jokingly called the Rutherson tubes. Malcolm engaged Percy to come up with a silver coating that was sensitive enough to detect the psychic energies, but would not blow up when placed near the idol. Finally, he worked with Quentin to devise a portable version of the machine. They finally settled on pulling apart a voltmeter, so that they could use the gauge to measure the strength of the signal from the Rutherson tube.

Over the course of two weeks, fifteen blown tubes, and two burnt out voltmeters, they perfected a functioning machine. The group decided that they would name their creation a psychometer. The final design was a simple wooden box with a gauge mounted on its face. A strong flexible wire went to a metal tube that Albert had fabricated to hold the Rutherson tube. The metal tube could be brought close to any kind of object, and the gauge would measure the strength relative to the idol. The centre point of the gauge represented measurement of the field from the idol. It would be instantly possible to determine the strength of the psychic energy relative to that of the idol.

Malcolm dutifully report his success to Geoffrey, and within an hour, Mycroft, Nigel, Joan, and Saxon travelled to Malcolm's dungeon workshop to see the contraption. Nigel brought several relics with him; a piece of the True Cross, the Shroud of the Virgin Mary, and a nail used in the Crucifixion. Nigel gingerly set each relic out, one at a time, on the lab bench. On a separate lab bench some distance away, Malcolm placed the idol.

"To demonstrate how the psychometer, as we've taken to calling it, works, we'll start with measuring the idol," Malcolm began. "If you'll follow me to the far workbench, we'll begin." The group gathered around as Malcolm carried the surprisingly portable psychometer to the bench. Malcolm plugged it in, grabbed the metal tube, and held it near the idol. The gauge's needle instantly moved to the centre of the gauge.

"That's amazing," said Saxon. "But why are we measuring this, and not the relics?"

"Because this is the standard against which we will measure the relics. We know that we are looking for a relic whose psychic strength is greater than the idol. We've calibrated the psychometer so that the idol reads dead centre of the gauge. Now we'll measure one of the relics, and see how it compares."

The group returned to the lab bench containing the three relics. "Nigel, can you leave just the piece of the True Cross on the table, and set the others on another workbench away from both this and the idol?"

Nigel nodded and moved the other relics. Malcolm waited until Nigel returned before beginning again. "I asked Nigel to move the other relics so the strength of each individual relic can be measured." Malcolm again took the metal tube and placed it near the relic. To everyone's disappointment, the needle on the psychometer's gauge rose, but was still some distance away from the desired strength. "I'm going back to measure the idol, so I'm assured that we're still measuring correctly." Malcolm and the group followed him to the idol, and watched as the gauge's needle again rose to the centre point.

"That's disappointing," said Malcolm.

"Why do you say that?" asked Mycroft.

"I thought this might actually be strong enough to save us from going through the crates of artifacts we collected. That is the next step, correct?" asked Malcolm.

"Yes, it is. As you said, this is most disappointing. Please try to measure the other artifacts as quickly as possible." He sighed heavily, and looked at Joan and Saxon and said, "I believe it's time for the two of you to start planning to implement your task. I, too, was hoping it wouldn't come to this, but I tend to agree with Malcolm that it is unlikely we'll find an artifact in our keeping that can compete with that," he said, as he pointed at the idol.

"Malcolm, I'd like you to construct two more of these psychometers as you call them. The first would be so that we can measure more artifacts; for the second one, I'd like you to make it portable, say able to be held in a briefcase. Can you do that?"

Malcolm looked at his assistants, and they all nodded in agreement. "Yes, we can," Malcolm said. "We'll start on the first today, so that if we have any luck, we'll have it ready tomorrow. Now that we know what to do, it's relatively simple to recreate it."

"Excellent," said Mycroft. "Nigel, tomorrow, you and Malcolm will begin measuring the items in our inventory." Mycroft turned and started toward the door, when Joan cleared her throat. Mycroft stopped and turned to the room. "Excellent work, everyone," he mumbled as he left the room.

Joan immediately came over to Malcolm. "Excellent job, Malcolm. I know this wasn't easy for you, but I am so proud that you figured this out."

Malcolm smiled. He was proud. He had invented something that no one else had built. He'd had a great deal of help, especially from Ernest Rutherford, who helped set Malcolm on the correct track. He thought about patenting the psychometer, but he had his doubts that such a device would ever be used again.

"Thank you," Malcolm said to Joan. "Perhaps we can celebrate tonight?"

"Perhaps," she said huskily, and gave him a wink. She turned and headed for the door, and Malcolm just couldn't take his eyes off her. When she left, he paused to clear his head and saw Saxon waiting with a bemused look on his face.

"Yes?" Malcolm asked.

"I am amazed that, even after all this time, she still captivates you so much. Shake it off, man, you're making the rest of us look bad." Saxon said with a smile.

"And why haven't I ever seen you pining about a woman?" Malcolm asked.

Saxon hesitated and added, "I guess I just haven't found the right one." He paused for a moment before adding, "Excellent work, Malcolm."

"Let me second that," Nigel said, shaking Malcolm's hand enthusiastically. "This is an impressive feat; quite frankly, I wasn't even sure that it could be accomplished. This will revolutionise my studies, Malcolm. Now that we can demonstrate a physical reaction to psychic and supernatural forces, the paranormal might become a valid field of study, as much as physics, chemistry, or biology. We'll prepare the artifacts today, and we will arrive bright and early tomorrow morning!"

Nigel and Saxon took their leave, and Malcolm was left with his assistants. He turned and said, "Well, no rest for the wicked, lads. Let's get to work."

CHAPTER 19

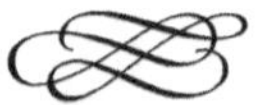

Malcolm and his assistants worked into the evening, and created another psychometer. Joan brought food to the men, who would not leave until the work was done. The longest part of the process was building the actual Rutherson tube. Once that was finished, it was a relatively quick process to rewire the voltmeter. They tested the second psychometer on the idol, and replicated their previous results. Malcolm returned to his quarters, feeling for the first time, in a very long time, that he had accomplished something. It was a feeling he had not felt since coming to the Secret Service.

That good feeling vanished later the next morning when the process of measuring and cataloguing all the artifacts started in earnest. By mid-morning, Malcolm had had enough of the tedium of measuring the reactions, and recalibrating with the idol. Many of the artifacts barely caused the needle to move. The measuring and cataloguing seemed endless. Each day, Nigel brought a cart full of artifacts. Mixed with the crucifixes, rosaries, scraps of cloth, and other objects, were reliquaries containing various body parts of saints.

One morning, Malcolm's heart nearly leapt out of his chest, when he removed the cover from the cart, and found himself staring at the mummified head of a nun, complete with wimple. "Good Lord, what is this?" Malcolm asked Nigel.

"This is the Sacred Head of St. Catherine," Nigel said.

"How are we supposed to use this to fight that thing?" Malcolm asked, holding up the reliquary. "Beat it over the head?"

"No, Malcolm," Nigel sighed. "We won't use it to beat anything over the head. But if we can somehow quantify the energy, we can use that to defeat… the entity. I'm loath to say its name, because it gives it energy."

"Really?" Malcolm asked, as he set up the psychometer to measure the relic.

"Names have great significance. Throughout history, cultures have held that knowing one's true name gave them great power over that person. In the stories of Ancient Egypt, Isis tricked Ra into revealing his true name, and used that power to install her son Horus as the king of the gods. Take the case of Rumpelstiltskin; when the girl learned his name, he was ruined."

"You don't believe any of that, do you?" Malcolm asked.

"Specifically? No," Nigel said. "But if you think about it, there's a glimmer of truth. Biologists have gone to great lengths to create a taxonomy to identify all creatures."

"So? Knowing I'm described as homo sapiens does not provide any power over me."

"True," Nigel said. "But naming things, particularly our fears, gives us great power. Fear of the unknown is one of mankind's greatest fears. When you name something, you define it, and it loses some of its power. When you were a child, did you ever fear that some monster would attack you in the middle of the night, only to find it was only shadows? Once you defined it as shadows, did it scare you anymore?"

"Perhaps you're right," Malcolm conceded. "It still doesn't explain why I'm spending my days measuring the psychic energy of severed heads, scraps of cloth, or even a sandal."

"Belief is energy. The saints were conduits for belief, as well as generating their own energy with their belief. I had hoped that these items would hold that energy, and we could find a way to harness it." Nigel watched Malcolm as he dutifully measured the reliquary's psychic energy. "What do you believe in, Malcolm?"

"I've never given it much thought," Malcolm said. "I believe in science, and the natural laws of the world."

"What about faith?" Nigel said. "Do you believe in God?"

"Yes," Malcolm said. "I'm just not so sure I believe in religion."

"What do you mean?" Nigel asked.

"It seems to me that the church puts far more stock in you attending services every week, than how you live your life the other six days of the week."

"That is sometimes true. But I find that the ritual and practice of the church service allows you to set aside the noise of the world, and allows you to think about God. And being a part of a community of like-minded people also deepens that faith."

"How so?" Malcolm asked.

"It is an experience that's both shared, and intensely private."

Malcolm raised an eyebrow. "How did you ever end up working for such a notorious skeptic as Mycroft?"

"Not long after I graduated, my fiancé Cybil was murdered. I had a crisis of faith. I wondered how God could take Cybil away from me. After a time, I returned to the one thing I was good at: studying. I delved into the works of ancient, and even lost, civilisations, looking for a means to destroy the murderous creature responsible."

"What did you find?" Malcolm said.

"I found much. I've read books containing the most foul and blasphemous knowledge. I have travelled the world, and observed all manner of strange phenomenon. In the end, I found that the most powerful weapon in battling these creatures is faith. Belief in all that is holy and good has a powerful effect on supernatural creatures. While materials such as silver, and symbols, such as a crucifix, are effective in dealing with the supernatural, the most important weapon is faith." Nigel paused and regarded Malcolm. "Do you have faith?"

Malcolm swallowed. He had never stopped to think about it before. "Yes," he answered with uncertainty in his voice.

"I fear that your faith will be put to the test," Nigel said.

"Yes, I supposed you are correct," Malcolm said. "Come," he said, changing the subject, "let's get to measuring these relics. They aren't going to measure themselves."

Malcolm and Nigel spent the rest of the day measuring the relics. If he forced himself to stop and assess the work, he knew that they were making good progress on the task, but Malcolm hated every single second of it. One week became two, and then three, with no end in sight. Halfway through the fourth week, they had completed their measurements. And to Malcolm's dismay, none of the artifacts did better than the fragment of the True Cross; in fact, most barely registered at all. Malcolm spent a day summarising the results, and sent the report to Mycroft.

CHAPTER 20

Malcolm awoke the next morning and started for the laboratory, not sure what he was supposed to do now. He hoped that he had done his bit for the Secret Service, and could go back to being captain, when he was intercepted by Geoffrey Pembroke. "Ah, I found you before you made it to the laboratory. Mr. Holmes needs you to attend a meeting. Please, follow me."

Malcolm stopped, not wanting to take another step further. He resented marching to Mycroft's tune, and this was probably another ploy to prevent him from leaving. Malcolm sighed, realising that being obstinate was not going to get him anywhere, and followed Pembroke. They soon arrived at the library, where Malcolm found Saxon, Joan, and Mycroft already seated. After Malcolm was seated, Pembroke brought him a cup of tea and left the room.

Mycroft began. "Thank you, Malcolm, for joining us."

"Like I had a bloody option," Malcolm muttered.

"Beg your pardon?" Mycroft asked.

"I said, my pleasure," Malcolm said in a monotone.

"Yes, I rather thought as much," Mycroft said. "Let me begin by thanking you, Malcolm, for the meticulous work you did in measuring and cataloguing all of the artifacts that we collected.

Unfortunately, it appears your efforts were in vain; not a single arti-fact has the necessary power we need to address our bigger problem."

"So you drummed me out of the Air Service for nothing?" Malcolm exploded.

"No, Malcolm. Will you stop nursing that particular grudge and let me continue?"

Malcolm crossed his arms and just nodded, knowing if he opened his mouth, he would say something that would only make matters worse.

"We have been planning for this eventuality from the beginning. We believe there is still one artifact that might be up to the task at hand."

"Then why did I bloody well waste four weeks in the laboratory testing those useless relics?" Malcolm said.

"Because," Mycroft said, cutting him off, "the artifact in question is locked in the Imperial Treasury in Hofburg Palace in Austria, so we can't just go and get it." He looked at Malcolm sharply, and Malcolm held his gaze for a moment before looking away.

"The artifact in question is the Holy Lance, sometimes called the Spear of Destiny. It is purported to be the spear used to pierce the side of Jesus at the Crucifixion to determine if He was actually dead."

"So we plan to just waltz into Austria and ask for the spear?" Malcolm asked. "You do realise that we are one catastrophe away from being at war with them?"

"Yes, I'm fully aware of the situation with the Hapsburg Empire; far more than you. But as a matter of fact, we *are* going to waltz in there, in a manner of speaking. Madame De Marnier, perhaps you had best explain the plan to our recalcitrant captain."

"For some time," Joan began, "Mycroft has been concerned that we might have to acquire the Spear of Destiny, and he tasked Charles and I with developing a plan. As it turns out, the Austrians are very eager to see an end to the Italo-Turkish War. They are right between the two warring nations, and have no desire to see the conflict spill over to their borders. As luck would have it, in two months, a British diplo-matic mission will be sent to assist in these talks."

"Diplomatic mission? That rules me out," Malcolm said.

"*Oh contraire, mon Capitaine,*" Joan said. "While it is true that you may not make an ideal diplomat, you make an excellent resource for acquiring the spear."

"And why is that?" Malcolm asked.

"Because," Saxon added, "the Imperial Treasury has a highly technical security system. While we have a great deal of information on the system, we need somebody technical, with a proven ability to think on his feet, and improvise solutions not obvious to most people." Saxon paused for a moment. "I am talking about you," he added with a smile.

Malcolm softened somewhat. At least this sounded like a duty to which he was suited. "Fine. What is our plan?"

"The three of us will be part of the diplomatic delegation. There will be a formal state dinner held at the palace. We will slip away and gain entry to the Treasury. Once there, we will use the portable psychometer you built to ascertain whether or not to take the Spear. If it is as strong as we think, we will take the Spear, and leave a duplicate in its place. We will leave the palace and be on our way to Switzerland before anyone knows better."

"Oh, that should be easy," Malcolm said dryly. "Nothing could possibly go wrong with that plan."

"Malcolm," Joan said, with a hint of anger in her voice, "stop being childish; of course, the plan isn't that simple. Charles and I have worked out a very detailed timeline and plan. You will begin training immediately for your part in this plan, and we will drill it until you can do it in your sleep. Based on our intelligence on the security of the Treasury, we have built a replica of the Treasury, and the three of us will begin drilling on the steps necessary to infiltrate it, and remove the Spear. When we are finished here, you will begin intensive training in hand-to-hand combat, and security systems, from the experts here in the Secret Service. Once you have completed that satisfactorily, you will join Commander Saxon and I in rehearsal. May I remind you that you are an Agent of the Secret Service, and are duty bound to complete this assignment. Is that clear?" Joan found herself irritated with Malcolm's sulking, and as she explained his duties to him, she found herself getting madder by the minute.

"Crystal clear," Malcolm said, with a note of ice in his voice. His anger rose, as he considered how the Secret Service had manipulated him into this position in the first place.

"Good," Mycroft said. "Everything is set in motion. Madame De Marnier, perhaps you'll join me in my office to discuss the details. Commander Saxon, if you would be as kind as to escort Captain Robertson to the gymnasium, where he'll begin his training."

The meeting broke up, and Saxon approached Malcolm cautiously. "Malcolm, you could at least try to be civil to Mycroft."

"Why? He destroyed a career that took me years to build. I was just getting acclimated to being a captain, and he ripped it away from me, with as much regard as you would give ripping a newspaper." Malcolm couldn't suppress his anger; he knew he shouldn't take it out on Saxon, but neither could he hold it back any longer.

"Come along," Saxon said. "Your first training session will be hand-to-hand combat. You can take your anger out on the punching bag, and not me." Malcolm noted a hint of anger in Saxon's voice, and felt horrible.

"I'm sorry, Charles," Malcolm said. "I'm being an ass. It's just... I feel so lost. The only life I've known as an adult has been taken away from me, and it doesn't feel very good." Malcolm sighed wearily. "Perhaps taking it out on a punching bag would be better than taking it out on you and Joan."

Saxon nodded in sympathy. "Malcolm, I know this is hard on you. You have worked hard for everything you have achieved, and it must hurt to have it taken away by Mycroft. Try to remember that there is a bigger picture. In fact, if we don't succeed, there may not be anything to be angry about any more."

Malcolm sighed. "You're right, Charles." He paused for a moment. "You seem to be taking this in your stride," he said.

"Well, for one thing, my career is not as long as yours, so I'm not as invested in it. And, I believe I have an actual aptitude for this. While I think I'm a capable second-in-command, I don't see myself ever becoming Captain. And the thought of filling out the rest of my days never achieving more than I have now scares me. This offers me a fresh start, new challenges, and a future."

Malcolm jolted. "You intend to make this position permanent?" he asked in disbelief.

"I very well might, Malcolm. You are my best friend, and I literally owe you my life, but this is something that genuinely excites me."

Malcolm considered his friend for a moment. As Joan had said, there were advantages to working with the Secret Service, and he saw how they might attract Saxon. He sighed again, and said. "You better get me to my training, or Joan will have both of our heads."

Saxon left Malcolm at the gymnasium to the tender mercies of James MacIlhenny, a former drill sergeant for the Royal Army, who thought little of the Royal Navy, and even less of the Royal Air Service. First, he made Malcolm endure a regimen of calisthenics that he had not endured since he first entered the Royal Navy. His arms were hurting, and he was out of breath, when he was forced to run through an obstacle course that involved jumping over hurdles, crawling under barriers, and climbing walls. When Malcolm finished that, he spent the remainder of his time sparring with MacIlhenny who kept saying, "What a molly you are! Can't you hit any harder than that?" Malcolm spent most of the sparring match picking himself up off the floor. By the time the afternoon ended, every muscle in his body felt sore, bruised, or both. He limped to his quarters, and sat in his bath tub for a very long time before dressing for dinner.

When he arrived for dinner, Joan looked at him and smiled. "I see you have met Mr. MacIlhenny, our physical combat instructor."

"Bloody Marquis de Sade, more like," Malcolm grumbled as he pulled the chair out for Joan.

"Yes, he rather is, I'm afraid. How did it go?"

"I haven't done that many calisthenics since joining the Royal Navy. Between that and jumping over hurdles and climbing walls, I was exhausted by the time we got to the self-defense. It was no wonder he was calling me a molly. I could barely lift my arms by that point."

Malcolm though he saw a flash of anger across Saxon's face, but it happened so quickly that Malcolm wasn't sure. Saxon was silent for moment, and then smiled. "Oh, go on, Malcolm, you must be exaggerating."

"If you think I'm exaggerating, you're more than welcome to join me, and show me how it's done."

"I may very well join you tomorrow afternoon; if that doesn't upset our schedule," Saxon said to Joan.

"No, that will be fine; at this point, we need to integrate Malcolm into the plan," she said. "Just so you know, MacIlhenny is infamous for his love of pushing people to their limits."

"Oh, I'm sure of that," Saxon said darkly. He smiled and changed the topic of conversation. Malcolm watched his friend, and could tell that he was deliberately being nonchalant, but something was bothering him.

The next day, Malcolm spent the morning learning the intricacies of locks, and the science of how they worked. While not the most stimulating field of study, Malcolm was thankful to turn his mind to something that he understood; the mechanical world. No more tedious laboratory work, or theoretical work. He was back to the world of gears and physics; he felt like he had come home. The morning sped away, and Malcolm was surprised when Saxon turned up to go with him to the gymnasium.

The afternoon was nearly identical to the day before; calisthenics until he felt nauseous, running the obstacle course until his arms felt like lead, and finally the sparring. "Which one of you sorry mollies wants to go first," MacIlhenny spat derisively at the two men. Saxon was breathing hard, but offered, "I will."

Malcolm was relieved that he was not going first. Saxon caught his breath and put his hands up, ready to defend himself. "Come on, you molly," MacIlhenny said. "Let's see what you've got. I doubt a molly like you will even land a blow. Come on, or are you afraid of breaking a fingernail?" MacIlhenny kept baiting Saxon, trying to get him to punch first. Saxon refused to take the bait, but his face darkened with every insult. MacIlhenny, impatient with Saxon, took a step to deliver a haymaker. Saxon, with a speed that Malcolm had never seen before, kicked the man's knee so hard that Malcolm heard a sickening pop. The haymaker now lost all its energy, and Saxon grabbed MacIlhenny's fist, spun him around, and pulled his arm behind his back. MacIlhenny was roaring with pain, from both his knee and his shoulder, as Saxon threatened to dislocate it. Saxon put his mouth close to MacIlhenny's ear and hissed angrily. "If I ever hear you call anyone else a molly, I will pull this useless arm off your body, and beat you with it." He let go and pushed MacIlhenny to ground, and strode off to the changing room. Malcolm stood there, dazed and shocked for a second, before he had the presence of mind to alert one of the instructors to get medical attention for MacIlhenny. Malcolm rushed over to see what he could do to treat him. His knee was no longer directly in line with the rest of the leg, and Malcolm's stomach turned at the thought of the amount of pain the man must be experiencing. He thought the shoulder was dislocated as well. After several minutes, a doctor came and attended to MacIlhenny. Malcolm turned and stalked to the changing room.

He stormed in, and found Saxon sitting shirtless on the changing bench with a towel over his head. "What the bloody hell was that about?" Malcolm asked, with a mix of anger and concern. "Whatever did that man do to you?"

Saxon was silent for a long moment before he spat out, "He was a bully."

"Of course he was a bully," Malcolm said. "Have you forgotten our basic training? Every single one of them was a bully!"

Saxon sat silently with his head down. He seemed as if he wanted to speak, but didn't know what to say. And he was clearly upset. Malcolm knew something important was bothering his friend. He sat down next to him and asked gently, "What's wrong, Charles?"

Saxon looked up at Malcolm for a long second, before getting up and turning away from Malcolm. "God," he said. "I have no idea how to begin, except to just start."

"Begin what?" Malcolm asked in confusion.

Malcolm saw Saxon take a deep breath, as if girding himself for a challenge. "I believe that you have remarked, on more than one occasion, about the absence of a woman in my life? Have you ever wondered why that might be?"

Malcolm looked at Saxon with confusion. "No, I just assumed that you hadn't met anyone."

"Don't you find it odd that I haven't attracted any female companionship? I am connected to the Royal Family, however distantly. There are many who want that connection, no matter how remote."

"I suppose that's true," Malcolm agreed.

"So why am I still single?" Saxon asked.

"You just haven't met the right person yet, Charles. There's nothing wrong with that. It's taken me this long to find Joan."

"Oh, Malcolm, you can be so dense sometimes! Now I know why Joan gets so perturbed with you." He paused and took a deep breath. "Malcolm, I'm not mooning over not being married. The truth is," Saxon paused, and seemed to be bracing himself for a backlash. "Malcolm, I'm a homosexual."

Malcolm was caught completely off guard by Saxon's remark. "You're a what?" Malcolm asked, barely able to process the words.

"I'm a homosexual; I'm a buggerer; I like to have sex with other men," Saxon spat angrily. He took another breath and forced himself to calm. "Certainly it explains many things; you rarely see me in the company of women, and I never talk about my love life. You asked me what Mycroft used to blackmail me out of the Air Service. This is it. If I'm exposed, not only do I go to jail, it stains the reputation of the Royal Family. I had no choice but to comply."

Saxon continued, "I had merely meant to knock MacIlhenny on his fat ass. But when he kept on calling me a molly, it was like I was hearing every single person in my life calling me out. I snapped. MacIlhenny was on the receiving end of all my years of stored up anger; anger for being different; anger for loving men, and not being able to express it; anger for having to live a secret life, and put up a false face to society, for fear I would be imprisoned. It just boiled up every time he repeated that word, and I lost control." Saxon turned and looked at Malcolm. Tears flowed down his face. "I'm sorry. I hope you don't despise me."

Malcolm's mind was reeling. He struggled to find words, but the shock of finding out his best friend was homosexual wiped everything from his mind. Malcolm backed away, paused as if to speak, and walked out of the room. Saxon leaned over, putting his face in his hands, and started to cry in earnest.

Malcolm returned to his room and sat in his chair, thinking about what Charles said. "It can't be true," Malcolm thought. But even as he did, memories popped up of instances where Saxon withdrew from conversations about women, and often deflected Malcolm's attempts to learn more about his private life. It explained so much. Malcolm realised that Saxon had not told him while he was his commanding officer, as Malcolm would be duty bound to dishonourably discharge him, and send him to prison.

Malcolm's thoughts churned between revulsion, and his own bond of friendship with Saxon. He couldn't get his mind around the fact that his best friend in the world was homosexual. And had kept it from him. He was lost in these thoughts when he was startled by a knock on the door. He answered, and saw an exasperated Joan. "Well, are you coming to dinner, or not? Everyone is waiting for you!"

"What? Dinner time? Really? I lost track of time. Come in, and I'll change," he said, realising he had not even changed out of his workout clothes.

Joan let out an exasperated sigh, and was about to chastise Malcolm when she saw the pained look on Malcolm's face. "Are you alright?" she asked.

"Yes," Malcolm replied. Joan gave him a sharp look. "No," he sighed.

"What's wrong?" she asked.

"I assume you heard about what happened to MacIlhenny?"

"Yes," she replied. "It seems Charles gave him quite a thrashing. Is that what's bothering you?"

"Yes. No," Malcolm said. He paused, and took a deep breath. "Do you know what Mycroft used to force Charles to resign from the Air Service?"

"Yes," she said softly. She was silent for a second and then started. "He told you, didn't he?"

"Yes," Malcolm said softly.

"What was your reaction?" she asked gently.

"I was stunned. I left without saying a word. I've been here ever since, trying to understand how someone who is such a good person could be that way."

"Malcolm, his being 'that way' has nothing to do with the person he is. Charles is a very good person, his being a homosexual has nothing to do with that."

"How can you defend that? It's wrong and unnatural!" Malcolm said, more angrily than he'd intended.

"Says whom?" Joan asked. She held her hand up and stopped Malcolm's reply. "The Bible? The Bible says a great many things are unnatural and abominations; such as pork, shellfish, tattoos. In my travels, I've met many homosexuals. They are people like you and me. They are not inherently evil or good. They are people who wrestle with the same angels and demons, with which you and I wrestle. They have the added burden of having to keep a great deal of who they are hidden from the world. I watched my uncle get ostracised from the family. My father rarely spoke of him, and never communicated with him, despite the fact my uncle frequently sent letters."

"Once I started in the Secret Service, I used my position to find out where he lived. I went to his townhouse in London, a very shabby place for someone of my uncle's lineage. When he answered the door, I saw a sad, faded-looking man who appeared to have little to live for anymore. I introduced myself to him, and he almost shut the door in my face. I explained that I was there of my own accord and wanted to meet him. He cautiously let me in and we chatted politely over tea. I was so curious as to why he had been exiled from the family."

Joan stopped for a moment and then continued. "We chatted that afternoon and he was glad that someone in the family had taken an interest in him. I met weekly with him for tea. He had barely left his townhouse in decades, and it was an enormous effort to get him to go outside. In time, we took strolls in Hyde Park. All the while, he never told me why he had been ostracised. I started investigating on my own, having all the resources of the Secret Service at my disposal. I found out that he, like my father, had been in the Army; in fact, my uncle held a higher rank than my father. My uncle mysteriously resigned his commission and left. Further investigation indicated that he had been caught with another man, and he'd resigned, instead of facing the ignominy and shame. I instantly knew why my father had cut him out of his life. I love my father, but he has very strong opinions and can be bullheaded."

She continued. "The next week, when I met with him for tea, I told him I knew why he left the military. He sighed and got up. 'How much do you want?' he said as he got up. I said, 'I don't want anything. I just wanted to tell you I knew. I love you for who you are.' At that he crumpled into his chair and broke into sobs. Apparently, I was the first member of his family who hadn't attempted to blackmail him about his secret. He just sobbed as I held him. His family had cast him aside, and my father had threatened to cut off any family money if he ever found out that my uncle was having a relationship with anyone. This man had been alone for thirty years of his life. I was the first one to reach out to him, and show him any affection, in thirty years. You talk about homosexuality being unnatural. How is that natural?"

Joan stopped talking, approached Malcolm and held his hands. "You and I have no idea how difficult it must have been for Charles to admit the truth, not knowing how you would react. Thankfully, you were too shocked to respond with your usual 'react first, think later' approach. Malcolm, Charles is the same man you've come to know and trust. In fact, he has shown a great trust in you by sharing who he is. I can't tell you how to think, but you need to tell him how you feel, for good or ill. I'll make excuses for you at dinner, but come as soon as you can." She raised his hand to her mouth, and gave it a kiss before releasing it and leaving.

Malcolm hurried to dress, thinking about Joan's story, and his own feelings. He hurried to the dining room, sure he looked as disheveled as he felt. The conversation at the table, which had been low, stopped when Malcolm entered. "Sorry," he said. "It appears my afternoon session tired me out more than I realised, and I fell asleep. My apologies," he said as he sat down. He looked at Saxon, who assiduously avoided his gaze.

Dinner that night was a gloomy, sombre affair. No one offered much other than platitudes about the quality of the meal and wine. Malcolm kept trying to catch Saxon's gaze, but Charles was uncharacteristically unengaged in the little conversation that took place around the table. As Malcolm watched Charles, his own heart seemed to break a little. Malcolm had felt like an outsider during his whole military career. As a Scot, who had nothing to recommend him other than his intelligence and hard work, he often had to play a role that was not truly who he was.

The dinner seemed to drag on forever. As soon as it was done, Saxon immediately rose and excused himself to leave. "Wait," Malcolm said. "I'd like a word, Charles."

"I'm tired, Malcolm, perhaps another night," Saxon said, still moving to the door.

"No, please, I need to say something to you, and it can't wait for tomorrow. I'd rather say my piece privately, but I will say it right now."

Joan rose immediately and yanked Pembroke to his feet. "Come Geoffrey, you can escort me back to my room while we let these two talk." Joan put her arm in Geoffrey's, and quickly dragged him out of the room.

When they left, Charles turned towards Malcolm. "You don't have to do this, Malcolm."

"I absolutely must," Malcolm said. He took a deep breath. "I owe you an apology. I should not have walked off this afternoon. You told me something very personal, and I walked away."

"Thank you, Malcolm," Saxon said emotionlessly.

"And I also want to say," Malcolm continued, "it makes absolutely no difference to me if you are homosexual or not. Who you love doesn't change my feeling for you. You are my friend, and brother, now and always."

Saxon looked at Malcolm, tears welling in his eyes. "Thank you, Malcolm. I thought after you left…"

"It was a bit of a shock, and I didn't know what to say. To be honest, I didn't know how I felt. But Joan talked to me and she put things into perspective for me."

"She knows?" Saxon asked.

"I would guess she's known for a very long time," Malcolm said.

"Oh," Saxon said.

The two men stood in silence. Malcolm broke the silence by giving his friend a hug as he done many times. He thumped Saxon on the back, and when he broke the embrace, he said, "I don't know about you, but I could certainly use a drink."

CHAPTER 21

Over the next weeks, things fell into a rhythm; mornings were spent learning basic locks. Malcolm quickly mastered the knowledge necessary to pick locks, but sometimes had issues with the manual dexterity required. He moved on to safes; learning how to defeat the locking mechanism, but also dealing with the various types of safeguards such as re-lockers, that shoot hardened steel pins into the frame if the lock is comprised in certain ways. Malcolm found he had more talent for this kind of work, as it required attention to detail, more than manual dexterity. He graduated to other security devices such as pressure plates, electrical alarms, and trip wires. Malcolm excelled at defeating these devices, because he had intimate knowledge of the mechanics or electrics involved.

Afternoons were spent doing calisthenics, traversing obstacle courses by climbing walls by handhelds, shimmying up a rope, crawling through tight spaces, and jumping hurdles, and finally, hand-to-hand combat training. As the days progressed, Malcolm found that his body began to gain a chiselled look, and he found muscles that had long since been dormant. At first, he felt ashamed that he'd let himself get out of shape, until he remembered that he had one of the best physical training scores for senior officers at his last assessment.

When Joan felt that Malcolm was ready to participate, only one week remained before they left for Austria. They had a map of the palace, and a general outline for the Imperial Treasury, or *Kaiserliche Schatzkammer*, as Joan was fond of calling it. She insisted that Saxon and Malcolm use the German name for it; it came easily to Saxon who spoke German, but Malcolm struggled to spit out all the consonants.

A very rough set of the courtyard leading to the Imperial Treasury had been constructed in one of the large gymnasiums. When Malcolm and Saxon arrived on the first morning of rehearsal, Joan was waiting for them. "Come along you sluggards, we haven't got all day!" Malcolm looked for some hint at humour on her face, but she was deadly serious. Suppressing an inner groan, Malcolm and Saxon fell into line as Joan began walking back and forth in front of them.

"Before we begin, let me get one thing straight," Joan began. "I am in command of this mission, and I will not tolerate any insubordination. Especially from you, Malcolm."

Malcolm took a breath as if to protest, saw the look on Joan's face, and softly exhaled.

"You will do what I say, when I say it, and how I tell you to do it," she continued. "With input from Charles, I developed several scenarios that we might encounter. I've instructed the logistics group to create a simulation, using one or more of the scenarios. We will attempt to complete the simulation. Once we complete the simulation, we will analyse our performance. During this time, the simulation will be reset, and the scenario will change. We will attempt the simulation and again analyse our performance. Overnight, the simulation will be changed, and we'll repeat the exercises all over again. Any questions?"

Malcolm tentatively raised his hand. Joan's glare indicated she would brook no questions, just like one of Malcolm's drill instructors, although admittedly, much more attractive.

"Yes?" she asked in an exasperated tone.

"Are there going to be other people involved? It seems to me that we'll have to deal with guards," Malcolm asked.

Joan relaxed a little. "That's an excellent question, Malcolm. Yes, we'll have to deal with guards. Several Secret Service personnel will also participate. All participants will be armed with these," she said, as she pulled out what looked like an oversized pistol. "The guns shoot a small bag of red dye that explodes on contact. This will indicate if anyone is wounded during the exercise, although they do sting quite a bit, and you will see the bruise the next day. For a non-lethal weapon, such as a jack, it's typically a soft item coated with something, to indicate if you have been hit. Your ability to down an opponent, and avoiding injury, will be evaluated as part of the exercise."

The general plan for the simulation was the same. Because there was no way to recreate the whole palace, the scenario started at the point that they would enter the courtyard. The mission was to get to the Treasury, gain entrance, test the Spear of Destiny, take it, replace it with the replica, and leave without a trace.

Joan gave Malcolm and Charles specific clothes. She ordered them to change, and get any tools they thought they would need for the mission. Malcolm put on a black tail coat which had several secret pockets along the inside, places all along the cuffs to keep tools, and a special pocket, that doubled as a holster near his left arm, that did nothing to give the appearance that he was armed. Likewise, the white waistcoat also contained many hidden pockets. Even the black oxfords he wore had a hollow heel that could be detached to hide items.

Generally, Malcolm detested formal clothing, as it was always tight fitting and generally inflexible. Not so with this outfit; it gave the illusion of being tightfitting, but allowed more movement than even his athletic clothes. Malcolm looked at himself in the mirror when he was finished, and almost didn't recognise himself. The reflection that stared back at him looked like a distinguished gentleman, and not the uncomfortable looking Scotsman. He had stopped shaving some weeks before, and had now grown out a full salt and pepper beard. With the grey that had already appeared on his temples, he looked like a distinguished gentleman. He had been ready to shave it off some time ago, but Joan insisted that he keep it. He could now see why; his very own mother might not recognise him.

Malcolm met Saxon at the Quartermaster's, and they added various accessories to their outfits, in addition to receiving their guns for the exercise. Malcolm chose a set of lock picks, a set of miniature screwdrivers and wrenches, a hand drill that could be disassembled and reassembled, a listening device consisting of a small amplifier tied to a collapsible head set, and cufflinks that contained a small amount of explosives. Saxon focused on logistical items and weapons: a small thin metal line that was both strong and flexible, a grappling hook that simply looked like a metal rod until a button was pushed that released four hooks, several throwing knives, a couple of small daggers, and, like Malcolm, the exploding cufflinks.

Malcolm and Saxon met Joan who dressed in a dazzling black gown draped with a scarlet red silk wrap. Malcolm thought that it left very little to the imagination, and he wondered how anything could be hidden there. But Malcolm knew better. He wanted to make Joan proud, and vowed to himself that he would follow her orders to the letter. She produced a stopwatch from her clutch, activated it, and told them to go.

They slipped into the space designated as the courtyard. As soon as Joan went through the door, she slipped immediately into the shadows. Charles was likewise successful at blending into the shadows. As Malcolm stepped through the doorway, he slipped and fell to the ground with a crash. The two men serving as guards at the Treasury entrance immediately came over to him, weapons pointed. Malcolm saw them, and immediately started to slur his words. "Pardon me," he said after letting out a large burp. "This isn't the head, is it?" Malcolm looked down at his feet and said, "My shoe's untied." As they looked down, Malcolm produced two saps and hit them both over the head. Tagged by the flour on the sap, the guards played unconscious, and Malcolm joined Joan and Charles in the shadows.

"What the hell are you doing?" Joan hissed in a low voice. "I told you to do as I said."

"Well, I tried that, and I bloody well fell on my ass," Malcolm whispered. "I was spotted, and did the best that I could."

Joan drew breath to answer when Saxon interrupted. "Perhaps this can wait until afterwards? I believe we have a spear to steal?"

The trio attempted to regroup, but things went from bad to worse. They made it through the outer door, but when Malcolm attempted to open the vault door that led to the Treasury, he triggered the re-lockers, and the vault was now inaccessible.

When it was obvious that they had failed, Joan wheeled on Malcolm. "You're doing this on purpose!" she yelled. "You don't want to do this, and you're doing your damnedest to get dropped from the mission."

"Hold it right there, lassie," Malcolm said. "You're right; I don't want to do this. I want to be captaining my airship. But I gave you my word that I would do my best, and that's what I'm trying to do."

"Your best isn't good enough. You must be better. At this point, you're a liability to the mission."

"What the bloody hell did you expect? You gave me three bloody weeks to become a safe expert. Did it ever occur to you that I have little practice actually opening a safe? And you expect me to do it while you're constantly nagging me to hurry up?"

"Nagging? I'm trying to get you to do your job," she yelled back.

"Breathing down my neck and second guessing everything I do isn't going to help me do it any better," Malcolm retorted.

Saxon stepped between them and raised his voice. "Alright, you two! That is quite enough from both of you." He wheeled on Malcolm. "You, go and take a shower and cool off. We will meet for our debriefing this afternoon. Until then, make yourself scarce."

Malcolm blinked at Saxon. Why was Saxon ordering him around? Malcolm was about to take a deep breath to offer a response. Saxon glared at him and Malcolm's breath turned into a snort, as he stomped out of the training area.

Joan said, "Thank you, Charles. He was being so unreasonable..."

Saxon cut her off. "No, Joan, Malcolm was not being unreasonable; you were. The reason I told him to leave was so I could talk to you privately."

"Me? Unreasonable? I'm the leader of this operation, and it's my duty to make sure everyone is performing at his top level."

"And Malcolm was," Saxon said gently. "Joan, we both know Malcolm. Subtlety is not his forte. He is rather much like the proverbial bull in the china shop."

As he said this, the tension in Joan's shoulders visibly released. "Yes, I suppose you're right." She paused and sighed. "It is rather part of his charm." She shook her head. "But why are you so capable at it, while Malcolm is so… bad?"

"A lifetime of keeping secrets, and learning how to not attract attention," Saxon said. "While I am told that I can be charming, I rarely try to attract attention to myself. Attention invites scrutiny, which as you know would be detrimental to me."

Joan put a hand on Saxon's shoulder. "I understand," she said softly. "But what are we going to do about Malcolm? At this point, he's a liability to the mission."

Saxon considered for a moment. "Well, for starters, don't yell at him when he tries to correct a problem."

"But he wasn't following the plan!"

"Because the plan had already failed when he slipped. He had the presence of mind to recover, and take the two guards out in the process. He accomplished the goal of dispatching the guards, but not in the way you planned. Malcolm has always been one for thinking on his feet. If you try to make him rigidly follow your plans, he will balk out of sheer stubbornness."

Joan sighed. "You're right. God help his Scottish stubbornness. Charles, you know him better than anyone. What do I do?"

Saxon considered this for a moment. "Malcolm works best when he can work within a set of general guidelines. He's never been one for following an exact prescribed set of steps. He needs to clearly know the problem that needs to be solved at each step. Let him think of a solution. And Lord knows, give him room to work. If you hover over his shoulder, he'll be just as likely to walk away and tell you to do it yourself."

"I suppose I was looking over his shoulder too much," Joan sighed. "Do you think he'll ever be ready?"

Saxon nodded. "I do. Since you rather indelicately told him he was a liability to the mission, he will redouble his efforts just to prove you wrong. He's done that his whole career. I rather think he enjoys proving everyone wrong."

Joan laughed. "Yes, he does. Come along, let's get changed and see if we can find our troublesome engineer."

Joan and Charles changed into their regular clothes. They looked, and found Malcolm in his room, nursing a whisky. "Come around to yell at me some more? Tell me how awful I am?"

"No, Malcolm," Joan said contritely. "It has been brought to my attention that I was perhaps a little harsh in my assessment of your performance."

"A little harsh?" Malcolm interrupted. "I'm trying my damnedest to do my bloody best, at a job for which I'm clearly not suited, and all you do is tell me I'm a 'liability to the mission'."

Joan's face started to redden, and Saxon arched an eyebrow. She caught herself, and took a deep breath. "Malcolm, I'm sorry. I handled the situation inappropriately. I know that you're trying, and this is difficult for you. I lost sight of that this morning. You know I think the world of you. Perhaps it isn't fair to expect you to become an agent, and an expert in safes and security systems, but you are what we have right now. And if there's anyone who can do it, in that short a time, it's you."

Malcolm sat in silence, then drained the remainder of his whisky. "Apology accepted," he said less glumly. "So what do we do now?"

"First," Saxon said, "we have lunch. Then we'll discuss what happened this morning." He paused, looking at each in turn, and added, "In civilised tones. We need to figure out what went wrong, and how to correct it."

"Fine," Malcolm said, getting up from his chair. "I'm starving."

Lunch consisted of pea soup, roast chicken, French-cut green beans, and roast potatoes. Malcolm was truly hungry, and attacked his lunch, as much not to say anything as he was hungry. Joan, for her part, pecked at her food, not eating much. Saxon ate because he too was hungry, but his attention was not fully on the task, as he tried to maintain non-threatening conversation. After a while, he gave up and just ate his lunch. The strain of the forced civility was almost a palpable presence. All of them seemed to dawdle over dessert; no one was looking forward to reviewing the morning's activities. When the last crumb was finished from the eclairs, and the teapot drained, the three of them looked at each other, and silently headed to the meeting room.

To Malcolm's surprise, Mycroft was waiting for them. "I didn't realise that you would be joining us," he said, with little warmth in his voice.

"I thought I would stop in and see how things are going," Mycroft said. "A great deal relies on your mission; I simply want to do what I can to help it succeed."

Get me off the mission, Malcolm thought to himself. He thought Joan had been correct; he was a liability to the mission. He barely had a grasp of what he had to do, and defeating the security measures relied totally on him. He took his chair with little enthusiasm. He was not looking forward to a two-hour discussion of his failings.

Joan smiled, but Malcolm could feel that she wasn't happy. "Mr. Holmes, it wasn't necessary to take time away from your busy day. You must certainly have something more important than to listen to the exercise review."

"Nonsense," he said. "I look forward to seeing where we stand. It's vitally important that this mission succeed without any issues."

"We're honoured that you are taking such an interest," Saxon said, trying to help. He knew that the conflict between Joan and Malcolm would help neither of them, and tried to do what he could to defuse a potentially messy situation.

"Madame De Marnier, please begin with a step-by-step explanation of what occurred."

Joan began at the very beginning, and had only reached the part where Malcolm slipped and fell, when Mycroft interrupted.

"Malcolm, is it true you slipped?" Mycroft asked.

"Yes," Malcolm replied glumly. "I apparently can't walk in oxfords."

"Ah," Mycroft said. "Madame De Marnier, send a note to the Quartermaster to redesign the oxfords, starting with Malcolm's size, to have more grip on the bottom." He turned to Malcolm and said, . "I have, on more than one occasion, had issues with those shoes myself." Malcolm was relieved to hear that he wasn't the only one who had issues with those damnable things. Mycroft turned to Joan. "Continue," he said.

Joan continued, and detailed how Malcolm pretended to be drunk and dispatched the two guards. "Excellent work, Malcolm," Mycroft said. "One of the most important skills an agent needs is to think on his feet. Excellent work. Continue," he said.

Joan nervously continued to the point where Malcolm triggered the re-lockers, and they were unable to gain access to the vault. Mycroft paused for the moment and turned to Malcolm. "What happened while you were trying to open the vault door?"

Malcolm squirmed a little in his chair, suddenly feeling like a mischievous schoolboy caught in the act. "I, um, failed to adequately examine the vault door." He stopped and looked at Joan. "I was in a bit of a hurry."

"Why were you hurrying?" Mycroft asked, in a very neutral tone.

"Um, because, um, the plan called for the vault door to be opened within two minutes of entry into the Imperial Treasury."

Mycroft nodded. "Why the short amount of time?"

Joan answered tentatively. "From our intelligence on the guard rotation, we have at most 15 minutes before a new set of guards come to relieve the current guards. Working back from our estimates, we only have two minutes to get the vault door open."

"Alright," Mycroft said. "Let's begin there. What can we do to give our erstwhile safecracker more time?"

For the next few hours, the group went step–by-step through the plan, looking for different ways to allow Malcolm more time to adequately inspect the vault. When they were done, they had a new plan that would give Malcolm more time to examine the vault door.

"Excellent work all. I look forward to seeing how you perform tomorrow. Mr. Saxon, you may leave. I'd like to talk to Madame De Marnier and Mr. Robertson." Saxon hesitated for a moment, nodded and left.

"Mr. Robertson," Mycroft said, as he was writing something, "I believe that this might assist you. Give this to the Quartermaster tomorrow. I believe it will come in handy. You are dismissed," he said, handing a slip of paper to Malcolm. He took the paper from Mycroft's hand, looked at Joan, and left.

Joan sat and looked at Mycroft, who stared back. In frustration, Joan blurted out. "You knew it wouldn't go well, didn't you?"

"I rather suspected it," Mycroft said. "But it went better than I expected, so that is promising."

"Really?" Joan asked in astonishment. "I can hardly see how it could have gone any worse."

"The fact that Mr. Saxon was able to get you and Malcolm back on task was very encouraging. He seems to have a knack for knowing when to say the right thing. You should not be afraid to use his skills, especially when it comes to you and Malcolm. I might suggest that you may not be completely objective in regard to his performance."

Joan sighed. "Yes, sir. I suppose you are right. Is there any way you can see that this mission will be successful?"

"Absolutely," said Mycroft. "I trust your experience, Malcolm's ability to think on his feet, and Charles' ability to mediate between the two of you."

"Perhaps we should use other operatives," Joan said. "While Charles has caught on quickly, he has no field experience. And let's say that Malcolm is not my first choice for an operation that requires a great deal of subtlety. Surely, there are operatives better suited for this mission."

"There might be," Mycroft said, "but I doubt it. While we might have operatives that are experts in safe cracking, we have very few with security system experience, and even fewer who could make things up as they go. We do an excellent job of creating agents who can plan operations down to the second, but we tend to do a lousy job of preparing them for the cases where reality refuses to comply with their plan."

He paused for a moment. "Malcolm has all of the skills he needs to succeed in this mission. He really only lacks two things; belief in himself, and belief that you think he can do it."

"But, I'm not sure if he can," Joan said quietly.

"Why on earth not?" Mycroft asked.

"He bulls through things. There is a time and place for that, but not on this mission," she said.

"Are you sure? I would suggest that you find places where you can handle the subtlety, and then let Malcolm loose like a bull in the proverbial china shop."

"But I need to control the operation. I need to know that when I give orders, they will be fulfilled exactly as I say."

"Which is why you're such an excellent operative," Mycroft said. "However, there are many unknowns in this mission; we do not have nearly enough intelligence on the Imperial Vault, and all we're doing is guessing. It's vital that you enter and leave completely undetected. I'm counting on you, as there is no one better suited for it than perhaps me. But I feel that Malcolm is right for this task; it is not a small part in why I engineered his resignation."

"Are you kidding?" asked Joan incredulously.

"Madame De Marnier, have you ever known me to kid about an operation? Malcolm is smart, and has a keen tactical mind. He is also, surprisingly, an excellent judge of people, and uses that to manipulate them to react exactly how he wants. He shares that trait with you. True, he tends to do it by angering them, but anger makes people do stupid things, which he uses to his advantage. During the mission to Russia, he got Frye to react exactly the way he wanted. Because of his actions, we are here having this discussion. He also has an uncanny intuition, which he uses to take the few facts he has and deduce the truth. He is one of a handful of people who deduced my role on a mission. For those reasons, I felt he was the right person for this mission."

Joan was silent. She knew the truth of Mycroft's words, but she was still troubled. Malcolm was an unknown; sometimes that was good, sometimes it could be bad. When things went bad on a mission, people tended to die. And the thought that it might be Malcolm scared her.

"What do I do?" she asked.

"Give yourself time to come up with a new plan, playing to the strengths of the three of you. If you can, involve Malcolm and Saxon. I think that by merging your talents, you will undoubtedly be successful."

"How can you be so sure?" asked Joan.

"I'm not, but we honestly have few options. If what the Martian Crown Prince said is true, this unspeakable evil is going to rise from the ocean, and that will be the end of our world."

"I was looking for some words of comfort," Joan said.

"Madame De Marnier, I'm surprised at you. How long have we known one another? When have I ever thrown myself over to such sentimentality?"

"Never," she said, as a smile crossed her face. "Thank you, Mr. Holmes."

"You know what you need to do, now execute it perfectly," he said. "For all our sakes."

CHAPTER 22

*D*inner that evening was quiet. Malcolm hoped that Mycroft had not been too hard on Joan. He had made a bloody mess of the plan, and he didn't want to be the cause of its failure. As dinner finished, the three rose to return to their rooms when Malcolm said, "Madame De Marnier, may I have a word? Alone?"

Saxon raised his eyebrow inquisitively, and Joan said, "Yes, Malcolm." She looked at Saxon and nodded slightly. He took the hint, and quietly left the dining room. Malcolm watched Saxon leave. When he turned to look at Joan, her body was stiff, as if bracing for a blow.

"Joan, I'm sorry," Malcolm said softly. "I didn't mean to make a mess of things. I'm just not cut out for this kind of thing. I'll try harder. I've got a pile of vault construction blueprints in my room. I'll do my best to memorise them before tomorrow morning. I know this is important to you, and I don't want to let you down. The last thing I want is to have you see me as a disappointment."

Joan's body relaxed, and a small smile played across her lips. "Malcolm, you are many things, but you are most definitely not a disappointment."

Malcolm looked at her for several seconds before speaking. "Was Mycroft hard on you?"

"No," Joan said. "He actually thought it went better than he expected."

"Seriously?" he asked. Joan nodded. "That's surprising. I'm not sure how it could have gone any worse."

Joan gave a short laugh. "I said nearly the same thing."

Malcolm paused. "So what do we do now?"

"Well," she said, as she drew nearer to him, "you will go to your room and memorise blueprints. I will retire to my room to rework the plan, and we try again tomorrow." As she said this, she drew closer and closer to Malcolm until they were nearly touching. "If we do better tomorrow, I think I'll have to find a way to reward you for your hard work," she said, as she gently touched a finger to his lips.

Malcolm kissed it. "Is there any way I can get an advance on that reward?"

"No, mister, you must earn it," she said in a sultry whisper.

"Well, let me get to those blueprints," he said.

"Yes, you should," she said in a husky whisper.

Before either was aware, they fell into each other's arms and shared a fiery kiss. After several seconds, Malcolm tore himself away. "If I'm to earn the reward, I think I should leave now before I won't want to leave. I'll have those blueprints memorised." He paused. "Right after I take a cold shower." He took her hand, gently kissed it, and left the room.

The next morning was much more relaxed. Joan detailed the new plan she had worked on during the evening. Her plan left the stealth portions to her and Saxon; all Malcolm had to do was stay quiet until signalled to move. It also gave more time for Malcolm to deal with the vault. The trio seemed more upbeat as they went over the plan. They left to change and acquire any gear that they might need. Malcolm remembered the slip of paper that Mycroft had given him, and took it to the Quartermaster.

When Malcolm arrived at the Quartermaster's, he dutifully filled out the forms for the same equipment, and handed the Quartermaster the slip of paper. "Mr. Holmes told me to give this to you."

The Quartermaster read the slip and raised an eyebrow. He looked at Malcolm, and hurried off to retrieve something. He returned with what looked like a very small bottle, looking very much like a container for rubber glue. As he handed it to Malcolm, he said, "Be very careful with this Palmer Fluid. It is only to be used on inanimate objects, and sparingly at best. This is all we have."

"What is it?" Malcolm asked.

"You don't know?" the Quartermaster asked, and Malcolm shook his head. "Palmer Fluid has the capability to make anything transparent."

"You mean, it makes things invisible?" Malcolm asked.

"Yes, haven't you been listening?" the Quartermaster chided. "Whatever you do, don't ingest the stuff. Sure, it will make you invisible, but it will drive you insane."

"Alright, thank you for the warning," Malcolm said as carried the pot gingerly. He started out of the Quartermaster's office then stopped. He understood why Mycroft offered this; Malcolm could see the complete inner workings of the safe, and could open it without tripping any of the countermeasures, provided he could figure out how the safe worked.

The trio began the new mission plan. Joan and Saxon took care of the guards, allowing Malcolm to cross the mock courtyard easily. Malcolm realised that Mycroft had been true to his word; his oxfords had much more grip than the day before. They reached the vault easily.

Malcolm carefully removed the top from the Palmer fluid, which had a small brush attached to the top, and painted a small amount around the area of the tumbler. Within seconds, the metal of the vault door vanished, and Malcolm could see the inner workings of the locking mechanism. He analysed the locking mechanism, and realised that it was a combination of two different mechanisms that he had memorised the night before. He started to turn the tumbler, and watched as gears around the tumbler interacted. Within a minute, he had successfully opened the vault door. With a smile, he stood up and gestured to the open vault door. "After you," he said.

Joan smiled. "Don't get cocky; we've only just started." She and Saxon slipped through into the vault, and began cautiously moving into the room beyond; Malcolm trailing behind.

The rest of the simulation proved easy. As they entered each room, they searched for any sort of security device, and Malcolm would quickly disable it. They made their way to the Spear, retrieved it, and replaced it with the duplicate with relative ease. They slipped back through the rooms, and escaped within the allotted time for the exercise.

When they exited the simulation, Joan was beaming. "That went extraordinarily well! You were tremendous, Malcolm!" She gave him a quick peck on the cheek. "Do I get my reward tonight?" Malcolm whispered before she pulled away.

"We'll see," she smiled coyly.

"Alright, you two. I believe there is still some Secret Service regulation about fraternising on the job!" Saxon said. "Or if there isn't, there should be."

Lunch was a far different affair from the previous day, and the trio chatted enthusiastically about the session. Their spirits remained high as they began their debriefing session. They reviewed the reports from the observers. It turned out that they'd tripped a silent alarm in the room containing the fake Spear of Destiny. Malcolm had disarmed the audible alarm in the room, and was positive that he had been successful. They returned to the simulation area, and searched for something they had missed. Finally, they disassembled the bottom of the display case. Malcolm found a strip of metal running around the perimeter of the glass case. After some detailed analysis, Malcolm concluded that the strip was photovoltaic metal, that generated a small electrical current from the light of the display case. When they had removed the front glass panel, the light stopped hitting the photovoltaic metal, breaking the circuit, and triggering the alarm.

The discovery of the failure did not discourage them, and instead emboldened them to think of other ways that they might be detected.

The discussion went well into the evening, and they ate a very late dinner, which consisted of cold sandwiches and soup. When dinner was finished, Joan returned to Malcolm's room, and he was rewarded for his work.

The rest of the practices continued much the same for the rest of the week. With each run, the group overcame a series of increasingly harder obstacles, and eventually retrieved the Spear with no trace of their incursion. The last days were spent reviewing diplomatic protocol, and the roles that each would take during the negotiations. Joan and Saxon would be interpreters, given their fluency in both German and French, the language of diplomacy, while Malcolm would play the role of personal assistant to one of the diplomats. His job, as near has he could ascertain, was to be a valet to his diplomat; retrieve papers, hand them to his diplomat, pour his drinks, and wait on his every whim. "I'm not a bloody butler, I'm an engineer," he said.

"Since we have no need at the diplomatic table for an engineer, what job do we give you then?" Joan asked with a bemused tone. "Do you want to be an interpreter, secretary, or diplomat?"

"I can't do any of those jobs," he said softly.

"Which is why we selected this job which, while not particularly suited to your temperament, is within your capabilities."

"Fine," Malcolm said.

The sessions continued until Malcolm's head was spinning at the demands of diplomatic protocol. Seemingly trivial details from where everyone was seated, to the placement of water and other refreshments, to body language were crucial. Malcolm did find that his ability to stand at attention for long periods of time, built over years in the military, would be of use.

The night before they were to join the delegation headed to Austria, the trio left the Secret Service headquarters, and emerged from Charing Cross Station. It was the first time that Malcolm and Charles had been outside in months. He'd missed the acrid smell of the air in London, the glow of nightlights, and people. The Secret Service building was a hive of activity during the day, but was often quiet and eerie at night. He hadn't realised how much he missed being in the presence of people, if only as a passive observer. The night was clear, and Malcolm suggested that they walk to the Savoy instead of hiring a taxi. Saxon and Joan readily agreed, and the trio strolled along the Strand to the Savoy, taking in the scenery. Even at this time of the evening, the street was abuzz with steam-powered cars, and lorries making deliveries to the many shops. The sidewalk was filled with people partaking of the night life of London.

After several minutes, they arrived at the Savoy. As they entered the foyer from the Strand, Malcolm was taken aback by its grandness. Black and white marble tiles graced the floor, while dark wood wainscotting and trim were a contrast to the white plaster ornamented ceiling. A chandelier illuminated the area; making it feel both light and airy, as well as dignified and solemn. Before Malcolm could take it in, a black-coated butler approached. "Ah, Madame De Marnier, we are so glad that you have returned. I have taken the liberty of preparing your usual room. Will you be staying with us long?"

"Unfortunately not this time. I'm off again on business, Whitford. Are the rooms ready for my associates?"

"Yes, Madame. We have given them the adjoining rooms. Their luggage has already been brought up, and dinner clothes laid out."

"Thank you, Whitford," Joan said. "I don't know what I would do without you."

"This way," Whitford said, as he led them to a room through an open doorway. The room was small, but decorated in the same style as the lobby. It contained a small couch and two chairs. "Please," Whitford said, "sit down. In one moment, we will be on your floor." He pushed a brass button on the wall, and a door closed across. He then pushed another button and there was a momentary sense of movement, but it was as if nothing had happened. If Malcolm hadn't experienced this when entering the Secret Service headquarters, this would have excited him.

The ascending room came to smooth stop, and Whitford pushed another button and the door retracted. He led them down an ornate hallway and came to three rooms, Joan's room in the centre, while

Malcolm and Saxon had the rooms on either side. The three agreed to meet for a late dinner in the Grill.

Malcolm entered his room and was nearly overwhelmed by the elegance. His room contained a large bed, a writing desk and a rather comfortable armchair. Off the room was his own private bathroom with a shower. The room contained several electric lamps, and had a small electric light hanging from the ceiling. Malcolm found his tuxedo laid out on the bed for him, and his toiletries laid out in the bathroom.

Malcolm showered and changed into his tuxedo. Inspecting himself in the mirror, he almost didn't recognise himself. The time spent training had toned his body, and the little paunch he had developed was now gone. His beard and mustache, now fully grown, gave him an air of maturity that he certainly didn't feel. He looked the image of an Edwardian gentleman. *I might just be able to pass as a diplomat's assistant*, he thought to himself.

He left his room and knocked on Joan's door. She opened the door and Malcolm lost his breath for a moment. Joan wore a red dress patterned with faded star bursts, while black velvet circled her wrists and neckline. The dress drew tight around her waist, and again tight near her ankles. She wore a wide-brimmed hat filled with plumage, and a delicate black lace veil over her face. Joan looked at Malcolm appraisingly and said, "You clean up fairly well. If I didn't know better, I'd mistake you for a gentleman."

Malcolm took her hand and gently kissed it. "And you have never looked more breathtaking."

"Charmer," she said with a smile. "I bet you say that to all of the women you meet."

"No, only one," Malcolm said in all seriousness. Joan looked away from his gaze and said, "We should get Charles. It would be rude to not have our full party together." They knocked on Saxon's door. He too, looked dapper in his evening clothes. He had acquired a mustache in his time at the Secret Service, and it made him look suave and debonair. The three of them called the ascending room, and made their way to the Savoy Grill. Upon arriving, the maître d' had already reserved a table for Joan and her companions. As he led them to their table, Malcolm tried not to gawk at the other patrons. He was sure he saw no less than three princes, and many other royalty bedecked in their finery and medals. Malcolm suddenly felt very out of place and conspicuous.

After they were seated, their waiter promptly arrived, and asked Malcolm if they would care for wine. Malcolm felt a momentary sense of panic before replying, "We are entertaining Madame De Marnier tonight. I think she should pick the wine." Joan quickly assessed the wine list, and ordered a cabernet sauvignon. The waiter recited the menu, and left to get their wine. Malcolm's head was swimming with the choices. He whispered to Joan, "I have no idea what to order. Any suggestions?"

Joan thought for a moment and said, "I believe that you would like the Chateaubriand. It is one of their specialties."

"Very well," Malcolm said. "What is it?"

"It's steak with a sauce poured over it," she said, trying to keep it as simple as possible. "It's usually served with potatoes".

"That sounds like something I might enjoy," Malcolm said.

The waiter returned with the wine. Thankfully, the waiter asked Joan to taste the wine, sparing Malcolm the opportunity to look like a dolt. When Joan tasted and approved the wine, the waiter took their orders: Malcolm ordered a pork pie appetiser because it was the only familiar option, and the Chateaubriand; Joan ordered caviar and blinis as an appetiser and Beef Wellington; and Saxon ordered *foie gras* for his appetiser and *côte de bouef*.

When the waiter left with their order, Malcolm asked Saxon, "What exactly did you order?"

"Goose liver as an appetiser, and a rib of beef." Saxon said with a droll smile.

"Goose liver sounds disgusting," Malcolm said with a grimace.

"Says the man who eats haggis. It's a delicacy. It's been far too long since I've enjoyed it."

"To each his own," Malcolm said.

Malcolm looked down at the array of cutlery laid out on his plate.

Only a few years ago, Malcolm would have panicked at the sight of a formal dinner. With Joan's assistance, he'd learned the etiquette of fine dining, and now knew his water glass from his wine glass, and his fish fork from his dessert fork. Malcolm looked around the sumptuous dining room, and was in awe. He never imagined that he would be having dinner in one of the most exclusive dining areas in all of London.

The appetisers arrived. Malcolm took a bite of his pork pie, and it tasted like no pork pie he had ever had. It contained pickled vegetables, and spices that he would not associate with a normal pork pie. Malcolm looked at Joan's caviar, and did not have the courage to try it. He looked at Saxon's *foie gras* that he spread on a toasted piece of bread. It looked equally unappetising. Malcolm tasted his wine, and found it agreeable, but he'd never had an appreciation for wine.

When dinner arrived, Malcolm was pleased with his choice. It was the best beef he had ever tasted, and the sauce complemented the beef perfectly. He looked at both Joan's and Saxon's dishes, and realised that he would have enjoyed either dish. By the time he finished, Malcolm thought he couldn't eat another bite, until the waiter listed the desserts. Malcolm thought he'd try the Peach Melba, named for the famed Covent Garden opera singer, Joan had a dainty chocolate torte, while Saxon ended with a crepe stuffed with strawberry and ricotta. After finishing his dessert, Malcolm was full, but did not regret eating his dessert.

The trio retired for the evening. As they approached their rooms, Malcolm and Joan seemed to hesitate. Saxon took the hint and bid the two goodnight. Joan looked at Malcolm. "Do you want to come in for a nightcap?" she asked.

"Is that wise?" he asked.

"I don't know if it's wise, but I do know that it might be the last time that we can be together until after the mission is completed." She paused to gather her composure before she continued. "Despite our success in the simulations, there is an excellent chance that one or both of us will be captured or killed. This is life or death, Malcolm.

And if this is our last chance to spend time together, I don't want to miss it."

"Neither do I," Malcolm said. "Let's have that nightcap."

Joan took Malcolm's hand and led him into her room. A few moments later, a hand reached out and put a 'Do Not Disturb' sign on the doorknob.

CHAPTER 23

$\mathcal{E}$arly in the morning, Malcolm returned to his room to shower and dress for the trip. As he dressed, he looked at himself in the mirror and, for a second, thought he saw a banker or businessman from the City looking back. The charcoal grey suit, waistcoat, and a red and blue striped regimental tie completed the transformation. A bowler and umbrella sat on his bed, and when he added that to the outfit, he looked like he would fit in at any accountancy in the City. Malcolm joined Saxon and Joan in the Grill for breakfast. Saxon also sported a similar suit, that seemed to fit him much better than Malcolm's. Joan was dressed in a grey woollen jacket and long black skirt giving her a severe, matronly look.

After a full English breakfast, Malcolm, Joan, and Saxon, took a taxi to Hendon Aerodrome where they would join the entourage that would attend the diplomatic mission in Vienna. The trio talked little as their taxi drove through the city to the aerodrome. The work day had just begun, and Malcolm watched store owners opening their businesses, deliverymen unloading their steam-powered lorries, people filling the streets. It all looked like an anthill after it was kicked; a flurry of activity with no discernible purpose.

Malcolm watched as they passed the British Museum and Regent's

Park, before passing into the districts outside of the City proper: Hampstead, Brent Cross, and Colindale, before reaching the Aerodrome. The Aerodrome was a lush green field in the middle of rows of flat houses. Around the edge of the Aerodrome, Malcolm saw the tall smoke stacks of factories, and rows of large warehouses scattered around the periphery. As they entered the gates from the southeast, they approached the hub of the Aerodrome, the station from which they would embark. Several airships were already tethered around the aerodrome, and Malcolm could see more that were waiting to leave the protective cover of their hangers. As they approached the station, Malcolm looked for their transport and started. He nudged Saxon and pointed, and he too started. It seemed that the airship that would take them on their trip would be none other than the *HMA Daedalus.*

Malcolm and Saxon looked at each other and shook their heads. Joan asked, "What's the matter?" She looked up and simply said *"Merde."*

"You do realise that this will make it nearly impossible to keep a low profile?" Malcolm asked.

"Yes, I realise that this is going to be difficult," Joan hissed. "When we get to the station, I'll see what I can do." When the taxi came to a halt, and before the driver could open the door for her, Joan jumped out of the taxi and bustled into the station. As Malcolm and Saxon took possession of their trunks, Malcolm could see Joan in a very passionate discussion. Malcolm watched as she hung up the phone, slumping in defeat for a moment before taking a deep breath, straightening her spine, and returning to Malcolm and Saxon.

"It appears that the Foreign Service insisted on arriving in the flagship of the Air Service. Mycroft tried to arrange a different ship, but the Foreign Service would not settle for anything less. God help us, the two of you must keep a low profile. Perhaps, you should both wear your hats to help hide your faces. And whatever you do, and I mean you, Malcolm, do not say a single word more than is necessary." Malcolm saw the look on Joan's face, and decided to follow her orders.

The trio kept a low profile as the rest of the Foreign Service entourage arrived. Joan pointed out to Malcolm the gentlemen who would serve as their superiors. Malcolm's superior, Sir W. Chauncy Cartwright, Chief Clerk, was a slight man with thick black-rimmed spectacles, and a pencil-thin moustache. He was very softly spoken and when Malcolm was first introduced, he found it very difficult to hear the man in the noisy station. Soon, Malcolm was separated from Joan and Charles, as he joined the other members of Sir Cartwright's staff. Many looked at Malcolm dismissively; Malcolm deciding that these were the career personnel looking for promotion. Malcolm, despite his age, contented himself to work with the young clerks fresh out of university.

For the next few hours, the arrival of diplomats and cargo kept the station in a whirlwind of activity, and Malcolm succeeded in keeping attention focused away from him. When it was time to board and present his papers, Malcolm started to panic. He followed the rest of the party up the gangplank, and waited to be let aboard. He tried to identify the officer taking names, and he was grateful that it was someone he did not know. Looking at the officer's uniform, he noted his rank as Commander. Malcolm kept his head down as he approached the officer.

"Name," the officer said, barely looking up from his paper.

"Howardson, Magnus Howardson," Malcolm said. Malcolm had not been keen on the name, but it was similar to his own, so it was easy to react to it.

"Yes, you've been assigned to Cabin 1F-23. Airman Curtis will escort you to your quarters."

"That won't be necessary," Malcolm said, before he realised what he was saying. There was no way a low-level diplomat would know how to find his cabin. "It's not that big," Malcolm said disdainfully. "It can't be that hard."

Malcolm could tell he had irritated the officer, which was his hope. If Malcolm appeared like one of those arrogant diplomats, the officer wouldn't think twice of Malcolm's earlier remark.

"I insist that you follow Airman Curtis. He will take you directly to your cabin. Much of the ship is off limits to *non-military* personnel."

"Thank you, Commander…," Malcolm trailed off.

"Davies. Commander Reginald Davies," the officer replied. Malcolm looked him over. He was slightly older than Malcolm. His high forehead promised a quickly receding hairline. His wispy blond hair was parted conventionally, and shaved short on the sides in traditional military style. Davies had a long face with a long skinny nose that came to a point. His dull grey eyes didn't acknowledge Malcolm.

"Thank you, Commander Davies. I believe I'm supposed to ask 'Permission to come aboard?'"

Davies sighed heavily, "Permission granted. Now, go on and get going. Some of us have real work to do."

"As you wish, Commander," Malcolm said. He looked up to see Joan staring daggers at him from across the cargo bay. He shrugged and followed Airman Curtis to his room.

Malcolm did remember Airman Curtis, who was a capable, amiable man. As he escorted Malcolm to his cabin, Curtis pointed out some of the interesting and important places in the *Daedalus*. Malcolm had to stop from laughing, as it was the very same presentation he had given time and again, as the *Daedalus* hosted dignitaries. To minimise the chance that Curtis might remember him, Malcolm kept his responses to non-verbal grunts.

Curtis pulled up sharply. "Here's your room, sir. It's not much, but you'll only be staying with us for a short time. Let me take your trunk, sir." The airman reached down and picked up the trunk to carry it into the room. He stopped and looked quizzically at Malcolm. "Pardon me, sir, but have we met before? Have you ever been aboard the *Daedalus* before?"

"No," Malcolm replied in as low a voice as possible. "I've never been on an airship before."

"Really?" the airman asked. "I have this strange feeling that I know you." He looked at Malcolm for a few more seconds, and shook his head. "I'll remember where I've seen you before." He brought the trunk in the room. "It's not much, but the best we could do under the circumstances. The head, I mean the WC, is three doors down on the left. I'm afraid that it's a communal wash room. You're probably not used to that, I imagine."

"You'd be surprised," Malcolm said.

"Please stay in your quarters until after we lift off. The Captain is holding a formal dinner for all our guests. I'll come back at six bells, I mean 7:00 PM, to escort you to the Officer's Mess. I believe the dress is formal."

"Thank you, Mr. Curtis," Malcolm said.

"You don't have to call me mister, sir, I'm just an enlisted man. The officers are misters."

"More's the pity, you've been very helpful, Airman Curtis."

"Thank you, Mr...."

"Howardson, Magnus Howardson," Malcolm said, offering his hand. The airman hesitated and shook Malcolm's hand. "Please call me Magnus."

"Very well, Mr., I mean Magnus. I'll come and get you just before six bells. Captain Bromley is very prompt."

"Bromley?" Malcolm asked.

"Yes, Captain Charles Bromley. He became Captain a month ago. His brother Arthur served on this very ship. Until he was killed, that is."

"Killed?" Malcolm said, feigning interest. Malcolm was all too familiar with the events that led to Commander Arthur Bromley's death.

"An explosion on the bridge set off by a German spy who was disguised as an engineer. Killed the whole bridge crew. If it weren't for Captain Malcolm..." The airman trailed off. He looked again at Malcolm. "Are you sure we haven't met?"

"Positive," Malcolm said. "I shouldn't keep you from your duties. Thank you for showing me to my cabin."

"Right," Curtis said, still eyeing Malcolm. "I'll be back at six bells." The airman turned and left down the hall, but not without stopping a few times to turn around and look at Malcolm.

Malcolm shut the door, sat on the bed, and buried his face in his hands. He had barely avoided being discovered by a crewman he didn't see often; what would he do when confronted by any of his officers? Malcolm sat in thought when he heard a knock on the door. Cautiously, Malcolm made his way to the door. "Yes?" he asked before opening the door.

"It's Charles," the voice said. Malcolm opened the door, and Saxon slid into the room quickly. "What are we going to do? I swear that Lieutenant Brown recognised me as I was escorted to my cabin."

"I don't know," Malcolm said. "Airman Curtis, who escorted me, nearly recognised me. I was able to miss the officers, but I daresay that we can't give them the slip for three days, especially at the formal dinner tonight."

"Well, you have been complaining about not being on the *Daedalus*," Charles chided.

"Very funny. Do you have any useful ideas about what we can do?"

"No," answered Charles glumly.

"Do you know where Joan is staying?"

"I believe she's staying in Cabin 1A-23. I believe it's the same cabin she used the last time she was here."

Malcolm had an idea. "Excellent. Can you give me a boost?"

"I beg your pardon?" Charles asked.

"The air vents. If you can hold me there, I can unscrew the cover, and manoeuvre my way to her cabin. I can talk with her without anyone seeing me. She must have some ideas of what we can do."

"Fine. But it's a good thing that you worked off some of that paunch if I'm going to lift you up," Saxon said, as he walked over to the vent.

Malcolm grabbed a couple of screwdrivers from the tools hidden in his trunk. Saxon cupped his hands and bent over to give him a boost. Malcolm stepped up and Saxon grunted, as he found the screws to the cover. Malcolm quickly had all four screws off, and was in the ventilation system before Saxon had a reason to further complain.

Malcolm scooted down the shaft until he came to the junction. He pictured the blueprints in his head; blueprints memorised what seemed like a lifetime ago, but never forgotten. He continued past the junction, took a left at the next junction, followed by a right. He continued until he thought he was in the right area and followed the vent to the cover. He looked through the slits in the cover, and thought he had the right room. He thought he could make out Joan's trunk, but it was difficult to tell from this angle. The room seemed empty, the only light coming from the porthole window. Malcolm waited and a few minutes later, Joan entered the room, looking very distraught.

"Joan," Malcolm hissed. He always tried to refer to her as Madame De Marnier, but this situation reminded him of when the two of them hid aboard the *Daedalus* while the crew thought them both dead. "Joan! Here in the vent!"

"Malcolm?" Joan asked as she looked around the room, before seeing the vent next to the ceiling. "What are you doing here?"

"I'm trying to figure out how Saxon and I are going to go three days among our former crew, without being recognised."

"I was trying to figure that out myself. I think I have an idea, although I don't think you will like it."

"Let's hear it. I'm flat out of ideas," Malcolm said.

Joan went to her trunk and rummaged around for a few moments before producing two small vials of a thick brown liquid. "Here's the way to keep you from the crew."

"What is it?" Malcolm asked with great trepidation.

"Syrup of ipecac. It induces vomiting within minutes of ingestion."

"That's your plan? To make us vomit? How long does it last?"

"The vomiting? I believe it lasts for several hours, and then you just feel awful for another twenty-four hours afterwards."

"Lovely," said Malcolm. "So what is your plan?"

"You and Charles will make an appearance at the Captain's dinner. I would suggest slipping the ipecac into your cocktail at slightly different times. I think perhaps Charles should go first, because he's slightly more recognisable than you; that beard hides so much of your face."

"At which point, shortly thereafter, we will vomit all over the buffet and be escorted back to our rooms, where the good doctor will think we are airsick," Malcolm finished.

Joan smiled. "And there we are. Anyone who knew you would know that you are not prone to airsickness, and the ipecac will make you look the worse for wear."

"Excellent, I can't wait to share the news of this plan with Saxon; I'm sure he'll be so excited," Malcolm said sarcastically.

CHAPTER 24

$\mathcal{M}$alcolm slithered his way back through the ventilation shaft to his cabin. As the room came into view, Malcolm saw Saxon pacing. When Malcolm got within earshot, he said. "Charles, you're going to wear out the carpet. Give me a hand down from here."

Saxon moved to the vent, and caught Malcolm as he tumbled out into the room.

"Did Joan come up with anything?" Saxon asked earnestly. Malcolm could see the nervous perspiration on Saxon's forehead.

"Yes, but I'm afraid you aren't going to like it very much," Malcolm deadpanned. Malcolm explained that the use of the ipecac would induce vomiting, and provide a reasonable cover of airsickness.

Saxon took his vial from Malcolm and looked at it. "There truly isn't another way?"

"Not that I know of," Malcolm said.

"Very well," Saxon said. "I'll take mine just before I'm escorted to the Captain's dinner." Saxon took his leave and Malcolm was alone. He lay on the bed. *Here I am, back on the Daedalus,* Malcolm thought, *and I'm a stranger.* It was inevitable that he would have had to give up his command someday, either through promotion or retirement. He just never thought it would be this quickly. He looked out the port-hole window and could only see water; they must be somewhere over the Channel. *God, do I miss this*, he thought. He felt like he had been trapped in the bowels of the Secret Service. He hadn't seen the sun in weeks, or was it months? He had long ago lost count. He stared out the window wistfully, mourning his former life, then he shook his head and closed the cover over the porthole. He had a job to do, and although he hated what he was doing, he would still perform to the best of his ability. Because that is what an airman does.

Malcolm sat at the pull-down desk and reviewed the myriad of papers that he had to study. Diplomatic terms in French, proposals in German, correspondence in all three languages. Malcolm was expected to keep track of all the correspondence, reports, and propos-als, and produce them at a moment's notice. Although Joan had spent some time with Malcolm and Saxon, explaining and preparing them for their assignments, Malcolm felt like a fish out of water. He hadn't felt this way since he had been thrust into command, and he didn't relish the return of that feeling.

Malcolm closed his eyes and took a deep breath. It didn't help; he would take that up again with Joan when given the chance. He looked at the pile of papers. *What is the problem I'm trying to solve?* Malcolm thought. *To give Mr. Cartwright the information he needs. The only way I can do that is to categorise it*, he thought.

For the next two hours, Malcolm went through each of the docu-ments and categorised them: background information, proposals, counter proposals, etc. Once Malcolm had classified the information, he kept them in their own binder, in which he assembled a 'Table of Contents' to organise the information within each binder. By the time he had to get ready for the formal dinner, he had categorised much of the paperwork, and felt more prepared to fulfill his role.

Malcolm dressed in the tuxedo furnished by the Secret Service. He picked up the vial, held it to the light, and watched as the thick brown liquid slowly oozed down the vial. *The things I do for my country*, he thought. He finished dressing and with just a few minutes to spare,

Malcolm answered the knock on his door, and followed Airman Curtis to the Officer's Mess.

Airman Curtis was outfitted in dress uniform, and Malcolm caught himself wishing he too, were in his dress uniform. Malcolm brushed away the thought and concentrated on his role as a taciturn junior diplomat. Airman Curtis, brought him to the door, guarded by two airmen in full dress. Malcolm took a deep breath, opened to door and entered the Officer's Mess.

It seemed exactly how he'd left it, but something was different. Malcolm recognised many of his former officers, but there were also a few new faces. As he surveyed the room, he saw Captain Bromley holding court with the senior diplomats. Commander Davies, who must be the second in command, followed the conversation like a terrier waiting for a scrap to fall from the dinner table.

And then Malcolm realised what was different. It was the tone of the room. The diplomats were not at ease around the military, and the military didn't quite know how to handle the civilians. But there was more to it than that. Malcolm looked at his former officers and realised that there was a certain amount of strain in their smiles and responses. Several times, Malcolm caught his men stealing furtive glances at their captain, trying to gauge the level of approval or disapproval. And it hit Malcolm; what he felt when coming into the room was the dread of spending an evening in the company of the captain. This was not the usual dread of dressing up and employing manners; this was palpable dread of spending any time with the captain.

Malcolm procured a Manhattan; he hated the thought of ruining perfectly good whisky with vermouth, bitters, and that ghastly cherry. But he needed something brown to hide the ipecac that he slipped into his drink. *Besides,* he thought, *this appalling affront to whisky would likely speed the effects of the syrup.* And he wasn't surprised that when he took the first swallow of the vile concoction, he almost gagged.

Malcolm continued to observe from the fringes, occasionally making small talk, but careful to avoid anyone who knew him. He spotted Saxon, who seemed paler, and had developed a sheen of perspiration on his forehead. It was not long before Saxon raced from the room, his hand over his mouth. Malcolm could already feel his stomach starting to roil from the combination of the alcohol and the drug.

As the roiling continued, Malcolm circled the party. The new ship's doctor returned to inform everyone that Saxon had become taken with a severe case of air sickness, and would be confined to his quarters for the duration of the trip. Malcolm burped quietly, feeling an acidic aftertaste. He knew his time was coming, and he too would have to run from the room. Or would he?

Malcolm gradually made his way to the circle gathered around the captain. His stomach lurched within him, and he felt the need to burp more frequently. He felt his head become sweaty. He managed to work his way into the knot of ambassadors circled around Captain Bromley. He managed to get close to Bromley, doing his utmost to keep swallowing down the feeling in his stomach.

Bromley finished the story about how he had taken command of the *Daedalus* and made it run as the flagship of the Empire should run, when he noticed Malcolm. "I daresay, sir, you don't look very well," Bromley said.

"I don't feel very well," Malcolm said. "I find this floating very disconcerting and…"

Malcolm vomited over Captain Bromley's dress uniform. There was a cry of alarm, as wave after wave of nausea came over Malcolm. He eventually fell to his knees. When there was nothing left, he offered a very weak, "I'm terribly sorry, Captain, I don't think air travel suits me."

"Here, let me take you to your cabin and examine you," Doctor Farmer said, lifting Malcolm by the elbow and guiding him out of the room. Although Malcolm felt awful, a part of him gladdened. As Bromley sputtered, trying to seem above it all, the officers all covered their mouths trying to stifle a laugh.

Malcolm stopped once on the way to his room, and vomited again. He didn't know that he had anything left in his stomach. He again felt bad that some poor airman would be forced to clean up the mess, but he began not to care. The doctor led Malcolm back to his room and set him in his chair. An airman brought a basin and sat it in Malcolm's lap.

"You must not, under any circumstances, lie down. Until the vomiting stops, you must remain seated. I don't want you asphyxiating on your own vomit. I say, I don't think I've heard of two such violent cases of air sickness."

"Lucky, I guess," Malcolm murmured, before vomiting again.

"I'll check on you during the night. Try to drink some water; it's important that you don't dehydrate yourself."

The doctor left, and Malcolm tried to drink a glass of water. No sooner did the water hit his stomach than it was back up. He repeated this cycle for nearly two hours, until the muscles in his stomach were cramped. When he could keep a glass of water down for first fifteen minutes, and then a half hour, he crawled on the bed and collapsed.

His head throbbed, his stomach ached, and he felt like he had been drugged. Eventually, he drifted off into a restless sleep.

CHAPTER 25

*J*oan's plan worked to perfection; both Charles and Malcolm were confined to their cabins for the duration of the flight. That suited Malcolm, as it seemed to take a whole day for the ipecac to work its way out of his system. It was like he was hungover, without the pleasant effects of drinking. He spent most of the day in bed enjoying the dark; the few times it was punctuated with light, when the doctor came to visit, or an airman brought some broth, it was too much to stand.

By evening, Malcolm began to feel more human, and roused himself to dress in a suit. He eventually resumed the classification and cataloguing of all the information for the upcoming talks. He stopped for a moment as he felt the difference in the engine, and he realised that they were slowing, and likely dropping in altitude. They would likely land in Austria in tomorrow.

Malcolm's thoughts were interrupted by a knock on the door. Cautiously, Malcolm went to the door and called out, "Who is it?"

"It's Madame De Marnier. Sir Cartwright asked if I would enquire about your health," Joan said very formally.

Malcolm opened the door and Joan darted inside quickly, after being assured one was watching. Once inside, she swatted him on the arm with her fan. "Why did you have to vomit all over the captain of all people? He was apoplectic when you left; he threatened to leave you in Paris. You could have blown your cover. What were you thinking?"

"First, I was thinking that if everyone knew how I couldn't keep my stomach in the air, no one would ever believe that I was Malcolm Robertson. Second, I did it for the men. You must have noticed the dread that hung in the room from the officers. They couldn't stand to be in his presence one more minute than necessary."

Joan sighed. "Very well, I suppose what you say is true. And don't get a big head thinking that your former officers find Magnus Howardson a bit of a hero for vomiting all over Bromley."

"I wish I could say that I enjoyed it more, but that truly wasn't the case," Malcolm said.

"How are you feeling?" Joan asked.

"Better. My body feels like I was run over by a train. But, I've kept some broth down, so all in all, I believe I'm on the mend."

"Good, I talked to Charles and he said he was feeling better," Joan said.

"What's our plan?" Malcolm asked.

"We arrive in Vienna in the late afternoon. We'll be whisked away to our hotel, and we will work over dinner to prepare for the talks. The talks are scheduled to last up to one week. One week from tomorrow, we will be scheduled to attend the formal dinner to recognise the work. That's when we will take our opportunity to grab the Spear."

"Do you think we will have an opportunity to see the vault before we try to break into it?" Malcolm asked.

"I think it's likely," Joan said. "I'm sure that the Austrians will wish to show off the Imperial Treasury. I'll do my best to make sure that at least one of us goes if the opportunity arises." She paused for a moment, and circled the room. "What are you doing here?" she said, indicating the desk.

"Just organising the information for Sir Cartwright," Malcolm said.

Joan picked up the binder. "A Table of Contents and tabs for all of the documents. I daresay, Malcolm, you would have made a fine bureaucrat in the Foreign Service. Is there anything you can't do?"

"Apparently, be a captain of my airship," he said bitterly.

Joan put down the binder and moved to Malcolm. "I'm sorry," she said, with real concern in her voice. "This must be desperately hard on you. Not just losing your command, but being replaced by that blowhard." Malcolm looked at her quizzically. "Fine," she said with a huff. "What you did to Captain Bromley was the right thing to do, and accomplished several things at once. But you know how upset I get when you deviate from the plan!" she said.

Malcolm stepped towards her and wrapped his arms around her. "Perhaps we should do something to loosen you up?" he said in a husky whisper.

Joan pushed against his cheek, and freed herself from Malcolm's embrace. "I can tell you're feeling better," she said. "Unfortunately, now is not the time or place. In fact, I'd best be leaving." She turned and started to open the door, then stopped and turned to Malcolm. "I'm very proud of you. I know this has been difficult, and being back aboard the *Daedalus* has made it even worse. But even though you hate it, you still give it your all, and produce better results than people who spend their career doing it. Why?"

"I want my ship back, and the only way that will happen is by finishing this mission. When I want something, I don't give up until I get what I want," Malcolm said softly.

The two stared into each other's eyes for several seconds, before Joan looked away. "I should leave," she said softly, as she opened the door and left the room.

Malcolm went to the door and peered out to watch Joan as she bustled down the corridor. Malcolm thought that he saw Joan take out a handkerchief and dab at her face, and he sighed, closing the door. He turned and looked at the desk, and sighed again at the work still awaiting him.

Malcolm worked well into the early evening. He had the massive amount of information organised, so that he could produce any document quickly. An airman brought him a very simple meal consisting of broth and ship biscuits. The dry, salty biscuits were flavourless, but they were filling, and didn't seem to react with Malcolm's stomach.

When Malcolm awoke the next morning, he could tell that the *Daedalus* had begun its final descent to Vienna. He went to the porthole window and his suspicions were confirmed. The *Daedalus* soared over the hills and mountains on its approach to Vienna, which Malcolm could just make out in the distance. As the hills flattened, Vienna seemed to spread in every direction from either side of the River Danube. At this distance, it was impossible to pick out individual buildings, but Malcolm had a sense of the location of the Imperial Palace, as he had studied the maps of Austria and Vienna specifically. Although not a great navigator, Malcolm could find his way by map through the spotting of landmarks. In Malcolm's case, it was a learned skill, as the landmarks on the map often looked different when viewed from the sky.

He wished that he were on the bridge where the view was magnificent; the wide windows providing a one-hundred-and-eighty-degree panoramic view. He sighed and stepped away from the porthole, and prepared to depart. Within a few hours, an airman came to collect his trunk, and Malcolm followed the airman, carrying a small black briefcase that held the carefully sorted documents. As he left, Malcolm checked in his mirror to see that everything was in order. His charcoal grey suit, complete with vest and the bowler hat he wore to hide his face, made Malcolm think he was looking at the reflection of a banker in the City, and not a former airship captain. Malcolm smiled wistfully; happy that he looked the part, but he missed the airship captain that used to look back at him. With a final sigh, Malcolm turned and followed the airman out of the room.

The airman escorted Malcolm through the corridors of the *Daedalus*, and while Malcolm tried to keep his face the picture of neutrality, he couldn't help but want to smile as he passed the spot where he had rebuilt the navigation controls. He saw the corridor branch off to the Engineering section, and he wanted nothing more than to return to the comfort of the Engine Room, and get his hands dirty again. With a heavy heart, and great effort, he assumed an attitude of disdain and followed the airman mutely.

They reached the cargo bay, and the main gangway off the *Daedalus*. Malcolm longed to turn around, to drink in the sight of the *Daedalus* one more time, but resolutely focused on the duty at hand. A line of officers waited to wish farewell to their guests. As Malcolm worked his way down the line, he shook each hand and mumbled a 'Thank you' and tried to not make eye contact with any of them. When he shook hands with Gunnery Officer Brown, the officer whispered, "No, thank *you*," when Malcolm offered his thanks. Malcolm looked up and saw the officer give him a quick wink. As Malcolm made his way down the line, he decided it would be best to avoid the captain and his first officer, so he melted into the crowd ebbing and flowing out of the airship.

He joined the diplomatic party, and many enquired after his health. After reassuring them that he was fine now that he was on the ground, they began to gather into groups for transport into Vienna. At best, Malcolm presumed that they were at an aerodrome some distance from the city. As the personal assistant to Sir W. Chauncy Cartwright, Malcolm was assigned to ride with Sir Cartwright in a sleek Horch Phaeton. The car was silver, with a long boxy bonnet that held the engine, wood-spoked tires, two large headlights in the front that gave Malcolm the impression of fish eyes, and a canopy that swooped over the top of the car and connected to the windscreen. Malcolm held the door for Sir Cartwright and closed it behind him, circling around the car to his side.

"Thank you, son," Sir Cartwright said. "You come very highly recommended from Mycroft," he said with a wink.

"Thank you, sir," Malcolm said. "I have taken the liberty of organising your papers."

Sir Cartwright glanced at Malcolm's work. "I'm sure it's satisfactory," he said. "Since you are filling in as my assistant, I am counting on you to perform your duties to my satisfaction."

"Yes, sir," Malcolm said quietly. He hadn't counted on being an integral piece of the actual diplomatic mission.

Sir Cartwright smiled. "I'm sure you'll do your best. Are you ready for your first…" he paused before continuing, "diplomatic adventure?"

Malcolm was sure that the diplomat was talking about Malcolm's real mission. "Yes, I do believe I am."

"Very good," Sir Cartwright said. "I do hope this thing moves soon, so that we get this mission underway."

Silence fell over the two men as they waited for the convoy to assemble and drive into Vienna. Twenty minutes later, the convoy made its way out of the aerodrome and headed east towards Vienna. As he had seen from his vantage point in the sky, Malcolm guessed they were still some distance from Vienna. Malcolm watched in silence as they passed the fields and small villages. The distance between the villages grew shorter, until there was no way to tell where one village started and the next ended. The chalets and cottages started to give way to multi-story stone buildings with terraces, balconies, and verdigris mansard roofs, whose graceful curves contained attic windows and apartments. Malcolm soon lost his sense of direction as the car navigated through the narrow streets.

As they reached the city proper, Sir Cartwright pointed out many historic sites.

"You seem to know much about Vienna. I assume you have been here many times?" Malcolm asked.

"More times than I care to admit," Sir Cartwright said. "The Hapsburgs do much to keep us on our toes." Sir Cartwright soon launched into a story about negotiating a resolution when the Austrians annexed Bosnia and Herzegovina, much to the consternation of Serbia, Montenegro, and Great Britain. "There is no love lost between the Serbs and Austrians over that, I'm afraid. The day will come when Serbia and Austria will come to blows." Cartwright sighed and slumped in his seat. "Ah, here we are at our home away from home; the Pension Neuer Markt; the best pension in all of Vienna. Largely because it is close to the palace."

Malcolm looked at Cartwright quizzically. "Pension?"

Cartwright smiled. "A pension is a boarding house or inn. You have never stayed in one on your travels?"

"No, I'm afraid I haven't," Malcolm said. "I tended to stay near the ship when we landed. And honestly, I've never been afforded the opportunity to visit Vienna. We tend to avoid flying over Austria, Hungary, and Germany, as the skies can be..." He paused before continuing, "a tad unfriendly."

"Yes, as I might imagine," Cartwright said. "For my money, this is the best pension in Vienna. Besides its proximity to the Palace, my favourite restaurant is just down the street, as well as an excellent coffee house. Do you drink coffee?"

"No, I don't care for it much. I'd much rather stick with tea," Malcolm said.

"More's the pity," Cartwright said. "You won't find a decent cup of tea in this whole city."

When the car came to a stop, Malcolm jumped out and ran around the back of the car to open the door for Sir Cartwright. The protocol came second nature to Malcolm as at the start of his career, he'd often attended to ranking officers. Once Sir Cartwright exited the car, Malcolm collected their luggage and engaged a porter to help him bring the bags and trunks inside. As Malcolm started inside, he noticed that the sunshine they had enjoyed on the drive into the city had given way to grey clouds, and a cool wind began to blow.

The reception area was brightly lit with electric lights that added to the glow of the yellow walls. The cherry parquet front desk seemed to give extra warmth to the room. Upon seeing Cartwright, the concierge moved quickly from behind the desk. "Ambassador Cartwright, it is so good to have you join us again! Everything is ready as you requested. I have taken the liberty of reserving your usual room."

"Thank you, Josef," Cartwright said. "Please work out the details with my assistant, Mr. Howardson. The others will arrive shortly. Magnus, I am retiring to my room. Please call for me at 4:00 this afternoon when we will meet to discuss the agenda for the next week."

"Very good, sir," Josef said. He turned to Malcolm. "Mr. Howardson, I am Josef, the concierge for the Pension Neuer Markt. I am at your service," the man said, extending his hand.

Malcolm shook his hand. Josef looked to be in his twenties. His coal-black, slicked-back hair, dark eyes, and thin mustache gave him a cosmopolitan air. Malcolm felt his stomach turn, as this man would quickly realise that Malcolm was not a diplomat's assistant. "I'm Magnus Howardson. Pleased to meet you, Josef. Let's go over the arrangements."

"Very good, sir," Josef said. "Come this way," he said, indicating the reception desk. Much to Malcolm's relief, he soon realised that all he had to do was solve a logistical puzzle, something his experience as Captain made much easier. As he reviewed the layout of the pension with Josef, he managed to have Joan and Saxon assigned rooms close to his own. Josef called the assembled staff of porters for Malcolm's review. Malcolm couldn't help but smile; he felt like a visiting officer inspecting the troops. And quickly, the smile dissolved from his face at the realisation that he wasn't an officer. He feigned a smile as he turned to Josef and said, "Excellent. Now let's assign these fine gentlemen to each of the entourage." As they agreed which porter would attend to which person, Josef barked orders to each porter. Thanks to Joan, Malcolm had a list of the members of the party, and could estimate the order in which the vehicles would arrive, so that the porters could be ready for each vehicle.

As Malcolm and Josef finished, the vehicles started to arrive. As Malcolm surmised, the Foreign Service had a pecking order not so different from the Air Service. The higher-ranked diplomats would arrive first, and receive the choicest rooms. Malcolm and Josef managed the chaos of the mass arrivals, and got everyone to the correct rooms quickly and efficiently. He caught a quick glimpse of Joan, looking just as ravishing as she had when he last saw her. For a second they locked eyes, before Joan was pulled away by another conversation. Malcolm watched as one of the young clerks seemed to be falling over himself to do anything for Joan. He started to feel hot jealously burning in his stomach, which dissolved into laughter, as he watched the clerk try to pull Joan's steamer trunk from the car. Malcolm remembered nearly throwing his back out trying to do the very same thing on one of their stolen weekends. After letting the young diplomat suffer for a few moments, Malcolm directed one of the porters to take over.

As quickly as the diplomats arrived, they disappeared to their rooms. Once Malcolm was satisfied that everything was in order, he entered the pension and started for his own room. He started to pass Joan's room and stopped. After knocking, he heard a clearly perturbed Joan answer. "Yes? Who is it?"

"Madame De Marnier, it's Magnus Howardson, I just wanted to check that your accommodations are in order."

Malcolm heard Joan scamper across the room and open the door. Before he could say a word, she grabbed him by the tie, pulled him into the room, shut the door, and covered his mouth with a kiss. Malcolm returned her kiss with equal passion, and after several, long moments, they parted to catch their breath.

"To what do I owe this pleasure?" Malcolm asked.

"I've been trapped with that sappy young diplomat Eggerton for the whole car ride here. There is nothing more annoying than a young man who thinks he's smitten."

"Except an older man who's smitten?" Malcolm asked, as he raised one eyebrow.

"Stop it," Joan laughed, as she playfully smacked his chest. "We have a few hours before we have to be anywhere," she said huskily, as she put her arms around him and pulled him closer.

"That we do," Malcolm said.

CHAPTER 26

alcolm found himself unprepared for the unexpected rigours of a diplomatic mission. At 4:00 PM, exactly, Sir Cartwright assembled the delegation and worked well into the night, establishing positions and conditions for the talks. The diplomats hardly stopped to eat the buffet brought by the staff. Malcolm was surprised that most of the dishes seemed to be based on beef or veal. He had heard of *wiener schnitzel* and recognised it immediately. He did not recognise many of the other dishes, but gamely tried them. He ate the *wiener schnitzel* as well as *tafelspitz* which was boiled beef; *selchfleisch*, smoked pork, served with *sauerkraut* and dumplings; and *beuschel*, a stew made from veal lungs and heart. The *beuschel* appeared to turn off many members of the diplomatic corps, but Malcolm enjoyed it immensely. Although different, it reminded him of haggis.

As they worked into the evening, Malcolm found it difficult to keep his attention on the work. The heavy meal had made him drowsy, and he was having trouble concentrating. Much to his consternation, tea was not served after dinner, however large pots of coffee had been brought into the room. Desperate to stay awake, Malcolm poured himself a cup of the dark, bitter beverage. He sipped carefully and wanted to spit it out almost immediately. He found a small pitcher containing cream, and a bowl of demerara sugar. He poured the cream into the cup until the coffee turned a light tan colour, then added several spoonfuls of the brown sugar crystals, until the coffee was as sweet as candy. Finally, Malcolm found this acceptable, and could drink the coffee.

With his concentration restored, Malcolm worked to keep up with the work of the evening. When Sir Cartwright needed information, Malcolm consulted the overall index of documents that he had created, and quickly produced the desired document. Malcolm saw more than one look of envy and hatred from some of the clerks. He was surprised that the clerks spent more time kowtowing to their superiors, than they did doing what their superiors wanted. The group broke up late that night. Sir Cartwright announced that they would return for an early morning breakfast meeting to complete their work before leaving for Hofburg Palace.

The next morning, the delegation was again hard at work over a traditional Austrian breakfast of a roll called *semmel*; a cereal of rolled oats and dried fruits called *muesli*; a selection of cold meats such as ham, cut sausages, and something resembling bacon; and boiled eggs. Once again, the only thing to wash it down with was coffee. Malcolm once again diluted the coffee with copious amounts of cream and sugar, so that he could stomach it. He wished for even a cup of the thick sludge that doubled for tea on the *Daedalus*. He feared that Sir Cartwright was right about not finding a good cup of tea in this city.

When the meeting finished, Malcolm escorted Sir Cartwright to the waiting car. He assisted Sir Cartwright into the long Horch Phaeton and walked around to the other side to enter. After Malcolm shut the door, sweat started to bead on his forehead, and he put a finger inside his shirt collar to loosen it. Sir Cartwright watched Malcolm for a moment before he smiled and said, "You'll be alright, young man. If you can face off against an enemy, you can handle a few diplomats."

"If you say so, sir," Malcolm rasped, his voice suddenly very dry.

"Diplomacy is not that different from war," he said. "Both sides are arrayed against one another, each with their own needs. Both sides attack, and counter-attack, until they get what they want."

"Or are destroyed," Malcolm pointed out.

"Yes," Sir Cartwright chuckled. "The big difference between diplomacy and war is that we tend not to destroy the other side. Diplomacy is the art of making everybody equally unhappy with the outcome." He thought for a moment. "Magnus, write that down. I may wish to use it someday." He looked out of the window and saw that the rest of the delegation were ready. "Once more into the breach, eh?" he said, as he indicated the driver to leave.

Instead of riding in an automobile, Malcolm had the sensation of floating in a boat on a river between two canyons. The buildings on both sides rose to four to five storeys, with quaint little stores on the ground floor, rising to two or three floors of balconies, followed by what could only be attic apartments whose windows broke the graceful slope of the mansard roofs. After a couple of turns, Malcolm was quickly disoriented. He couldn't even see the sun to get his bearings. A few minutes later, the car turned into a giant circular plaza, that came up to the gates of the Hofburg Palace. Opposite the palace stood a large church.

"That would be *Michaelerkirche*, or St. Michael's Church. One of the oldest churches in Vienna," Sir Cartwright said, as he pointed to the Romanesque church. The spire rose several stories above the circle. Malcolm turned to face Hofburg Palace. A two-story gated arch sat in the center of the palace, as two wings extended on either side around the plaza, ending with two fountains; one representing Austria's power of the sea, and the other its power of the land. Two smaller gates flanked it on either side. Four towering marble statues of Hercules sat on either side of the three gates. Behind the facade of the building, Malcolm saw a great verdigris bronze dome rising above the statues that decorated the top of the building.

The car stopped in front of the massive gate. Malcolm saw two guards stationed at either side of the gate. Malcolm immediately recognised the blue grey of the Austro-Hungarian Army, and the high collars that all military uniforms seemed to require. The young sergeant, Malcolm guessed from the colour and pips on the collar, was expressionless and stood at rigid attention. He was relieved that this was not his duty; while he was physically able to stand at attention for long periods of time, he loathed every second of it. Malcolm smiled to himself, and assisted Sir Cartwright out of the car. They were immediately met by a young blond man in a dark suit. "Welcome, Sir Cartwright. We are pleased that you are attending the talks." The young man spoke English with only a hint of an accent. *He probably speaks better English than me*, Malcolm thought.

"Thank you, Leopold. This is my assistant, Magnus Howardson," Sir Cartwright said. Malcolm extended his hand, but Leopold looked at it with disdain, so he smiled and withdrew his hand.

"If you and your assistant will follow me, Sir Cartwright, I'll take you to the conference room. Many of the other delegates are already there." Leopold led them through one of the many ornate doorways leading out of the dome, and to an ornate staircase. They travelled up and entered a hallway before entering a large room. The room was dazzling. Gold accented the trim along the ceiling, on the ceiling, and along the various wall panels. Two massive gold chandeliers, holding a hundred candles each, threw flickering light that further illuminated the gold, making the whole room glow. A large central table was set at the centre of the room. At the table were several flags, each representing the diplomats involved in the talks. Arranged around the outside of the room were a similar set of tables, where the chief diplomat's staff would work. Malcolm followed Sir Cartwright to his chair, and started for the table where the rest of the delegation was settling.

"Where are you going, my boy?" Sir Cartwright said. His eyes were twinkling.

"I thought I would be joining the rest of the delegation," Malcolm said sheepishly.

"You are my assistant. You will stay right here," Sir Cartwright said. "However, you will be standing for the proceedings. I hope that's not a problem."

"None whatsoever," Malcolm said. "But are you sure you don't want someone more qualified?"

"Nonsense," Sir Cartwright said. "You are far more capable than my past assistants, who only wanted to scrape and bow, in hopes that it would advance their career. You want to do a good job. That's what I need."

"Thank you, sir," Malcolm said.

The room gradually filled up with delegates from the two parties engaged in the conflict, Italy and the Ottoman Empire. In addition to the British delegation were delegations from France, Germany, and Austria. Joan arrived and was seated next to Sir Cartwright, as the official translator for the diplomat. Malcolm saw Saxon working with the other members of the British delegation. The noise in the room was a mélange of languages that kept Malcolm on edge. He couldn't pick out most of the words from the other delegates, and he felt like he was in the Tower of Babel.

Suddenly, a trumpet sounded and everyone in the room rose. Emperor Franz Joseph entered the room, and the conversation ceased immediately. The Emperor's white hair and bushy mustache made Malcolm think of a walrus. He wore a military jacket, festooned with medals and decorations. He walked into the hall and Malcolm gasped. Immediately behind the Emperor was a young blond man with an eye patch over his left eye, and his right hand gloved. Malcolm recognised him immediately as his former friend and assistant, Matthew Frye, who was actually Matthias Frietag, German agent. Frietag had planted the bomb that destroyed the bridge of the *Daedalus*, thrusting Malcolm into command. Frietag had tried to kill Malcolm several times during that mission, and almost succeeded, until Malcolm sabotaged a gun that blew up in Frietag's face. Malcolm took a quick step behind Sir Cartwright and looked down, hoping that Frietag hadn't recognised him.

The Emperor began his remarks and Malcolm immediately heard Joan translating the Emperor's words. "Greetings and welcome! It is our pleasure to host such an august body. We wish you luck through the next week, as we attempt to resolve this dispute in a manner equitable to all parties. At the conclusion of the week, we invite you to attend us at a State Dinner given in your honour." With that, the Emperor turned and left the room. Malcolm thought that Frietag had glanced in his direction as he followed the Emperor from the room. Malcolm dropped his file close to where Joan was standing. He moved behind her and whispered in her ear. "Frietag is guarding the emperor," before squatting to pick up the file. Joan, imperceptibly moved her head. Malcolm knew immediately that she'd heard as he saw her body stiffen, and her hands balled into fists.

As he stood up, she whispered. "We'll talk later. Tell Saxon."

"Agreed," he whispered. He pulled a piece of blank paper from the table and scribbled 'Frietag is here'. The diplomats were beginning to sit down and start the talks. Malcolm leaned close to Sir Cartwright and said, "Sir, I find I need another file. I shall return in a moment."

"Very good, Magnus," Sir Cartwright said.

Malcolm made his way to the table of the British delegation. Saxon was busy transcribing something when Malcolm interrupted him. "Excuse me, can you fetch this file for Sir Cartwright?"

Saxon grabbed the paper without even looking up. He read the note and looked up at Malcolm. He simply nodded to Saxon who slipped the note into a pocket. "I don't believe I have it here, sir. I can arrange to get it to you later. Would that be sufficient?"

"That will do. Thank you," Malcolm said, before turning to return to Sir Cartwright. Malcolm took his place behind Sir Cartwright and very shortly, the talks began. At least that's what Malcolm assumed was happening. There seemed to be a great deal of yelling and passion. Joan was busy translating for Sir Cartwright, but even Malcolm guessed she was not relaying a word for word translation. After a while, Malcolm felt the talks fall into a rhythm; first a repre-sentative from either Italy or the Ottoman Empire would make a statement, the other side would immediately erupt with another statement, then there would be much arguing before someone from the German or French delegation would say something, and the talks would progress for a short time.

The talks continued uninterrupted all morning. As near as Malcolm could discern nothing had happened, and Sir Cartwright, as head of the British delegation, had so far offered nothing. At 1:00 PM, the talks adjourned for lunch. Before lunch was served, Malcolm caught the attention of both Joan and Saxon before he left the room. A few moments later, they joined him in the hallway.

"What do we do? Do you think Frietag recognised us?" Malcolm asked.

A voice behind Malcolm answered. "Why, yes, Malcolm, I did recognise you. Even with that ridiculous beard. Oh, look the whole crew is here. Charles, how good to see you again."

Malcolm turned and studied his former assistant. Frietag still kept his blond hair cropped in the military style. Like Malcolm, he no longer wore a uniform, but was dressed in a richly appointed suit. As Malcolm had observed in the audience chamber, Frietag wore a black leather eye patch over his right eye, and a black leather glove on his right hand.

Frietag smiled. "I see you are observing your handiwork, Malcolm. I lost my eye and the use of my hand. Until very recently." He pulled off the glove to reveal a hand made of brass. Gears and pulleys replaced joints and tendons. As Frietag opened and closed the fingers, Malcolm heard the clack of the gears. "Alas," he said, as he raised the mechanical hand to brush Joan's cheek. "I'll never feel the softness of a woman's face, but it does have other uses." With lightning speed, the mechanical hand closed around Joan's neck.

Malcolm tensed, ready to jump Frietag. He balled his hands into fists.

"Go ahead, Malcolm," Frietag sneered. "It will be my pleasure to crush the life out of her before you take a step."

Malcolm stopped and took a deep breath. "What do you want, Matthias?"

"Very simply, I want to destroy you, as you have destroyed me. I will start by finishing off your love."

"Matthias, are you sure you really want to do that? Killing an innocent member of the British delegation? There could be international consequences to such an act," Malcolm said calmly.

Frietag glared at him. After a moment, he pushed Joan towards

Malcolm. "What are you doing here? Why aren't you captaining that piece of junk you call an airship?"

Malcolm bristled at the insult to his ship, but he replied calmly. "I'm sure you already know that I resigned from the Air Service. I decided to apply my skills to the Foreign Service."

"Then why the assumed name, Magnus Howardson?" Frietag spat derisively.

"Very simple," Malcolm said. "I knew my name might cause... certain difficulties. So I changed my name."

"A likely story," Frietag said. "But knowing you as well as I do, Malcolm, I know that you're too stubborn to tell me anything. I will figure out the real reason you are here, mark my words."

Malcolm looked at Frietag. He knew that he would keep them under close observation, spoiling almost any chance for them to complete their real mission. Unless of course, he was busy doing something else. "Frietag, after watching your many incompetent attempts to kill me, do you really think I'm scared of you?" Malcolm asked.

Frietag's face turned bright red and he sputtered. "Do not be too sure of yourself, Malcolm. The Palace grounds can be... very dangerous for those who wander off unattended."

"If they're guarded by you, I very much doubt it," Malcolm said, egging on Frietag. "How did you get the job as the Emperor's body-guard? Surely the ruler of the Austro-Hungarian Empire can do better than a one-handed cyclops..."

Malcolm stopped talking as Frietag's mechanical hand circled around Malcolm's throat and began to tighten. "You will die for such insolence."

"What is going on? What are you doing to my assistant?" Malcolm looked over to see Sir Cartwright standing in the doorway to the audience chamber.

Frietag hesitated for a moment. The hallway began to fill as diplomats spilled out to get fresh air. Frietag saw the eyes on him. He released Malcolm and hissed. "This is not over." He stalked through the crowd, pushing people out of his way as he stamped away.

"Good heavens, whatever was that about?" Sir Cartwright asked.

Malcolm struggled to catch his breath. "An old friend."

"With friends like that, who needs enemies?" Sir Cartwright said. "Nevertheless, I will file a formal grievance that you were roughed up by one of the Emperor's ruffians, and make sure that he is nowhere near the conference."

"Thank you, sir. I'd appreciate that," Malcolm said. His voice was still raspy, but it seemed no permanent damage was done.

"Very well. When you've gathered yourself together, please return. We have much to do before lunch."

"Yes, sir," Malcolm said.

When the diplomat was out of earshot, Saxon hissed. "What the devil were you playing at, Malcolm? You nearly got yourself killed and blew our cover!"

Joan interrupted. "That was brilliant, *Magnus*," she said, correcting Saxon. "You have a knack of getting under Frietag's skin, and you tricked him into attacking you without apparent provocation. In front of witnesses. As Sir Cartwright said, he will be nowhere near the conference for the next several days." Joan frowned.

"What is it?" Malcolm asked.

"I'm worried," Joan said. "You wounded Frietag again, Malcolm."

"So?" Malcolm asked.

"Like animals, people are most dangerous when they are wounded," Joan said.

CHAPTER 27

The trio returned to the audience chamber, and after a buffet meal of various meats, cold sausages, bread, and pickles, the talks resumed. From what Malcolm could work out, the whole of the first day was all about posturing. Italy claimed they were protecting Italian citizens living under Ottoman rule, while Turkey decreed that the land was theirs by conquest. The French seemed to throw their support behind the Italians, while the Austro-Hungarians seemed to care only about appeasing the Ottoman Empire. Germany and Britain remained neutral in the proceedings. In fact, both sides said little in the opening stages of the negotiations. Malcolm thought that the day ended where it started, with nothing accomplished.

On the drive back to the pension, Sir Cartwright turned to Malcolm and asked, "What is your assessment of how things went today?"

"Well," Malcolm said sheepishly, "it seemed to me as if nothing happened at all."

Sir Cartwright smiled. "Yes, in many ways nothing happened. But one important thing happened. Both sides got the opportunity to express their case in front of several interested parties."

"Pardon my ignorance, but why are we, I mean, Britain, interested? This doesn't seem to have anything to do with us."

Sir Cartwright smiled. "In many ways, you're correct. However, Egypt is sandwiched between Libya and the Ottoman Empire. We also own the Suez Canal; the only passage from the Mediterranean to the Red Sea. With the Ottomans preoccupied with the Italians, they aren't looking at Egypt." Sir Cartwright sighed. "The Ottoman Empire is not as strong as it once was, but that does not mean it should be underestimated. Also, the Germans have taken an active interest in the fate of the Ottoman Empire, and have done what they can to support the current government. Unfortunately, we have lost our influence, and the government hears only Germany."

"It's a delicate spiderweb of alliances and influence; one good push and the web is destroyed. Maybe not immediately, but soon. And then the whole continent may be engulfed in war." He paused for a moment. "Now that the pieces have been arranged on the board, the game can commence in earnest."

And Sir Cartwright was correct. The next day, the talks moved from hard lines drawn in the sand, to a framework for discussion of the issues. Each side accused the other of hideous slaughter, and tried to use that to obtain the moral high ground. Malcolm watched it as he would a battle. Italy and the Ottomans were intent on strong frontal assaults; intent on demolishing the other side. Malcolm observed as both the German ambassador and Sir Cartwright played a subtler game of sly attacks and counter attacks. Malcolm watched as Sir Cartwright sat silent for hours, and then asked a question, or offered an observation, that steered the conversation towards his desired outcome. The German diplomat, Johannes Kriege, was Sir Cartwright's chief nemesis in the discussions. While the Italians and Ottomans made charges and counter charges, with the French and Austrians supporting their respective allies, none of them saw the attacks and counter attacks happening at the periphery. Germany wanted nothing more than a full victory for the Ottomans. The British response was more nuanced. While they supported the Italians, the British did not wish to anger the Ottomans by embarrassing them at the negotiation table.

Malcolm found it very hard to keep up with the games within games going on within the talks. The talks continued until early evening. "That was a very productive day, don't you think?" Sir Cartwright said.

"If you say so, sir," Malcolm said. "I am out of my element here."

Sir Cartwright turned and looked at Malcolm appraisingly. "I must disagree. I think that you see more than you believe you see. I think that what you lack is not talent, but experience. Tell me what you observed today."

Malcolm described it in the only terms that he knew, as a series of attacks, counter attacks, feints, and blocks. When he finished, he asked, "Are they always like this? Fencing with words?"

"Fencing with words? I've never thought of it like that," Sir Cartwright said. "But, yes, I suppose it is. You have a very intuitive grasp of what's said and what's unsaid." He looked up. "Ah, we are here. Thank you, Magnus, I believe I will retire early tonight. I have no assignments for you."

"Thank you, sir," Malcolm said. He escorted Sir Cartwright to his room and returned to his own room. He quickly scribbled two notes asking Joan and Saxon to meet him in the lobby in an hour, and slid the notes under their doors. He went to the lobby and, through the assistance of the concierge, secured reservations at a restaurant not far from the pension.

One hour later, Malcolm entered the lobby to find Joan and Saxon already waiting for him.

"It's about time you got here," said Saxon, looking at his pocket watch. "We've been waiting a whole forty-three seconds."

"Must be this civilian life making me soft," Malcolm said, as he smiled. "I believe we'll still be able to make our reservations."

"Reservations?" Joan asked. "Where are we going?"

"To an excellent restaurant recommended by the concierge," Malcolm said.

"Do you think that's wise?" Joan asked.

"I don't understand," Malcolm said, as his brow furrowed.

"I wouldn't put it past Frietag to watch our movements. Since we are not at the Palace, he might have more freedom to carry out his threats."

"Let him," Malcolm said. "I welcome the chance to settle the score with him."

"As do I," said Joan. "But this may not be the time or place."

"Let's decide one way or another, because I am, frankly, very hungry," Saxon said.

Joan was silent for a moment. "I suppose we can go. The three of us should be more than a match for him. Come, let's go before we are late," Joan said, as she offered her arm to Malcolm.

As the trio left the pension, the lanterns on the tall, ornate lamp posts bathed the streets in a yellow glow as they made their way down the *Tegetthoffstraße*. Malcolm felt Joan tense up as they reached the corner of *Maysedergasse*. "What is it?" he asked.

"I'm sure that we are being followed. Don't turn around, but as we turn the corner, there is man about fifteen feet behind us. Blond hair, thin beard."

As they turned the corner, Malcolm shot a look down the street and quickly found the man that Joan had described. He noticed that he had short-cropped hair in a military style. Joan stopped at a window front, and pulled Malcolm to her. "Oh look, isn't this darling? You should buy it for me!"

Malcolm looked in the window and was confused. They had stopped in front of an apothecary, and the only thing Malcolm could guess that she was pointing at was a hot water bottle. "What do you need a-" he asked, before Joan's elbow connected with his rib. Now he understood. She was waiting to see what the follower would do. "Now, Madame, we've gone over this time and time again, the budget does not allow for us to buy every trinket you see."

"You never let me have any fun," Joan said as she turned to Malcolm, and looked past him to their tracker. "All we do is look, I never get to have any fun," she said as she arched her eyebrows to indicate the man behind Malcolm. Malcolm grabbed Joan's hand, turned around, and pretended to drag Joan away from the window. "Madame, you know we're on a strict budget. May I remind you that you are still paying off your last spending spree?" He now walked towards the man, who momentarily froze. The man pulled out his pocket watch, pretending to check the time. Malcolm kept pulling Joan along behind him, and when he got close enough to the man, he gave Joan a strong tug, and directed her towards their tracker. Joan collided with the man.

"Oh, I beg your pardon," she said in perfect German. "I am so sorry. My manservant forgets his place sometimes."

"No pardon is needed, Madame," said the man. "But I think your manservant treats you poorly."

"Oh, he is just following my orders," Joan said. "Most of the time, I don't like my orders."

"Ah. Good evening," the man said, tipping his hat and walking hurriedly down the street.

"What did you find?" Malcolm whispered after the man was some way down the street.

"He had a gun and a wallet. I did leave him the pocket watch, though," Joan said.

"How thoughtful," Saxon quipped.

"Oh, look, I do believe he is part of the *Evidenzbureau*, the Austrian equivalent of the Secret Service," she said, as she showed Malcolm and Saxon a card spirited away in a hidden sleeve of the wallet. "Rather clever, these wallets."

"Come along," she said, as she dropped the wallet on the sidewalk. "There, let him think he dropped it." She took Malcolm's arm, and continued down the street. She saw a postal box and surreptitiously dropped the gun in the box.

"I daresay, the postman will be in for a surprise tomorrow," Saxon said under his breath.

The trio continued a little farther down the street. Joan looked up, her eyes wide. "Malcolm, you didn't?"

"Yes, I did. We are eating at the Hotel Sacher."

"I haven't been here since I was a child!" Joan said with excitement.

"I don't remember much, but I do remember the torte!" Joan wanted to hug Malcolm fiercely, but since they were in public, settled for squeezing his hand.

"I remembered once you said how much you loved it. I asked the concierge to get us reservations. I may have already spent my salary on this meal, so let's enjoy, shall we?"

"I must say, Malcolm. I am very impressed," Saxon said. "Who would have thought you would have such refined tastes?" Saxon smiled and Malcolm laughed. They approached the opulent hotel, a far cry from the much more modest pension where they stayed. The hotel stood several storeys high. Windows and pediments covered every side of the building. A green awning extended over the entrance way, supported by two wrought iron columns, each holding a hanging electric light.

Once inside, the restaurant was immediately on their left. The room was long with green carpeting, and painted green panel frames with walnut trim. One side of the room was decorated with large windows draped in emerald green cloth, trimmed with gold. Electric light chandeliers and wall sconces provided bright illumination. Two rows of tables lined each side of room.

Malcolm announced the party to the maître d', who summoned their server, dressed in a red uniform with black pants, and shoes with enough shine to see one's reflection. The server led them to a table by the window. The window had a view of the *Maysedergasse*, and the trio watched the comings and goings of the pedestrians and traffic. Their server returned and took their drink orders; Malcolm was surprised to find they had a decent whisky selection, and ordered his whisky neat. Saxon stuck to his usual Gimlet, while Joan chose a Stinger. After the server returned with their drinks, Joan said, "Wait, don't drink them just yet." She reached into her purse, and after a moment pulled out three strips of paper, and handed one each to Malcolm and Saxon. She placed hers in her drink and after a few seconds, the paper turned blue. "Go ahead," she indicated.

Malcolm and Saxon looked at each other, shrugged, and dipped the paper into their drinks. After a few seconds, the paper also turned blue.

"Very good. They're safe. Cheers!" she said, raising her glass.

"Cheers!" the men echoed. After sipping his whisky, Malcolm asked, "Why did we stick paper in perfectly good drinks?"

"That was rather the point. To make sure they *were* perfectly good drinks. The Secret Service devised these strips to detect common poisons or knockout drugs. They aren't foolproof, but given our run-in on the street, I didn't want to take a chance."

"It's a good thing," Malcolm said. "I'd be heartbroken to have to abandon perfectly good whisky."

They ordered their meals; braised beef ribs for Malcolm, baked cod for Saxon, and a potato goulash for Joan. Discussion soon fell to the talks.

"I swear that if I have to transcribe any more documents, I'm going to go stark, raving mad," Charles said as he sipped his gimlet.

"I am so tired from listening in one language and speaking in another. This is the break I need. Thank you, Malcolm," Joan said.

"You're both very welcome," he said.

"And how is it that you have been sheltered from the monotonous jobs, Malcolm? You seemed to be very involved in the proceedings," Saxon added.

"You give me too much credit. I am really a glorified butler, delivering and receiving papers."

Joan sipped her drink. "Sir Cartwright seems to like you Malcolm."

"Oh?"

"Yes. During one of the breaks, he asked me about you, if I knew your plans. He would like to see you in the Foreign Service."

"Me? A diplomat? The poor man must be mad," Malcolm said.

"I would think so," Saxon said. "You? A diplomat?"

"I'm wounded," Malcolm said with a laugh. "Me a diplomat? Not bloody likely!"

"That's what I said. In more diplomatic terms," Joan said as she smiled.

Their food arrived, and the trio were quiet as each enjoyed their meals. Malcolm had never had beef as tender as this. It seemed to melt in his mouth. Each of them took the time to savour each bite. Soon, the server came to take away their dishes, and before the server could even ask, Joan said, "We would like three of your famous sacher-tortes." She turned to Malcolm and Saxon. "You must try these. They are absolutely the best torte you will ever have. I visited here when I was a little girl, and it was the best dessert I've ever had."

"Very well," Malcolm said. "I concede to your judgement."

Before long, the server returned with three plates. Malcolm looked at the dessert. The sacher-torte was a double layer chocolate cake, with what appeared to be apricot jam spread between the layers. The cake was covered in a dark chocolate frosting that was glossy, and reflected the light. On the side was a fancy dollop of whipped cream.

"I have waited so long for this," Joan said, as she took a forkful.

Malcolm took a bite of the cake. Joan was right; it was quite excellent, although it did seem to have a strange aftertaste. Joan appeared to be enjoying her dessert immensely, as Malcolm was certain he heard small moans escape every time she ate a bite.

When the desserts were finished, Malcolm spoke. "Not to spoil our current mood, but what do we do about Frietag? I'm not alone in supposing that our tracker tonight was sent by him?"

"I'm sure you are correct, Malcolm. I'm sure he has something planned for you. He can't touch us while we're in the diplomatic party, but if he were to catch us away from the entourage..." She stopped and sighed. "You really do know how to bring down a mood, don't you, Malcolm? This was exactly what Frietag hoped we would do."

"I'm sorry. I was just hoping that we could have a few minutes in private to go over our plans," Malcolm said. "So what do we do?"

"Yes, what do you do?" A voice asked from behind Malcolm. He turned and found Frietag standing behind him. "I hope you don't mind if I join you?" Frietag said, as he pulled a seat from a nearby table, and sat with them. "I see you had the sacher-torte. An excellent choice, I might say."

Malcolm turned towards Frietag, and found he was having trouble focusing on him. The room seemed to drift in and out of focus. And then the room started to spin. Malcolm could feel himself starting to lose consciousness. He shook his head to attempt to clear it.

"Ah, I should have said, the meal is with my compliments. Your desserts are a very special treat made to my specifications. You were smart to check your cocktails. I have been watching your little dinner party the whole time. It was child's play to doctor your desserts. And now, I think it's time for you to sleep."

Malcolm watched as first Joan and then Saxon slumped on the table. He turned to Frietag and slurred, "You bashturd," before he, too, slumped on the table.

CHAPTER 28

Malcolm struggled to open his eyes. His brain felt like oatmeal, and he found it hard to put together any thoughts. At first, all he could see was fog, but as his vision cleared, he realised that he was in a cell. *How did I get here?* he thought. *I was having dinner with Joan and Charles, and then... Frietag...* He tried to punch something nearby, and realised that his arms were chained over his head. *That explains why my shoulders hurt so much,* he thought. The anger started to clear the fog from whatever drug Frietag had put in his dessert. It was a shame; it was a very good dessert.

The cell was a five-foot by five-foot room bounded by three stone walls, and a sturdy set of iron bars. The room was illuminated by a single bare lightbulb protruding from a socket in the ceiling. The air was dank, and had a slight smell of mould. Malcolm assumed that meant that he was underground.

He took stock of his situation. The jacket and tie he had worn to dinner were missing, as was his belt and shoes. *Bloody hell,* he thought. *That's where I hid most of my tools. First things first,* he thought. *What do I have?* He assessed his situation. He looked up and realised that his cuff links were also gone, because the sleeves of his shirt were open. He tried to push his head down on his collar, but with his arms raised it was difficult to tell if the two thin picks he had snuck into his collar were still there. He wasn't certain, but he was sure his pockets were empty. He looked above his head, and saw that his chains were attached to the wall. The light was dim, so Malcolm could not see into the corners of the room. While trying not to make too much noise, Malcolm tugged on his chains and was not surprised that they were securely fastened to the wall.

Malcolm heard some noise in the hallway, and turned his head to see what was happening. Frietag appeared with a couple of guards. "Ah, I see you are awake," he said. "We have much to discuss."

"If you think I'm going to tell you anything," Malcolm snarled, "you'll be waiting for a very long time."

"I think I have a way to make you talk," Frietag said. He unlocked Malcolm's cell and nodded to the guards. Malcolm deduced that the guards were other intelligence agents, since they wore nondescript grey suits. They could just as easily be bankers or bureaucrats, which Malcolm realised was the whole point. The men handcuffed Malcolm first, then undid the manacles on his wrists. As soon as he was unchained, Malcolm fell hard on the floor. The two guards roughly snatched him up and put him on his feet. Frietag laughed and exited the cell. Malcolm was pushed along by the guards, and was taken down the hall to a room with a heavy looking table and two chairs. A fabric screen, like the type used in hospitals, closed off the back half of the room. Malcolm got a very queasy feeling in his stomach.

The guards pushed him into the chair, and locked his handcuffs to the table. Frietag slowly circled around the table, before settling into the chair. "That will be all," he said to the two guards dismissively. "I must say, it's nice to have an opportunity to brush up on my English. I haven't had much chance to use it." He smiled, and Malcolm had to swallow down the urge to spit in his face. "Let's catch up, shall we? What have you been doing since you cost me my eye and hand?"

"A little bit of this, a little bit of that," Malcolm said.

"You always had a talent for being spectacularly unhelpful," Frietag said. "Why did you leave the Air Service?"

"Time to try my hand at something new," Malcolm said.

"I find that very hard to believe," Frietag said. "Where have you been since you resigned your commission?"

"Out and about," Malcolm said.

Frietag pulled a file full of papers from his jacket. "We have no record of you, from the time you resigned until you arrived, under an assumed name, as part of this delegation. Do you care to explain?"

"Not particularly," Malcolm said. "What crime have I committed?"

"None yet," Frietag said. "But I wouldn't count on the law if I were you. The *Evidenzbureau* has a great deal of latitude in dealing with spies."

"Spies? Are you mad?" Malcolm said. "I'm working for the Foreign Service. I'm a diplomat."

"What is it you like to say, 'pull the other one, it has bells on it'? You and Saxon both resign from the Air Service, and suddenly both end up on a diplomatic mission. Why are you here?"

"Trying my hand at something new, like I just said."

Frietag sighed and shook his head. "I was hoping that you would be reasonable, but I see you intend to force my hand."

"Which one? The real one or the freakish mechanical monstrosity?"

Frietag backhanded Malcolm with the mechanical hand. The solid hit from the hard metal caused stars to appear before Malcolm's eyes. "I really have had enough of your insolence."

"That's too bad, there's plenty more where that came from," Malcolm said.

"Yes, I suppose there is. But I think it's time to change the tone of this conversation, and impress upon you the seriousness of the situation." Frietag got up and pulled the screen aside.

Strapped to the table was Joan.

Malcolm forced himself not to react, and took a deep breath through his nose. He put his hands together on the table, his right hand on top of his left. Hidden in his left hand was a very small needle-like lock pick that Malcolm had pulled from his collar when he fell in his cell.

"I have your acquaintance, a certain Madame Charlotte De

Marnier, I believe she calls herself? While I am a gentleman, I have a job to do. I know too well that you would sooner die than tell me anything. You might even be willing to let Saxon suffer, because you know he would accept it as part of his duty. But Malcolm Robertson is too much of a gentleman to allow this lady to suffer." Frietag smiled. "I, however, have no such compunction."

"Magnus, what is going on? Who is this Malcolm he keeps talking about? Why are we here?" Joan yelled.

"My dear, there's no need to make this difficult. You are a beautiful woman, and I would hate to do something irreversible."

"Magnus, don't tell him anything!" she said urgently.

"Perhaps you wish to be more forthcoming?" Frietag said. He waited for a moment. "No? Very well."

He wheeled over a tray containing some wicked-looking surgical instruments. Malcolm couldn't see very well, but he could make out several scalpels, and a very large set of tongs. Frietag turned from him to pick up the tongs. Malcolm feverishly worked with his pick, until he heard a soft click. Although still stuck around his wrists, he was no longer handcuffed to the table.

Frietag looked at the tongs with glee. He turned to Malcolm. "Do you want to talk yet?"

"What are you going to do, you monster?" Malcolm yelled.

"I think the lady needs to have her nails done," he said. Joan balled her hands into fists, but Frietag forced her hand open. He used the tongs to grab the fingernail on her index finger, and started to pull it back. Joan bit down hard on her tongue, trying not to scream out in agony. Malcolm could see the pain etched on her face, and he knew Frietag was right. He could never bear to see Joan hurt.

"Fine, I'll talk," Malcolm yelled. "Just let her be!"

"Very well," Frietag said. "Start talking. If I'm satisfied, I won't hurt her."

"Magnus, don't," Joan said between breaths. Malcolm could see blood, and he thought that the fingernail was half off.

"It's alright, Charlotte," Malcolm said. "I'm sure he knows enough already." Malcolm took a deep breath. "Yes, you're correct, Frietag. I am not part of the Foreign Service. When we resigned from the Air Service, both Saxon and I were recruited by the Secret Service."

"Ha! I knew it," Frietag said victoriously. "What were you doing before you joined the diplomatic mission."

"Training for our real mission."

Frietag moved to the table. "Yes, your mission. What is it?"

"To beat your sorry ass," Malcolm said. He leapt up from the chair, and head-butted Frietag as hard as he could. Both Malcolm and Frietag howled in pain, but Malcolm had delivered many head-butts in rugby, and knew how to do it with the minimum of pain to himself. While Frietag was still staggered, Malcolm came behind him and pulled the chain of his handcuffs tight across his neck.

Frietag instinctively reached for the chain, but Malcolm had already pulled it tight. The mechanical fingers couldn't find purchase under the chain. Malcolm was easily able to keep Frietag off balance, so that he couldn't land a punch with the mechanical hand. Minutes seemed to go by as Malcolm pulled the chain for all his worth. Gradually, Frietag provided less and less resistance until he stopped. Malcolm pulled for another ten seconds, and when he felt no resistance, Malcolm let go.

He fished through Frietag's pocket and found a set of keys. After several failed attempts, Malcolm unlocked his handcuffs. He immediately placed them on Frietag before going to Joan.

Her fingernail was a wreck, and blood was flowing everywhere. Malcolm looked around and found bandages. He made a makeshift bandage and released her from the bed. Joan immediately hugged Malcolm. "Dear, that was absolutely brilliant!"

Malcolm gave her a hurried kiss. "Are you alright?"

"I've had worse," she said. "Let's get out of here."

"Let's take care of the guards first. Do you think you can get them to come?"

"I think so," she said. They went to either side of the door, and Joan called in a fair approximation of Frietag's voice to have them retrieve the prisoners. Malcolm and Joan quickly dispatched the guards. They dragged Frietag back to Malcolm's cell, and chained him up. Malcolm took Frietag's handkerchief and made a crude gag.

They searched the hallway, and found Saxon in a cell next to the one that had been Joan's. They chained the two guards in the cells and likewise gagged them.

"Thank you," Saxon said. "But now what?"

"We leave," Malcolm said. "And since we need money and clothes, I suggest we help ourselves," he said, indicating the guards. Malcolm and Saxon donned the men's suits, and took their wallets with their badges. It wasn't a perfect fit; Malcolm thought if he took a deep breath, he might rip the jacket, and Saxon's pants were two inches too short. The worst part was the shoes. It was all either could do to put their feet in any of the shoes. Joan pulled her hair up and shoved it under one of the fedoras. Malcolm was amazed that she might be able to pass for a man at a glance. The trio also armed themselves with their captors' guns.

Slowly, they snuck up the hallway from the direction the guards had come, Joan leading, followed by Saxon, with Malcolm bringing up the rear. The hall ended in a steel door with a window, which was closed from the other side. Joan quickly found the correct key and unlocked the door. Cautiously, she opened the door and relaxed when she saw that it was at the foot of a staircase. The staircase rose and although it was dark, the trio could see another sturdy, steel door at the top of the stairs. They crept quietly to the top of the stairs. Joan listened and slowly turned the handle on the door. She slowly opened the door and peered through the doorway. Ahead, in the well-lit hall, Joan saw several doorways on either side of the hall; some open, some closed. At first glance, they appeared to be offices. The far end of the hall opened into a large room, and Joan thought she could see two outside doors at the far end.

Joan closed the door and told Malcolm and Saxon what she had seen. "I think we should pretend we're taking someone to the Palace for questioning. If we're stopped, someone is going to have to speak for us. I can't talk because my voice will give me away, and I know Malcolm knows no German. Charles, how is your German?"

"A little rustier than I would want in a situation like this," he said. "But I think if I just yell, and act like I'm in a bad mood, I can get us through."

"Alright. Who gets to be the prisoner? You or I?" Joan asked.

"I will," Malcolm said. "I'm more recognisable than you, so it will make sense that I'm the prisoner."

"Alright, are we ready?" Joan asked.

"As ready as I'll ever be," Malcolm said.

Saxon opened the door with purpose, and Joan and Saxon pushed Malcolm through the door, holding him tightly by the arms.

"Not so hard," Malcolm whispered.

"It's supposed to be convincing," Saxon whispered.

They proceeded down the hall, Saxon nodding and acknowledging anyone they met in the hall. They entered what had to be the lobby of the building. The floors were marble, and on their left as they came into the room was a large reception area, also carved in marble. A single guard, dressed in a suit, sat at the table reading a newspaper.

When he saw them, he asked *"Was ist das?"*

Saxon replied in German. The man paused for a second, then laughed. Saxon laughed too, as did Joan, and the trio exited out of the doors.

As they made their way down the street, Saxon asked. "Why did he laugh? I told him we had orders to deliver him to the Emperor."

Joan laughed. "Actually, Charles, you told him that you were delivering him *for* the Emperor."

"Oh," Saxon said. "Now I understand his amusement. At least we managed to escape. Now what?"

"We retrieve our equipment from the pension, and then we disappear," Joan said.

CHAPTER 29

"Shouldn't we hide first?" Malcolm asked.

"No, we have some time before they discover that we have escaped," Joan said. "We need to take that time to clear out our equipment, because they will make a bee-line for the pension. My hope is that we are gone before they arrive. Hold on, let me figure out where we are."

They travelled to the next corner, and Joan realised that they were just a block or two west and north of the Palace. The trio hurried down the streets while trying not to draw attention to themselves. Several minutes later, they arrived at the pension.

"Do we take the front door, or do we sneak in?" Malcolm asked.

"I think we sneak," Joan said. "We don't want the receptionist or concierge to see us. As far as they know, we left and never came back. Follow me."

Joan led them around the back of the hotel, and down an alley that was obviously used for deliveries. Joan tried the back door and was unsurprised that it was unlocked. "The staff get sick of having to get the keys every time a driver brings a delivery. You would be surprised the number of buildings you can get into this way."

They made their way through the back of the pension, and found a back stairway to the second floor. They snuck off to their rooms; Malcolm and Saxon returned in a few minutes, each with a large suitcase, and wearing a new set of clothes. Malcolm had packed the portable psychometer, his lock and safe tools, and the small flask of Palmer Fluid, in addition to a few suits and his tuxedo. It took a few more minutes before Joan arrived. "Sorry, I had information that I needed to destroy. We should go," she said.

And then they heard a great commotion down below. There was yelling and the barking of orders.

"Damn, they're here," Joan said. "It looks like the only way out is up."

"I was afraid you would say that," Saxon said.

The trio raced up the stairs as quickly and as quietly as they could. However, their luggage made it difficult to do either well. The stairs ended at a trap door. Joan carefully set down her luggage, and retrieved a key that unlocked the trap door. Malcolm wanted to ask her how she had a key, but thought better of it. She opened the trapdoor carefully, preventing it from making any noise. They clambered up into a large attic room, with large dormer windows running its length. There were no light fixtures in the room, but the glow of the streetlights below was enough to provide dim lighting. Dust cloths covered furniture shapes, while dozens of mattresses were stacked in one corner.

While it was an attic, it was obvious that it was kept clean; Malcolm breathed a sigh of relief, as he saw that there was no dust to show their footprints. Joan led them to the stack of furniture, and started climbing to the ceiling. When she reached the top, she started reaching around on the ceiling until she found a catch. This time, the trap door swung down, and Malcolm could see that it opened to the roof. When the trio was on the roof she pulled the door tight and on the roof, slid a bolt to prevent the door from being opened on the other side. While Malcolm and Saxon stood by the trap door, Joan made a sweep of roof along the street side. When she returned, her face was grim.

"It's what I feared," she said. "The streets below have been sealed off. There are several uniformed policemen milling on the streets. We aren't going to be able to get away on the street, at least for the foreseeable future."

"Where are we going?" asked Saxon. "We obviously can't stay here, and I don't fancy living up here until they go away. That is, if they don't find us first."

"There's a safe house several blocks from here. But you're not going to like how we're going to have to get there."

"What could be worse than being stuck on the roof waiting for them to catch us?" Saxon asked.

"You'll see," Joan said with a smile. "Follow me." She started running across the room to the eastern edge. The roof sloped down, and five feet below the edge of the slope was another roof. "Do as I do," she said. Joan put her luggage in her lap, still holding the handles. She slipped down the tin roof, and when she hit the end of the pension's roof, she fell lightly and landed on the roof below.

"She has to be kidding," Saxon said.

"Come on, let's get this over with," Malcolm said. They raced to the edge of the roof. Malcolm got up and sat on the edge. It was difficult, as he had both his luggage and the psychometer in his lap. He slid down, and prevented the psychometer from taking any damage, but he lost control of the suitcase, and it landed with a thud on the roof.

Saxon looked at the roof tentatively. "Come on," Joan hissed. "We don't have time. Either get over here, or stay to be interrogated by Frietag!"

Saxon muttered something under his breath; Malcolm was sure it was a curse. He sat on the edge, closed his eyes, and started sliding. Malcolm was sure that Saxon was going to do the whole thing with his eyes closed. But just as Saxon left the roof of the pension, he opened his eyes and landed softly. Joan nodded her approval and then took off across the roof. Again, she came to the edge of the roof and this time, another roof appeared in front of her, approximately two feet higher than the current roof. She slowed down and hefted her luggage up onto the new roof, and pulled herself up. Malcolm was sure that she wouldn't have stopped if it weren't for the luggage. He could see a small structure on the new roof, and Joan started for that. Malcolm and Saxon followed her example; hefting their luggage, and pulling themselves up. Malcolm suddenly felt glad for all the awful physical training they had done in London.

By the time Malcolm and Saxon caught up with Joan, she had opened the door to the structure, and was waiting for them on a staircase that descended into the dark. "We're going all of the way to the bottom. Be as quiet as you can. Pull the door tight when you come down; I've already re-locked it." Joan quickly descended into the darkness. Malcolm and Saxon looked at each other, shrugged, and followed her down.

After they descended from the roof, the stairwell had some illumination. They descended the stairs for several minutes; Malcolm quickly lost track of the number of floors they had descended. They passed doors which Malcolm assumed would take them to another floor, but he quickly lost track of them as he struggled with the luggage and the psychometer. They reached the bottom of the stairs, which stopped at a door. Joan said, "It's vital that you stay close to me. This is the part that you won't like very much."

"As opposed to the fun we've had so far," Saxon said.

Joan gave Saxon a look that would blister wallpaper, as she took out an electric torch from her bag. Malcolm was glad that he wasn't the recipient of that glare for once. Joan opened the door and they were clearly in a basement. Shelves of food in canning jars lined one side of the basement, on another was a small workbench with a smattering of neglected tools. Several crates, a dusty perambulator, and a crib were among the numerous items stored here. Joan continued to one of the shelves and went to the end, and fumbled with the shelf. There was a click, and the shelf swung away, revealing an opening. And suddenly a stench reached Malcolm's nostrils that almost made him gag. It smelled like a sewer, and Malcolm realised that's exactly what it was.

"We're not really going in there, are we?" Malcolm said.

"I'm afraid so. It's the only way we can get to the safe house at this point," she said.

Malcolm took a big breath of fresh air, and followed Joan through the opening. It led to another staircase that descended to a ledge that ran out of sight. The ledge was roughly three feet wide, and below that was the river of sewage. Joan waited for Malcolm and Saxon to fall back behind her. Joan said. "Stay close, you're not going to want to-" she said before there was a loud splash, "slip and stick your foot in there."

Malcolm gritted his teeth. "Thank you darling, I would never have guessed." Malcolm nearly lost his shoe as he tried to pull it from the effluent.

"Be careful," she said. "It is slippery, and you do not want to actually fall into the… river," she said sarcastically. She shone her light ahead as they started out.

The sewer arched from one side of the ledge to another ledge on the other side, and seemed to slope down slightly. Soon, another branch joined their branch. Joan stopped and shone her light around, looking for something. "Alright," she said. "We have to jump."

Joan made the three-foot span with ease. Malcolm and Saxon barely made it, and Malcolm came very close to putting the other shoe in the sewage. They continued until they came to a large circular area where multiple branches joined. To their right was a ladder, and much to Malcolm's dismay, Joan started climbing. Resigned to his fate, Malcolm sighed and started after her. They climbed nearly ten feet up, to a catwalk that circled the whole room. The trio gingerly picked their way around the catwalk, which to Malcolm's further dismay, had no railing. They circled to the other side of the room, to another ladder, and they descended.

This time, the tunnel seemed to angle slightly up. They continued for another five minutes when Joan stopped. She started to search the wall next to her, and within ten seconds tripped a latch, which caused part of the wall to open. She slipped inside and urged Malcolm and Saxon to follow her. When they got to the opening, Malcolm now saw two men holding rifles pointed at Joan. The trio was talking in animated German, and eventually the men put down their guns. "Malcolm, Charles, this is Medford Mayberry and Randall Tibbits from the Secret Service. We've reached our temporary home. Welcome to the Secret Service safe house in Vienna."

CHAPTER 30

$\mathcal{M}$ayberry and Tibbits left momentarily and returned with three robes. "You're probably not going to want to wear those clothes anymore. The odour down there has a nasty tendency to cling to the fabric," Mayberry said, as he offered Malcolm a robe.

"I'm sure," Malcolm said. "Any hope for these?" he asked, pointing to his excrement-coated shoe.

"I suppose," Mayberry said. "But you'll have to wash it off. Do you have another pair?"

Malcolm thought for a moment. "Yes, I do."

"Then burn it in the furnace. You'll be glad you did," Mayberry said.

Malcolm started removing his clothes when he heard a cough. Both Joan and Saxon were looking at him with disgust.

"What? I smell bloody disgusting, and I want to get out of these clothes right this second. When did the two of you become so bloody modest? You've both seen me in my undergarments before."

Saxon and Joan laughed and realised that Malcolm was right.

"Turn your backs, gentlemen," Joan said, as she started to pull off the dress she had worn to dinner. Malcolm and Saxon complied, and soon they were all given slippers, and they made their way through a basement. One side held shelves containing various jars of canned items. Malcolm looked back at the wall from which they'd entered, and the whole thing was lined with shelves of canned foodstuffs that Malcolm realised had been permanently attached to the shelves.

They climbed a rickety set of wooden stairs, and came into a pantry with an exterior door to the right. Shelves lined the walls of the pantry, which also contained canned foodstuffs in much less dusty jars. Malcolm could make out relishes and jams on the shelf. It quickly transitioned into crockery and bags of flour and sugar. They were ushered into a kitchen.

The room was dimly lit by candles, although Malcolm saw an electrical light fixture overhead. It was a modest kitchen; the cast iron coal-burning stove took most of one wall. There was a small sink with a cabinet just to the left, and the final wall held a small wooden table with two chairs. The walls were a dull beige, and a heavy black shade was pulled over the window above the sink. Malcolm thought the room looked very dreary.

"Welcome to your home away from home. I'm Medford Mayberry, chief of the Vienna bureau of the Secret Service. Do you want anything to eat or drink?"

"No, thank you," Joan said. "I am Charlotte De Marnier, and this is Magnus Howardson, and Charles Gothburg. We were abducted by the *Evidenzbureau* while at dinner, and we managed to escape."

"How did you know about our... sanctuary?" Mayberry said, ushering them into a small parlour that contained a couple of over-stuffed armchairs and a small sofa. Joan took one of the armchairs, while Malcolm and Saxon squeezed onto the sofa. Mayberry sat in the other chair, and Tibbits hovered in the doorway.

"I am a member of the Secret Service. You can verify my credentials by sending the following telegram to headquarters: 'The crumpets are soggy; the shortbread is stale; and the gateaux is runny.'"

"Tibbits, please verify that," Mayberry said. Tibbits left the room when Malcolm noticed that Mayberry had a gun pointed at Joan in his suit pocket. Malcolm decided that discretion was the better part of valour, and he would wait to see how this played out.

When Malcolm looked at Mayberry, all he could think of was a walrus. Mayberry was a rotund man, nearly as big around as he was tall. His cheeks were red, as if he was constantly blushing. His thin blond hair did little to cover his forehead. But what caught Malcolm's eye the most was the large bushy moustache that drooped over his upper lip, completely hiding it. Tibbits was tall and wiry with dark black wavy hair. The duo reminded Malcolm of the nursery rhyme about Jack Spratt.

"What did you do that warranted the *Evidenzbureau* to abduct you from your dinner?" Mayberry asked suspiciously.

"Actually, nothing. A few days ago, we had a run in with Matthias Frietag, the German spy who appears to be working for the Emperor. He bears us a grudge, and he sought to have his revenge."

Mayberry nodded dutifully, and suddenly bolted up straight. "Yes, I understand now. You were involved in the Tunguska Affair. I recognise you now." Mayberry pulled his hands from his suit jacket, and Malcolm felt himself release some of his pent-up tension. "I believe that you are here for the diplomatic talks?"

"Yes," Joan said. "However, our true mission is something else, which I'm not at liberty to share. You understand, of course."

"Of course," said Mayberry.

"We'll need to hide out here for two more nights, and then we'll need to leave the country in the middle of Friday night. It's vital that we get out of the country safely."

"Very well," said Mayberry. "I will see what I can do about transportation. In the meantime, let me show you to your rooms. I'm afraid we only have two rooms. You two," indicating Malcolm and Saxon, "will need to share. There's one small bathroom and precious little hot water so plan accordingly. We have some supplies to assist you on your trip, and they are at your disposal. For now, why don't you try and get some rest. I imagine that it's been a long day."

Malcolm stopped and took stock. He was in fact, very tired. It was late as they'd started dessert, and he had been out cold for at least four hours. At the mention of rest, it was all Malcolm could do to stifle a yawn.

Mayberry led them to their respective rooms. As Malcolm shut the door, Saxon said. "Oh, one bed. Is that going to be a problem, Malcolm?"

"Not for me," Malcolm said. "But it might be for you."

"Why is that?" Saxon asked nervously.

"I'm told I snore very loudly. Especially when I'm very tired."

Malcolm and Saxon stripped to their underclothes, and both were asleep shortly after their heads hit the pillows.

Malcolm slept fitfully. Every time he rolled over, he was rolling into Saxon. Unable to get back to sleep, Malcolm got out of bed, and was surprised to see that a small sliver of sunlight illuminated the room. He opened his suitcase to inventory the things he'd thrown into it at the pension. Three suits, his formal tuxedo, his lock and safe tools, as well as the psychometer. Malcolm realised that he would have to determine if it was still working. Fortunately, Malcolm had chipped off a sliver of the Cthulhu idol, and packed it with the rest of his tools. While he couldn't use it to recalibrate the psychometer, he was certain that he could at least use it to tell if the Spear still worked.

After putting on a new shirt and suit, Malcolm crept out of the room, and left Saxon sleeping. He walked gingerly down the hall and down the stairs. He found Mayberry and Tibbits sitting in the living room reading the newspapers. Malcolm spied cups on the small end table, and hoped that they contained tea.

"Aw, early bird," Tibbits said. "Can I get you some coffee?"

"I was hoping that you might have tea," Malcolm said hopefully.

"No. It's deucedly difficult to find it in this city, and we don't want to draw attention to ourselves. Would you like some coffee? I daresay it's a fresh pot."

"If I must," muttered Malcolm

"Beg your pardon?" Tibbits said.

"Yes, thank you," Malcolm said, remembering his manners. "Is anyone else up?"

"No, you are the first," Mayberry said, as he folded his newspaper and put it beside him. "Frankly, I expected you would stay in bed a while longer given your evening."

"Here's your coffee," Tibbits said, handing the cup and saucer to Malcolm. He looked at it and tried to suppress a grimace as he drank the hot, bitter liquid. *It's as revolting as it was the last time, but beggars can't be choosers*, he thought.

The three men just looked at each other until Malcolm broke the silence. "What is it that you do here?" Malcolm asked.

"We keep track of our Austrian friends." Mayberry said matter-of-factly. "We keep tab of important comings and goings."

"How long have you been doing this?" Malcolm asked.

"Ages," Mayberry said. "Nearly twenty years. Tibbits just showed up a few months ago. I think the plan is for me to show him the ropes, so to speak, and they can put me out to pasture."

"I'm sure that's not the case," Malcolm said.

"Oh, it's fine. I'm ready for a life that's less exciting," Mayberry said.

"What do you know about Frietag?" Malcolm asked. Malcolm saw the tiredness in the man's eyes, and knew he was weary of the life of an agent.

"Matthias Frietag. He showed up here about a year ago. I gather he was drummed out of the *Abteilung* IIIb."

"Section IIIb?" Malcolm asked.

"You speak German?" Mayberry asked.

"Not really. I've picked up a little from reading German technical journals, but I certainly can't speak it."

"Ah," Mayberry said. "*Abteilung*, or Section, IIIb is German military intelligence. As near as we can tell, Frietag worked for them up until he showed up in Vienna. We believe that he used his contacts to get a job in the *Evidenzbureau*, and has moved quickly though the organisation."

"When we were at the diplomatic talks, he seemed to be guarding the Emperor," Malcolm offered.

"Yes, we believe he uses that position as a front to spy on foreign dignitaries. Or rough them up," Mayberry said, indicating Malcolm.

"I'm no dignitary," Malcolm said. "But I know he blames me for his fall from grace. I'm sure he'll do anything to have his revenge on me."

"I know that I surely would like to get my revenge on him," Saxon said, as he came down the stairs. "If it weren't for Malcolm, I would be dead by his hand. I'm a good-natured man, but it is hard to get over that kind of thing."

"Coffee?" Tibbits asked.

"Yes, please," Saxon said, as he sat down on the small sofa next to Malcolm.

"Did you get some sleep last night?" Malcolm asked.

"Not bloody likely," Saxon said. "It sounded like I was sleeping next to a bloody sawmill. The only peace I had was when you got up."

"Listen to the two of you bickering like an old married couple," Joan said as she came down the stairs.

Tibbits returned to the living room, and handed Saxon his cup of coffee. "Coffee, ma'am?" He asked Joan.

"Yes, please," Joan replied sincerely.

Joan sat down and the room fell silent, until Tibbits returned with a cup of coffee for Joan. "Thank you," she said sweetly. She sipped her coffee and set it down next to her on the side table.

The silence continued for several more seconds before Joan finally said. "I must contact headquarters, so that our disappearance from the talks will be explained."

"What about our mission?" Malcolm said.

"Our mission remains unchanged," said Joan. She looked in the direction of Mayberry and Tibbits to indicate that this was not the place to discuss anything.

"I can assist you in sending a message, Madame De Marnier," Tibbits offered. "Our communications room is in the basement."

"Very good," said Joan. "Do you mind showing me the way now?"

"Not at all. Follow me," Tibbits said.

"May I come too?" Malcolm asked. "I'm curious at how you can communicate all the way from Vienna to London."

"It's highly technical," Tibbits said. "I doubt that you would understand."

"Try me," Malcolm said. "I used to be an engineer; I'm pretty sure I'll at least have a basic knowledge of the technology."

"Very well," Tibbits said, with a distinct note of condescension. Malcolm hated this type of person; the person who had extensive knowledge about a certain subject, and had to prove how much smarter he was than everyone else in the room.

Tibbits led them back down the staircase to the basement. He went to the wall of shelved canned goods near the wall they came through from the sewers, picked up a can, and a section of the wall opened into another room. As Malcolm approached, he saw a very small room with a set up that looked very similar to something he had seen in Mycroft's cabin when he was aboard the *Daedalus*.

At the centre of the desk, a typewriter sat connected to a standard computator by a bundle of wires. Even in the dim light of the basement, Malcolm could see the columns of brass gears glinting. Another typewriter, this one without a keyboard, sat next to its mate. It too, connected to the computator by a bundle of wires. As Malcolm looked more closely, he realised that the wires attached to the keys on each typewriter. Malcolm also spotted the telegraph transmitter, likewise attached to the computator. The telegraph had a long wire that snaked out of the back of it, into a hole in the wall.

"What we have here," began Tibbits, "is a marvel of the current age. The machine you see before you…"

Malcolm interrupted. "Takes input from the typewriter, pushes it through some kind of code pattern stored in the computator. The signal is sent via telegraph because you've spliced into the main telegraph lines for Austria, and is passed down the line, until it reaches a similar machine in London. At the other end, the computator decodes the message, and prints it out on the keyboard-less typewriter, thus ensuring secure communication. Does that about cover it?"

For one moment, Tibbits looked slack-jawed at Malcolm, before brusquely saying, "Yes, that's right." He composed himself and smiled at Joan. He consulted a book, and pulled out a couple of cards with holes punched in them and asked, "What did you want to send to headquarters?"

"Send the following: Had to leave the party early. Stop. Gone to visit Aunt May. Stop. Checking if we will attend banquet as planned. Stop. Yours, Charlotte."

Tibbits dutifully typed the information on the typewriter. Malcolm watched, as the wires connected to the keys were connected to switches left open or closed, which, in turn, set the gears for the computator. Malcolm watched the various gears turn other gears, until he heard the click clack of the telegraph transmitter. Although Malcolm disliked using a computator, he marvelled at the precision engineering used to create the device. And with a chuckle, he recalled how he found a way to program a computator to perform a series of operations that made it self-destruct. If he didn't need the information, he'd be tempted to program some punch cards, stick the cards into the computator, and wait to watch the look on Tibbits' face as the machine vomited gears all over the room.

Tibbits said, "Nothing to do now, but wait for the response. I'll stay here and wait. You should go up and rejoin your friend."

As Joan and Malcolm walked up the stairs to the pantry, Joan poked Malcolm in the ribs. "That wasn't very nice," she said. "You didn't have to act like a know-it-all."

"Me?" Malcolm said, as he rubbed his ribs. "What about his 'It's highly technical. I doubt you would understand.' Like I'm some idiot?"

"I suppose, but it still wasn't very nice," Joan said.

As they entered the room, they both saw Saxon slumped over on the couch. Malcolm thought he saw blood on his head. They both started towards him when Mayberry swung around from beside the entryway, and levelled a shotgun at them.

"That will be far enough," Mayberry said.

"What is the meaning of this?" Joan said. "You saw our credentials; you know who we are."

"You are absolutely correct, Madame. Which is why I will receive quite the reward when I turn you over to Frietag." Mayberry said.

Saxon began to stir on the sofa, and reached up to touch his head. He looked at the blood, looked up to say something, then just sighed and said, "Bloody hell, not again."

"You are another plant? Been an agent for Austria this whole time?" Joan said disdainfully.

"No, actually my employment with the Emperor is a relatively new position, as it were. I can see the writing on the wall. I'm to be shuffled off to a desk job, and eventually pushed out. I have spent twenty years of my life away from my home. I have no friends and no family. And for that, I'm expected to let some young upstart take over my life's work while I churn papers. It did not take a great deal of convincing from Tibbits to entice me to work for Frietag." He paused for a moment. "Tibbits? Yes, he's a plant from the *Evidenzbureau*. I didn't realise until after Frietag made me such a generous offer."

Tibbits returned with a printed sheet in one hand, and a revolver in the other.

"You received a reply?" Mayberry asked.

"Yes," Tibbits said. "It reads: Banquet still a go. Stop. Bring an umbrella. Stop. Hope Aunt May has recovered from cold. Stop."

"Are you going to tell us what that means, or are we going to have to drag it out of you?" Mayberry asked. Saxon, Joan, and Malcolm all stared at Mayberry and Tibbits with a look of utter contempt. "Very well, no matter." He motioned to the basement. "Come along quietly, and no one gets hurt."

Malcolm waited for a cue from Joan, but she meekly started forward. Saxon followed quickly. Malcolm was surprised that they wouldn't try something, as the odds were clearly in their favour. Malcolm decided to follow along, but was already looking for an opportunity to escape.

Tibbits and Mayberry prodded the trio down to the basement, and through the hidden passage to the sewer. The group followed the sewer for several minutes as near as Malcolm could tell, before they took a turn into a tunnel that led to a platform above the sewer. There was dim light in this area, and Malcolm could make out several people. Malcolm's stomach dropped when he saw a glint of metal where the man's right hand should have been.

"Malcolm, we meet again," Frietag said, with a grin that made Malcolm shiver.

CHAPTER 31

alcolm's mind started to turn over the situation. It appeared that Frietag had two cohorts with him. In the dim light, Malcolm couldn't be certain, but he thought they were the two officers from the station. It didn't surprise him; they were probably eager to cover their mistake. With Mayberry and Tibbits on Frietag's side, the odds were no longer in their favour.

They came to a small ladder that led to the platform some five feet above the walkway next to the sewer. As Malcolm got closer to the platform, he could see four wheels that must be used to open and shut the valves used to direct the sewage to one of four different passages leading out of the passage. Malcolm searched the wall, and was comforted to see a very large pipe wrench leaning against the wall, not that far from where Frietag and his henchmen were standing.

"I swear you reappear more than a case of the Shanghai clap," Malcolm said. "Which reminds me, did you get that taken care of before or after you buggered your mother?"

Frietag stiffened, and took a breath before responding. "Tsk, tsk, Malcolm. Using such language in front of a lady."

Malcolm kept his face even, but was happy that he could still provoke a reaction from Frietag. Malcolm knew that Frietag made mistakes when he was angry, and Malcolm knew just how to antagonise him. One by one, the trio climbed the ladder, and were led towards Frietag and his men. Malcolm was concerned as it appeared that Saxon was woozy after he climbed the ladder. Malcolm remembered the blood on his head, and was worried he had a concussion. Saxon walked uncertainly before falling to his knees in front of Frietag.

"Look, how the mighty have fallen," Frietag said. "One bump on the noggin, and he's crawling around on his hands and knees. So much for the superiority of royal blood."

Malcolm and Joan were led to Frietag and his men. As they approached, Mayberry said, "You have your prisoners. Where's my money?"

"Yes, your money. You see, I've decided that I no longer have any need for you." Frietag said, as he started to draw his gun.

In one single motion, Saxon rose from his hands and knees, and punched Frietag in the groin with all his might. The gun that Frietag had started to draw dropped from his hand, as he immediately doubled over in pain. Malcolm heard a crack, and saw that Joan had dropped one of Frietag's men with a sharp kick to the head. A gunshot rang out in the chamber, echoing repeatedly. Deafened by the roar, Malcolm turned to see Mayberry moving his gun from Tibbits to the other guard, before pulling the trigger again.

Tibbits looked down with confusion, and saw blood pouring from his abdomen. He looked up at Mayberry, started to speak, and then fell to the ground. Malcolm looked up, and saw the last henchman had pulled out his gun. Before the man could point the gun, Malcolm charged the man, and put his own finger behind the trigger as he tackled him. Before the man could try to pull the trigger, Malcolm forced the gun out of his hand. He flailed around before barely reaching the pipe wrench, using it to smack the man across the jaw.

Saxon had jumped on Frietag, and was holding him down. "May I borrow that?" Saxon asked, as he indicated the pipe wrench.

"Absolutely," Malcolm said, handing the pipe wrench to Saxon. He swung the wrench, connecting with Frietag's jaw and Frietag went limp. Malcolm made a move towards Mayberry, but Joan said, "It's fine. Mayberry is on our side."

"How do you know?" Malcolm asked, not taking his eyes off Mayberry.

"The message. 'Aunt May has recovered from her cold.' It means that Mayberry has come out of cover."

"How did *you* know?" Malcolm asked Saxon.

"While you were learning the intricate details of safes and locks, I was learning how to be a spy. How to code messages, and how to interpret them. Everyone thought that one of us should know what to do if something happened to Joan."

"So I'm the only one who didn't know what was really happening?" Malcolm huffed.

"I didn't know until we received the reply. Until that point, I was as in the dark as you."

"I hate to interrupt," Mayberry said. "Although it is the sewers, the gunshots are bound to attract some kind of attention. Follow me, I have another safe house – one whose existence no one else knows."

Mayberry started down the tunnels, and Malcolm drew close to Joan. "Can we trust him?" he whispered.

"Yes, he has been vouchsafed by headquarters," Joan said.

"How do you do it?" Malcolm whispered.

"Do what?"

"Never trust another soul, for fear that the person is an agent?"

"You place your trust very carefully," Joan said. "Like you. And Saxon. I trust both of you with my life. It's why I requested you for this mission."

"Requested us?" Malcolm asked, raising his voice. "You requested us? Does that mean you were a party to the blackmail that got both of us booted from the Air Service?"

"I... no... I mean," Joan stuttered. "Now's not the time or place to talk about it."

"It never is," Malcolm muttered, and strode ahead catching up with Mayberry. "What should we do with them?"

Mayberry drew a long, sharp knife from a hidden sheath. "We should probably finish the job," he said, as he started over to the unconscious man that Malcolm had tackled.

"No. We can't kill them. It's heartless to kill them while they're helpless," Malcolm said.

"Do you think they would give you the same consideration? I doubt that they would."

"Which is exactly why I won't," said Malcolm. "Perhaps there's another way." He looked around. "Do they work?" Malcolm asked, indicating the wheels.

"I have no reason to believe that they don't. Why?" Mayberry asked.

Malcolm moved to the wheels without answering. While trying each of the wheels, he found the combination that would close the valves, so that there was no escape for the sewage down any of the other tunnels. Malcolm searched Frietag and his men, and found three sets of handcuffs. He handcuffed Frietag's mechanical hand to an overhead pipe, and handcuffed his other hand to his unconscious henchman. "There. They won't be going anywhere for a while."

Mayberry muttered. "It would have been much easier just to kill them, and dump the bodies in the sewer."

"Yes, it would," Malcolm said. "And that would make us no better than them."

"If we're done here," Mayberry said impatiently, "we have to clear out of the safe house, and put some distance between that and us."

Mayberry led them back the way they had come. In the end, they left Tibbits and the dead henchman next to Frietag.

"Tibbits was a double agent the whole time?" Malcolm asked.

"Apparently," Mayberry said. "I was disillusioned with my job, running the safe house, but never really being part of the game. And it was true that Tibbits had been sent to become my replacement. I had let slip some of my frustration. After a while, Tibbits made comments suggesting that there was more I could do. I think he thought me an easy mark to convert. I've been at this game longer than he's been alive. I pretended to go along with him, and he slowly tried to entice me to join him. I got word to headquarters, and they asked me to play the part of a triple agent. The reply you received also told me that it was time to let my cover go, to do whatever I needed to do to assist you."

Malcolm listened, but said nothing. He couldn't understand how one could live their life never trusting another person. Being paid to see conspiracies behind every bush. The constant accumulation of secrets that could be used as currency. When Malcolm was captain, trust was integral to operation of the *Daedalus*. Malcolm had to place his trust in his crew, and the crew, likewise, put their trust in Malcolm, to keep them safe and return home.

Malcolm remembered Joan's remark about requesting him and Saxon for this mission. Had she deliberately helped to destroy his career, for the sake of this mission? Here he was, trudging around in the sewers of Vienna, no closer to finishing the mission than he was when he started. His face felt hot, and he felt the anger rise within him. *How could she?* he thought. *She knew how much the Air Service meant to me. She erased all of my work, just so she could have me on her precious mission?*

Malcolm stopped. Wasn't that exactly what he was asking Joan to do by marrying him? Give up her career, just so he could have her closer to him? Malcolm understood her point of view. He still hated it, and was mad at her, but he understood. Despite her protests, she did want him around. And apparently she would stop at very little to make that happen. He was less angry, and he would be happy to accept her apology. But that was totally up to her.

The group trudged back to the safe house in silence. Quickly, they assembled their luggage and gear. It did take Mayberry some time to gather his things. "Malcolm," Mayberry said. "Could you assist me in disassembling the computator?"

"I'd be happy to assist," Malcolm said. It felt good to do something he understood. He laughed to himself; usually he was trying to hurry to repair something. It was always much easier to break something.

Malcolm and Mayberry went to the basement, and started tackling the disassembly of the computator. Malcolm analysed the computator for a few minutes, while Mayberry disconnected the typewriters. He had no trouble destroying the typewriters, and sending the remains splashing into the sewage.

Malcolm went to work on the computator and, within minutes, it was nothing but a pile of gears, cogs, and metallic rods. Malcolm and Mayberry likewise disposed of the remains of the computator in the river of sewage. Like the typewriters, the metallic corpse of the computator sank quickly. When they returned to the small room that had contained the computator, Mayberry closed the door, and cut the cable to the can that was the mechanism to open the door. Without the cable, there was nothing to unlock the hidden room. Malcolm found the solution highly ingenious.

When they returned to the main floor, Malcolm could see that Joan was upset. "What's the plan now? Where do we go?" she asked with a sharp edge in her voice.

Mayberry looked at her, and raised an eyebrow. "We leave now. If I could have some assistance getting this trunk downstairs, I'd appreciate it."

"Can't it stay?" Joan said. "What do you need with it?"

"Madame," Mayberry said coldly. "I'm leaving the only home I've known for the last twenty years. I don't suppose it's too much to ask to take one steamer trunk and a suitcase."

"I'm sorry," Joan said. "You're right. Please forgive me. I'm... I don't know what's wrong with me."

"Come, I have a car hidden a couple of blocks from here. We'll take the sewer, and we can leave from the garage."

"Do you only ever use the sewer?" Saxon said. Malcolm could tell by his expression that Saxon did not relish yet another trip through the sewers.

"No, only most of the time," Mayberry said.

Malcolm gave Mayberry the portable psychometer, and used his free hand to take one end of the steamer trunk, while Saxon took the other. Joan followed behind, her head bent down. The group went back down the stairs and into the sewer. While the secret door to the sewer was open, Mayberry again sliced the cable to the can used to open it from the basement. When the door closed behind them, there would be no trace that there was ever an entrance into the sewer system.

As Mayberry said, the trip to the car was quick. Again, Mayberry clicked a secret switch, and a door appeared in the sewer wall. Beyond the door was a small room with a ladder. Mayberry climbed the ladder and opened a trap door at the top. He disappeared through the top and after a few moments, stuck his head through the hole. "Hand up the luggage, and we'll get out of here," he said. Malcolm and Saxon handed the luggage up to Mayberry, and then everyone climbed the ladder.

They emerged into a large garage. In the centre of the garage was a large steam-powered delivery truck. Malcolm could hear the engine coming to temperature to make the steam. The vehicle had two seats at the front, and a large boxed-in section behind. Mayberry had already loaded the luggage in the back. "I know it will be a bumpy ride, but I suggest that the three of you ride in the back. As soon as the engine comes to temperature, we'll leave."

Malcolm and Saxon lifted Joan into the back of the truck, and clambered in after her. Mayberry pulled the doors shut, and the trio were in utter darkness. Joan turned on her electric torch, and set it on the floor to illuminate the area. They sat there silently for several minutes, before they heard the truck being put into gear, and they lurched forward for a few seconds before stopping again. Malcolm could only assume that Mayberry had stopped to close the garage behind him.

For several minutes, the silence continued. They were bumped and jolted constantly, as the truck traversed the cobbled streets of Vienna. Malcolm heard Joan take a deep breath to speak. "Malcolm?" she said tentatively.

"Yes?"

"Can we talk about what I said? That I requested you for this mission?"

"Yes. Then it's true?" Malcolm asked.

"I suppose. You see, Mycroft asked me who I would trust to have with me on this mission, because he was aware of the likelihood of having to steal the spear. I off-handedly said 'I'd trust Malcolm, but he probably wouldn't want to come without Saxon.'"

"Malcolm," she continued, "you must understand, I had no idea he would actually make it happen. I know how much the Air Service means to you, and I, in no way, wanted to destroy your career. Or yours, Charles. I only meant that you are the two people in the world I trust the most. I will do anything I can to make it right when we finish this mission."

Malcolm reached over and took her hand. "I believe you," he said. "I won't lie, I *was* furious with you. But I had a sudden revelation in the sewer. You wanting me to be on this mission, is like me asking you to marry me. We both want to be together, but neither of us wants to give up anything."

"I think I may be sick," Saxon murmured. "While I appreciate the fact that I may not have to referee both of you, what is the plan now? Do we tell Mayberry about the mission?"

Joan removed her hand from Malcolm's, but not before giving it a squeeze. "I suppose we must. What day is it? I'm losing track of time."

Malcolm pulled out his pocket watch, and squinted through the darkness. "It appears to be late afternoon on Wednesday, I think. The banquet is scheduled for Friday. How are we going to get into the palace? I'm sure that Frietag will have doubled the guards to try to catch us. I assume he thinks we're up to something with the diplomatic talks."

"I think we have to move up the timetable for the mission, but I'm not sure how we get into the palace now," Joan said. "I say we have no choice, but to trust Mayberry with the mission. We're going to need his assistance in getting out of the country. If we can get to Italy, we can make our way back home with comparative ease."

"I agree," Saxon said. "I do think he's on the up and up. I think he would like one last chance to play an active role in a mission. He knows that returning to Britain now likely means a desk job for the rest of his career."

"Are we ready?" Malcolm asked. "I think I have everything I need, but I have no idea if the psychometer survived all of its recent travel."

"We have to be ready," Joan said. "If the Crown Prince is correct, and we don't retrieve the Spear, I shudder to think of the consequences."

CHAPTER 32

The trio sat in silence for the rest of the journey. Malcolm reached over and took Joan's hand, but nothing was said; each of them contemplating the implications of failure in this mission. The truck came to a stop for several moments. Malcolm started to rise when the truck lurched forward again, causing him to fall. A few seconds later, the truck came to a stop. The trio waited until they heard Mayberry unlatching the back of the truck. The doors swung open, and even the dim light flooding in seemed blinding.

"Sorry about the ride, but this is the most anonymous method of transportation through Vienna," Mayberry said. He helped all of them out of the truck, and they unloaded their luggage. They were in a small warehouse. Stacked next to the truck were rows of crates. There were two large lights hanging from the ceiling that provided dim light throughout the warehouse. In one of the corners of the warehouse, a set of stairs led to a room that overlooked the rest of the space.

Mayberry led them to an area towards the stairs. The area was almost a room, as it was bound on two sides by the stacks of crates, and the warehouse walls on the other. In the centre of this area was a table and six chairs. They settled into the chairs, and looked at one another expectantly, waiting for someone to speak.

Mayberry spoke first. "We'll rest here for a few hours, but we must leave Vienna, and Austria, immediately."

"Medford, we can't leave yet." Joan said. "We have to complete our mission; many lives are at stake if we fail."

"What is your mission?" Mayberry said suspiciously.

Joan sighed. "We have to steal the Spear of Destiny from the Imperial Treasury."

Mayberry laughed contemptuously. "Oh, something simple. Why do you bloody well need that relic? It's not actually valuable. Why aren't you stealing the crown jewels?"

"I can't tell you that, Medford," Joan said. "But please believe me when I say it is of the utmost importance."

"Fine," Mayberry said. "What was the original plan?"

Joan explained the details of using the formal dinner as the diversion necessary to break into the Treasury. When Joan finished, Mayberry considered everything for a moment. "That was a pretty sound plan before you gained Frietag's notice. I think we're going to have to act tonight, before Frietag has an opportunity to do anything." Malcolm could almost see the man's mind turning, as he thought through the options. "Yes, we'll have to do it tonight. I believe I can get you inside. I'll wait in the truck, and I'll be ready to pick you up, then we'll drive to Italy. I don't suppose any of you know how to drive?"

Malcolm, Saxon, and Joan all shook their heads. Malcolm was ashamed; he knew many of the mechanical underpinnings of the vehicle – the steam-powered engine, the transmission, the brakes, and the steering. But he hadn't learned how to drive one. *But*, he thought, *can Mayberry pilot an airship?*

Mayberry sighed. "Very well, that will be up to me."

"How are we getting into the palace?" Malcolm asked.

"How do you think?" Mayberry said with a mischievous smile.

"Not the bloody sewers again," Saxon said.

"Yes, the bloody sewers," Mayberry said. "There's a sewer grate just a few blocks from the palace, which leads into a grate in the corner of the central courtyard. I have used that on more than one occasion to get into the palace. From there, you should be able to follow your plan accordingly. Once you've retrieved the Spear, return to the sewer, and come back the way you came. I'll be waiting with the truck, and we'll start for the Italian border."

"I will stay at the rendezvous point until dawn. If you have not returned by then, I will leave without you, and assume you have been captured."

Malcolm was about to speak, but held back. Mayberry was right. If they were captured, someone had to get word back to London, so someone could try again. The mission was much more important than any of them.

"We should rest. We're all going to need it to be sharp tonight. Madame, you're welcome to use the office." Mayberry said, indicating the room at the top of the stairs. "There's a cot there with a proper pillow." He turned towards Malcolm and Saxon. "Unfortunately, I don't have much to offer you other than a crate or the floor."

"Do you have one on the other side of the warehouse?" Saxon asked. "This one," he said, as he pointed at Malcolm, "snores like a band saw."

Joan took the stairs to the office, and Malcolm watched her as she went. When she closed the door to the office, he sighed and reluctantly staked claim to a couple of crates that seemed to be softer than the concrete floor. Once Malcolm settled, Saxon walked off to put some distance between himself and Malcolm.

It took a few minutes to find a position on the crate that wasn't excruciatingly uncomfortable, but Malcolm dropped off to a fitful sleep. He dreamt of long tunnels, and being pursued, only to find Frietag waiting for him at almost every turn. Before he knew it, Joan was shaking him. "Malcolm, time to wake up."

He tried to rise quickly, but his back shrieked in agony. He felt stiff and old as he climbed down from the crate. It took several minutes of stretching and movement before he felt like he could walk again. He looked and saw that everyone was gathered around the table. There was a pot, which Malcolm could only assume was coffee, and a plate with a few sandwiches on them. Everyone else was eating and drinking. Malcolm joined them and poured himself a cup of coffee, and grabbed a couple of sandwiches. As he bit down, he realised it was just a slice of ham between two slices of bread, but it was as good as a gourmet feast. He was hungry. He realised that it was rather late in the day, and he hadn't eaten since their aborted dinner at the Hotel Sacher.

"How do you do that?" Saxon said.

"Do what?" Malcolm asked.

"Fall asleep so quickly? I barely found a place to lay before the roof was shaking with your snoring!" Saxon said.

"I don't know; natural talent, I guess," Malcolm said with a smile.

"It's nearly 6:00 PM," Mayberry interrupted. "It would be best if we left here at 8:00. That gives us an hour to get to the palace. From past experience, there's a five-minute window of opportunity, where the guards can't see the sewer grate during their circuit of the courtyard. If you are quiet, you should be able to sneak out of the courtyard to the Treasury building. I will park over the sewer grate you'll use to enter; there's a trap door in the bottom of the truck that can be used to exit and enter unseen. When you get back, bang on the back wall. That will be my cue to leave. If I hear the alarm bells ringing, I will attempt to make three circuits around the palace. After that, I will need to leave, so as not to draw undue suspicion. I will assume that you've been captured."

"That's encouraging," Saxon said dryly.

Mayberry rose and took another sandwich. "I'm going to the office to get a few more things. I suggest you prepare yourselves for the mission." He trudged to the stairs, and shut his office door behind him.

Malcolm, Saxon, and Joan gathered their luggage, and started to pull out the items they needed for the mission. Malcolm looked at his equipment, and he wished he had more. He still had the gun that he took from the *Evidenzbureau*, but not the streamlined sidearm and holster he had been issued at the Secret Service. He examined his lock picks and tools, and thought he had everything he needed. And he smiled with relief when he saw that he still had the metal flask of Palmer Fluid. Malcolm picked up the psychometer, and set it on the table to inspect it. He unscrewed the screws, opened the casing, and carefully examined the inside. The Rutherson tube seemed to be intact. He closed the device and turned it on. The battery indicator was green. Malcolm took the sliver from the idol, and held it to the detector. Immediately, the gauge registered activity. He turned off the psychometer, satisfied that it was working.

Malcolm then turned to the issue of clothing. Although he still had a few suits packed, the only clothing that he had that could hold all his tools and equipment was his formal dress tuxedo. Malcolm went to the water closet and changed into the tuxedo. As he opened the door, he felt absurd and horrendously overdressed. While Saxon also shared Malcolm's quandary, and was also dressed in a tuxedo, Joan had packed her tight-fitting jacket and trousers that she favoured when on a mission. Malcolm carefully stored his picks and tools in the carefully tailored compartments. There was no holster for his gun, so he was forced to put that in his trouser pocket.

"Don't you look dashing?" Joan said.

"I feel like a right git," Malcolm said.

"I do believe we are a tad overdressed for the sewers," Saxon said drolly.

"But, the two of you will fit in at the palace. On any given evening, there is usually some formal dinner," Mayberry added.

Mayberry produced a map of the sewers, and pointed to their entry point. "You will enter here. When you climb down the ladder, you will see a large arch to your left. If you get disoriented, you should see a small crown painted on the stone. Take that tunnel. You will pass four passages on your right. Take the fourth passage, and you will travel a short distance. Take the first passage on your left, and you will see the ladder just ahead, on the right side of the passage."

Joan laid out a map of the palace that she had retrieved, and they reviewed the mission again. She quickly spotted the location of the sewer access on her map. Fortunately, access to the Treasury wing was near the grate. They still had to deal with the guards in the courtyard, as well as any guards stationed in the entrance to the Treasury. From there, they would travel up the stairs to the Treasury proper. Malcolm would open the safe, and disable any security devices he could find. They would carefully make their way through displays of the Burgundian treasures, the baptismal treasures, and finally, to the holy relics, where the Spear of Destiny resided. Malcolm would disable any security devices on the Spear itself, replace it with the replica, and they would quickly make their way back.

"How are we going to get past the guards?" Malcolm asked.

"With these," Joan said, holding out two rubber balls in her hand. As Malcolm looked closer, he realised that the balls were not solid, but a rubber membrane, like a child's balloon. "They are filled with ether," Joan said. "When the membrane breaks, the ether is released as a gas. We must be careful as it is very flammable."

"This looks terribly easy," Saxon said sarcastically. "What could possibly go wrong?"

The trio drilled the plans over again, each memorising the map so that, if separated, they could always return to the sewer grate. They reviewed their resources for the mission. Malcolm had tools; the lock picks, a miniature electric torch, a revolver, and the psychometer. Joan had rope, her large utility gun; which could handle several types of ammunition, from large calibre bullets, to a small grenade, to a grappling hook attached to a length of rope, four ether grenades, and a knife. Malcolm was sure she also had several other items hidden on her person. Saxon also had a revolver, a miniature electric torch, maps of the palace in a small flipbook, and several official looking forms and letters that might be used to gain access.

It was still another hour before they would leave for the palace. No one talked, just wandered aimlessly throughout the warehouse, willing the time to go quickly. Malcolm's stomach was doing somersaults. He couldn't remember a time when he was this nervous. And he flashed back to a night on his first mission as captain, when he knew four German zeppelins would attempt to catch the *Daedalus* in an ambush. While he'd had a ship full of people counting on his outrageous plan, he felt more nervous now. There were far too many variables for his liking, and the plan wasn't his. He had to admit he liked being the one to determine the plan of action, and he was having a hard time being just a participant.

After an hour that seemed like three, Mayberry looked at his pocket watch. "It's time."

CHAPTER 33

They loaded their luggage into the back of the truck and Malcolm, Saxon, and Joan climbed into the back of the truck and into nearly pitch darkness. Within moments, the truck was in motion and driving through the streets of Vienna. In the dark, the anxiety built as Malcolm, Joan, and Saxon visualised the steps in their heads, their trips through the sewer, and the map of the palace.

At some point, Malcolm reached over and grabbed Joan's hand. She gave his hand a squeeze and pulled herself close to Malcolm, so she was leaning against him. He put his arm around her, and she slipped her arm around his back. They sat in the silence, content to just hold one another in the minutes before the trip.

The trip kept them all on edge. Every time the truck stopped, they each held their breath, wondering if they had reached the palace. And after a few seconds, the truck would begin to move, and they would collectively release their held breath. The trip to the palace was longer than their escape from the safe house, which told Malcolm that their warehouse was quite a distance from the palace. Malcolm had assumed they were near the Danube somewhere, because there were many warehouses near the river as it held a great deal of commercial shipping.

After a series of false starts, where they thought they had reached their destination, the truck halted. After a few seconds, Malcolm heard a knock on the wall of the truck, the signal that they had reached their destination. Malcolm and Saxon opened the trap door in the bottom of the truck, and the sewer grate was directly below them. They used two long, hooked iron rods to remove the sewer grate, and slide it to the side. Malcolm shone his light into the sewer, and the light quickly dissolved in the inky blackness. But he knew they were in the sewer as the hideous odour of sewage rose, and filled their noses. Malcolm thought he would be glad when this mission was over, and he would never have to travel in a sewer again. Saxon climbed down first, followed by Joan. When they reached the bottom, Malcolm handed down the psychometer, and climbed down the ladder. He opted to leave the sewer access open, in case they needed to make a quick escape.

Malcolm and Saxon turned on their electric torches and they got their bearings. They found the arch marked with a crown, and followed Mayberry's instructions. When they turned into the passage that contained the ladder, they turned off their torches and let their eyes become accustomed to the darkness. They could see a very dim light coming from above. It was not enough to illuminate anything, but it gave them the direction they needed to travel. They slowly inched up until they reached the ladder. Saxon climbed first, and stopped at the top. He reached into his pocket and pulled out what looked like a long rectangular box. He held the bottom to his eye, and put the top through the rungs of the grate. He attempted to turn as far as he could to either side, then he suddenly pulled it down and packed it away. It was only then that Malcolm realised that he had a periscope that he had used to view the courtyard. Saxon climbed halfway back down the ladder and stopped. Within a few seconds, Malcolm heard footsteps and conversation in German. One set of footsteps stopped right near the grate, and Malcolm's heart leapt into his throat. He heard someone hack up and spit into the grate, barely missing Saxon. Malcolm knew that even now, Saxon was contemplating any number of ways for getting revenge on the guard that nearly spat on him.

Saxon waited several seconds before climbing back up, and carefully sending the periscope above the grate. After a few seconds, he was satisfied and very gingerly pushed the sewer grate up and to the side. Malcolm was amazed that Saxon did it with the minimum of noise. Joan clambered up the ladder quickly and quietly. Malcolm struggled with the psychometer, and when he got close enough, handed it off to Saxon. He quickly climbed up, and together he and Saxon noiselessly put the sewer grate back in place. Malcolm looked around to get his bearings. They were in a courtyard near one of the corners. He could see the guards approximately one hundred feet ahead of them. He noticed the corner covered them in shadows. Malcolm looked up at the sky, but it was filled with clouds, which reflected the light from the city.

Joan motioned to them and they moved close to the wall. She took the lead as they crept beside the walls of the courtyard, until they came to a set of large oak double doors. She motioned Malcolm over to the doors as she slowly turned one of the handles. The handle seemed to only turn halfway. Malcolm got out his lock picks, and within a few seconds of work, he heard a satisfying click. Joan slowly and carefully opened the door a crack to peer into the room.

Malcolm, squatting behind her, also peeked and saw two Austrian guards in dress uniforms; one was reading the newspaper, the other a book. From what Malcolm could tell, they were seated on either side of a hallway that extended into the building. Malcolm thought he could make out the stairs to the Treasury, as well as a doorway just past the Treasury stairs. Joan counted on her fingers, down from three. When she reached one, she opened the door, threw one of the ether grenades into the room, and closed the door. Within a few seconds, Malcolm heard one thud, and then another. Joan put a mask over her face, slipped into the room, turned off the lights and opened the door. After another thirty seconds, she lifted the mask off her face, sniffed, and waved in Malcolm and Saxon. They quickly darted inside, closing and locking the door behind them. Joan produced a flask, and splashed alcohol on the fallen guards. Malcolm identified it immediately by the smell; peppermint schnapps. If anyone found them, they would assume they had passed out from drinking.

They crept through the outer chamber and down the hall. The hallway opened immediately to a grand marble staircase, and the hallway continued for a few more feet, before ending at a door with a frosted window. Malcolm checked the door and it was locked. There were words on the frosted glass: *Restaurierung und Reinigungslabor. Whatever that means*, he thought.

Malcolm and Joan looked for any sign of security devices before starting up the stairs. They kept to the inside of the staircase, because Malcolm thought it might be harder to plant any sort of pressure-sensing device in the smallest part of the tread. They carefully made their way up the staircase, and arrived at the landing with a large vault door in front of them.

This was Malcolm's cue to get to work. First, he checked the exterior for any wires that might feed electricity to an alarm. He felt carefully along the edges of the vault, and found three sets of wires on the left side. Malcolm removed the flask of Palmer Fluid from his coat, took the top off, and used the brush attached to the lid to trace the wires in the vault door. It took him no time to see that the wires were meant to detect if the door was opened. Taking a book of matches from his supplies, he lit the match and held it over the thin wires. As he expected, the insulation melted, exposing the wires. Malcolm cut a small strand of wire and secured it over the exposed wires. He was counting on the fact that the alarm circuit would trip, because the current would stop flowing. He repeated this for the other sets of wire. He examined his work and when he was satisfied, he turned to the lock.

First he painted the area around the tumbler, and the handle, with more Palmer Fluid, so that he could see the internal workings of the lock. As he looked at the results, he breathed a sigh of relief. Near the tumbler was a series of glass plates, which would have shattered if he'd had to drill into the face of the vault door. But even though he could see the workings of the safe, he still needed concentration to discern the combination to the safe. Inside were five disks; the first disk turned anticlockwise as he turned the combination clockwise. When he reached the number, the pin slid into a groove on the disk. If he turned the combination the other way, the first disk stopped moving and the second disk turned, again opposite of the combination.

Malcolm slowly turned and watched the pin fall into the notch on the second disk. He started to turn the combination lock in the opposite direction, and he saw the pin begin to slip out of the notch. He stopped and turned it back until the pin stayed in place. He turned the combination in the other direction, and was relieved to see that the third disk started to move. He repeated his careful manipulation of the disks, and was rewarded when the bar that prevented the locks from disengaging moved out of its locking position.

He nodded to Joan and Saxon and whispered. "Here goes nothing." He turned the handle, and could feel the locking mechanisms retracting into the door. He carefully pulled on the door and slowly opened it. To his relief, the only sound he heard was the slight protest of the vault door's hinges as the vault opened to reveal the Imperial Treasury.

The Treasury seemed to be more of an ornate museum display than a safe. Malcolm saw several oak display cases ahead of him, with paintings and hutches on either side. Malcolm shone his electric torch into the room, and the light reflected against gold, silver, and jewels. He swept the entryway for any additional traps, such as an electric eye. He carefully checked the floor in front of the vault for pressure plates. When he was confident that there was nothing there, he stepped in and looked around the back side of the vault door. He spotted the alarm bell, and followed the wires back to the door. He carefully stepped into the room one more step, looking for any sort of alarms. When he reached the middle of the room, he motioned for Saxon and Joan to follow him. Saxon and Joan did their best to attempt to follow in Malcolm's footsteps, knowing that a deviation may set off an alarm.

The trio slowly made their way through displays of ornate cloaks, jewel-encrusted medallions, crosses, and swords. The room then turned to the left, and they entered another wing of the Treasury. Here were the relics of the Holy Roman Empire: crowns, sceptres, and robes. Accompanying them were other jewels, and trappings of power: ornate crosses, gold gilt swords, and jewelled medallions. They continued to the end of this hall, where the room turned to the right.

Malcolm, still checking carefully for alarms, held his breath as they entered. This was the Ecclesiastical wing, where the holy treasures were kept. With even more care, they crept into the wing and examined every display case without touching it. The cases contained gold crosses, ornately-carved crucifixes, golden chalices, censers for holding incense, ecclesiastical robes in gold, reliquaries, and tabernacles. As they searched each display case, there was no sign of the Spear. At the far end of the hall, Malcolm noticed an empty display case. With a sinking feeling in his stomach, he carefully made his way to the display case. Inside the case, on the bottom, lay a note. He signalled for Joan and Malcolm to come over, and he pointed at the note. He whispered, "What does it say?"

Joan and Saxon peered at the note, and in near unison said, "The Spear of Destiny has been temporarily removed for cleaning."

"Bloody hell," Malcolm muttered.

CHAPTER 34

"Now what?" Malcolm asked, trying to keep his voice to a whisper. "The bloody thing could be anywhere!"

"Keep your voice down," Joan said. "Let me get the map and think." Joan got the map out, and made to spread it out on a display case when Malcolm hissed, "No, you'll likely trip an alarm!"

"Alright," she hissed back. She scanned her map for several seconds before sighing in defeat. "I don't see anything here that tells me where it might be."

"Let's think about this logically," Saxon said. "If you were going to remove a priceless artifact for cleaning, you likely wouldn't take it outside of the vault. That means it has to be here somewhere."

"There was a door just past the staircase." Malcolm said. "It had a sign on it that said something like 'Restaurant rings and Reingold labour'."

"What are you talking about, Malcolm?" Joan said angrily. "Restaurant rings and Reingold labour… Wait. Was it *Restaurierung und Reinigungslabor?*"

"I think so," Malcolm said. "You know German is not my strong suit. That's why we have the two of you."

"Malcolm," Saxon said. "'*Restaurierrung und Reingungslabor*' means Restoration and Cleaning Laboratory."

"Oh," Malcolm said. "Then what are we waiting for?"

They carefully made their way back through the displays, and back down the staircase. Malcolm led them to the door. He took his lock picks and, with a minimum of effort, picked the lock. Before opening the door, he carefully searched around the door frame to see if there were any alarms. He noted that the frosted window on the door had an alarm set to go off if anyone broke the window. He opened the door with caution. He saw a large room with several rows of laboratory benches. At regular intervals on the benches were individual work areas. Some contained large magnifying glasses and collections of fine, soft brushes and picks. Others contained jeweller's pliers, small screwdrivers and other tools for repairing jewellery. Other areas looked like they were equipped for painting restoration, and fabric repair. At the far end of the room was a large safe bolted to the floor.

They fanned out across the room, and examined each workstation. They quickly avoided the areas meant to deal with paintings and fabric, and concentrated on cleaning and jewellery repair. Although there were a few of the larger treasures at some of the workstations, the bulk of them were empty.

Malcolm made his way to the safe. He set down the psychometer, and started to get out the Palmer Fluid, when he heard a sound outside of the room. Joan jumped, and when she did, she knocked him over, right onto the psychometer. The psychometer slid hard into the metal safe, and Malcolm heard the tinkling of glass. Even more alarming, the flask of Palmer Fluid fell out of his hands and spilled on the floor. Malcolm started to curse when he heard someone check the door. Malcolm, Joan, and Saxon quickly squeezed into spaces between the chairs and the laboratory bench to hide. Malcolm cursed to himself as he realised that the empty flask of Palmer Fluid, and the psychometer, were left in full view.

The door opened and the beam of an electric torch swept the room. Malcolm pulled himself back into the space as far as he could, and held his breath.

"Was ist das?" a voice said. The guard had his revolver drawn, and moved to the empty flask and the psychometer. He examined both and suddenly stood up, shining the light around the room.

"Herauskommen. Ich weiß, dass du da bist," the guard said. Malcolm had no idea what it meant, but he was sure that it was something he didn't want to do. The guard began to check in each of the rows of laboratory benches. He turned around and started on Malcolm's row. The guard shone his light at the work bench next to Malcolm, and pulled the chair out of the workbench. He pushed it back in, and moved towards Malcolm's hiding spot. When the guard started to put his hand on the chair, Malcolm kicked it with all his might and the chair knocked into him. The guard fell with the chair on top of him, and Malcolm heard the gun clatter to the floor. He leapt from his hiding spot and jumped the guard. Before the guard could do anything, Malcolm socked him hard in the jaw. His hand exploded in pain, but it had the desired effect; the guard lay motionless on the floor.

Joan and Saxon raced over, and Joan leaned over and kissed the guard. Before Malcolm could say a word, she peeled something from her lips and stuck it in her pocket. Malcolm then realised it was some knockout agent that would keep the guard unconscious.

"Come on, Malcolm. Let's get going. It won't be long before the other guard comes looking for his friend," Saxon said.

"I'm going to have to do this the hard way," Malcolm said, pointing to the Palmer Fluid. He could see into the basement below, as the Palmer Fluid had made the concrete floor transparent. "Be very quiet."

Malcolm pulled out a specially-designed stethoscope, made for listening to safes. He decided to try the opposite direction from the vault safe. He guessed by the size, and that fact it was used daily, that the combination would likely be three numbers, and relatively simple. Each second seemed to linger for minutes, as he tried to discern the combination. Once he heard the first click, he knew that he was on his way to solving the problem of the safe. Each successive click was easier to find. After three successive clicks, he turned the latch and opened the door.

Alarm bells rang shrilly, filling the room with noise. Malcolm cursed himself for being in a hurry, and not checking for another alarm. He opened the vault and quickly searched through the shelves. He saw something covered in cloth and quickly unwrapped it, and there it was; the Spear of Destiny. Or rather the head of the spear. It was nearly two feet long with had two blades that came together in a point. The two sides were bound to the central spine, and each other, by leather and wire. A space was left between the two blades, where a long iron pin was attached to the central shaft of the spear head. The bottom third of the head was covered in thin gold sheet. But despite its construction of iron, and the addition of the gold, the spear head was surprisingly light.

Although he was sure it was broken, Malcolm turned on the psychometer to see if this was the real Spear of Destiny. Although the psychometer's power light lit up, there was no register on the gauge. To determine if the psychometer was not working, Malcolm gingerly set the Spear of Destiny on the floor, and brought out the splinter from the idol. Before Malcolm could even get the splinter near the psychometer, the Spear began to glow with a white light that filled the room. He quickly put the splinter away. "I think we have the real thing," he said. Quickly, he replaced the Spear with the replica designed by the Secret Service. To his eye, no one would tell the difference. He wrapped the replica in the cloth, and placed it back into the safe where he'd found the Spear. He started to close the safe door when he had an idea. He rummaged through the safe until he found a jewel-encrusted cross medallion, covered in hundreds of diamonds and emeralds. He put the medallion in the unconscious guard's hand, and motioned for Saxon and Joan to leave. Malcolm collected the broken psychometer, and the empty Palmer's Fluid flask, and moved as quickly and quietly as he could. As he left the room, he saw Joan and Saxon hiding in the shadow of the staircase, and he could hear running from above towards the staircase. He left the door open, and darted into the shadow of the staircase.

Within mere seconds of Malcolm reaching his hiding place, the guard scrambled down the stairs, revolver drawn. The trio collectively held their breath as the guard ran past them, and into the laboratory. They raced for the door and, as they did, they heard an argument in German behind them. Malcolm couldn't understand what was being said, but there was a lot of shouting. They darted out of the main doors as quickly and quietly as they could. Malcolm was amazed that he could hardly hear the alarm once the doors were closed. Thankfully, the guards on the far end of the courtyard seemed to pay them no mind. They slunk through the shadows to the sewer grate. Malcolm and Saxon lifted the grid and slid it to the side, then Joan and Malcolm descended quickly, by placing their shoes on either side of the ladder to turn the descent into a controlled fall. Saxon climbed down and pulled the sewer grate back in place. It fell in place with a soft thunk.

The trio started back to Mayberry's truck, and had returned up the passage when they heard alarms sounding above them. Without looking, and with no light, it was a nightmare journey to the truck. They only had their sense of touch, because they didn't dare turn on a light for fear that it might somehow be seen from above. In the pitch-black, every sound put them on edge. They held hands so as not to get separated. When they thought they had reached their original entry point, they dared to turn on the electric torch and sighed in relief when they saw the crown. They climbed up the ladder and into the waiting truck. As Saxon manoeuvred the grate into place, Malcolm pounded on the back wall of the truck and received two knocks back. The truck moved, just as Saxon put the grate in place. Joan grabbed him, and prevented him from slipping through the trap door in the bottom of the truck. He pulled himself up and shut the trap door.

They leaned against the back wall of the truck, collectively breathed a sigh of relief, and visibly relaxed. Malcolm's heart was still pounding like a drum, but a glorious sense of relief began to settle over him. The weeks of work had indeed been worth it. Although things had not gone exactly to plan, they were successful. Malcolm had an idea. He crawled away and opened his suitcase.

"What are you doing?" Joan asked. It was the first words they had spoken since leaving the Treasury.

Malcolm didn't say a word as he searched through the trunk, until he found his Granda's flask. Malcolm had filled it before leaving London to drink in celebration or depression. Holding the flask triumphantly, he closed his suitcase and returned to the back of the truck. Raising the flask, he said, "To our success," and took a long drink from the flask. He handed it Joan.

"This isn't that beastly whisky you like so much, is it?" she said hopefully.

Malcolm raised his eyebrow. Joan sighed. "Of course it is. But it is better than nothing, and I daresay we deserve a drink." She took a respectable draught, but when she finished she couldn't breathe. It felt like her throat was on fire, and her eyes were watering. She passed the flask to Saxon while she tried to regain her breath.

"Here's to us," Saxon said, taking a much more measured sip than Joan. Although he preferred gin, he was used to Malcolm's penchant for whisky, and had grown accustomed to its taste and fiery characteristics. He passed the flask back to Malcolm, who took another long sip. He felt the whisky warming and relaxing him. He felt lighter than he had in months.

"It's a relief to be done with this," Malcolm said, as he drank another sip from the flask.

Joan was finally able to speak, and took the flask from him. "I hate to disappoint you, Malcolm, but this was only the beginning. The real mission still lays before us," she said, as she took a much smaller sip of whisky.

CHAPTER 35

After a few more sips of the whisky, the trio fell asleep. They awoke nearly four hours later when the truck came to a stop. Mayberry opened the back, and asked if they wanted to eat and relieve themselves. They heartily agreed. Before they got out of the truck, Mayberry warned them to speak only in German to not arouse suspicion. Malcolm started to ask how he was to get along, but thought better of it. They were parked on the main street, which appeared to be the only street, and quickly found a small bakery.

Malcolm stuck close to Joan, and when the baker asked him something in German, Malcolm pointed to a roll with raisins in it, and Joan ordered for him. He heard Joan order *"zwei kaffee"*, and he knew he would have to make do with that hideous coffee. He couldn't wait to get back to England, indeed even France, where he could get a decent cup of tea. Mayberry paid for the food, and they sat at a small table in the front of the bakery. They sat in silence and ate their meal. Malcolm thought the roll was quite good, but could have used some butter. Once they'd eaten and refreshed themselves, they climbed back into the truck. As they returned to the truck, Mayberry explained that they still had another four hours until they crossed the border into Italy, and even longer before they stopped in Tolmezzo for the night.

The trio slept for most of the rest of the journey. When they finally stopped five hours later, Mayberry was exhausted. They found an inn and took four rooms. Mayberry handed Joan a wallet full of various currency, and retired straight to his room to catch some much-needed sleep. In flawless Italian, Joan asked for directions to a good restaurant, and the host was kind enough to direct them to a bistro. They enjoyed a meal of spaghetti, red sauce, and meat balls, and a bottle of a sweet red wine. Malcolm did not have a great deal of experience with eating spaghetti, and tried to emulate Joan's use of the spoon and the fork to twirl the pasta. Despite the mess he made, Malcolm enjoyed the meal and felt almost too full to move. They returned to the inn and, despite the sleep they'd had in the truck, they all fell asleep quickly and soundly.

They rose early the next day to get to their destination: Venice. The trip would only take about four hours. Now that they were past the border, Mayberry invited someone to join him in the front of the truck. Saxon quickly volunteered, because he sensed that Malcolm and Joan would rather be alone. Breakfast consisted of pastries, and an extremely bitter variation of coffee called espresso. All Malcolm could think was that the more he tried coffee, the better he liked tea.

Joan and Malcolm climbed in the back of the truck. They were both quiet and didn't say a word. Malcolm put his arm around Joan and held her close. She melted into the hug and snuggled up to him. Before he knew it, his mouth found hers, and they started kissing. He hadn't realised how long it had been since they'd had even a moment like this together. Their kissing became more insistent, and soon they were lost in one another.

When they had recovered, Malcolm said, "That was unexpected, but very worth it. It feels like forever since we've been alone."

"I agree," Joan purred. She snuggled next to him with her head on his chest.

"Do you think we'll ever get a chance to spend more time together?" Malcolm asked.

"We do have our trip to London. We can pose as a married couple."

"That's all we ever seem to do," Malcolm said. "Pretend to be married."

Joan sat straight up. "What do you mean by that?"

Malcolm's stomach sank. He hadn't meant to start this fight again. "Nothing, Joan. I understand. You don't want to be married. I even appreciate the reason more than I did before. I just meant that we only get these stolen moments, and I don't know if that's enough."

"Oh," Joan said rather curtly. She moved away from Malcolm, and started to find her clothes. "What do you suggest?" Malcolm could almost feel the iciness in her voice.

"I don't know. I do know that I love you, Joan, and I know that I want to spend as much time with you as I can. But I know we both want different things. I want to return to the Air Service; you wish to continue working for the Secret Service. You have no desire to be tied down, and I understand. I was livid when I thought you'd had me drummed out of the Air Service, just so I could be on this mission with you. But I realised that's exactly what I was asking of you, by asking you to marry me."

Joan did not respond, but lowered her head, so Malcolm could not see her face. "Malcolm, I wasn't lying when I said I had no idea that Mycroft would do that. I wish to God I had never said a word."

Malcolm reached over and took her hand. She didn't pull away. "I know," he said gently. "Besides, it hasn't been all bad. I've spent more time with you in the last few months than for the two years I've known you."

She still couldn't look him in the face. "But you've lost so much because of me. I hate that I had anything to do with that."

"It's fine," he said. "It made me realise why you hate the thought of marriage. One of us must sacrifice to make the other happy, and we're both too stubborn to do that. Which is why I've decided that whenever we get done with this mission, I'm going to sell the engagement ring."

Joan removed her hand from Malcolm's. Confused, he asked, "Isn't that what you wanted?"

"Yes, no… I don't know!"

Malcolm said nothing, waiting to see if she would say more. "What's the matter? I thought you didn't want to get married."

"I don't," Joan said. "I would have turned you down, but I think deep down, I wanted to be asked. Even if I said no."

"Joan, that makes no sense," he said gently.

"Don't you think I know that?" she snarled. "You're so damned logical about everything. Everything is black and white to you; if it's this, then it's not that. My world isn't black and white; everything is shades of grey. In my mind, it's not contradictory to want to be asked to be married, and yet not want to be married. It's two different things, to know that someone cares about me enough to ask me to spend the rest of their life with me, and another to accept that I will be bound in a role for the rest of my life."

"Surely you know how I feel? I've tried to talk to you about marriage many times, and you push me away every time. How am I supposed to ask you when you won't let me?"

"I don't know!" she blurted. In the dim light of their electric torches, he could see tears flowing down her cheeks. "I'm sorry, Malcolm. I'm not trying to be difficult on purpose." She sniffed, and used her hand to wipe her face. "You're right," she said. "You probably should just sell the ring. I'm not being fair to you by making you hold onto it."

Malcolm reached for her hand. He expected her to pull it away, but she didn't. "I love you, Joan. I want to spend the rest of my life loving you. But if it's only a collection of stolen moments, so be it. I won't do anything hasty about selling the ring."

She squeezed his hand, and looked up at him with a wan smile. "Thank you, Malcolm. I know I sometimes make it hard to love me. And I…" She hesitated. "…love you, too. God, why is it so hard for me to say that? I absolutely feel that way about you, but why is it so hard for me to put it into words?"

"Maybe because you live in a world where you can't trust a single soul. Being in love is trusting a part of yourself to someone else."

She turned to him, and brushed a stray lock of hair from his face. "When did you get so wise about love?"

"I learned from the best," he said, gently caressing her cheek.

"Flatterer," she laughed. "Malcolm, why do you put up with me?"

"Because I love you. The Lord Almighty knows that you are a challenge, but I really like the making up."

"Me too," she said. Her eyes flashed as she pulled him close, and kissed him urgently.

Again, the spark between them ignited a fire that neither could resist. When they were spent, they put on their clothes and held each other, as they drifted off to a contented sleep.

The next thing they knew, the doors opened, blinding them with light. It took a few seconds for their eyes to become accustomed to the daylight. When both could see, Malcolm jumped out of the back of the truck, and helped Joan down. He looked up and found that they had reached Venice. It wasn't the Venice of the famous canals, but the Venice that was still attached to the mainland of Italy. They had arrived near the *Piazzale Donatori di Sangue*. They walked to the British Consulate's office, a nondescript building that looked as if it could equally be home to an accountancy.

Upon entering, they were immediately greeted by a young clerk in bright-sounding Italian. Malcolm had always thought that the lilting quality of Italian made it sound happy, or at least passionate. Joan replied in perfect Italian, and then switched to English for the benefit of everyone else. Once Joan introduced the party, the clerk immediately ushered them into a meeting room. Within a few minutes, he returned with a tray of small sandwiches, pastries, a pot of coffee and, to Malcolm's great delight, a pot of tea. Malcolm went straight for the tea, and poured himself two cups before anyone else could have it. When they looked at him, he said, "I have been forced to drink coffee for the last week, and I am making up for lost time."

Once they had finished eating, and Malcolm had drained the dregs from the teapot, the clerk brought in a man who was near Malcolm's age, and introduced him as Assistant Diplomat Tipton Banks. The diplomat joined them at the meeting table, and nodded to the clerk in dismissal. When the clerk closed the door, Banks said, "I am very glad that you have arrived here. We were concerned when you vanished from the conference, and more so when we received your message. We didn't hear anything else until we heard the news about the attempted robbery at the Imperial Treasury of Vienna."

"Robbery?" Joan asked.

"Yes, apparently one of the guards was caught red-handed with a gem-encrusted medallion worth a small fortune. He claims that there was someone else in the Treasury, and he has no memory of taking the medallion." He paused. "You wouldn't have anything to do with that, would you?" he said with a smile.

"Not at all," Joan said.

"When we didn't hear from you after Mr. Mayberry's message, we were worried. We figured that given your choices, you would come here. I am glad that I was correct." He opened a file he'd brought with him, and handed the four of them a large envelope. "You'll find four new passports, tickets, and lodging reservations for the trip to England, in addition to money split out into the currency of the various countries."

"I must contact the Home Office. Am I to say that your mission was a success?" Banks asked.

"Yes," Joan said. "Apparently, a complete success."

"And Mr. Mayberry," Banks said. "I have been instructed by Mr. Holmes to convey his deepest thanks for your service on this mission, and to advise you that you will have your choice of assignments when you return to London."

Mayberry, who until this time had seemed bored, perked up. "Thank you, sir. Please relay my thanks to Mr. Holmes."

"I will do that. We have arranged for you to stay at a nearby hotel, and tomorrow you will take the train from Venice to Geneva. After a brief stopover in Geneva, you'll take another train to Paris, and then a chartered airship to London. Until tomorrow, please enjoy all that Venice has to offer. If you'll excuse me, I must report back. *Ciao.*"

Within moments, the young clerk came back to show them out of the consulate, and to provide directions to the hotel. Their luggage from the truck was already waiting for them when they arrived, and had already been taken to their rooms. To Malcolm's and Joan's delight, they found that their passports listed them as Mr. Malcolm and Mrs. Joan McGuffin, and that their arrangements had been made as a married couple. Malcolm was relieved that he would not have to find a way to sneak around so that they could be together.

Malcolm and Joan settled into their room, and both took luxurious showers, finally getting the opportunity to wash the stink of the sewers off themselves. When they were finished, they laid together on the bed, just holding one another. They finally roused themselves, and returned to the lobby to meet Mayberry and Saxon for dinner.

Joan had visited Venice many times on her travels, and knew exactly where to go. She took them to a small *ristorante* on the waterfront, where they could look out and see the Venice famous for its canals, bridges, and gondolas. When the server came to take their orders, Joan translated for the party, and took the lead in offering suggestions. She ordered *sarde in seor*, an appetiser of fried sardines, marinated with vinegar, onions, and raisins. For the primo, or main course, she suggested *fegato alla veneziana*, calf liver and caramelised onions on polenta, for Saxon and Malcolm. For Mayberry, she suggested *polenta e schie*, fried shrimp on polenta; while for herself she ordered *bigoli in salsa*, an anchovy and onion sauce, served with a very wide pasta. Malcolm was thankful for a choice that did not involve pasta, as he still had not mastered the art of eating it. No one was disappointed in the choices that Joan had made for them.

They sat outside, and as the sunlight faded, they watched the lights of Venice turn on, until it was a glow of gold in the midnight blue of dusk. They talked, ate, and drank, and thoroughly enjoyed themselves. Mayberry was an accomplished raconteur; his stories of his time in the Secret Service kept them in stitches.

Reluctantly, they tore themselves away from the restaurant, and returned to the hotel. Bidding everyone a good night, Malcolm and Joan returned to their room. He immediately went to the bathroom and changed into his night clothes, before getting into bed. When he left, Joan said, "Don't get too comfortable in bed. I may have a surprise for you if you stay awake," as she winked at him and closed the door of the bathroom behind her.

Malcolm lay there, and he was having a hard time trying to stay awake. He felt contented, and the meal they'd had made him feel satiated. In fact, he couldn't remember the last time he had felt this at peace. He felt his eyes start to close when he heard the bathroom door open. He opened his eyes and sat up with a jerk.

Joan stood there in a black corset over a black silk chemise and drawers. A pair of black garters held up her black silk stockings. "Was this worth the wait, Mr. McGuffin?" She climbed into the bed, and Malcolm swore that she almost slithered to him.

"Most definitely," he said as he kissed her.

CHAPTER 36

hey rose early to catch their train. Before they left the railroad station, Joan purchased a copy of *Il Gazzettino*, the local newspaper. As Banks had said, the issue had a sensational story about the guard, who was thwarted in his audacious attempt to steal a treasure of the Austro-Hungarian Empire. The story had maintained that the guard, one Johann Reisinger, gassed his partner with ether, and attempted to steal a jewel-encrusted Grand Cross of the Order of Maria Theresa. Reisinger maintained his innocence, and insisted that there were one or more intruders in the Treasury that he had attempted to apprehend. A military tribunal was scheduled, where Reisinger would be charged with treason. Malcolm sighed and Joan said, "Don't feel bad, Malcolm. He would have killed or captured you. Then it would be you facing the charges, or more likely all of us."

"For the record, not me," Mayberry said. "If you had been caught, I would have made for Venice anyway."

Joan shot him a withering look, and Mayberry put up his hands and turned away from the conversation.

"It still doesn't make it easier to know that I have condemned an innocent man to die." Malcolm said.

Joan squeezed his hand. "I know, Malcolm. It's one of your more endearing qualities. But try not to let it bother you."

The train chugged its way west through Padua, Verona, and Bergamo, before turning northwest at Milan, and heading into the mountains and Switzerland. The closer they got to Switzerland, the more the guard's fate played on Malcolm's mind. He had shot at men, likely killed them, and it didn't bother him. Maybe because the men he'd shot were firing back, and it was 'kill or be killed'. But this felt like he had put a loaded gun to the head of an innocent man, and pulled the trigger. He was sullen and withdrawn. Joan's attempts at conversation were met with grunts, or no response at all. After a while, he left the dining car and returned to his cabin.

After some time, Joan entered the cabin. Malcolm was lying on the bed. She sat next to him on the edge of the bed. "What's wrong, Malcolm? You haven't said two words to me since this morning. Is the honeymoon over already?"

Malcolm didn't reply.

"It's that guard, isn't it?"

"I don't want to talk about it," Malcolm said.

"Clearly you need to talk about it, because you're acting like a sulking baby," she said.

"I'm not sulking," he said. "For your information, I'm brooding."

"Oh, is that what it is?" she said. She reached for his hand. "I know it's hard, Malcolm. It's never a good thing to think that you are responsible for someone else's death. And I won't tell you to just get over it." She paused and whispered. "If you do, it becomes that much easier the next time, and before you know it, there is no regret."

Malcolm said nothing for a long moment. "Then what do I do?"

"For now? There's nothing you can do. When we get to Geneva, I'll make enquiries to see if something can be done for him."

"Really? That would help a great deal." Malcolm said.

"On one condition," Joan said.

"What?"

"That you provide your new wife, Mrs. Joan McGuffin, with a splendid honeymoon," she said, settling on the bed next to him.

Malcolm took her in his arms and kissed her. "Thank you, Joan."

She smiled. "You're welcome."

Malcolm was struck with a sudden thought. "You said we're stopping in Geneva? Maybe we should try to see your mother while we're there."

Joan bolted out of his arms and sat upright. "Absolutely, under no terms whatsoever, am I taking you to meet my mother."

"Are you ashamed of me?" Malcolm asked.

"I'm ashamed of her!" Joan said. Malcolm could see that she was all but shaking. She paused for a moment, and took a deep breath before continuing. "And I haven't told her I'm alive, so it would come as something of a shock if I just showed up."

"You haven't told her you're alive? Why not?"

Joan sighed. "It's complicated. My mother never approved of my career in the Secret Service. She thought I should try to marry one of the nobility of Europe to restore our name. She thought that marrying my father would help her fortunes, and it did."

"My mother is selfish; she only looks at people with a view to how she can use them to her advantage. Take me. In her eyes, all I was good for was improving the family station by marrying. When I wouldn't do that, I was of no use to her."

"And…" Joan continued, "if I brought you to meet her, she would eat you alive. I know interrogators who could learn a few things from her."

"Sounds just like my mum," Malcolm said.

"She's as good at reading people as I am; it's probably where I get it from."

"Why haven't you told her you're alive?"

"I think she would be happier thinking that she had been right that I shouldn't have joined the Secret Service, than happier that I'm not dead. Sometimes mothers and daughters can't get along."

"What about your father?" Malcolm asked. "Does he know?"

"Yes, I went and told him. I get along famously with my father," she said. "That wasn't always the case, but he thinks that the Secret Service is much like the military, so he thinks I've followed in his footsteps. He was a Colonel in the Army. At first, I think he and Mum were happy. But sometime while I was growing up, they drifted apart. I imagine that my father began to see my mother for who she is. My father has been more than decent to my mother, far more than he owes her, I daresay. But they stopped the pretense of their marriage some time ago. He returned to Britain while I was at university, and she stayed at their villa in Geneva."

"After I told you I was alive, I found out he was staying in at his estate in Kent. He cried tears of joy when he first realised it was me, but quickly covered them up, claiming he had something in his eye. We sat and talked for quite some time, and I try to stop by when I can."

"Your family has an estate? I'm not surprised, but I never suspected," Malcolm said. He realised exactly why she didn't want him meeting her mother. He could only imagine what would happen if the daughter, that she sought to marry to a nobleman of Europe, arrived home with the son of a welder and his wife, who lived in a flat over a greengrocer.

"Fine, scratch visiting your mother as a colossally bad idea. What would you like to do while we're in Geneva?"

"There are a few places I haven't seen since university. I would like to share some of them with you, Mr. McGuffin," Joan said. She was smiling now, and Malcolm could hear the excitement in her voice.

They spent the rest of the journey in their cabin, content to just hold hands and watch first the Italian, and then the Swiss, scenery fly by in a blur. They reached Geneva at nearly nine o'clock. They took a carriage to the hotel, and found a small café where they could get a light meal, before turning in for the night.

Malcolm and Joan left early the next morning, leaving a note for Saxon and Mayberry that they would be back to pick them up for dinner that night. They walked among the shops that lined the streets, holding hands. Joan showed Malcolm the school she attended when she was young, and the library where she spent much of her time as a teenager. They purchased a picnic lunch from street vendors, and ate a relaxing lunch at a park with a view of Lake Geneva. They walked to a secluded part of the park, and she showed Malcolm where she received her first kiss. When everyone met for dinner, Joan led the party to her favourite restaurant in Geneva: *Café du Soleil*. Joan introduced them to the Swiss tradition of fondue; dipping cubes of bread into melted cheese, held in a special ceramic pot called a *caquelon*. She ordered a *valaisanne* plate, consisting of dried meats, ham, cheese, and bacon, served with rye bread, tomatoes, and gherkins. By this point, they decided to skip an actual entrée, and instead went straight to dessert; a round of green tarts called *carac*. The green came from a layer of fondant, over a shortbread crust, filled with Swiss chocolate. Malcolm found himself eating more than he should have, as he loved the contrast between the chocolate and the shortbread crust.

When they returned to the hotel, the fresh air, exercise, and the meal, had left Malcolm very drowsy and he promptly fell asleep. They awoke the next morning and boarded the train for Paris. The train brought them into Paris in the early evening, where they found a car waiting to drive them nearly twenty miles south to the aerodrome Port Aviation, which Malcolm thought was a very fitting name. As they drove into the aerodrome, Malcolm looked at airships docked there. He recognised the colours of the commercial airship lines from France, Britain, and Germany.

At the far end was a much smaller airship. Its skin was a patchwork of material; patches of burgundy, mustard, royal blue, white, silver, and black, gave the ship the appearance of a giant quilt. Malcolm wondered how the airship could hold any air. The gondola looked like it could barely hold two people; four seemed completely out of the question. Much to Malcolm's consternation, it quickly became clear that the decrepit-looking airship was their destination. As they approached the patchwork airship, Malcolm tried to assess the ship's airworthiness. The balloon skeleton appeared to be in good shape; there was no distortion that he could see. On further examination, he could see that the balloon had been patched with great care, and he now withdrew his assessment that it would leak. He examined the single propeller that drove the airship. Malcolm guessed, based on the size, that the little airship would be nimble. His rising excitement quickly dissipated when he saw a single exhaust line rising straight up from the rear of the gondola, and saw black stains on the balloon's fabric. Malcolm surmised that the engine was often out of adjustment and burning oil.

When the car came to a stop, they all got out and retrieved their luggage. Malcolm watched as a very tall man approached with a lurching limp, and he soon realised that one of his legs was mechanical. The man wore a military jacket, cut off at the sleeves, over a long sleeve shirt. He wore jodhpurs, tucked into long black boots that had not seen polish in quite a while. He was bald, and his black skin glistened with sweat. He held out a huge hand, and with a deep voice said. "I'm Colfax Mingo, Captain of the *RAS Uhuru*. Welcome aboard!"

Malcolm shook the proffered hand, and his own was crushed by the firm handshake of the captain. Saxon and Mayberry also tried to mask a wince when the mountain of a man shook their hands. But with Joan, he was a gentleman; kissing her hand gently, and helping her into the gondola.

"Saxon and I know our way around an airship. Do you need a hand with anything?"

"No, I'm fine. I've set my operation up so I can do this all on my own," Colfax said. "Just settle in, and we can talk once we're in the air," he said, and turned to untying the tether ropes.

Mayberry, Saxon, and Malcolm loaded the luggage into the airship. The area near the gangplank, that would be the cargo hold, seemed too small for a commercial vessel. As Malcolm looked around, he understood. A door in the wall, at the tail of the airship, obviously led to the engine room. Looking toward the front of the airship, the wall of the cargo hold opened into a hallway. As Malcolm approached the hallway, he realised the corner was hinged. As he moved down the hall, the wall had a door, that opened into a small room that contained a pull-down bed. Malcolm realised that this wall was then pinned to the next set of walls that made the next cabin. He now understood; the walls of the rooms could be folded back to increase cargo space, or, as it was now, to be used as passenger space.

They placed their luggage in the rooms and Malcolm explored. The bed folded down from the side of the wall, and Malcolm was pleased to discover a toilet that pulled up from the floor. Everything in the room was made to fold away, so that the space could be used for cargo if needed. He travelled up the hallway and past the temporary cabins, and he found permanent spaces. On one side was a complete washroom with a shower, and past that, what could only be the captain's cabin. On the other side was a single room, which Malcolm could see was the galley and dining area. The hallway ended in the cockpit of the airship. Despite wanting to look around the cockpit, he would never invade the space of another captain.

Within a few minutes, Colfax pulled himself into the gondola, pulled in the gangplank, and shut the door. Seeing Malcolm, he said, "It will probably be best if you sit in the galley until we get aloft. There are ropes that can be used to tie you into the seat." Colfax disappeared behind the door at the front of the airship.

Saxon looked at Malcolm and he shrugged. He led them into the galley. He found the seats were bolted to the floor. They sat around the table, and Saxon and Malcolm used their knowledge of naval knots to tie first Joan, and then Mayberry, to their respective chairs, and then their own. Within a few minutes, Malcolm heard the engine start to chug. There was an ever-so-slight lurch, which indicated that they had lifted off from the ground.

After about twenty minutes, the door opened and Colfax joined them in the galley. "We have a successful lift off. You can untie yourselves now. Can I get anyone a drink?"

"That would be wonderful," Joan said.

"Let's see if I've got this right," Colfax said. "Vodka for the lady, whisky for you," he said, indicating Malcolm. "Gin for you," he said, pointing to Saxon, "and brandy for you," pointing at Mayberry.

"I'm impressed," Joan said. "How did you know?"

"I didn't really; I guessed. I was given specific orders about what to stock. Since I brought four bottles and there are four of you, I surmised that each of you had distinct tastes. He…" Colfax said, pointing to Malcolm, "is obviously a Scot by accent, so I was confident he would have the whisky. You," he said, indicating Saxon, "have the look of a gin drinker, and I guessed by your age," he said, pointing now to Mayberry, "that you would favour brandy. That left vodka for you," he said, nodding to Joan.

"Impressive," Joan said. As drinks were poured, they introduced themselves to the captain properly. Malcolm said, "Charles and I used to serve on an airship; we would be honoured if we could tour your ship."

"You've seen most of what there is to see," Colfax said jovially. "What did you do?"

"I was an engineer and…" Malcolm hesitated, realising that Saxon's rank of gunnery officer would mark him as military.

"And I was a navigator." Saxon added. Malcolm tried to keep a straight face, because navigation was never Saxon's strong suit.

"Must have been a pretty big vessel to pay for an engineer and a navigator. Commercial or military?" Colfax asked,."Military," Malcolm said. He figured it would be easier to be truthful than to lie.

"Really?" Colfax asked. "What ship?"

"HMA *Firefly*," Malcolm said, which in fact was one of the first airships where he'd served as an engineer.

"I'm familiar with her." Colfax said. "Not a bad ship, if a little underpowered."

"I agree," Malcolm said. "I was constantly doing anything I could to coax more power out of her over-worked engines." He took the proffered glass of whisky, and waited for everyone else to be served. When everyone had a drink, Malcolm raised his glass. "A toast to our captain. May he have untroubled air, and safe passage home!"

"Since this isn't a military ship, you can bring your drinks and I'll give you the grand tour. We are in the galley and mess hall for the military types, or the kitchen and dining room for the civilians. If you'll follow me," Colfax said, indicating the door.

"Over there," Colfax said, pointing to the door almost directly across the hall, "is the shower. You all have toilets in your rooms, in case you hadn't discovered them." He continued down the hallway to the small cargo area. "This is my cargo bay. The cabins that you have…"

"Fold into the walls when you need more space in the cargo hold," Malcolm interrupted. "Sorry, I shouldn't have interrupted you. I just thought it was such a brilliant design."

"Thank you," Colfax said. "The rooms were my design, so that I could make money taking personal charters, as well as haul cargo." He continued over to the last door. "And here is the engine room, such as it is." Colfax opened the door, and the smell of machine oil, engine exhaust, and fuel oil, brought Malcolm back to the engine room on the *Daedalus*. Although he learned to enjoy being the captain, there were times that he would have given anything to tear down one of the engines. It was what Malcolm had expected: one giant engine housing, sitting in the middle of the room, with a mismatched collection of ductwork and hoses running everywhere. Spare parts, some in good condition, others disassembled with their guts all over the floor, were strewn everywhere. The tool box was open, and it looked like some of the tools had returned to their place, the others lying around the open box. For a moment, the two captains locked eyes, and Malcolm could tell Colfax was embarrassed by the state of his engine room. "Come," Colfax said. "Let me show you the bridge, although there's only enough room for one at a time."

When it was Malcolm's turn, he was impressed. Although it was compact, everything was laid out so that the captain could see it easily. While Malcolm had grown to like the ship's wheel on the *Daedalus*, the *Uhuru* used the more standard lever system to control vertical and horizontal movement. The advantage was that the lever had a locking mechanism, whereas Malcolm had had to fashion his own. Malcolm noted a co-pilot's seat, but it was currently filled with stacks of maps and charts. Malcolm was sure it had not been used by a person in a very long time.

They returned to the galley to finish their drinks. "I should have you in London by tomorrow morning. The *Uhuru* isn't the fastest ship, but she will get us where we need to go."

"It must be tough being a one-man crew, even on a ship of this size," Malcolm said.

"Most of the time, it's manageable," Colfax said. "It's only when the engine acts up, while I'm trying to navigate around a storm, that it gets a little dicey."

"How did you acquire your ship?" Malcolm asked.

"Do you mean how could someone like me afford an airship?" Colfax said, arching an eyebrow.

"No, I meant..." Malcolm stammered.

"I didn't purchase it. I won it in a bet," Colfax said with a smile.

"Really? This sounds like an interesting story," Joan offered, trying to help Malcolm out of his situation.

"I suppose I should start at the beginning," Colfax said. "I'm from Kenya, if you couldn't guess. My father was an educated man, and worked for the Imperial British East Africa Company, as a translator for the local tribes. My family was better off than many of my people, and he used his position to allow me to attend a church-run school. The staff there saw great potential in me, and they arranged for me to attend Cambridge on a scholarship for engineering."

"I jumped at the chance," he continued. "However, what they hadn't told me was that the terms of my scholarship involved serving the British Empire in some capacity after I graduated. I had no desire to be a clerk, stuck between the Empire and native people. I joined the Air Service. But despite my degree in engineering, I would not be accepted into the officer corps, so I had to serve as an enlisted man."

"It wasn't awful, but I did resent the engineering officers, because I knew more than they did, and I was only fit to do the manual work. But I learned a great deal."

He paused. "I'd probably still be serving if it weren't for this," he said, pointing to his mechanical leg. "I was serving aboard the HMA *Mars*. We were travelling to Kenya, when the ship was hit by a terrible storm. The captain panicked, overreacted, and we crashed in the Mau Forest. During the crash, my leg was crushed by one of the engines, when it came loose from its housing. At this point, we were nearly forty miles from a village of any size, and roughly eighty miles from

Nairobi. Most of the crew survived, but we lost many of the bridge officers as we went down nose first. Most of the remaining officers were barely out of the Academy, so I took charge. We stripped the *Mars* of anything useful, handed out the provisions, and started walking our way out of the forest. The officers didn't like it at first, but acquiesced when pressed about what we should do."

"We walked for four days until we encountered a village. The village was too small to have any way to contact Nairobi, so we simply traded for more supplies and kept on walking. I handled the dialogue with the villagers, as I was the only one who could speak Swahili. We made it to Nairobi nearly a week after the crash. I had kept up by splinting my leg heavily, but the jungle is not a good place to have a broken limb. By the time I got to Nairobi, I was feverish, and the leg had turned green and smelled awful. Truly, I didn't notice the smell, because after a week of travelling through jungle and plains, I honestly couldn't tell."

"I was hospitalised immediately, and the doctor removed the leg, thus ending my career in the Air Service. Before they booted me out, I did receive a notice for my role in securing our return. There I was, a one-legged engineer with no future. I returned to my home, and clerked with my father for a while. I also started work on this," he said, as he tapped his mechanical leg. "When I was satisfied that the leg was working, I started looking for work as an airship mechanic. Despite my degree from Cambridge, and my impeccable grasp of the King's English, most colonials didn't think I could possibly know anything about engines. I did manage to get a job at the Nairobi Air Ship Repair Company, owned by Newton Monroe, solely because he knew he could pay me almost nothing. I worked for him for a couple of years, when I noticed that this ship was never maintained, never flown. I asked Monroe about it and he said, 'That thing? We haven't been able to keep it in the air for more than a day at a time. I think the thing is cursed. If you can fix it, you can have it. Good riddance!' I asked for that in writing, and he looked at me funny. He laughed and said, 'If you can get that piece of crap to fly, you deserve it. But, you still have to do your regular work.'"

"Every spare moment I had, I started working on it. I pulled it apart and put it back together again, piece by piece. When Monroe realised that I might succeed, he started doubling my workload. But I kept at it, and almost two years after I started, I took Monroe up in my airship. Although Monroe was always a bit of a scoundrel, he did honour his agreement, and I left his employ. Now I travel the world, taking passengers and cargo to any place I'm asked. And," he said meaningfully, "I don't ask any questions."

"I assume the name, *Uhuru*, is Swahili. What does it mean?" asked Saxon.

"*Uhuru* is the Swahili word for 'freedom'. I thought it an apt name. And, despite the superstition of bad luck in changing a ship's name, I have had no trouble since rechristening her. I think she just didn't have the right name," Colfax added.

They continued to talk as Colfax made a simple meal of chicken soup and dumplings, which was a welcome relief from the rich food that they had been eating since they arrived in Venice. Drinks and conversation flowed easily. Colfax was an excellent storyteller, and kept them all enthralled with several of his somewhat dubious adventures, which included smuggling a concubine of the Emir out of Riyadh, and back to Britain, after her cover as an agent of the British Empire was revealed.

As they settled into their small cabins for the night, Malcolm was impressed by the ingenious use of space. The cabins could be configured into two small cabins, like they were now, or combined into one large cabin. The toilets, that remained hidden until needed, made the cabins seem less primitive. The bed was not forgiving, but he would only spend one night on it, and Malcolm had slept on much worse in his career.

The next morning, Malcolm arose to the smell of toast, bacon, and fresh-brewed tea. He hurried to the galley and found a rack full of several pieces of toast, a jar of marmalade, a plate full of bacon, and a pot covered in a cosy. Malcolm wasted no time in pouring a cup of strong, black tea. He piled his plate with several rashers of bacon, and toast, buttered and slathered with marmalade. He helped himself to a second cup of tea, and when he was finished, he went to the cockpit and knocked on the door.

"Come," Colfax said.

"Sorry to bother you, I was just wondering when we would... Oh, never mind," Malcolm said. Through the cockpit's window, he could see the White Cliffs of Dover.

"I'd say another four hours," Colfax said. He reached over and pushed the maps and charts off the co-pilot's chair. "Please, have a seat. I could use the company, and it seems no one else is up yet."

"I daresay, I hope I left them enough food," Malcolm said sheepishly. "I assumed I was the last one up."

"It appears that your friends may have imbibed a little too much last night. What about you?"

"Right as rain," Malcolm said, as he squeezed into the co-pilot's seat.

"Are you really an engineer?" Colfax said.

"Absolutely," Malcolm said. "I got my engineering training through the Navy, and went back to learn about airships. My first posting was a coal-burning ship and, as a midshipman, I got the pleasure of stoking the fire."

"Ah, but at least you were an officer," Colfax said.

"I'm sorry that you were never made an officer. From what you've done with this ship, it obviously was the Air Service's loss."

Colfax turned and looked at Malcolm. He was trying to determine if Malcolm was just being diplomatic, or if he meant it. Malcolm appeared earnest. He smiled and said, "You know, Malcolm, if you ever want to get back on an airship, I could use someone like you."

"I heartily appreciate the consideration, but I'm afraid I'll have to decline," Malcolm said, a little disappointed.

"I understand, the missus wants you to stop flying, and settle down," Colfax said.

"The missus? What, no," Malcolm stammered, and then remembered his cover as a married man. "Actually, yes. She wants me to settle down to a boring desk job."

"She must be someone special to make you give this up," Colfax said, indicating the sky before him.

"Yes, she is," Malcolm lied. He honestly didn't know if he could give up the air for her, or for anyone for that matter. "I've taken enough of your time. I'll let you get to it, sir," Malcolm said, and threw a smart salute to Colfax as he left the cabin.

rue to his word, the *Uhuru* touched down four hours later at Hendon Aerodrome, and they found a car waiting to take them back to London. As Malcolm departed, he stopped to shake Colfax's hand. "It was a pleasure to meet you, and I wish you fair skies."

"Thank you, Malcolm," he said. "Who knows? Maybe our paths will cross someday," he said with a smile.

"I hope so," Malcolm said. When he turned around, he realised that the luggage had already been packed away, and everyone was already waiting in the large coach. Although the skies were generally clear, the smoke of the chimneys and factory smoke stacks left everything in a foggy haze. It seemed to be uncomfortably warm, and the humidity made the air feel like a thick, wet blanket. As the car took them back to the centre of London, the oppressive nature of the weather began to increase. The car dropped them off at Charing Cross, and Joan led them to the secret train line that took them to the Secret Service. Before they could even unpack, they were summoned for a meeting with Mycroft Holmes.

They met in the large library meeting room, where Malcolm and Saxon had first joined the Secret Service only a few months ago. *Had it only been a few months?* Malcolm thought. Mycroft Holmes and Nigel Sinclair were sitting at the table. On a cart near the table, Malcolm recognised one of the psychometers he'd built, and something shrouded in cloth, which Malcolm assumed was the noxious idol.

"Hail the conquering heroes," Mycroft said dryly. "Congratulations on a well-executed operation. So far, there has been no discovery that we now possess the true Spear of Destiny. However, to make sure, I asked to have a psychometer brought in, as I understand that you were unable to measure it while you were in Vienna. Malcolm, would you do the honours?"

Joan carried the Spear, still wrapped in cloth, and set it gingerly on the table. She uncovered it, and perhaps it was a trick of the light, but Malcolm thought the gold shone brighter than it should. He walked over to the shrouded item, and was not surprised to uncover the idol of Cthulhu. It made his insides cold just looking at it. He turned on the psychometer and measured the spiritual energy from the idol, using that to set a baseline. The needle moved to the centre of the gauge just like he expected.

He covered the idol and set it on the floor, several feet away from the table and the Spear. As he wheeled the cart closer to the table where the Spear lay, the needle on the psychometer started moving. When he was still a yard away, the needle was nearing the maximum level on the gauge. Malcolm lifted the detector wand, and brought it closer to the Spear. The needle on psychometer went to the far-right side of the gauge. As he brought the wand closer to the Spear, the psychometer emitted an audible hum. The closer Malcolm brought the wand to the Spear, the higher and louder the sound became. The volume pitch intensified until there was suddenly a loud pop. The psychometer's needle fell to the far left, and a puff of smoke drifted up from the device.

"It appears that you were successful. This must be the Spear of Destiny," Mycroft said.

"I should say so," Malcolm said. "The psychometer was calibrated on a logarithmic scale. That means each number represents ten times the amount of psychic energy of the number before it. The baseline reading was five, and the maximum of the gauge was ten. That means at the time that we stopped measuring it, it was already ten thousand times stronger than the energy from the idol."

"I should say, we may never have the opportunity to study an artifact like this again," Sinclair said in awe. The group stood around the Spear, each looking at it with new appreciation.

"I'm afraid we won't have much time for that now," Mycroft said, indicating that they should take seats at the table. "While you have been travelling the continent, I have had our people scouring the globe for news of a planetary alignment. And as luck would have it, we found a news article from one H. Lovecraft in the *Providence Tribune*. It describes a rare conjunction of Earth, Mars, Jupiter, Saturn, and the star Antares, predicted by the staff at the Ladd Observatory. We described this conjunction to our guest, and he believes this is the alignment that will cause Cthulhu to rise."

Mycroft continued. "I've asked our associates in the Royal Astronomical Society for any information about this conjunction, and they were deucedly unhelpful, calling it a trivial event that means nothing in true science terms."

"But we are running out of time. The article says that the conjunction will be visible from one spot on earth in just over a month's time. In the last few months, there have been a marked increase in the number of people committed to asylums for delusions. Traditional weather patterns have been disrupted, and there have been an increased number of reported earthquakes. All of this points to some sort of disjuncture in the order of nature."

"I daresay that my contacts in the world of the supernatural feel a great sense of foreboding," Nigel interjected. "The number of attacks by vampires, and other creatures, has risen over the last few months."

"We need to find out where the conjunction will occur, and I think the only way we're going to find that out is to talk to Mr. Lovecraft," Mycroft said. "I've taken the liberty of creating new papers for Malcolm and Charles, to appear as members of the Royal Astronomical Society, intent on speaking to Mr. Lovecraft. Meanwhile, Nigel has asked to spend some time at Miskatonic University, which is not far from Providence, or so I'm told. He will try to find any information that might help you in your task."

Mycroft paused. "I don't think I have to remind you of the gravity of your task, but I will. You must confront, and prevent, this entity from rising and stretching its shadow over the world. Failure in this mission means the world as we know it comes to an end, and we all fall into madness."

Everyone was silent. Malcolm realised the enormity of the task that there were about to undertake. Mycroft's voice shook him out of his daze. "Malcolm and Charles, gather any gear you may possibly need. I have no idea if you are going to Africa, or Antarctica, or any place in between, so gather a bit of everything. Charlotte, you and I will work out the logistics of the trip. Nigel, you will mount the Spear, and prepare it for the trip."

"The four of you will leave tomorrow for America. You will fly straight to Providence, Rhode Island. Malcolm and Charles will talk to Mr. Lovecraft, and Joan and Nigel will travel to Miskatonic University. Once their business is completed, you will contact one of our embassies to relay the coordinates to me, and arrange for any other equipment you might need."

"After that, all you must do is defeat a god," Mycroft said, with a hint of sarcasm in his voice. "In all seriousness, I have complete faith that the four of you will be able to see this task to its completion."

"And if we don't?" asked Malcolm.

"I'd rather not think of the consequences," Mycroft said.

The rest of the day was a whirlwind of activity, as Malcolm and Charles went to the Quartermaster and nearly cleared him out of all manner of portable equipment: ropes, grapnels, underwater breathing apparatus, parkas, boots, snow shoes, rain coats, and various guns of many calibres. In addition, they gathered multiple changes of clothes, in all manner of fabrics and weights, to anticipate whatever conditions they could encounter. Malcolm saw little of Joan and, in fact, ended up eating dinner with Charles. When he returned to his room, he was happily surprised to find his steamer trunk packed with his personal effects from the *Daedalus*. As he opened it, he found the icon of St. Nicholas laid on top, and an envelope. He tore the envelope open and sat on his bed to read it.

"Dear Captain Robertson,

As ranking member of the crew, I was asked to pack your effects from your office and quarters. I do this duty with a heavy heart. There is too much here for an inventoried list, but I did my best to gather all your books, manuals, and items. If you find there is something missing, please let me know and I will endeavour to get it to you.

I don't know what circumstances caused you and Commander Saxon to resign your commissions. The crew is upset that they didn't find out until Captain Bromley showed up with orders that he and Commander Davies were taking command of the Daedalus. There was nearly a mutiny, if I may add.

Although I often felt like I couldn't be a good enough engineer for you, I have since found that not to be the case. Our new captain knows nothing about engineering. He ignores the important matters and fixates on the trivial. When you were hard on me, I realise that you wanted to me focus on the truly important things, and you didn't care about the minutiae unless it was relevant.

Thank you for all that you taught me. I feel I'm a better engineer and officer for serving under you. Should you ever require a chief engineer, please let me know; I would be happy to serve with you again.

About the icon: Bromley saw that on the bridge and was apoplectic. Something about not wanting such heretical claptrap hanging on his bridge. He was about to destroy it when I explained it had been a gift from the Patriarch of the Eastern Orthodox Church, and destroying it might not be a wise diplomatic action. He took it down and gave it to me saying, 'Get it off my ship!'. I don't know what your plans entail, but I thought you should have it, as the Patriarch did give it to you, and I feel that you may need a saint looking out for you.

Best of luck and regards,

Thomas Jennings"

Malcolm felt his eyes water, and he had to rub them to prevent a tear from splashing on the page. He was again reminded of everything he had lost and suddenly, the elation of retrieving the Spear of

Destiny evaporated, and he felt the cold, wet feeling of loss envelop him. He knew that their new mission was important, and that if they failed, it wouldn't matter if he were an airship captain. But it didn't make the pain and loss any easier.

He stared down at the letter in his hand. He had been a good captain. Jennings was right that Malcolm probably had been too hard on his engineering work, yet Jennings thanked him for it, and would work under him in a heartbeat. He pulled his flask out from his jacket pocket. He searched through his personal effects and found a half empty bottle of Auchentoshan, his favourite whisky. He refilled the flask, and took a draught straight from the bottle. He decided to see what Jennings had succeeded in sending him. He was happy to find his books, and his framed photograph of Joan. He also found a lacquer box containing a beautifully painted fan, along with a white silk kimono that he had intended to give to Joan; a katana that had been given to him as a gift by the Japanese, when he had given a talk last year about airship technology; and an African carving of a giraffe. This, and little more, was all he had for his time in the Air Service.

He took another drink of the whisky. Assuming he survived the current mission, Malcolm had no idea what lay in front of him. Mycroft had promised he would get him reinstated to the Air Service, but chances were good, he would be banished to a desk job; especially now that Bromley had his hands on the *Daedalus*. He took one more drink before putting the bottle away. As he saw it, his options were to either fail at this mission, and die in a world of pain and insanity, or go back to the Air Service, likely in a desk job where he could watch his soul bleed from him through a thousand paper cuts. Neither sounded particularly appealing. Maybe he could be a private flyer like Colfax. Hell; maybe Colfax would still hire him. He was sure he would not wish to work for the Secret Service any longer. He closed the trunk, but on a whim, decided to pack the katana, the icon of St. Nicholas, and the ring he had bought for Joan. He considered the katana to be a possible weapon, and the icon a blessing that they might need. He just wanted the ring with him, in case the worst happened and he could give it to Joan. He tried to fall asleep, but his mind was buzzing with thoughts of the mission, and what would come afterwards. When he did finally sleep, he slept fitfully all night, having a recurring dream where he couldn't get the budgets to add up correctly while he was chained to a desk.

He joined Joan, Saxon, and Nigel for breakfast.

"Good God, man, you look awful," Saxon said.

"And a good morning to you, Charles," Malcolm said as he grabbed his cup, in search of tea.

"What's wrong?" Joan asked, decidedly more diplomatically.

"Nothing really. Just didn't sleep well last night."

Conversation was at a minimum at the breakfast table. Malcolm helped himself to multiple cups of tea, hoping it would shake the fog in his head, but he was only moderately successful. Again, they left through the private underground train, and arrived in Charing Cross to find a car waiting to take them back to Hendon Aerodrome. The car once again travelled down the strip to the patchwork *RMA Uhuru*. When they got out of the car, Colfax was in the exact same pose as Malcolm had seen him in Paris.

"Let me guess, Mycroft had already acquired your services before we left Paris?" Malcolm asked.

"Part of the trip. Deliver four passengers to London, deliver four passengers to the United States, deliver the four passengers to destination unknown, and return everyone to London. And I didn't mind, since the mission sounds easy and the money was good."

"Let's hope so," Malcolm said uncertainly. The truck with their supplies arrived, and it became a logistical nightmare trying to squeeze the equipment into the storage space available aboard the *Uhuru*. In the end, Malcolm and Joan agreed to share one room, and Charles and Nigel agreed to share the other. The ship was cramped, but they had packed for any destination, with the hope that once they determined the exact location, they could offload some of the equipment.

Malcolm, Joan, Charles, and Nigel tied themselves into their chairs in the galley. Nigel, who was seated next to Malcolm, had a bit of a pale complexion. "Are you nervous about the flight?" Malcolm asked.

"Need a little liquid courage?" he said, as he offered the professor his flask.

"I'm not nervous about the flight itself; I'm more worried about what we will find at the end of the flight," Nigel said, downing a swallow of whisky. "The end of this mission will be unlike anything any of us have ever encountered."

"Is there nothing we can do to prepare?" Malcolm asked. Now, it was his turn to partake of the liquid courage.

"Yes, I think there is," Nigel said. "While we're travelling, I'll teach some exercises in resisting psychic dominance. These exercises are meant to develop and strengthen our own natural resistances."

"Professor, I don't to pretend to understand any of this, but I trust your experience and knowledge. As an engineer and a man of science, I have a hard time believing that there is a whole world outside of what we can observe, and describe with science. But I've seen it; hell, I've measured it. I will try my best to put my natural skepticism aside and put my trust in you, and the power of the Spear."

"Thank you, Captain," Nigel said.

"Please call me Malcolm; I'm no longer a Captain, and I think it will confuse our situation on the ship."

The takeoff was smooth; even Malcolm and Saxon had difficulty telling that they had lifted off. Once Colfax brought the *Uhuru* to cruising altitude, he left the cockpit and informed his passengers that they were free to move around the ship. He heated a kettle of hot water and made a large pot of tea. Malcolm was thankful that he could drink tea and not coffee. Although he quickly realised that, depending on where they ended up travelling, he may very well be forced to drink coffee. For now, he vowed to enjoy the tea while he could get it.

After lunch, Nigel began teaching exercises to build psychic defences and resistance. The first exercise involved visualising a white light around themselves to keep out the psychic energy. Malcolm was eventually able to visualise it. Then Nigel made them visualise this white light while reciting The Lord's Prayer. Malcolm thought they would have no idea if this worked, but to his surprise, Nigel had brought a psychometer aboard, and used it to measure everyone's psychic energy. Malcolm and Saxon barely budged the needle. Joan succeeded in budging it a little. Malcolm measured Nigel and he made the needle move some distance on the scale. They all decided that when it came time to confront the entity, he would wield the Spear of Destiny. They had taken to calling it 'the entity' as no-one wanted to speak its name.

As they were discussing the results, a thought occurred to Malcolm. "Excuse me a moment," he said, and left the galley. The others looked at him quizzically, but said nothing. Malcolm went his cabin, and within a few minutes, returned with the icon of St. Nicholas. He walked down the hall and knocked on the cockpit door.

"Yes?" Colfax answered.

"Sorry to bother you, but I wonder if you would allow me to hang this in the galley? It's an icon of St. Nicholas, patron saint of Air and the Tempest. It was given to me by the Patriarch of the Orthodox Church. I would have your permission before I would hang it on your ship," Malcolm said.

"Getting superstitious, are we?" Colfax asked. He looked at the icon for a moment before smiling. "Please feel free to hang it. I personally can use all the help I can get, be it divine or mundane."

Malcolm found an empty nail on the galley wall, and hung the icon. When they returned to their lessons in psychic defence, Malcolm focused on the icon, and saw a noticeable improvement in the strength of his psychic energy.

"What a capital idea, Malcolm. I wish I had thought of it. We could have each packed a small artifact that had personal meaning to each of us, to act as a focus." Malcolm looked puzzled, so Nigel continued. "The connection you feel with this piece, gives you something around which your psychic energy can coalesce, or focus."

"Did we have anything from the patron saint of lost causes?" Saxon muttered.

"I believe we had several relics purported to belong to St. Jude, patron saint of lost causes," Nigel said. "I curse myself for not having the foresight to think of that."

Nigel encouraged each of them to find one thing on their person that meant a great deal to them, and use that to help focus their psychic energies. Malcolm used his granda's pocket watch; Joan used the cross on her necklace; while Saxon focused on his gold ring. During the afternoon exercise, Nigel again measured them, and their scores had increased noticeably.

However, as the day turned to night, the travel became noticeably rougher. Strong winds seemed to buffet the ship. On more than one occasion, Colfax ordered them to strap down. After a half hour of the storm buffeting the ship, Colfax called for Malcolm.

"Yes, Captain?" Malcolm asked.

"Ever piloted in a storm?" Colfax asked.

"On several occasions," Malcolm said.

"Excellent! You're going to be my eyes. I need you to keep track of the thunderheads. We want to stay well away from them," Colfax said.

"Why?" Malcolm asked, and he knew the answer as soon as he asked. The balloon was filled with hydrogen. While certainly the lightest gas known to exist, it was also incredibly flammable. "Bloody hell," he said. "If you're using hydrogen, how come you have a stove on board?"

"Because I bloody well like to eat a warm meal," Colfax growled. "In case you didn't know, fractional distillers, that can produce helium, are bloody expensive. Too expensive for someone like me, that flies from assignment to assignment. Now, if you'll pay attention to the weather, we should be able to get through this in one piece."

Malcolm watched Colfax's mastery with the ship. When Malcolm pointed out the flashes of light in the clouds, Colfax lightly touched the controls, and avoided every spark of lightning. Malcolm expected that they would eventually escape the grasp of the storm, but as the hours went by, Malcolm saw no relief. "Were the weather charts this bad?" he asked.

"Funny you should ask, but no. The weather charts indicated clear skies all the way to Nova Scotia."

"We're still over land, aren't we?" Malcolm asked. "Should we put down and wait out the storm?"

"From what I understand, we're under a pretty tight schedule. Can we afford to wait, especially since we don't know anything about this storm?" Malcolm remained silent. "Besides," Colfax continued, "we've got St. Nicholas on our side, right? Patron Saint of the Air and Tempests?"

Malcolm laughed. "Very well. St. Nicholas, save and protect us!"

They debated trying to fly above the storm, or going below it. From what they could tell, in the miasma of grey and black in front of them, the cumulonimbus clouds towered high above them. It quickly became apparent that they would not be able to climb above them. Colfax gently angled the *Uhuru* down below the clouds. But this was worse. The winds that buffeted the airship now threatened to throw it out of the sky. Malcolm looked over, and saw that Colfax's hands were white from gripping the control levers so hard.

Nigel, Saxon, and Joan managed to make some sandwiches for dinner along with several pots of strong tea. Colfax and Malcolm ate in the cockpit; Colfax doing his best to pilot the ship, while Malcolm helped navigate, and watch for lightning. The clouds had a greenish and purplish cast, as if the very sky was bruised. When the lightning flashed, on more than one occasion, Malcolm was sure he saw the shape of an octopus head in the clouds.

After another couple of hours, Colfax was rubbing his eyes, trying to keep awake. "Can you take over for a while? If I'd known that I would be piloting through a storm, I would have slept later this morning," he asked.

"Are you sure?" Malcolm said, trying not to let his eagerness show. He hadn't realized, until this instant, how much he missed being behind the controls.

"Yes. I can barely keep my eyes open. I'll send your friend up, so you can take turns piloting and navigating. I'll be back in a couple of hours to relieve you." Colfax locked the control levers into place, and left the cockpit. A few minutes later, Saxon stuck his head into the cockpit and said, "You've only been with him a few hours, and you've driven the captain away?"

"You know me; I'm so demanding," Malcolm said sarcastically.

"Why don't you make yourself useful, and help me navigate this ship?" Saxon settled into the co-pilot's seat, and arranged the maps so he could get his bearings.

After several minutes, Saxon looked over at Malcolm. "You really do miss being a captain, don't you?"

"What? Yes, I suppose," Malcolm said. "Why do you ask?"

"I haven't seen you this at ease since we left the *Daedalus*. I know this is not easy work, but despite the concentration, you are relaxed."

"I'm not that bloody relaxed," Malcolm said. "Between trying to keep this thing on course, and avoiding lightning strikes, it's hardly a walk in the park."

"Come now," Saxon said. "You don't fool me for one minute. You are enjoying every single second of this."

Malcolm was silent for a minute before he smiled. "I guess you're right. It's just, for the first time in I can't remember when, I feel like I'm doing something I understand."

"You miss the Air Service?" Saxon said.

"God help me, yes I do. It's all I've known for my whole adult life. And I'd like to think I'm a decent captain, despite what some in the Admiralty think."

"Malcolm, you are a good captain, and it is the Admiralty's loss. But are you sure you want to go back, even if you could?"

Malcolm considered this. "Yes, I would. What about you?"

Saxon smiled. "I think we both know I can't return." He put his hand up before Malcolm could interrupt. "We both know that, even if Mycroft convinces the Admiralty that the charges are falsified, there will always be the cloud of suspicion hanging over me. Every word, or accidental touch, will be scrutinised. If there's only one thing I'm glad about, through all of this, it's that you know who and what I am. When we were in the Air Service, there was no way I could tell you, without forcing you to either betray your oath as a Captain, or betray me." He sighed. "I hate to admit it, but Mycroft really did me a favour. And I find, I like this cloak and dagger stuff. Maybe because I'm good at hiding things."

"The Secret Service is getting one hell of a good man," Malcolm said.

"You sure you don't want to join me? And Joan?" Saxon asked.

"I'm sure. I hate this slinking around, hiding in the shadows, lying about everything, and not knowing who to trust. I don't know how anyone can do it!" Malcolm said.

Saxon laughed. "Malcolm, you have just described my life, up until this very moment. And I've become very good at all of that."

"I'm sorry, Charles. That's not what I meant," Malcolm started.

"I know, Malcolm. And I know you well enough to know that you would be utterly miserable if you stayed in the Secret Service. What will you do if Mycroft can't get you reinstated?"

"I don't know. Maybe I'll work for Colfax," Malcolm said.

"I don't see that. You've been a captain; you'd want to be a captain again."

"Maybe. But I've been an engineer far longer than I've been a captain. I can always go back to that."

"What does Joan think?" Saxon asked cautiously.

"I don't know," Malcolm said. "We haven't had much time to talk, and I dare not bring it up." Malcolm related the discussion he'd had with Joan about the engagement ring, and her reaction.

"Ah," Saxon said. "I don't pretend to know anything about women, but I think the two of you need to figure out what you really want. I know that you both love each other, deeply, I might add. But you're both too stubborn to compromise. And I think that's what you're going to need to do to be happy."

Malcolm nodded, but offered no response. The ship was buffeted by another strong wind, and Malcolm and Saxon's full attention went to navigating through the storm. The weather didn't relent for several more hours, until sometime near three o'clock in the morning. Joan and Nigel kept Malcolm and Saxon well supplied with tea, but by the time the storm had diminished, Saxon too was bleary-eyed and looking for sleep. At nearly five o'clock, Malcolm finally kicked Saxon out of the cockpit to get some rest.

Malcolm was wide awake despite not having slept. He was energised, and felt like he could take on the world. From up here, his opportunities seemed endless. He could see the horizon, and as morning began to break, the east began to glow with orange and pink, that seamlessly merged into the midnight blue of the early morning sky. He chuckled to himself, remembering how nervous he had been to pilot the *Daedalus* out of its hangar, after it was rebuilt in St. Petersburg. He had come a long way from there. He knew that he wasn't a great pilot, but he was perfectly serviceable.

There was a knock on the door, and Malcolm nearly jumped out of his seat. "Yes?"

"Are you still here?" Joan asked. She had pulled a thick cotton robe over her diaphanous nightwear.

"Yes. Someone has to keep us up in the air," he said. "Come in, keep me company."

Joan climbed into the co-pilot's seat. Malcolm was amazed at how she made that seem graceful. "Where are we?" she asked.

"Hand me that map," Malcolm said, pointing to the map to her left. He stared for a minute, and held it up to compare the map to the view from the cockpit. "Unless I'm totally lost, I think *that*," he said, as he pointed to a mound of twinkling lights far to the right, "is Kilarney in Ireland. If we'd taken the scenic route via Iceland, we might have been able to see my home."

"That's a shame. I'd like to see it sometime," she said.

"There's not much to see. It used to be a farming village, until the train came and people realised that they could live in Kilmacolm, but work in Glasgow. I'd guess that most of its inhabitants spend very little time living there now."

"Your parents still live there?"

"Yes," Malcolm said. "My dad's leg is really bothering him, so he doesn't get out as much as he wants. They still live over the shop that used to be my granda's. It's a greengrocer now. They collect rent and the occasional extra produce."

"Do you miss them?"

"I do. I know they wanted me to see the world, and were happy that I could escape the shipyards, but part of me misses home." He chuckled. "I didn't really realise just how much I missed it until just now. I'm so close, but I may as well be a million miles away. Maybe after this is over, I'll visit my parents. It's been far too long since I've seen them."

Joan took a breath as if to speak, and then shook her head.

"What?" Malcolm asked.

"Nothing," Joan said.

They sat quietly together for nearly half an hour when the door opened. "You still at it?" Colfax said. "Why didn't you get me when the storm passed?"

"I had things under control, and I thought that at least one of us should get some sleep."

"I suppose. But I don't want you to get too comfortable sitting in my chair." Colfax said with a grin. "You are relieved, Malcolm."

"I am relieved," Malcolm said, completing the standard response. He locked the controls into place, and started out of the cockpit. "Are you coming?" Malcolm asked Joan.

"In a moment," Joan said.

Malcolm shrugged and left the cabin.

"Did you want something?" Colfax asked.

"Yes," Joan said. Before Colfax arrived, she had thought that she would try to dissuade him from trying to hire Malcolm to work for him. But seeing Malcolm at the controls this morning, it occurred to her that he would never be happy unless he was working aboard an airship. "I don't know your circumstance, but I assume that since you freelance for the Secret Service, you must have some resources. I would very much like it if you hired Malcolm at the end of this mission. I'm in a position within the Secret Service to make it worth your while."

"Really?" Colfax said, arching one eyebrow. "That's very funny. When I told him I could use a man like him, he turned me down. He said he was giving up the air for a boring desk job for you."

"He... what? Really?" Joan said. She was taken aback. She didn't want Malcolm to be miserable just for her. "Thank you, Captain. I've taken enough of your time." Joan left and, as she walked the few steps down the hall, her anger began to rise. She stalked down the hallway and ripped open the cabin door. She was about to speak when she saw Malcolm asleep on the bed, in the clothes he had on when he left the cockpit.

The anger evaporated, and she just watched him. He snored like a band saw, but she couldn't help but think that he looked like a little boy, despite the grey at his temples. She carefully removed his shoes. She took off her cotton robe, carefully got into bed, and curled up next to him.

CHAPTER 38

Malcolm woke alone in his bed. He fumbled for his pocket watch and, through bleary eyes, saw that it was after noon. He stumbled out of his room to the communal wash room, and splashed cold water on his face, and half walked, half stumbled to the galley in search of tea. To his great joy, a fresh pot was waiting for him. Nigel, Joan, and Charles were in the middle of one of their psychic defence lessons. Malcolm was thankful for the silence, and the tea, so he could get his own thoughts together. While they continued with the lesson, Malcolm slipped from the galley, and knocked on the cockpit door.

"Come in," Colfax said. "Look who finally rose from the dead?" He laughed when he saw it was Malcolm. "You didn't have to fly all night through that storm. I told you to get me in a few hours."

"I know, but I was having so much fun evading thunderheads that it slipped my mind," Malcolm said sarcastically.

"Well, thank you. It was nice to have a second set of hands. It's been some time since I've had help."

"Did you have a co-pilot?" Malcolm asked.

"Yes. Adele Winterset." Malcolm looked at him quizzically. "Yes, a woman. Smart as a whip and, truth be told, a better pilot than me."

"What happened?" Malcolm asked cautiously.

"Nothing dramatic. Adele was a firebrand. She was the youngest daughter of landed gentry. She ran away, because she refused to be married off to some boring rich bloke. She cut her hair, and pretended to be a boy, so that she could apprentice with a commercial airship company. When she learned everything she could, she left, and came looking for someone to hire her. As someone who was always overlooked, I decided to take a chance on her. And I don't regret it for one second. Adele and I must have circled the globe a dozen times, and got in even more scrapes. About a year ago, she wanted to go it alone, and I wouldn't stand in her way. Last I heard, she's doing fairly well."

"So you've been doing this by yourself for the last year? Isn't that a little dangerous?" Malcolm asked.

"Probably. It keeps my costs down though. I keep a good eye on the weather, and I typically sleep for about an hour every couple of hours. I can't do that for too long, but usually long enough to get where I need to go. I mostly haul cargo, so I usually don't have any passengers to protest."

"I'm willing to take the night shift," Malcolm offered.

"We'll see," Colfax said. "You seem awfully eager to pilot. Didn't you say you were an engineer?"

Malcolm hesitated. He decided that, since Colfax was mixed up in this at Mycroft's request, it wouldn't matter. "I did, but I wasn't strictly telling the truth, to avoid disclosing my identity. I'm Malcolm Robertson, previously Captain of the *HMA Daedalus.*"

"The *Daedalus?* Good God, man, what are you doing here?"

"It wasn't exactly my choice to leave, if you understand."

"Ah. Mycroft needed you and got you." Colfax said.

"You sound like you have first-hand experience?"

"Yes," Colfax said. "Mycroft is the reason Adele went out on her own. He's been trying to make it up to me by offering charters like this."

"Ah," Malcolm agreed. "I won't lie; I miss being a captain, and flying the airship."

"Why did you say you were an engineer?"

"Because I was. I was Chief Engineer of the *Daedalus* before I became her captain." Malcolm told Colfax about the bomb that destroyed the bridge of the *Daedalus*, leaving him as ranking officer. "We were quite a distance from Britain, and were told to continue with our mission. When I returned, the Admiralty made me captain, and gave me the *Daedalus*."

"And Charles?" Colfax asked.

"He was my second in command. Truthfully, neither of us are great at navigating, but I believe I am better at navigating from a map than he is."

"It seems we have a ship full of commanders and no crew," Colfax laughed.

"No, there's only one captain on this ship, and that's you."

They started discussing the route, and Malcolm called Saxon to join them. Colfax laid out the route and, now that he knew that there were two other capable pilots, he divided the day into three eight hour shifts. Once the shifts were established, the trip became rather routine. Because he had slept so late this morning, Malcolm landed the midnight to eight o'clock shift, while Saxon took the four o'clock to midnight shift. Malcolm worked with Nigel after dinner on building his own psychic defences, ate dinner with the group, and after kissing Joan good night, settled into the cockpit.

For three days, the cycle continued. Just before Malcolm's shift began, they reached the first land they had seen since their first day, as they passed over Nova Scotia. The *Uhuru* continued over the ocean, before stopping at a small airfield in Quincy, Massachusetts. Malcolm walked Joan to the gang plank, as she and Nigel prepared to leave.

"Be careful," Malcolm said as he held her hand.

"I always am," she said, and Malcolm looked at her ruefully. "Alright, most of the time."

"We'll see you in Providence in two days' time. With any luck, we'll know where we have to go."

"Be good," Joan said. "Don't give Charles too much of a hard time. And stay out of trouble."

"I'll try," he said, as he reached down to hold her hand. "But trouble seems to have a way of finding me."

"Am I trouble?" she asked, using her husky voice to its full advantage.

"Most definitely," he said, as he kissed her hand. "But the kind I like the most."

. "Flatterer," she said.

"Good luck," he said, as he pulled her into an embrace, and kissed her. The kiss lingered for several seconds before she finally pulled away.

"I've got to go," she said, with a hint of nervousness in her voice. "Nigel is waiting."

Malcolm nodded and let her go. She gathered her things, and walked off to join Nigel, who was already waiting for her at a car that they had hired to take them to the University. Malcolm watched as she got into the large black car, whose bonnet was easily six feet long, and took up half of the car's length. It pulled away slowly, belching a cloud of exhaust. Malcolm remembered they were in America, and remembered the American fondness for using gasoline to power vehicles. He turned and saw Colfax standing in the doorway.

"Ready to go?" Colfax asked.

"Yes, let's get going," Malcolm said, as he walked onto the airship.

Within minutes, the *Uhuru* was in the air heading to Providence. A short two hours later, they touched down in Blackstone Park. At the park, they found a trolley stop, and Charles and Malcolm took the trolley into town. After stopping several people for directions, they located the offices of the *Providence Tribune*. As they opened the door, they felt like they had been blown into a maelstrom of activity. They stepped into a large room full of men and women seated at desks, with typewriters tapping out the rhythm of the daily news. The clack and whirl of the printing presses combined, to create a ritual drumming in the background. The office was hot, and smelled of ink and sweat.

"Pardon me," Saxon said to the first person he could stop; a young woman dressed conservatively, in a long white blouse and black skirt.

"Yes?" she said, with a great deal of irritation. As she turned to Saxon, her attitude softened, as Saxon smiled at the her. "What can I do to help you?" she asked enthusiastically.

"I'm looking for Howard Lovecraft? I believe he writes for your newspaper?"

"Lovecraft? Oh, yes, Howard. He submits a monthly article. He doesn't work here."

"Oh. You see, I'm from the Royal Astronomical Society of Britain, and my colleague and I wanted to speak to him about a recent article."

"Oh," the woman said in surprise. "Someone actually reads his articles?"

"Yes, my colleague and I are devoted readers."

"What do you know about that?" she said.

"Do you know how I can get in touch with him?" Saxon asked.

"No, but the boss would. You should probably talk to Mr. Rathom, our editor. That's his office over there," she pointed. In the corner of the room was another room, with frosted glass windows. On the door was painted *John R. Rathom, Editor and General Manager*.

"Thank you, miss. You've been most kind," Saxon said.

"The pleasure was all mine," she said demurely.

Malcolm shook his head and followed Saxon, as they worked their way through the seeming labyrinth of desks. Saxon knocked on the door, and a voice boomed from the other side. "What is it?"

Saxon slowly opened the door. Large green file cabinets filled the back wall. In front of them was a large oak desk, covered with stacks of papers. Seated behind the desk was a rotund man, with dark hair that was receding in the front. He wore a three-piece suit, much like Malcolm and Saxon, but the buttons on his vest were threatening to burst.

He looked up and barked, "Who are you, and what do you want?" He spoke with an accent that wasn't American, and wasn't British. Malcolm had heard it before, but couldn't place it.

"Sorry for the intrusion. My name is Charles Saxon, and this is my colleague, Malcolm Robertson. We are representatives of the Royal Astronomical Society of Great Britain. We have come across the sea to speak with your reporter, Howard Lovecraft, about an article he wrote."

"You want to speak to Lovecraft about an article? What's wrong? Did he mess it up so badly that you came all this way to correct it?" Rathom said. It was then that Malcolm placed the accent. The man was Australian.

"On the contrary, his article intrigued us greatly, and we wanted to talk to him about it." Saxon said.

"I never would have guessed that," Rathom said.

"We've come all this way to speak with him," Charles said. "Do you know where we can find him?"

"He's either at his home, or at the observatory. He doesn't get out much. He doesn't even come in to drop off his articles. He just mails them in." Rathom rose from his chair and leaned against the door frame. "Gladys, where does Lovecraft live?" A young blonde woman left one of the desks nearest the office, and began searching through a file cabinet. After about 30 seconds, she said, "Howard Lovecraft lives at 598 Angell St."

"There you have it, gentlemen. 598 Angell St. Do you know how to get there?"

"No, we just arrived in your fair city," Saxon said.

"Gladys, give these gentlemen directions to Lovecraft's house when they leave," Rathom said. He closed the door and returned to his desk. "I'm sure that you'll credit our newspaper, should Lovecraft's article amount to anything," Rathom said. "It would mean a great deal to the credibility of our paper."

More like give you more publicity, Malcolm thought. He had taken an instant dislike to the man, and his desire to profit rubbed Malcolm the wrong way.

"Most assuredly," Saxon said, with a charming smile. Malcolm rarely saw this side of Saxon, and was amazed at how easily he could charm many people.

"What's with your friend?" Rathom asked. "He hasn't said two words since you came in. Is he mute?"

Malcolm took a breath to speak, but Saxon interjected. "My

colleague is much more at home in the world of astronomy and maths. It was all I could do to persuade him to come with me, and get him out of the observatory."

"I see. One of those intellectual types with his head in the clouds," Rathom snorted.

"Yes," Saxon said, barely able to suppress a smile. He rose, and Malcolm followed suit. "We've taken enough of your valuable time. Thank you for your assistance." Saxon offered his hand, but Rathom stayed seated at his desk and had already turned his attention to something else. "We'll see ourselves out," Saxon said.

They left, closing the door behind them. They stopped at the desk of the young woman, who had answered to the name Gladys, and asked for directions to Lovecraft's house. As Gladys gave Saxon the directions, Malcolm could not help but notice that the young woman seemed disarmed by Saxon's presence. He thought that she might be blushing. Saxon flashed her a dazzling smile, and thanked her for her trouble. They took their leave and, as Malcolm left, he saw that the young woman was watching them the whole time.

As they started towards Lovecraft's house, Malcolm said, "You really enjoyed that, didn't you?"

"Yes," Saxon said smugly. "Especially when he called you an intellectual with his head in the clouds. I thought for sure I was going to burst out laughing."

"Thank you," Malcolm said bitterly.

"Malcolm, you are not someone I would describe as having his head in the clouds, except in the literal sense that you are an airship captain. You are a man of action, grounded in reality, and not what ifs. But," he continued, "I was perfectly content to let him think that, if it got us what we needed. And it did. Will it make you feel better if I let you do the talking when we meet Lovecraft?"

Malcolm sighed. "No," he said reluctantly.

"Then stop being so gloomy, and let's meet Mr. Lovecraft so we can get on with this."

They realised that it was nearly a two mile walk from the newspaper to Lovecraft's home. Both men decided it was a good day for a walk, and that they had been stuck inside the airship for too long. The sky was overcast and threatened rain, but they soon found themselves removing their jackets. They walked past the brick shops and offices of Providence's downtown, and crossed the confluence of the Woonasquatucket and Moshassuck Rivers. From here, the streets started to rise, and the architecture changed. Wooden clapboard houses lined the streets. Although the houses were all interconnected, Malcolm was amazed at the size. In similar neighbourhoods in London, there might be two houses in the space of one here. The street continued to climb, and when they turned onto Angell St, they found themselves walking parallel with the end of a university or college. Malcolm assumed it must be Brown University, the home of the observatory.

Their walk down Angell St was a study in contrasting architecture. As they walked alongside the University, everything was neo-classical, and built of stone or brick. As they passed the university, they saw houses decorated with gables, towers, and widow walks. These large houses were often painted extravagantly in multiple colors. As they progressed, the houses became more modest clapboard houses. Malcolm remarked at the number of trees that lined their route; he thought that he had seen more trees on this walk than he had ever seen in London.

After nearly an hour, they arrived at a modest two story house. Two sets of bay windows sat on top of one another, making the front of the house look like it was bulging out. Two gable dormers perched at the top of the house. A plain wooden door, with an iron knocker, was set on the left-hand side of the house.

"Shall we?" Saxon asked. He led the way up the short walk to the front door and knocked. After some moments, a pale young man, dressed in a dark suit, opened the door. "Hello," he said.

Saxon extended his hand with a card. "Good afternoon, are you Howard Lovecraft, astronomy correspondent for the *Providence Tribune?*"

"Yes," Lovecraft said. His voice was high and sounded shaky, as if he was unused to talking. Malcolm couldn't help but notice his long face, and very pale skin. Malcolm wondered if this was the most sun the young man had seen in weeks.

"I'm Charles Saxon, and this is my colleague, Malcolm Robertson. We're from the Royal Astronomical Society in Britain. We wish to speak to you about one of your columns."

"You've read my columns? In England?" the young man said incredulously.

"Yes. If we are not disturbing you, we wish to discuss them with you."

"Oh, yes, certainly," Lovecraft said. "Come in, come in."

Malcolm and Saxon stepped into the house. A staircase rose to the second floor, and there was a small hall that ran next to it. Lovecraft ushered them into a parlour to his right. The bay window dominated one wall of the room, but the room was dark from the heavy curtains drawn across the window. A fireplace centred one wall, while the wall opposite the bay window contained a built-in bookcase stuffed with books. A small writing desk was stuffed in the corner next to the bookcase. Centred around the fireplace were two settees, and an upholstered chair.

"Please, sit down." Malcolm and Saxon sat on one of the settees. "Can I get you something to drink? Water? Iced tea?"

Iced tea? Malcolm thought. *How absolutely revolting.* How anyone could take tea, and drink it cold, was beyond him. Truthfully, he had to admit to himself that he drank cold tea many times in his life, because he got engrossed in his work and forgot that it was sitting there. But to intentionally make it cold was something he simply could not understand.

"Water would be fine," Saxon said.

"I thought you would be inclined to have tea," Lovecraft said.

"I would if it were served in a civilised fashion," Malcolm muttered.

"I beg your pardon, what was that?" Lovecraft asked.

"Water would be fine," Malcolm said.

"I'll be back in just a moment," Lovecraft said as he left the room.

"And you wonder why I don't let you talk?" Saxon whispered.

"I'll try to do better. But you must admit that putting ice in a perfectly good cup of tea is absolutely barbaric!"

Before Saxon could respond, Lovecraft returned with a pitcher of water and three glasses. He poured water for his guests and, after filling his glass, he asked, "Which of my articles did you want to discuss?" Malcolm could see that it had been all that Lovecraft could do to observe the niceties, before asking about the article. Malcolm felt bad that they were allowing him to think he had been noticed by the Royal Astronomical Society.

"Yes, we wanted to talk to you about the article you wrote about the conjunction of Earth, Mars, Jupiter, Saturn, and the star, Antares. What can you tell us about that?"

"I spend a great deal of time at the Ladd Observatory. Professor Upton mentioned it in passing, when I was asking him about upcoming astronomical events. He noted that this was a particularly rare conjunction."

"That is fascinating," Saxon said. "It is a rare astronomical phenomenon. You mentioned that there was a single point on Earth, where one would have the best chance to see this?"

"Yes. I asked Professor Upton about it and he said, 'Figure it out for yourself'. He doesn't think a conjunction of stars and planets, no matter how rare, is worth his time." Lovecraft paused for a moment. "I am loath to admit it, but I don't have the skills in mathematics to be able to discern the location."

"Have you tried to use a computator to do the calculation?" Malcolm asked.

"No, I have no luck with those infernal contraptions. And you must know what to program to get an answer. I'm afraid I'm of no use," Lovecraft said dejectedly.

"Do you have the information about the conjunction?" Saxon asked. "My colleague is adept at these calculations, and should be able to find the location."

"No. Professor Upton is very strict about retaining anything that belongs to the Observatory. He won't so much as lend me a pencil or a piece of paper. Perhaps if I introduce you, Professor Upton will be willing to share the information. I daresay the fact that you are members of the Royal Astronomical Society will certainly have an influence."

Lovecraft rose. "Come, let's go to the observatory immediately. I'm most curious to see where the conjunction will take place!" Lovecraft took their glasses, placed them on the tray, and whisked it out of the room. He returned momentarily. "Well? Are you ready?"

Malcolm took a breath to speak, but looked at Saxon, who glowered at him. Turning to Lovecraft, Saxon said, "Yes, of course. Lead the way, good man."

They left the house, and walked back through the tree-lined avenue towards the centre of the city. They soon turned right and headed north. "I walk this way often," Lovecraft said. "I spend a great deal of my time at the observatory."

"Are you considering a career in astronomy?" Saxon asked.

"I would love that more than anything. However, I find the complex mathematics above my ability. So, I chose to write about it instead. It's such a fascinating field, don't you think?"

"Well, yes; otherwise, I wouldn't be a member of the Royal Society."

"Tell me," Lovecraft said. "What is it that attracts you to the study of astronomy?"

"Well," Saxon said uncomfortably. "It's many things."

"Such as?" Lovecraft prodded.

Saxon glanced at Malcolm, appealing for assistance. Malcolm smiled, waiting for two seconds to see the look of desperation in Saxon's eyes, before he spoke. "If I can speak for my colleague, I think it's both peering into the unknown, and the thrill of discovery."

"I feel the same way! The opportunities I have had to look into the telescope are magical. I can see the cosmos, and all of creation. It is both humbling and depressing."

"How so?" Malcolm asked.

"To see the beauty of the whole universe, and to think we are alone."

"Don't be so sure about that," Malcolm muttered.

"I beg your pardon?" Lovecraft said.

"What my colleague said was that there are millions of stars in the universe, and there must likely be millions of planets," Saxon interjected. "The likelihood that we are the only planet that supports life is highly unlikely."

"True. I often suppose that we are not alone, and that there are things far more ancient and alien than mankind."

"Really?" Saxon said.

"They are just idle fancies really. I write the stories to entertain myself. Maybe one day, I will get them published. Until then, I write for the *Tribune*."

Saxon steered the conversation towards the history of Providence, a subject about which Lovecraft knew a great deal. He told Malcolm and Saxon about the founding of Providence by Roger Williams, a clergyman expelled from Massachusetts. After the Revolution, it became renowned for jewellery making. In recent years, it had become very successful, buoyed by its industrial base of precision tool making, steam engines, silverware, and textiles. Lovecraft boasted about the technological advances made in automation, while bemoaning the increase of the immigrant population that manned the factories. "It's as if Providence no longer belongs to the people who are steadfast New Englanders."

Malcolm thought of the prejudice he'd had to endure in the Air Service, for having the audacity to be born Scottish. Involuntarily, his fists started to clench and he took a breath to speak when Lovecraft pointed ahead. "There's the observatory."

The observatory was a large brick and stone rectangular building, merged with an octagon. The octagon thrust out of one side of the rectangle, with stone steps rising to a stone portico over the door. On top of the octagon rested a cylindrical brick wall, with a large metal dome covering the cylinder. The front of the observatory was covered with ivy, making it impossible to see the building material underneath. The only surfaces not covered by the greenery were the windows and the door.

Lovecraft consulted his watch. "It's late afternoon; there's an excellent chance that Professor Upton will be in his office. Because of the nature of his work, he tends to start late in the afternoon and work into the night. I'm sure you understand."

"Yes, of course," replied Saxon.

Lovecraft took them to a door on the far side of the observatory. Here the ivy was less plentiful, and Malcolm could see the brick and stone of the structure. The interior reminded him of many of the buildings where he had attended university. The large hall ran the length of the building, and was broken by a series of doorways. Some led into small classrooms, complete with desks, chairs, and a blackboard; others were offices. Lovecraft led them down the hall, until they reached the office of Professor Winslow Upton. Malcolm knocked on the door and heard a somewhat irritated voice respond. "Yes, what is it?"

"Professor Upton, it's Howard Lovecraft."

"Howard, please go away. I am very busy right now, and I don't have time to talk to you."

"I have two visitors that I think you'll want to meet. They are from the Royal Astronomical Society."

"Really? Come in." he said. Lovecraft opened the door and ushered them into the room. The room was filled with bookcases, each with books meticulously placed on the shelves. The desk itself was orderly, with only an open journal on the blotter, with a slide rule by its side. Professor Winslow Upton rose as they entered. Silver, bushy hair circled the sides of his head, and cascaded into a full beard and mustache. He had dark, sharp eyes that keenly appraised the two visitors. "I'm Professor Winslow Upton. And you are?" he said as he offered his hand.

"I'm Charles Saxon, and this is Malcolm Robertson. We are from the Royal Astronomical Society. It's a pleasure to meet you."

"The Royal Society? How is it that I've never heard of you before?"

"We actually work for the Royal Society. We do fieldwork on behalf of the Royal Society. Here are our credentials, if that will assuage your doubts." Saxon handed Upton the false letters of introductions, extolling the skills of Saxon and Malcolm, and requesting the receiver to supply any assistance that could be offered.

"It seems to be in order," Upton said. "Please, sit." He indicated the chairs in front of his desk. "What can I do for you?"

"We read Mr. Lovecraft's article in the *Tribune* about a rare conjunction of Earth, Mars, Jupiter, Saturn, and the star, Antares."

"I told him not to publish that. You know, as well as I, that just because planets and stars align, there's no supernatural meaning to it. Why, there's no real meaning in it at all!"

"Be that as it may," Saxon said. "The Society asked us to come here to find out where the optimum viewing place would be to see the conjunction. I believe that one of the Fellows, in addition to being a brilliant astronomer, is a Spiritualist, and believes that it will open a conduit to the spirit world. I know that it's all claptrap, but what can one do when one's employer demands you follow his dictates?"

Upton snorted. "And he sent the two of you all of the way from London to Providence just to find out where he can see this conjunction?"

"Yes," Malcolm offered. "He has more money than sense, it appears."

Upton laughed. "That is true. Let me look at my journals. When did you report this, Howard?"

"Nearly two months ago," Howard said. "You mentioned it after having a particularly frustrating night of observation, where everything was obscured by clouds."

Upton followed a line of journals on the wall until he found the journal. "I believe this is the correct one." He brought it back to the desk and leafed through the handwritten journal. "Here it is," he said. "I can't believe I'm wasting my time with such superstitious nonsense. But if it furthers the aims of the Royal Astronomical Society, who am I to say otherwise? Perhaps one of you would be able to assist me, and verify my calculations?"

"It would be my honour," said Malcolm. He had been looking forward to this part, as there were few things Malcolm enjoyed more than solving mathematical puzzles. While he had never studied orbital mechanics, his familiarity with navigation and particle dynamics were of great use to him. Upton and Malcolm filled pages with their calculations, and their fingers flew over their slide rules. Lovecraft fetched a globe from a classroom to aid their calculations. After an hour of continuous calculations, Malcolm and Upton looked at each other and nodded.

"The optimum place on Earth to view the conjunction is 47°9' S 126°43' W," Upton said.

Saxon looked at the globe, and pointed to a location in the middle of the Pacific Ocean. "Our patron will be most disappointed," he said. "It couldn't be farther away from land if it tried."

CHAPTER 39

alcolm and Saxon thanked Professor Upton for his time and left with Lovecraft. "What will you do now?" Lovecraft asked excitedly.

"We must confer with our colleagues in London, to determine our next steps. But should anything come of it, we'll make sure that you and Professor Upton will receive due credit."

"Thank you. That is most kind," Lovecraft said. "Is there anything else I can do for you gentlemen?"

"Yes," Saxon said. "Could you direct us to the nearest trolley stop?"

Lovecraft walked them to the trolley stop nearly four blocks away. He shook their hands enthusiastically. "Thank you so much. This means so much to me that my articles are read, and viewed with such regard, by the Royal Astronomical Society. I can't tell you what an honour it has been to assist you."

"The honour was all ours," Saxon said, and Malcolm though he detected a note of sadness in Saxon's voice. "I don't wish to get your hopes up; nothing may come of this at all."

"I know," Lovecraft said. "But it does encourage me to keep at it."

"As it should," Saxon said. "Thank you again, and best of luck in the future."

"Thank you," Lovecraft said, as he took his leave. Both Malcolm and Saxon watched him walk, with what appeared to be a spring in his step. Malcolm shook his head. "This is why I can't do this job. We've deluded this poor young man into thinking that he wrote something worthy enough to appeal to the Royal Astronomical Society."

"True," Saxon said. "But perhaps we've also inspired him to keep writing. Perhaps he will write something important one day."

"Perhaps," Malcolm said. They stood in silence and waited for the trolley. After a winding trip through Providence, they returned to Blackstone Park. When they arrived back at the *Uhuru*, they showed the coordinates to Colfax. "This is where we need to go," Malcolm said.

"Bloody hell! That's literally in the middle of nowhere!" Colfax said. "I certainly hope there's something there when we get there!"

"So do I," Malcolm said.

Colfax announced that he needed to go into the city to order supplies and more fuel. The trip to the coordinates was much longer than the trip across the Atlantic. They would need to fly the length of the America eastern coast, cut across Florida, the Gulf of Mexico, cut through Guatemala, before flying over nearly five thousand miles of ocean, to reach the point of the conjunction. "Malcolm, would you come with me to help order supplies? I'm not always treated well when I arrive in the States. They can't believe someone like me can fly, let alone own an airship. It's one of the reasons that Adele was so handy; she got cooperation where I received hatred. While you don't have her feminine wiles, you'll have to do."

"Why not use Charles? He's the charming one. So I've been told," Malcolm said.

"No, I think you are the man for the job. You strike me as someone who knows how to wield authority. And dressed as you are, you have the air of someone with money, which is the only thing most of these bandits respect."

"Alright," Malcolm said, not particularly looking forward to another long walking trip of Providence.

"I have been here before. I believe we can secure what we need not very far from here. And it can be delivered."

Malcolm and Colfax walked back to the trolley, leaving Saxon alone with the *Uhuru*. Instead of taking the trolley into town, they took the trolley down to the harbour south of their landing spot. Malcolm and Colfax walked the harbour for some time, until they found a general supply company. They entered the office; a shabby affair overlooking the harbour. Behind a counter of cheap, painted wood, sat a young man intently reading the newspaper.

"Excuse me," Colfax began. "I'd like to arrange for this list of supplies to be delivered to my airship at Blackstone Park." Colfax slid the list over the man's newspaper.

The clerk looked up and crumpled up the list. "I'm sorry. I don't take orders from someone like you."

Malcolm stepped from behind Colfax. "And why on earth not? Why would you not serve my partner?"

"Partner?" the clerk said incredulously. "I won't serve him because..."

"What? Because he's tall? Muscular? Too good looking?"

"No, he's..."

"He's what?" Malcolm asked.

"Never mind. Let me see what we have," the clerk said, as he uncrumpled the list, and tried to smooth the paper flat. After several seconds, he nodded. "I can have everything delivered as you require."

"I think you need to say that to my partner, and not to me," Malcolm said. "Look him in the eye as you say those words, or we will take our business elsewhere." Malcolm guessed he was making an idle threat, but he decided to try it anyway.

The clerk locked eyes with Malcolm. "Very well. Come along, Colfax, no need to waste our money where it's not wanted." Malcolm moved to the door and opened it.

"Alright," the clerk yelled. He turned to Colfax and looked him in the eyes. "I can have everything delivered as you require."

"Sir," Malcolm said.

"Sir," the clerk said unenthusiastically.

"That wasn't so hard now, was it?" Malcolm asked. "Thank you."

"We should expect the supplies to be delivered tomorrow morning?" Colfax asked.

"Yes," the clerk said, this time looking at Colfax. "Sir," he added, as an afterthought.

Colfax and Malcolm walked to the trolley stop to return to the *Uhuru.* "Do you always face that treatment?" Malcolm asked.

"Almost every port of call. America is the worst," he said. "They still haven't figured out what to do with people who were property only fifty years ago. Europe is bad enough, mind you. There I'm treated as an aboriginal. They can't believe that I could possibly speak the King's English as well as I do. The only places where I truly am treated well are places that see no colour, but the colour of money, or at home in Africa."

They returned to the *Uhuru* in silence. Malcolm was at a loss for words at seeing the treatment that Colfax endured constantly. For nearly his whole career, Malcolm had been treated as an inferior by other officers, most of which were sons of nobles. But at least, they treated him as a human being. The contempt in the clerk's eyes, when dealing with Colfax, made Malcolm ashamed to feel sorry for his lot in the Air Service.

Dinner was a simple affair of sandwiches and soup, and the three men talked and drank well into the evening. The next day, the trio spent the day in the *Uhuru*; the supplies arrived mid-morning, and Colfax put Malcolm and Saxon to work as they loaded the *Uhuru.* By early afternoon, the *Uhuru* was ready to begin the long trip; they only needed the last two passengers.

It was late on the next day when a car drove up and deposited Nigel and Joan. Nigel looked paler than Malcolm remembered, and Joan had a worried look on her face. "Is everything alright?" he asked.

"Let's wait until we're in the air, shall we?" Joan said.

Within a half hour, the *Uhuru* rose into the sky to begin the long trip. They gathered in the galley to discuss the mission to Miskatonic

University, and the trip ahead. Nigel and Joan seemed reluctant to discuss what had happened, so Malcolm told them how Saxon was successful in finding their destination.

"So that will be where R'lyeh rises," Nigel said softly.

"Beg your pardon?" Malcolm asked.

"R'lyeh is the home of… the entity. The books that I consulted, while in Miskatonic, talked about the conjunction that will occur, and when it does, the entity and his forgotten city will rise."

"Tell us about your trip," Saxon asked.

Nigel said nothing. After a few seconds, Joan started. "It began easily enough. Once we made it into Boston, we took a train to Arkham, and arrived late in the afternoon. We went straight to the university, but I felt a sense of dread the whole time we were in Arkham. Mycroft had made arrangements for Nigel to consult some rare books in the library's collection that might have some bearing on our mission. It was a good thing, as the Head Librarian, Dr. Henry Armitage, was very hesitant to allow Nigel to see the books, and permitted no note taking whatsoever. Nigel did some preliminary research, but made little progress before closing time."

"Nigel and I found a quaint inn at which to stay. Typically, it was used as a boarding house for students, but since it's nearly summer, they had quite a few vacancies. Arkham was a nice enough town, filled with large gabled houses. But I had the distinct feeling that someone was following us."

"We rose the next morning, and were waiting on the steps for the Library to open. Dr. Armitage brought Nigel to a room so that he could read the books undisturbed, or apparently not disturb anyone else."

"What do you mean?" Malcolm asked.

"Although I was in an office outside of the reading room where Nigel worked, I could tell every time he opened one of those insufferable books. I could feel it. The room seemed to darken, and the temperature would drop. I eventually had to leave because it was too much for me. I left the library and walked around the college and into the town. All the while, I felt that sense of dread, and of being watched."

"I was on my way to get Nigel, when I was ambushed near the college by three men. I couldn't tell what nationality they were; they looked Asian or Polynesian, but I couldn't say. They were jabbering something, including the name of that... thing. I dispatched them easily enough, but I was shaken at this point. I hurried to the library, and there was a large commotion in front of the library."

"At first, I couldn't get in, but I eventually convinced a policeman to let me inside. When I got to the place where I left Nigel, I found the police talking to Dr. Armitage, and there was a corpse, covered with a sheet on the floor. It turned out, the victim tried to force entry to the rare books. Professor Armitage pulled a revolver from one of his drawers, and shot the man. Apparently, Armitage has been authorised to use deadly force to prevent people from seeing the books. After the ambulance arrived to take away the body, the police left after Armitage gave them his statement."

Joan continued. "I waited there until closing, and when Nigel finally emerged from the room, he was pale and acted almost stunned. We left the library and immediately took the last train to Boston. After we found a suitable place to stay, we ate, and I fed Nigel a few stiff drinks. He came around enough to say that he was feeling much better."

"Did you find the information that you needed?" Malcolm asked.

"Yes," Nigel answered. "The books that I read are some of the most hideous books ever written by mankind. The things that are detailed in the books have driven lesser minds mad. I have been slowly building my psychic energy back, after a day and a half of consultation. But, yes. I did find a few things that may assist us." He addressed Colfax. "I assume that we will stop near a city at some point in our travels."

"Yes," Colfax said. "We don't have much slack in the schedule if we are to make it to those coordinates in time for the conjunction. But we must stop a few times for fuel and food. I can radio ahead, and arrange to have anything you need delivered."

"Thank you," Nigel said. "How long will it take us to reach... our destination?" Malcolm noticed that Nigel hesitated before the word destination; he couldn't bring himself to utter the name.

Colfax laid out a navigation map over the table. "We are here," he said, pointing to the approximate location of Providence. "Our coordinates, 47°9' S 126°43' W, are here," he said as he drew a cross at the point. Taking a long ruler, he drew a straight line from Providence to the coordinates that followed the eastern coast of the United States until Florida, where it cut across the state, through the Gulf of Mexico, before cutting across Central America, continuing through the South Pacific. "I'll need to do some specific calculations to determine where we need to resupply, but I think it will take roughly seventeen days."

"What if we took a slight detour to New Orleans?" Nigel asked. "As I look at potential places to get the supplies I need, I think New Orleans might be the best. How much time will it add?"

Colfax considered for a moment before speaking. "Probably another two days of travel."

"How long do we have before the conjunction?" Joan asked.

"Twenty-four days," Saxon said.

"It appears that gives us enough time to swing by New Orleans," Joan said. "Is that alright with you, Captain?"

"I'm being paid by the mile, plus expenses. If you're good for it, I don't care if we go the long way around the world," Colfax said with a smile. "I'm going to suggest that we all disembark when we arrive in New Orleans. While I love my airship, even I need to get out of here occasionally. And as many of you know, seventeen days in a small airship can seem much longer. Give me another hour or so, and I'll devise a proper itinerary to get us to the coordinates in twenty-four days."

While Colfax returned to the cockpit, the four decided it was best to resume the psychic defence training they had started on their trip across the Atlantic. At first, Saxon, Joan, and Malcolm were a little rusty, and it took most of the session before they could make the needle on the psychometer move. But by the end of the session, all except Nigel had reached their previous level of psychic defence.

When they finished, Nigel said, "If you don't mind, I think I would like to lie down for a bit. The events of the past two days have been taxing, and I would very much like to rest."

Saxon said, "I should go do... something so the two of you can talk."

"Why?" Joan said. "Is there something I should know about?" she asked, turning to face Malcolm.

"No," Malcolm said, putting his hands up defensively.

"I meant, rather," Saxon said, "that you have not had a chance to talk to one another in the past several days, and I thought that my presence might prevent that. Now that I've made a mess of things, I'll leave," he said as he left the galley.

They sat in silence for several seconds, before Joan reached over and pulled Malcolm into a long kiss. "What was that for?" Malcolm asked. "Not that I'm objecting, but why the urgency?"

Joan frowned. "I don't know. Ever since we arrived at Arkham, I've had a terrible sense of foreboding. I have not been able to shake it. And feeling the influence of those books, even as far away as I was, has left me anxious. I can't imagine how Nigel is holding up."

"He does seem worse for wear," Malcolm said. "Do you think he's alright?"

"I think he will be. From what little he's told me about those books, horrible things happen to those who read them. One of the authors, an Arab whose name I can't remember, was said to be seized by an invisible monster and devoured in broad daylight. I only hope that he doesn't meet such a horrible end. I was like you; at first I didn't believe this claptrap about an evil entity, and the Spear and all. But now, I think it's all true and that frightens me."

Malcolm pulled her close. "You're frightened?"

"Yes," Joan said, softly. "I am very frightened."

Malcolm cupped her face in his hands. "I can't promise you that everything will be fine, but I promise you this. I will do whatever I can to keep you safe."

"I know," she said. "And I promise to do whatever I can to keep you safe."

Saxon, who had returned for a drink, stood in the doorway and said, "Such sweetness; I may vomit."

CHAPTER 40

The flight of the *Uhuru* was different from the initial plan that Colfax had laid out. They flew past New York City, and saw the tall buildings shooting up from the island of Manhattan. From the air, it reminded Malcolm of a porcupine with its quills. But instead of flying along the coast, the *Uhuru* turned inland and flew over the Appalachian Mountains, past Atlanta, and on to New Orleans.

They landed outside of New Orleans three days after departing Providence. Given the events of Arkham, they decided that there was safety in numbers and travelled together. At Colfax's insistence, they stopped for *café au lait* and *beignets* at *Café du Monde*, in the French Quarter market. Malcolm conceded that the coffee was almost palatable. Colfax led them into the French Quarter, with its narrow streets, and wrought iron balconies. It was in the French Quarter that Nigel found a shop that promised to sell charms and talismans, in addition to numerous magical powders and elixirs. Although Nigel had been reluctant at first to enter the shop, fearing it to be a hoax, he was happy when he left, his arms filled with two bags, loaded with an assortment of liquids, powders, and five talismans. The talismans were each inscribed with a line and five branches; three on the left, two on the right. "Please wear these at all times, even you Colfax. They offer some protection against the entity."

They left the French Quarter and headed to the port, where Colfax had no problems re-supplying the *Uhuru* with water, food, and fuel. After finishing that errand, they returned to the French Quarter for shopping. Joan bought several dresses, jackets, and hats, while Malcolm, Saxon, and Nigel nearly had to be dragged out of one bookstore, where books were piled on nearly every available surface. The books ranged from the science books that Malcolm enjoyed, to the histories favoured by Saxon, to the obscure favoured by Nigel. When they left the French Quarter, everyone but Colfax had their arms filled with their purchases.

It was late in the afternoon, and the party was famished. Eager to also sit, the group took a streetcar along St. Charles Street into the Garden District. As they travelled, the houses became bigger and grander; a mixture of Italianate, Greek Revival, and Victorian styles. When the trolley reached Washington Street, Colfax indicated that they should disembark. They walked along the oak-lined street, and travelled a block, before they saw a walled-off block.

"What is that?" Malcolm asked.

"That," Colfax said, "is Lafayette Cemetery #1. When we pass the front gate, you might notice something peculiar. There are no headstones, only standing crypts."

"Why is that?" Malcolm asked.

"Because the city is built on a swamp. If you dig, you'll hit water. So, the dead are put in these tombs. But that's not why we're here," Colfax said. "If I can direct your attention to ahead of you, and to the left." The group looked, and ahead was a large blue and white building, with a sign that read 'The Commander's Palace'. "That," Colfax said, "is where we will eat tonight."

Although it was early for a fashionable dinner, the group was famished. They were seated at a table. "If you are game, I would like to order for you," Colfax said. "I come here every time I am in New Orleans. If you want to try the local cuisine, I would be happy to order."

Malcolm looked at the menu, and read the strange mélange of English and French that made up the names of the various dishes. He folded the menu and said, "I'm game." One by one, the members of the party agreed. Colfax started them off with a round of *Sazerac* cocktails, a mixture of absinthe, cognac and bitters. Malcolm, never a fan of brandy, did not particularly enjoy it. For starters, Colfax ordered raw oysters, and taught them how to eat them. Joan seemed to have the stomach for the raw oysters, but Malcolm, Saxon, and Nigel politely declined after one. Dinner was mixture of several different dishes; *etouffee*, *gumbo*, and *jambalaya* were served from large tureens and ladled over rice. To Malcolm's surprise, the food was spicy, but not so spicy that he could not enjoy it. The meal finished with bread pudding, a treat that Malcolm had not had since he was a young man. Here they added a whisky sauce to the bread pudding, making it all the better. When they felt like they couldn't eat a bite more, the party left the restaurant and took the trolley back to the centre of the city, where they could secure a taxi to carry them back to the *Uhuru*. The mood that night was lighter than it had been since the start of the trip.

The next day, after the supplies were loaded, the *Uhuru* took to the sky and within hours, was soaring over the Gulf of Mexico. Their next stop was Mexico City, which would be the last stop on their trip. The group continued to practice their psychic defence, this time using the talismans purchased by Nigel.

"What are these things?" Malcolm asked.

"They are called Elder Signs. They are said to offer some measure of protection against things like... the entity. It's one of the things I learned from my reading. I am glad that we stopped in New Orleans, because there is a strong occult bent in that city. It's famous for its voodoo, but that is not the only occult energy there. There are cults that live in the swamps, far from human eyes, that worship the entity and his kin. It did not surprise me that a shop might have talismans like these."

"What else did you get?" Malcolm asked, this time with real curiosity.

"Some very specific mineral powders and elixirs. They are very common in the many pagan traditions for warding off evil spirits. The books I read seemed to indicate that they might have some effectiveness in dealing with the entity."

"Oh," Malcolm said. As a man of science, he was skeptical that the potions of the superstitious would have any effect, but he had also invented a device to measure psychic energy, so he couldn't dismiss it out of hand. Faced with the enormity of their task, Malcolm supposed every little advantage would help. He did note that using the talisman as a focus did seem to increase the strength of his psychic defences, so maybe there was something to this after all.

When the *Uhuru* landed in Mexico City, they decided not to leave the ship and simply procure what they needed as efficiently as possible, as they had landed in the early stages of a civil war. While there was no fighting in Mexico City, it was a bit of a powder keg ready to erupt, and tensions were high. They spent very few hours there before taking off for the final leg of the trip. It wasn't long before they had left land behind, and were flying across the South Pacific.

All they could see was water in every direction. The weather and the trip were unremarkable. Tensions started to rise the farther out to sea they travelled. Two days into their flight from Mexico City, the psychic defence classes started to falter. Malcolm started to have a hard time concentrating on creating the white light. "Malcolm," Nigel said, "you have to master this skill, or your mind will be destroyed."

"I am trying. Maybe if you weren't breathing down my neck, I'd be able to do it!" Malcolm responded.

"If you'd put some effort into it, you might succeed," Nigel said.

"What the bloody hell do you think I'm doing?" Malcolm said. "If I'm so bloody useless at it, leave me here when you go and battle that thing. I don't even want to be here!"

"That's obvious," Nigel muttered.

"Look, I'm only here because I was blackmailed out of the Air Service."

"We're never going to be able to defeat the entity with that attitude!" Nigel said.

"Well, blame your boss. I didn't bloody well ask for this. If I'm such a miserable failure, leave me out of this," Malcolm said. He took off the talisman of the Elder Sign and threw it at Nigel, before storming out of the galley, stomping to his cabin, and slamming the door.

A few minutes later, Joan stormed into the room. Malcolm was laying on the bed with his arm draped over his eyes. "What the hell was that about?" Joan said.

"Please, don't you start in on me too," Malcolm said. "I don't know. I feel like my nerves are on edge. Anything anyone says feels like it pulls a loose thread, and unravels more of my calm."

"I've felt the same way to a lesser degree," Joan said. "It probably has to do with the fact that we're getting closer to our destination."

"That's very likely," Malcolm said. He sat up suddenly. "I wonder something." Malcolm got off the bed and pushed past Joan without a word, and walked back to the galley.

"Nice of you to join us," Nigel sneered. Malcolm ignored him and walked to the idol that he had been using for calibrating the psychometer. Since they'd left Britain, he had not recalibrated it, as he only needed to know relative increases in the psychic energy they generated during their lessons. Malcolm uncovered the hideous statue, and thought he saw some sort of purplish energy crackle over the idol. He blinked to clear his eyes and it was gone. He turned on the psychometer and placed the sensor close to the idol. Instead of the needle landing in the centre of the gauge, it was nearly three quarters of the way across the gauge.

"Nigel, look at this, please," Malcolm said, as diplomatically as possible.

"What are you playing at, Malcolm?" Nigel said. "I've no interest in your silly gadgets."

"Please, Nigel. I need your expertise to help interpret what's happening," Malcolm said as humbly as he could. The irritation that caused him to explode earlier was threatening to rise into another outburst, but he kept trying to take deep breaths, and concentrate on the task at hand.

"Very well," Nigel huffed, and walked over to Malcolm with a great deal of reluctance, and with an air of condescendence. Malcolm took a deep breath before speaking.

"When I measure the idol for calibration, the needle usually lands about here," Malcolm said, pointing the middle of the gauge. "Watch what happens when I measure it now," Malcolm said, as he moved the sensor closer to idol again. The needle swung past the halfway point, and reached three quarters of the way to the right of the gauge. "See? The psychic signal from the idol is getting stronger. I don't pretend to understand this, but I'm guessing this is the reason I'm so on edge and irritable."

Nigel looked at the gauge. "I think you're right!" His curiosity took over the irritation. "That would indicate that this idol is acting like a psychic antenna back to the entity; receiving psychic energy, the same way a radio receives radio waves. This is wonderful!" he said. "We can truly demonstrate that artifacts are actually conduits for psychic energy. This could revolutionise the field of paranormal research!"

"That's wonderful and all, Nigel," Malcolm said. "I think we have a more immediate issue."

"And that is?"

"If you and I are at each other's throats, and we're still nearly five thousand miles from the entity, what's going to happen the closer that we get to it? Remember, each click on this gauge means the signal is ten times stronger than the previous."

"Oh," Nigel said. "I understand."

"What are the two of you going on about?" Saxon said, the irritation present in his voice. "Are we practicing or not?"

"Just a moment, Charles," Nigel said. "If you'll excuse me, for a moment. Malcolm, you'll want to turn off the psychometer, and perhaps relocate it to your cabin."

Malcolm nodded, turned the psychometer off, and carried it to his cabin and shut the door. Back with the others, he watched as Nigel returned with a long narrow case, nearly five feet wide. Nigel set the case down gingerly and opened it. In the case lay the Spear of Destiny, attached to a proper wooden staff. Malcolm noticed a layer of metal throughout the case. "Is that lead?" Malcolm asked.

Nigel finished a silent prayer and crossed himself, before picking up the Spear. "Yes," he said. "Based on your work, we thought that lead would help block the psychic particles, if you will." Malcolm watched as Nigel lifted the Spear and moved towards the idol. The Spear began to glow with a blue white light, which caused spots to appear before Malcolm's eyes. The idol began to emit the purple light that Malcolm thought he saw before, and the energies collided with an audible boom. Sounds of crackling energy, and the smell of ozone filled the galley. The energy from the Spear increased, and slowly pushed the purple light back into the idol. It crackled on the surface for several seconds, before the energy from the Spear completely enveloped the idol. The blue light completely ingested the idol until there was nothing left.

The Spear's light extinguished immediately. And Malcolm noticed that his mood was instantly lighter. It was as if a high-pitched sound that he could almost hear had been silenced.

"I imagine the Martians might be upset that we destroyed their statue," Saxon quipped.

"I think if we don't stop their god, they might be more upset," Joan said.

"Thank you, Malcolm," Nigel said. "I should have realised that the idol would pick up the energy from the entity." He carefully returned the Spear to its case, and put it back into storage. When he returned, he asked, "Perhaps we can try our class again? I don't know about all of you, but I feel much more at ease than I have in several days." Malcolm went to his cabin to retrieve the psychometer. They spent the next hour practicing, and without the distraction of the idol's presence, they created stronger defences.

With the destruction of the idol, the overall mood lifted on the *Uhuru* for a short time. Nigel spent nearly every minute teaching them more techniques to centre themselves, so that they could more quickly generate their psychic defences. After spending so much time in their own minds, they were eager for conversation, but the mental drain had tired them. Dinner had become simple sandwiches, as no-one had the energy to think of anything better. As the days went on, even the conversation seemed to drain away. Dinners were almost sullen affairs where no-one spoke, and almost immediately went to bed after dinner. And the effectiveness of the classes seemed to go down again. There seemed to be no more growth in their skill.

On the sixth day after they left Mexico City, Colfax made a course correction, unbeknownst to his passengers. During another psychic defence class, Malcolm suddenly noticed that the *Uhuru* seemed to be descending. He caught Saxon's eye, and knew that Saxon had felt it too. Malcolm excused himself and went the cockpit. He knocked on the door. "Come," said Colfax.

"Sorry to bother you, but are we descending? Is there some sort of problem?"

"Yes, there is. You and your friends need a diversion from this training."

"But we must be ready, and there's so much to be done," Malcolm said.

"Yes, but you're driving yourselves into the ground. The last three nights, we've had nothing but sandwiches, and none of you talk. You eat in silence, and then you go to bed. I don't know much about what you're doing, but I do know the way to prepare for something isn't to drive yourself to the point of exhaustion. I'm forcing everyone onboard to get off the ship, and to relax for one night. I know the perfect place that is just a slight detour from our goal. According to my calculations, we're actually ahead of schedule."

"Are you going to tell me where we're landing?" Malcolm asked.

"No."

"I didn't think so," Malcolm said. "How long until we reach our destination?"

"Another hour or two," Colfax said.

"Very well. I will tell everyone that we will be landing in a while, at an undisclosed location."

"Thank you," Colfax said with a smile.

When Malcolm broke the news to the group, Saxon and Joan immediately balked at the idea of not doing more to prepare. Nigel finally spoke up and said "I believe our captain may be correct. The work we are doing takes most people months to reach the level of mastery that you have achieved in several days. But the soul can't keep up the pace of a sprint over several days. I believe that, given the right place, a break may do much more good than continued study. In fact, let's break now."

They stopped, each secretly glad for the break. They took turns looking through the galley windows, to see if they could spot land, but saw nothing but unending sea. The *Uhuru* continued to descend and, within the hour, they saw their destination. At first, it appeared like a small rock in the ocean. As they grew closer, they saw a small island with a mountain rising near the north end of the island, and two smaller mountains to the south and east. As they grew closer, the green of the island's grass began to outshine the ocean. Colfax brought the *Uhuru* down gracefully. As soon as they neared the ground, he grabbed one of the ropes tied to the *Uhuru* and jumped out of the door, to tie the balloon down. He made a makeshift hammer out of a rock to drive a spike into the ground. When he felt that the *Uhuru* was truly tied down, Colfax lowered the gangplank.

"Welcome to *Rapa Nui*, also known as *Isla de Pascua*, or Easter Island. If my calculations are correct, we have a couple of days to spare before we reach our destination. We are not departing until the morning. In that time, as Captain of this ship, I order you to explore and enjoy the beauty of this island."

"Aye, aye, sir!" Malcolm said, with a mock salute. He stepped down the gangplank, very glad to be off the ship, and stopped suddenly. On either side of the *Uhuru*, some distance away, were rows and rows of huge stone statues, each resembling the upper torso of a person. "What is this place?" he asked, awestruck.

Nigel walked down the gangplank and said, "*Hanga Roa*. I've read about this place, but never thought I would ever see it. Thank you, Captain," he said, as he vigorously shook Colfax's hand.

Joan followed, and inhaled deeply. "It's beautiful," she whispered.

Saxon sauntered down the gang-way, pretending to be nonchalant. But as he stared across the landscape, even he couldn't keep up the façade. Grasslands stretched over the island, and up the mountains. Ringing the island on either side were the statues.

"Come back at sunset, and I will have dinner ready. We will eat and sit out under the stars. I would have fire, but alas there is not a stick of wood on this island."

"Do we need a fire?" Saxon asked. "To keep away any animals?"

"The only living things on this island are sheep," Colfax said. "I'm sure they won't bother us. Until sunset, enjoy the island!"

Joan walked over to Malcolm, took his hand, and they walked towards the eastern side of the island. Nigel, who had walked some distance, turned and jogged back to the *Uhuru*.

"Where are you going? I thought I ordered you off," Colfax said.

"Just getting my sketch pad and journals," Nigel said, as he ran up the gangplank. In a few minutes, he returned with a large sketch pad, and a leather-bound journal.

"Do you mind if I join you, Nigel?" Saxon asked.

"It might be very boring. I'm likely going to spend my time measuring, writing, describing, and sketching these statues. I believe they are called *moai*."

"I find archaeology fascinating. This may be the closest I ever come to participating in an archaeological expedition," Saxon said.

"Very well then," Nigel said. "You can start by carrying these," he said, as he handed the large sketchpad and journal to Charles.

Colfax laughed, and he realised that it felt good to laugh. He felt like he had not laughed in weeks. He sat on the gangplank, and looked up at the blue sky, breathing in the warm air of the island.

"This is the best part of being in the Secret Service," Joan said. "Getting these small moments, where you see things that you know very few people will ever see. I imagine it's the same with the Air Service."

"Yes," Malcolm said. "It's odd; just a few months ago I was flying past the Sphinx, and over the Great Pyramids, and now, I'm here among these giant statues. The engineering work necessary to accomplish this is just amazing. Why it would take-" Malcolm said before Joan pulled him close, and stopped his words with a kiss. After the initial shock, Malcolm eagerly returned the kiss until Joan pulled away. "What was that for?" he asked.

"To shut you up. Let's not think about engineering, or secrets, or anything else. Let's just enjoy what the island has to offer." They continued to walk along the coast of the island, talking very little, occasionally stopping to kiss or rest, while they looked out over the ocean. They looked at each *moai* and stopped for a short time, so that Joan could sketch several of them. As the sun approached the horizon, they turned back and headed for the *Uhuru.*

As they approached, they saw that Colfax had laid out a large tarp on the ground, to act as a picnic blanket, and laid out pillows from their beds. He'd wanted to bring out the table and chairs, but in the airship they were bolted down, so they didn't fly all over the place during turbulence. He'd made a ring of rocks to set a large pot. Malcolm could smell a combination of ginger, curry, and tomatoes, and suddenly he was ravenous.

"What is for dinner tonight? It smells delicious," Malcolm said.

"It is a dinner from my homeland," Colfax said. "Something about this island reminds me of my home. That, and I had all of the ingredients."

They patiently waited another five minutes, before Nigel and Charles arrived. They were in the middle of an animated discussion when they caught sight of the *Uhuru.*

"Good Lord, man, that smells fabulous," Saxon said. "I feel I could eat that whole pot."

"You might have a bit of an argument," Colfax said. "Come, sit." He began to ladle out the stew into the bowls, and pass them around. He also handed them pieces of bread, long stale, to sop up the juice. Malcolm enjoyed the stew; it had a tomato based broth with beef, onions, carrots, and potatoes, as well as the curry and ginger he smelled earlier.

Colfax produced five wine glasses, and a bottle of red wine that perfectly complemented the stew. When the first bottle was emptied, a second and then a third were opened. As they ate and drank, they talked and laughed. As the evening drew on, the sky became awash with stars.

"Nigel, what do you know about the statues?" Joan asked.

"Sadly, very little," Nigel said. "I know that most of the natives of this island have been decimated by slavery and disease. Experts seem to think that the statues represent the ancestors of the living, looking out for them. That's why all of the statues appear to look inward."

"Why so many of them?" Saxon asked.

"Again, I have no idea. We don't know what possessed them to build all of the statues all around the island. These statues are unique to Easter Island. I would hazard a guess that they are meant to protect the islanders."

"From what?" Saxon asked.

"I have no…" Nigel started to say, as he trailed off. He got up and went back into the *Uhuru*. In moments, he returned with the case for the Spear of Destiny. He took the Spear out and closed his eyes. Using his Elder Sign medallion as a focus, he gathered his psychic energy, and pushed it into the spear. Suddenly, a bolt of blue-white energy shot from the spear, and struck a nearby statue.

The eyes of the statue began to glow, and the energy began to expand from the Spear to the nearby statues. As far as they could see, in either direction, the blue white energy crawled over each statue before jumping to the next. In a few minutes, the energy became a shimmering wall of blue light.

"The statues are here to protect the island from the very entity that we are seeking," Nigel said.

CHAPTER 41

igel released the psychic energy and, within seconds, the wall dropped.

"You must be exhausted," Joan said.

"Actually, I'm not. With the Spear, it took a surprisingly small amount of psychic energy to create the shield around the island."

"That's good to know," Malcolm said. "Presuming we survive, we know we have a haven."

"Perhaps," Nigel said, with a tone of doubt in his voice. From his research at Miskatonic, he knew that there would likely be no haven in the world, if the entity emerged and gained full power.

Colfax, feeling the chill in the conversation, launched into a story about attempting to flee Hong Kong during the great typhoon of 1908. Colfax was a masterful storyteller, and kept them enthralled, taking their minds off the recent demonstration. The stories, and wine, continued for another hour before they all became drowsy, and made their way into the airship.

The next morning, they got a late start, and had a picnic breakfast. They were loath to leave, but knew they had to return to the mission. The group watched from the cargo hold as Colfax drew up the gangplank, and made the preparations for take-off. He gently nudged his ship skyward, and soon they were off towards the completion of the mission.

A sense of urgency entered their psychic training. This time, Nigel strictly enforced limited class times, and mandatory rest periods. He taught them how to meditate, so that they could regenerate their own psychic energy. Malcolm had a particularly hard time of quieting his mind and focusing, as he pondered what awaited them at their journey's end.

Dinner, although subdued, was animated as they told stories to buoy each other's spirits. After dinner, Nigel, Joan, and Saxon attempted to teach Malcolm how to play bridge. He found it difficult at first, but once he caught on, his mathematical mind allowed him to analyse the odds. By the end of the night, he and Joan became formidable opponents for Charles and Nigel.

The activities of the next days were much the same; carefully regimented exercises, and strictly enforced rest periods. After dinner, they again played cards. This time, Malcolm and Joan were nearly unbeatable. They had already played several hands, when Colfax poked his head in the galley and said severely, "You better see this."

They followed him to the cockpit, and struggled to squeeze in to get a view. In the dimming light of twilight, they saw a gigantic swirl of clouds still quite a distance away. The clouds looked like a horrible bruise in the sky; masses of green, blue, purple, red, and black, all swirling around a distant point they couldn't see.

"That storm is colossal," Saxon exclaimed. "We would never survive that."

"Most certainly," Colfax said.

"How far away is it?" Malcolm asked.

"My guess is that it's at least another fifty miles away," Colfax said.

Malcolm turned to Nigel, "I'm assuming this is probably not a natural storm?"

"I don't think so," Nigel said.

"Do you think it will clear before the conjunction?" Malcolm asked.

"It might. According to my research, it's vital that the alignment can be viewed. My guess is that the entity will ensure that the sky is clear that night. I believe that the entity is pulling in all the negative energy it can muster, and that storm is a manifestation of that process," Nigel said.

"What do we do?" Colfax said, as looked at Malcolm.

"Why are you asking me? I'm not in charge," Malcolm retorted.

"If it were my trip, I would avoid that at all costs," Colfax said. "But this is a charter. Someone needs to tell me what you want to do."

Malcolm looked at Saxon, Joan, and Nigel. None of them said a word, and all looked at Malcolm for his opinion.

"Fine," Malcolm huffed. "But none of you get to complain if you don't like my decision."

"Fair enough," said Saxon.

Malcolm sat in the co-pilot's seat, and reviewed the map. "Where are we?" he asked.

Colfax pointed. "Here."

Malcolm found the spot, and roughly measured the distance left to their destination. "Here's our dilemma: we're still nearly a thousand miles, or roughly two days' journey, from our destination. We have approximately three more days before the conjunction occurs. Hopefully Nigel is correct, and this storm will dissipate. I suggest that we fly near the edge of the storm, and wait for another day to see what happens. If we get an opening, we'll have to take it. That means Colfax, Charles, and I will need to take turns at the helm, so we can be ready to move when we get the chance."

"What if we don't get a chance?" Colfax said.

"We'll have to find a way over, or through, it," Malcolm said.

"I was afraid that you would say that," Colfax said.

"Charles, why don't you go ahead and get some sleep? If you can spell me at six bells, and Colfax could spell you at eight bells in the morning. After that, we will split the shifts more equitably. Colfax, you should get some sleep now as well. I think we're going to have a very interesting few days."

Malcolm was correct; keeping distance, so that the *Uhuru* would not be sucked into the storm, was no easy feat. Winds continually tried to push the small airship into the storm, and each pilot had to fight hard to keep the airship safe. In the middle of Malcolm's shift in the afternoon, Malcolm noticed that the clouds were pulling away from the *Uhuru*, as if the storm were shrinking in on itself. He immediately pointed the airship towards the storm, and kept pace with it, as it shrank away. They continued this tactic until nightfall, when it was impossible to see the boundary of the storm clouds. They let the airship drift in the general direction of their destination, but did not fly under power.

At first light, Saxon realised that the storm was out of sight, and applied full power. By the end of his shift, the ship had the edge of the storm in sight. This continued for another day, until the edge of the storm was only fifty miles out from their destination. They stopped and waited.

The skies were black and dark; the bruised colour of the sky was concentrated directly ahead of them. Although it was the middle of the afternoon, Malcolm thought it looked more like twilight.

Suddenly, the sea below the storm began to roil, as if it were boiling. The storm clouds below them began to swirl, and pick up speed. Malcolm watched as a waterspout seemed to spin up from the ocean, and reach to the skies, where it seemed to be drawing in the clouds and the storm.

"Everyone! Come here right now!" Malcolm yelled, as he opened the cockpit door. In seconds, everyone came running, and crowded around the cockpit and doorway.

"That doesn't look promising," Saxon said.

"Indeed," Nigel said.

"What's going on?" Joan asked. "I can't see through all of you."

"It appears," said Colfax, "that the sea, or something under the sea, is drawing in the storm."

"It's beginning," Nigel said.

"What's beginning?" Saxon asked.

"You may not remember, but when the Crown Prince showed us the idol, I said a phrase that I dare not repeat here. But roughly translated, it means 'In his house at R'lyeh, dead Cthulhu waits dreaming.'"

Nigel paused for a moment to find the correct words. "According to the books I consulted, when Cthulhu awakes, R'lyeh will rise from the sea. I believe that is what we are witnessing."

The storm clouds continued to swirl down the waterspout into the ocean. The storm gradually shrank, until the last of it spiralled down into the sea. The ocean began to thrash violently and soon, strange blocks of stone began to push through the water. They were the bright green colour of slime. The blocks curved in angles that looked acute, but were somehow obtuse. Staring at any of the blocks for too long made Malcolm dizzy.

When the island stopped rising, they saw a single promontory, crowned with a bizarre, fantastical, and blasphemous monolith; a fifty-foot-tall block of unnatural green stone that glowed, and gave off a green fog. The water caught by the land, on its way to the surface, turned the same sickly green. They watched as it flowed back into the ocean, polluting it with its taint.

Malcolm swallowed and said, "Alright, everyone. Prepare to land."

CHAPTER 42

Malcolm relinquished the controls to Colfax, and began to prepare for the conclusion of this long mission. The strangeness of the island made him feel unsettled. He closed his eyes, took a deep breath, and tried to focus while touching the Elder Sign medallion. It seemed to relieve some of his uneasiness, so he could focus on the task at hand. Although the weapon of choice against the entity would be the Spear of Destiny, Malcolm knew he would feel better with additional firepower.

He rummaged through the supplies that he had brought from England those many weeks ago. Saxon joined him, and together they armed themselves with a pair of revolvers each, and both carried rifles that could be used to shoot elephants. Malcolm also grabbed rope, a knife, a few sticks of dynamite, and matches. He returned to his cabin, and Joan was dressed for the mission, in a tight-fitting leather jacket, pants, and boots.

"I thought you never liked to wear the same thing twice," Malcolm said. "That's what you wore when you explored the Martian rocket."

"So nice of you to notice," she said, not looking up from her work. She was checking her two large custom guns, to make sure they were in proper working order. She looked through her trunk, and pulled out several large-size rounds, that fit the two oversized pistols she typically used. She packed her backpack with more rounds of ammunition, and pulled on a bandolier filled with hand grenades.

"I'll have to be careful about hugging you," Malcolm said. "I might actually catch a pin, and we'd go out with a bang."

Joan looked at Malcolm and smiled. He often used humour to disguise how utterly terrified he was. She used quiet and focus. She returned to review everything she had packed, and went through her mental checklist twice before she was sure.

She looked up at Malcolm and smiled. She walked over and pulled him close, so that her head was resting on his chest. "I'm scared, Malcolm," she whispered.

"So am I," Malcolm said. He brushed a stray tendril of hair away from her face. "Soon it will be over."

"I know," she said.

Malcolm reached into his pocket and produced a ring box. Before Joan could protest, he said, "If something happens, I want you to have this. Not as an engagement or promise ring, but as a remembrance. I love you, Joan."

"Malcolm." Joan said. "I..."

"Shhh," he said, as he put a finger to her lips. "Just kiss me, and leave it at that."

They kissed for a long time. It was not a kiss of fire and urgency, but slowness and gentleness. When they broke the kiss, they held each other for long minutes, before Saxon knocked on the door. "It's time," he said.

Malcolm and Joan joined the others in the cargo bay. Everyone was dressed in similar tight-fitting leather jackets, pants, and boots. When Joan and Malcolm arrived, Nigel addressed the group.

"The moment we step foot on that land, we are entering a quasi-dimension between our own reality and the entity's. I have prepared some potions that will help our minds absorb the odd reality of this island. It only affects our perception, not our judgement. Lord knows, we need our wits about us."

"We must go to the temple or crypt at the top of the hill," Nigel continued. "I'm sure that's where the entity lies. If we can get there before the conjunction, we might be able to stop the entity from waking."

"And if we're not that fortunate?" Saxon asked.

"The mission becomes exponentially harder."

"I was afraid the answer was something like that," Saxon said.

"Before we go outside, take a moment to centre yourself, and prepare your psychic defences."

"What's our plan?" Malcolm said.

"I will take the Spear of Destiny and stab it," Nigel said.

"Stab it? That's your plan? Stab it?" Malcolm said. "We travelled thousands of miles to get here, and that's our plan?"

"There really isn't any alternative. The weapons you are bringing will be gnat bites to the entity."

Malcolm stopped himself from responding.

"We're only going to have one chance, so we must make it count," Nigel said.

Colfax entered the cargo hold. "What are my orders?" he asked, looking at Malcolm.

"Keep the engine ready. We may need to leave in a hurry," Malcolm said.

They drank the foul-tasting potions and, within a few seconds, Malcolm felt like he had double vision. Things seemed to shift slightly when he looked at them. After a minute, Nigel nodded, and Colfax lowered the gangplank. When Malcolm looked outside, he could focus on the city in a way he hadn't been able to from the air.

They walked down the gangplank and surveyed the scene. Ahead of them were fifteen foot high stone blocks, covered in green slime, that formed a giant's stairway to the demented temple at the peak. The air smelled of seaweed, dead fish, and the sickly-sweet odour of decay. Malcolm tried breathing through his mouth, but the stench was no less oppressive. He and Saxon attached grappling hooks to their ropes, and tossed them to the top of the first block. They climbed the ropes and, when they reached the top, Joan followed them. Together, Malcolm and Saxon helped Nigel up. The quartet turned and looked toward the monolith, and counted at least nineteen more steps in this pythonic staircase.

As Malcolm turned to toss the grappling hook to the top of the next block, he realised that the wall was covered with strange markings that were foreign, and yet somehow familiar. He realised why they looked familiar. "Nigel, did you notice these markings? They look like the markings on the idol."

Nigel examined the markings more closely. "I think you're correct, Malcolm," he said. Ever the archaeologist, he got out a piece of paper and a charcoal crayon, and made a rubbing of the engraving. "No time to look at it now," he said. "Let's get up there."

The group laboriously made their way up the block stairway. Each block took longer to ascend than the last. By the time they were halfway up, Malcolm's arms felt like they were on fire. As they rose, the sky grew darker, as if night was falling. Malcolm checked his watch and, if the time was correct, it was much too early for nightfall. By the time they reached the twelfth step, they took out their electric torches, so that they could see the tops of the blocks.

With five steps left, they heard a strange low-pitched hum, almost at the edge of their hearing. They looked up at the sky and, in the east, at the heart of the constellation Scorpio, Antares began to shine brightly. They watched in astonishment as a beam of light shot from Antares, and targeted the monolith at the top of the hill. The beam intensified, bathing the monolith in an eerie purple glow, and the hum increased in both volume and pitch. They put their hands to their ears, and just when they thought they could no longer stand the sound, the light and sound vanished.

"It appears that the conjunction has occurred. We best hurry," Nigel said. They redoubled their efforts to scale the blocks. As soon as Malcolm and Saxon reached the top, Joan and Nigel were already on their way up, however, Malcolm and Saxon still had to help Nigel reach the top. Despite their best efforts, it was nearly ten more minutes before they made it to the top.

They stood and faced the monolith. Upon closer examination, it seemed to be more of a doorway than a solid monolith. The jambs and lintel of the door were carved in the same strange markings found all over the stones. In the centre of the monolith was a bas-relief of Cthulhu's octopod head, framed with two bat-like demon wings. While it obviously seemed to be a door, Malcolm could not tell if it was vertical or diagonal. He wasn't experiencing vertigo, but he was still having trouble telling up from down.

"I believe now would be an excellent time to invoke your psychic defences," Nigel said. He closed his eyes, breathing deeply several times. He opened his eyes, and walked to the monolith to examine it. He reached out and seemed to find a mechanism, as if he expected it to be there. There was a rumbling sound, and the great door seemed to dissolve diagonally into the jambs. The opening revealed nothing, as a wall of impenetrable darkness filled the opening. They shone their electric torches, and the light reflected off the darkness as if it was a solid substance. Malcolm and Saxon cautiously pushed their rifles through the darkness, and the rifles passed into the inky blackness.

Nigel unstrapped the Spear of Destiny from his back, and held it in both hands. The point of the Spear began to glow blue in the darkness.

"Shall we go?" he asked, and stepped through the opening.

CHAPTER 43

Malcolm took a deep breath to centre himself, and stepped into the darkness. He emerged in a large chamber, made of the same slime green stone. It gave off an unearthly glow that lit the chamber. Two sets of columns ran the length of the room, and rose out of sight, presumably supporting some unseen ceiling. The walls and columns were covered in strange markings, and alien sculptures of things only seen in nightmares. A wave of some sort of dark energy tried to wash over Malcolm, but he was pleased to find that this psychic defences had deflected the effect.

Malcolm's sight was soon directed some hundred feet ahead of him. In a pose reminiscent of the idol, sat Cthulhu on his throne. At forty feet tall, It filled the space at the end of this chamber. Its octopod head was tilted downwards, as if It were still sleeping. Long, clawed hands rested on Its knees. Its demonic wings curled around Its back. Malcolm sensed that there was more to his creature than his physical presence; somehow this creature existed both in and out of physical reality.

Malcolm concentrated with all his might to keep his defences in place. He was afraid if his defences slipped, his mind might be destroyed. His heart started pounding, and a chill went down his spine. His mind screamed to run away and abandon this horrific place. It was taking nearly all of his concentration to keep his breathing even and steady. He fished around in his pocket, and found the comfort of his granda's pocket watch. He focused on the watch, and the safety he'd felt when he worked with his granda. As the seconds passed, he could relegate the fear to a small voice. With a glance, he noticed that everyone's Elder Sign medallions had begun to glow.

Nigel nodded, and they slowly started down the chamber. Each step was a test of Malcolm's will, to step closer to the unnatural atrocity in front of him, and each step was harder than the last. When the group was within ten feet of the thing, Its two dark eyes flipped open, and they jumped back in alarm.

Nigel began reciting. *"Pater noster, qui es in caelis, sanctificetur nomen tuum."* The Spear began to glow and, as he continued to recite the Lord's Prayer, it burned brighter.

Malcolm felt searing pain slice through his mind. At first, he could see nothing as the pain assaulted his senses. Suddenly, he was somewhere else. He was back aboard the bridge of the *Daedalus*, and watched in horror as the bridge exploded in flame. He was burning, and then falling into oblivion. When he stopped, he was again aboard the *Daedalus*, reliving the moment when Frietag shot Joan. This time he shot her in the head, and she was dead before she hit the floor. Malcolm ran to her, and suddenly found himself trapped in the *Evidenzbureau* headquarters, and chained to the wall. Joan was strapped to the table, and Frietag was slowly carving away her flesh with a butcher knife. She screamed in agony. He strained against the chains that bound him, but he found he couldn't move. The air was thick with the smell of blood, seaweed, and decay.

A thought occurred to Malcolm. Seaweed. There is no seaweed in Vienna. Seaweed and decay. He gripped his granda's watch tightly. Joan's screams echoed in his head as he concentrated on the watch, and his granda. The vision slowly faded, and he found himself back in the chamber. He looked at Nigel, Saxon, and Joan, each frozen in a rictus of horror. He faced the abomination, raised his rifle, and fired.

The bullet impacted on the gelatinous skin; slime and oozing matter exploding from the impact. Almost instantaneously, the semi-liquid skin solidified and the hole closed.

It flicked a finger and Nigel stirred from his paralysis. He turned towards Malcolm, and he saw that Nigel's irises were completely black. Nigel drove the Spear of Destiny into Malcolm's abdomen.

Malcolm felt the sharp pain immediately, and his knees buckled. Nigel released the Spear and Malcolm was now holding it, watching his blood gush from the wound. *This is it*, Malcolm thought. *I'm done, and we failed.* He heard his granda's voice in his head; *"Ye aren't gonna give up now, are ye? Fight it!"* The sound of the voice enveloped him, like a warm blanket, and his pain diminished.

"But how, granda?" Malcolm said.

"Ye have the weapons, use them," his granda said, even as the voice faded away.

Weapons? What weapons do I have? Malcolm thought. He looked down and saw the blood oozing from his abdomen. Screaming, Malcolm pulled the Spear out of his flesh. He tried not to look down, but he was sure he had seen a piece of intestine hanging out of the wound. The blood flowed more freely now. He held the Spear vertically and, with his ebbing strength, pulled himself to a standing position. He was still doubled over from the wound, and looked like a hunchback.

Malcolm levelled the Spear at the horror in front of him. The light that Nigel had kindled within the Spear was gone, and he struggled to remember what Nigel had done. He felt light headed, probably from the blood loss. Nigel had recited the Lord's Prayer. Malcolm swallowed and began to speak. "Our Father, who art in heaven, hallowed be thy Name." He lurched forwards two steps, as the Spear began to glow with blue white intensity.

"Thy kingdom come, thy will be done." Two more steps.

"On earth as it is in heaven." Two more steps.

"Give us this day our daily bread, and forgive us our trespasses, as we forgive those who trespass against us." Malcolm was within reach of the monster. He was close enough that the abomination could swat at him with his giant claws, but It was frozen. The light from Spear was blinding, and Malcolm was having trouble seeing the monster before him.

"And lead us not into temptation, but deliver us from evil!" Malcolm felt his legs beginning to falter. Although blinded by the light of the spear, Malcolm could see the edges of his vision turning dark. Gathering the little strength he had left, Malcolm threw himself at the monster, and drove the Spear of Destiny into Cthulhu's abdomen.

The room exploded into a painful white light. "For thine is the kingdom, the power, and the glory forever and ever."

"Amen," Malcolm whispered as he fell to the ground, everything fading to white.

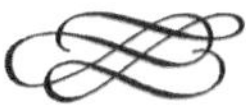

CHAPTER 44

Malcolm opened his eyes and everything was a fuzzy white. Something was blurring in his line of sight. As his eyes slowly focused, he found himself looking up at a white ceiling fan, lazily spinning. He realised that he was lying in a bed, in a white room. There was a curtained window to his right.

"Where am I?" he whispered. "Am I in Heaven?"

"Welcome back to the world of the living, Malcolm," a familiar voice said.

Malcolm turned his head in the direction of the voice, and saw Mycroft Holmes looking up from a book.

"Oh, I must be in Hell," he muttered.

"Always one for the drama. I assure you, this is neither Heaven nor Hell," Mycroft said.

"Where am I?" Malcolm asked.

"Christchurch, New Zealand," Mycroft said. "Colfax and Saxon brought you straight here."

"Is everyone alright? Was anyone hurt?" Malcolm asked.

"Everyone is uninjured, but I daresay they're a little shaken by what happened."

"How long have I been unconscious?" Malcolm asked.

"You've been unconscious for nearly two weeks."

Malcolm felt his abdomen. It was smooth, save for the scar he'd received from a knife attack in St. Petersburg two years prior. "My stomach? How is that possible?"

"I don't know. I have no explanations that are grounded in the rational world."

"What happened? Were we successful?" Malcolm asked.

"Yes. But perhaps I should let someone else tell you the rest of the story. Madame De Marnier has scarcely left your bedside. I had to order her to get some rest last night, as she was exhausted. I will get her and let her tell you what happened." Mycroft rose and started for the door. "One thing I should warn you about. There has been a change in your appearance. Try not to be alarmed," he said as left the room.

Malcolm turned over and saw a nightstand next to his bed. He rummaged through the drawers and found a small shaving mirror. He raised it and looked. The visage looking back at him looked much the same, but his hair, and beard, were now shocking white.

He put the mirror down quickly, and let out a breath, then slowly raised it again. He looked at the face staring back at him in the mirror. He still had the same square jaw, cheekbones, and piercing blue eyes, but they were now framed with snow white hair. He stared for several seconds before realising that things could be worse, and set the mirror back on the nightstand. He tried to remember what had happened. He remembered Nigel stabbing him with the Spear, and fighting with what he thought were the last ebbs of his life, to drive the Spear into Cthulhu. And then nothing, until just moments ago.

The door burst open and, before Malcolm could even see who it was, Joan threw herself across him and kissed him. He was shocked at first, but quickly had the sense to return the kiss.

"Malcolm! I'm so glad you're awake!" Joan said, as she released her clinch on him.

"If I knew you'd greet me like that, I think I should get stabbed more often," Malcolm said with a smile.

Joan's face blanched noticeably. "Malcolm, please. Never kid about that ever again!"

"I'm sorry. It wasn't a very funny joke," he offered apologetically.

"Apology accepted," she said, as she pulled Mycroft's chair as close as she could to Malcolm's bed. She reached across and held his hand between hers.

"What happened? The last thing I remember is pushing the Spear into that… thing."

Joan was silent for a moment. She took a deep breath before she spoke. "Malcolm, please bear with me. This is very difficult for me to say, so I may have to stop. But I will tell it."

She took another deep breath. "We approached the entity. All at once, all I could see were visions of you, being torn apart. I screamed and screamed and nothing happened. Then, my vision cleared enough for me to watch Nigel stab you with the Spear. But I couldn't move. I was frozen in my spot. I watched you pull the Spear out, and stagger towards the entity, muttering the Lord's Prayer. All the while, the Spear gave off more and more light. You stabbed the entity, and the chamber exploded in white light. You fell, and we were all released from Its control. Nigel was nearly catatonic, but he could still walk and follow orders. Just then, we felt the chamber shake, and we could see the door beginning to close. Saxon put you over his shoulders, I pulled Nigel along, and we moved as quickly as we could to the door. We barely got out before the door closed. I thought for one second, I saw a claw from that thing trying to reach through the doorway, but I didn't stop to look."

She stopped, and took several deep breaths. "We hurried down the way we had come, but the island was sinking back into the ocean. We kept moving down, but the water was rising faster. Colfax realised this, and manoeuvred the *Uhuru* to pick us up. Charles carried you on board, and I pushed Nigel inside. We shut the cargo door and Charles laid you on the floor. We both checked your pulse, and I swear that you were dead! I threw myself on you, and started to cry. Suddenly, you took a shuddering breath, and just like that, you had a pulse.

That's when I realised that your abdomen was completely healed. It was as if Nigel had never stabbed you."

"But you wouldn't wake up, or respond. I was afraid your brain had been damaged. As I said, Nigel was nearly catatonic. Colfax and Charles decided the best thing to do was to fly to New Zealand, as it was the nearest English-speaking nation. You've been in this hospital for nearly a week and a half."

"How is Nigel?" Malcolm asked.

"He's recovered somewhat, but he's eating himself up with guilt. He felt that he shouldn't have been dominated by the entity, that he should have had the knowledge to defeat it."

"Maybe that's the trick?" Malcolm said. "Maybe because he knew so much about it, the monster was able to use that against him. I'm too dumb to know better." He said with a smile.

"I would not call you dumb," Joan said, as she used both hands to raise his hand and kiss it. Malcolm noticed she was wearing a ring on the ring finger of her left hand. A ring with a diamond that looked very familiar.

"Is that…?" he started to ask.

"Shh," she said, putting a finger to his lips. "When I was holding you, thinking you were dead, all I could think of was that I would never see you, hold you, love you, ever again. In those moments, when I thought I had lost you, I thought my life was over. When you finally drew a breath, I knew that I had been granted a miracle; another chance. And I made a decision right there."

Joan left her chair and dropped down on one knee. "Malcolm Francis Robertson, will you marry me?" she asked softly, tears streaming down her face.

"It would be my pleasure, now and forever," he said. He felt almost compelled to mention that he was supposed to be the one on bended knee, but thought better of it. Joan once again launched herself at Malcolm, and he lost his breath for a second. Their lips met in a long kiss. When the kiss broke, they sat in silence, holding hands.

CHAPTER 45

Saxon stopped by later that afternoon. "What are you doing lying around?" he asked with a smile. "You act as if you died or something."

Joan gasped, "Charles, don't say that, even in jest!"

"I'm sorry, Joan. That was very unfeeling," he said. "How are you?" he asked in a gentle tone.

"I'm… alright, I think," Malcolm said.

"We… *I* was worried about you," Saxon said.

"I know," Malcolm said.

Joan let out an exasperated sigh. "Men!" She rose, kissed Malcolm on the forehead, and left the two men to talk.

"All kidding aside, Malcolm," Saxon said. "How are you? I would swear on my life that you were dead."

"I'm fine. I'm weak, but other than my sudden change in hair colour, I'm fine."

"What do you remember?" Saxon said.

"Not much," Malcolm replied. "I was losing consciousness when I drove the Spear into that thing. Everything exploded in a white light, and the next thing I knew, I was here."

Saxon filled in the details missing from Joan's account. He and Colfax flew day and night, as fast as the *Uhuru* could travel, to get to Christchurch. Once Malcolm was admitted, Joan cabled Mycroft, who left immediately from London. Mycroft apparently commandeered the *Daedalus*, and forced Captain Bromley to fly the *Daedalus* at top speed.

"From what Mycroft said, once he let slip that the trip was about you, the crew nearly set a speed record for the *Daedalus*."

"Are they still here?" Malcolm asked, hoping to see his ship.

"No, they left immediately. Bromley could not get out of Christchurch fast enough. I imagine that the return trip will not be as quick."

The two chatted for an hour before Malcolm grew tired, and Saxon left. Joan returned, but just sat holding his hand as he slept.

Now that Malcolm had regained consciousness, he had a steady stream of activity. Joan got him out of bed that first day, and made him walk down the hall. Each day, she prodded him to walk farther, and without anything to steady himself. His legs began to grow stronger, and he could see more of the hospital.

Five days after Malcolm regained consciousness, Nigel appeared at his door. "Hello, Malcolm," he said softly. "How are you?"

"I'm fine, Nigel," Malcolm said. "Please, come in."

Nigel hesitated before taking the seat next to Malcolm. He looked at Malcolm for a long moment. "Malcolm, I'm so sorry."

Malcolm looked at him. He saw immediately that Nigel's conscience was eating him alive. "Nigel, there is nothing for me to forgive. You are not responsible for what that thing made you do."

"But I am!" Nigel said angrily. "I'm the one who should have been able to resist It. I have the knowledge, and I thought my faith was strong enough. It should have been!"

"Nigel, I wish I could tell you how I was able to do it, but I don't know," he said. He paused before adding, "I think I had help."

"What do you mean?" Nigel said.

"When you stabbed me," Malcolm began, but stopped when he saw

Nigel wince at the words. "Sorry." He paused before beginning again. "After it happened, I didn't know what to do, and I was going to give up when I heard my granda's voice, telling me not to give up, and to fight. It could have been due to blood loss, but I really felt his presence."

"It is possible, Malcolm," Nigel said. "I think that love is just another form of energy. I like to think it lives on, even when our loved ones are gone." He paused for a moment. "He must have loved you very much, to appear to you when you needed him."

"He did," Malcolm said. "Nigel, please don't blame yourself for what happened. It very well could have been any of us. Please don't think any less of yourself. If it weren't for you, I would never have been able to resist."

"Thank you, Malcolm. That's very generous," Nigel said.

"What's next for you?" Malcolm asked, eager to change the subject.

"I think I will return to academia for a time," Nigel said. "I have had my fill of the supernatural for the time being. And," he said, smiling for the first time, "I must write a paper about the psychometer, and the ability to measure psychic energy. You will, of course, be a co-author."

"I've never been an author of a scientific paper. You'd better include Ernest Rutherford; he won't want us to have all of the credit."

"I imagine that, given his reputation, he would rather not be associated with the paper."

Malcolm laughed. "I'm sure you're correct."

Nigel rose and offered his hand. "Thank you, Malcolm."

"Thank you, Nigel," Malcolm said, shaking his hand.

"Til we meet again," Nigel said as he left.

Other than the change of hair colour, the doctors could not find anything wrong with Malcolm, other than a natural loss of strength from being bedridden. Two days after Nigel's visit, Malcolm was cleared to leave the hospital.

As he waited with Joan for his discharge, Mycroft swept into the room. "Malcolm, I need to talk to you." Joan started to rise, and

Mycroft said, "No, Madame De Marnier, you should stay as this involves you too."

"I should describe what happened in London, while you were confronting the entity. The Martian Crown Prince summoned me the instant that the conjunction occurred. He told me that he felt the psychic pull from the entity. And just as suddenly, the psychic pull vanished, and the Crown Prince knew that the mission had been a success. By the time Madame De Marnier cabled London, I had already acquired transportation on the *Daedalus*, and was waiting to know where to travel. You know how much I despise travel, so you should feel honoured that I came personally."

"I know, Mycroft," Malcolm said.

"It was the least that I could do," Mycroft said. "Your actions have saved not just one world, but two. You have the gratitude of the Crown, and the Martian Crown Prince."

"And to that end," Mycroft said, as he produced a letter from his suit pocket. "It is my great privilege to inform you, Malcolm Francis Robertson, that you have been appointed as Knight Commander of the Most Distinguished Order of Saint Michael and Saint George, for extraordinary non-military service in a foreign country. If your mission did not exemplify extraordinary service in a foreign country, I don't know what does. Once you return to London, His Majesty will confer upon you the title of Sir. And should you marry..." Mycroft said with a smile, as he looked at Joan. "Your wife will be granted the title of 'Lady'. Congratulations, Malcolm. It is truly an honour well deserved."

"Thank you, Mycroft. I don't know what to say," Malcolm said. In his wildest dreams, he never thought that the son of ship builder would ever become a Knight.

"I have one last thing. I promised you that I would return you to the Air Service, upon the successful completion of the mission. You have lived up to your end of the bargain, and now I must live up to mine."

He paused for a moment before continuing. "I could not secure you command of an airship." Malcolm started to protest, before Mycroft raised a hand. "Please, let me finish."

Mycroft took a deep breath. "I can't offer you the command of an airship, but I can offer you the position of Captain on the very first spaceship of the British Empire."

THE END

ACKNOWLEDGMENTS

It takes many people for a story to make its way out of the author's head and into the book you hold in your hands. This book would not be possible without the following people.

* * *

Thank you to my beta readers: Keven and Melanie Simmons, Michael and Donna Moren, and Bob Coulter, for letting me know I was on the right track and pointing out where I veered off!

* * *

Thank you to my editor Jeannette Armstrong of Collins Armstrong Editing for her patience and determination in cleaning up the manuscript. I can't wait to work with you on the next project! You can find out more about her work here: https://collinsarmstrong.wixsite.com/editing

* * *

Thank you to the writing community and especially, the four podcasts that have served as guidance and inspiration to me in this process. Thank you to *Write Now* podcast by Sarah Rhea Warner, *Horrible Writing...and Whining* by Paul Sating, *The Creative Writer's Toolbelt* by Andrew J. Chamberlain, and *The Creative Penn* by Joanna Penn. These podcasts have given me guidance, tips, and inspiration; I can't thank each of them enough for their work. You can find the podcasts here;

Write Now: https://www.sarahwerner.com/episodes/

Horrible Writing: https://www.paulsating.com/horrible-writing

Creative Writer's Toolbelt: https://andrewjchamberlain.com/cwtepisodes/

The Creative Penn: https://www.thecreativepenn.com/podcasts/

* * *

Thank you to my wife Colleen and daughter Holly for putting up with me either exiling myself to my office to write or blathering on about something driving me crazy in the book. Thank you also for your love and support. It means everything.

* * *

And finally, thank you to you, the reader, for giving this book a chance.

* * *

If you're interested in keeping up with what I'm doing, go to my website at http://www.reluctantauthor.com and sign up for my email newsletter.

* * *

And one last thing, if you could leave a rating or review wherever you purchased this book or on https://www.goodreads.com, it would really be helpful to me!

ABOUT THE AUTHOR

Michael Tefft is a software developer, musician, and writer who lives in Central New York. This is his second novel. Previously, he has written two one-act plays *The Job Interview* and *Musical Chairs* and the first novel in the *Reluctant* series, *The Reluctant Captain*.

Michael's other passion is music. In the spring, he can often be found playing trumpet in the orchestra for many high school musicals. In the summer, he can often be found playing in local community band concerts and in the winter, he plays in many holiday concerts.

When he's not doing the above, Michael is a fan of hockey, role-playing games, and Star Trek. He's proud that he's been a long time fan of Captain America and The Avengers, way before the movies made them cool.

facebook.com/ReluctantAuthor
x.com/Mike_Tefft
instagram.com/mtefft66